MARGARET OLIPHANT

(1828-1897) was born in Wallyford, near Edinburgh and lived in Scotland until the age of ten when her family moved to Liverpool and then Birkenhead. Her mother was an Oliphant by birth, but little is known of her father, Francis Wilson, except that he once "took affidavits" in a Liverpool Customs House. She wrote her first novel at the age of sixteen while nursing her mother through an illness, but her first published work was *Passages in the Life of Mrs Margaret Maitland* (1849), and in 1851 she was introduced to the Scottish firm of Black-woods, who were to be her principal publishers, and to whose *Blackwoods Magazine* she remained a regular contributor until her death.

In 1852 she married her cousin Francis Oliphant, an archi-tectural glass painter and associate of Pugin. The greater part of the family income, however, came from her journalism and Scottish regional novels such as *Katie Stewart* and *The Quiet Heart* (1854). In 1859 she found herself a widow with three small children and £1000 in debt: from then on she was always under pressure to write to educate her sons (her daughter died in 1864), and also to support her brothers, nephew and nieces.

One of the greatest women of the Victorian Age, Mrs Oliphant eventually published almost 100 novels, of which the best known are the "Carlingford Chronicles": *The Rector and The Doctor's Family* (1863), *Salem Chapel* (1863), *The Perpetual Curate* (1864), *Miss Marjoribanks* (1866), and *Phoebe Junior* (1876). Other important works include *Harry Joscelyn* (1881), *The Ladies Lindores* (1883), *Hester* (1883), *A Country Gentleman and His Family* (1886), *Lady Car* (1889), *Kirsteen* (1890) and *Sir Robert's Fortune* (1895). She also wrote supernatural tales, biographies, literary histories, translations and travel books. Her last years were overshadowed by the deaths of her nephew Frank in 1879, and her sons Cyril and "Cecco" in 1890 and 1895. Remembered by J.M. Barrie as "of an intellect so alert that one wondered she ever fell asleep", Mrs Oliphant died in Wimbledon at the age of sixty-nine.

Virago also publishes *Hester* and *The Rector and The Doctor's Family*.

VIRAGO
MODERN
CLASSIC

NUMBER

228

Chronicles of Carlingford.

SALEM CHAPEL

MRS OLIPHANT

WITH A NEW INTRODUCTION BY
PENELOPE FITZGERALD

Published by VIRAGO PRESS Limited 1986
41 William IV Street, London WC2N 4DB

First published in Great Britain by W. Blackwood & Sons 1983
Virago edition offset from W. Blackwood & Sons 1985 edition

Introduction copyright © Penelope Fitzgerald 1986

British Library Cataloguing in Publication Data
Oliphant, *Mrs*.
Chronicles of Carlingford.—(Virago classics)
Vol. 2 : Salem Chapel
I. Title
823'.8[F]'   PR5113.C/
ISBN 0-86068-723-6

Printed in Finland by Werner Söderström Oy

INTRODUCTION

"When I die I know what people will say of me," Mrs Oliphant wrote. "They will give me credit for courage, which I almost think is not courage, but insensibility." In the winter of 1861 she was living in a small house in Ealing, to the west of London. She had three young children to support, one of them born after her husband's death, and, except for what she could earn from publishers, she was penniless. Working, as usual, in the middle of the night, the only uninterrupted time she could count on, she continued her chronicles of provincial life with *Salem Chapel*.

At the heart of her new book is the unwelcome clash of the idealist with the world as it is. The world, this time, is represented by Salem – the Dissenters of Carlingford, in satisfied possession of their thriving shops and of the red-brick chapel which they have built themselves. Salem, in appearance, is modest. On the shabby side of Grove Street, the chapel is surrounded by the "clean, respectable, meagre little habitations" where the congregation live. They, of course, are condescended to by the gentry, they are tradespeople. But their independent worship and their free choice of their own minister, to be replaced if he fails to suit, give them an agreeable sense of power. Salem folk, the women in particular, are never happier than when they are "hearing candidates". As a community they are inward-looking – the poor of Carlingford are the church's business, not theirs – but there is warmth and dignity in Salem, the warmth of neighbourliness and the dignity of self-help. To them comes Arthur Vincent, their just-

elected minister, a gentlemanly young scholar fresh from
theological college, "in the bloom of hope and intellectualism", asking only for room to proclaim the truth to all men.
He is met by what Mrs Oliphant calls "a cold plunge".
Salem wants him to fill the pews with acceptable sermons,
and to do his duty at tea-meetings.

There is a strong hint, too, that the very best a young
minister can do is to choose a wife from the flock, which in
practice means the pinkly blooming Phoebe Tozer, the
grocer's daughter. He is told of another young pastor who
failed "all along of the women; they didn't like his wife,
and he fell off dreadful". Arthur's instincts prompt him to
escape. "Their approbation chafed him, and if he went
beyond their level, what mercy was he to expect?" As in
the two previous novels of the series, *The Rector* and *The
Doctor's Family*, Carlingford will prove a test for the
newcomer which is all the more painful because it is only
half understood. *Salem Chapel* makes no claim to show the
impact of Dissent on English life. There can be no kind of
comparison, for instance, with George Eliot's treatment of
Methodism in *Adam Bede*. Non-conformism is not even
shown as a significant moral force. "As a matter of fact,"
Mrs Oliphant admitted, "I knew nothing about chapels,
but took the sentiment and a few details from our old
church in Liverpool, which was Free Church of Scotland,
and where there were a few grocers and other such good
folk whose ways with the ministers were wonderful to
behold". One of her earlier editors, W. Robertson Nicholl,
pointed out that she got several of these details wrong. But
this, even if she had realised it, would not have deterred
Mrs Oliphant.

What she did understand, from the depths of her Scottish
being, was the power of the spoken word as a communication from heart to heart. Arthur Vincent's progress as a
preacher, through the length of the book, is from mere
eloquence to a painful success (which he no longer wants)
before an assembly which "scarcely dares draw breath". In

the second place, Salem, as she presents it, is a small community which, however comfortable and unassuming it is, claims a power which may be beyond the human range. Her concern is still with the urgent question which she had raised in *The Rector:* what does it mean for a man, living among men, to call himself their priest? Vincent has received his title to ordination, not from a bishop, but from the vote of the congregation itself, and when he first arrives in Carlingford he is proud of this. He agrees to deliver a course of lectures attacking the Church of England, a hierarchy paid for by the State. But the experience of ministry makes him question not only what he is doing, but who he is. If he is answerable to God for the souls of human beings, can these same human beings hold authority over him?

Almost certainly Mrs Oliphant had in mind two great unorthodox Scottish ministers, Edward Irving and George Macdonald, both rejected for heresy by their congregations. Only a year earlier she had been writing her memoir of Irving*, in which she let fly, with generous indignation, at the "homely old men, unqualified for deciding any question which required clear heads", who had passed judgement on the great preacher. And Arthur Vincent, like Irving, comes to dream of a universal Church, with Christ as its only head, "not yet realised, but surely real". Irving, however, was the son of a tanner, and Macdonald the son of a crofter. Both of them were giants of men, with their own primitive grandeur, quite unlike the dapper young man from Homerton. But the distant echo of their battles can be heard in *Salem Chapel*.

Arthur believes that his first duty is to save himself from "having the life crushed out of him by ruthless chapel-mongers", all the more so because he constantly risks the ludicrous. His meditation on his high calling as a soldier of the Cross is interrupted by Phoebe Tozer, who blushingly

*The Life of Edward Irving, Hurst & Blackett, 1862.

comes to offer him a left-over dish of jelly. But, at all levels, the conflict is not as simple as he believes. The real fighting-ground is psychological. He could, for example, have accepted the dish of jelly graciously, Mrs Oliphant tells us, if he had not been a poor widow's son. His poverty and his Dissent give a painful edge to his ambition. English society, he finds, in Carlingford as elsewhere, is "a phalanx of orders and classes standing above him, standing close in order to prevent his entrance". He had hoped to make Salem a centre of light. Now, as Salem's minister, he finds himself shaking hands 'which had just clutched a piece of bacon'. And in all the pride – not to say the vanity – of his intellect, he discovers not only how difficult it is to accept these people, but how easy it is to manipulate them. He sees himself as a teller of tales to children, and feels delighted, in spite of himself, with his own cleverness. This two-edged danger returns more than once. He grows disgusted with his own work, but "contemptuous of those who were pleased with it".

In Mrs Oliphant's novels, men turn for help to women. But in Carlingford the two women who mean most to Arthur act, in a sense, as his opponents without intending it or even knowing it. Beautiful Lady Western, with whom he falls so disastrously and pitiably in love, means no harm, either to him or to anyone else. She is quite conscious of her power, but not of the damage it is doing. Then there is Mrs Vincent, Arthur's mother. The formal distance between Mrs Oliphant and her subject is often very slight, particularly when she introduces these frail, anxious widows who come to the rescue of their families with the unexpected strength of ten. Evidently she is drawing on her own experience here, and indulging herself a little. There is too much about the widow's self-sacrifice, and far too much about her spotless white caps. But Mrs Oliphant is still able to take a clear look at Mrs Vincent. She loves Arthur dearly, her simple faith puts him to shame, and in his defence she confronts Salem, and even Lady Western, successfully, but she is a minister's widow, and to her the ministry is everything. Nothing can make her see beyond the limits of pastoral duty. For this reason, in the end, she can be of comfort, but not of help, to her son.

Arthur Vincent's struggle is a real one, and not only in terms of the mid-nineteenth century. He has enough to contend with, it might be thought, in Salem. Why did Mrs Oliphant feel it necessary to involve him, as she does, in such a lurid sub-plot? It starts off well enough with the mysterious, sardonic Mrs Hilyard, stitching away for a living at coarse material which draws blood from her hands. She and her dark sense of injustice are successfully presented, and it seems appropriate that she eventually puts the crucial question of the book, when she begs Arthur, as a priest, to curse her enemy, and he offers instead, as a priest, to bless her. But when the eagle-faced Colonel Mildmay makes his appearance ("'She-Wolf!' cried the man, grinding his teeth"), and Arthur and his mother begin to chase up and down the length of England to save his sister from "polluting arms", the effect is not so much mystery as bewilderment, turning, sooner or later, to irritation. Arthur himself is singularly inefficient – at one point he arrives at London Bridge just in time to "glimpse" not one, but two of his suspects gliding out of the station in separate carriages. Even Mrs Oliphant herself became doubtful about her contrivances. "I am afraid," she wrote to her publishers, "the machinery I have set in motion is rather extensive for the short limits I had intended."

Like her contemporary, Mrs Gaskell, she was not at ease with the "machinery", and this is the only time it appears in the *Carlingford Chronicles*. It is true that she was an admirer of Wilkie Collins (though not of Dickens), and in particular of *The Woman in White*. In May 1862 she wrote a piece for *Blackwoods* under the title *Sensation Novels*, which praised Collins for using "recognisable human agents" rather than supernatural ones. But the goings-on of Colonel Mildmay are not much, if at all, in the style of *The Woman in White*. They are stock melodrama – abduction, bloodshed, repentance – though admittedly there is nothing supernatural about them. Mrs Oliphant however, was determined to produce a bestseller at all costs, and she did. *Salem Chapel* began running as a serial in *Blackwoods* for February 1862, and came out in book form in 1863. "It went very near," she recollected, "to making me one of the popularities of literature". It paid the family's bills, at least for the time being, and gave her the courage to ask an unheard-of £1500 for her next novel.

This was a sturdy professional attitude, but I think she had another reason for the sensational elements in *Salem Chapel*. Arthur Vincent cannot come to terms with himself, or with his gift of words, until he has encountered what Mrs Oliphant (who knew something about it) called "the dark ocean of life". Poor though he is, he has been sheltered from the sight of absolute want and misery, and at Homerton he has never been led to think about such things. The shock of Mrs Hilyard's mysterious poverty drives him out to visit the slums in Carlingford, even though he has no idea how to go about it. He believes everything he is told, gives money to everyone who asks, and returns penniless and exhausted. This is a beginning. But the wild scenes of flight and pursuit in which he is soon caught up distance him from Carlingford altogether. This, I think, is the effect Mrs Oliphant wanted. When at long last he admits to Salem that his old certainties are gone and that now he only faintly guesses how God, being pitiful, has the heart to make man and leave him on this sad earth", he is talking about things which he could only have learned outside Carlingford, and beyond it.

When John Blackwood, however, said that the novel came very near greatness, but just missed it, he was probably regretting the disappearance of Salem for so many chapters. And if some of the readers thought that the book must be by George Eliot (this caused Mrs

Oliphant an indescribable mixture of pleasure and annoyance), they, too, were thinking of Salem. Mrs Oliphant inherited the Victorian novelist's birthright, the effortless creation of character. In Salem she is totally at her ease. She lets her readers know the people of Grove Street better than poor Arthur Vincent ever does. This is true even of those who only make two or three appearances. Mr Tufton, for example, Arthur's predecessor, is a homely old minister who has fortunately been "visited" by paralysis – "a disease not tragical, but drivelling" – giving the congregation an excuse to retire him with a suitable present. A bland self-deceiver, he has never admitted his own failure, and the congregation (this is a convincing touch) has forgotten it. They assume that it will do the new minister all the good in the world to visit the old one and draw on his wisdom. Arthur suffers agonies of impatience in the Tuftons' stuffy front parlour, dominated by its vast potted plant. But this place of amiable self-deception is, unexpectedly, also the source of truth. The crippled daughter, Adelaide, strikes the sour note of absolute frankness and absolute unpleasantness. Her eyes have "something of the shrill shining of a rainy sky in their glistening whites". She explains that she has no share in life "and so instead of comforting myself that it's all for the best, as papa says, I interfere with my fellow creatures. I get on as well as most people." She takes no pleasure in it, it is an "intense loveless eagerness of curiosity" which the complacent old Tuftons scarcely notice. At the end of the book Adelaide plays a curious small part in deciding Arthur's future. This kind of detail, a novelist's second sight, is characteristic of Mrs Oliphant.

Mr Tozer, the senior deacon of Salem, seems at first to represent the Victorian idea of the good tradesman. Never quite free of the greasiness of the best bacon and butter, he is proud of being "serviceable" to the gentry and is all that is meant or implied by "honest" and "worthy". He makes the familiar equation between morality and trade.

All accounts, financial and spiritual, must be squared, and
the new pastor's sermons must "keep the steam up". His
household, where the apprentices eat with the family, is
patriarchal, and, it is suggested, belongs to times past.
So, perhaps, does his unaffected kindness. Often, Salem
knows, "he's been called up at twelve o' clock, when we
was all abed, to see someone as was dying". All this is
predictable, but Mrs Oliphant refuses to simplify it. Tozer
is Arthur's champion, but partly, at least, because he
backed him from the first and can't endure to be put in the
wrong. When Arthur touches despair Tozer shows him
Christian kindness, but doesn't conceal his pride in
managing the minister's affairs. Arthur finds it hard to
bear Tozer's perfect satisfaction over his own generosity.
He feels, and so do we, that it would be "a balm" to cut
Tozer's remarks short, and to "annihilate" him. At this
point he is goodness in its most exasperating form. Yet we
can't miss the weight of his reproach when the wretched
young man "breaks out" (his sister is suspected of murder):
"Mr Vincent, sir, you mustn't swear. I'm as sorry for you
as a man can be; but you're a minister, and you mustn't
give way."

  Comic characters on this scale generate their own energy,
and grow beyond themselves. Tozer escapes from the
confines of his "worthiness". In his own way – although
Arthur feels he must be "altogether unable to comprehend
the feelings of a cultivated mind" – he is a connoisseur,
and even an aesthete. This appears in his description of a
tea-meeting, "with pleasant looks and the urns a-smoking
and a bit of greenery on the wall", and, more surprisingly,
in his tribute to Lady Western's beauty: "She's always
spending her life in company, as I don't approve of; but to
look in her face, you couldn't say a word against her."
Again, Tozer's reverence for education goes deep, although
he is too shrewd to expect others to share it. It would, he
thinks, be unwise to charge an entrance fee to Arthur's
lectures. "If we was amusin' the people, we might charge

sixpence a head; but, mark my words, there aren't twenty men in Carlingford, nor in no other place, as would give sixpence to have their minds enlightened. No, sir, we're conferring of a boon, and let's do it handsomely." He, too, has his battle to fight, with his second deacon, Pigeon, who cannot believe that Salem needs a highly educated minister. And, in practical terms, Pigeon turns out to be right, but we can never doubt Tozer's claim to authority. The last sight we have of him is his red handkerchief; he has drawn it out to wipe away a tear or so, and to Arthur, preaching for the last time in Salem Chapel, "the gleam seemed to redden over the entire throng". This is Tozer heroic. Mrs Oliphant herself, although she always refused to make any high claims of her own work, admitted that Tozer had amused her.

Salem can settle back to its own level, and find its own peace. "Unpeace" – this is Mrs Tozer's word – is at all costs to be avoided. But there is no easy solution for Arthur Vincent, who has been called upon for something less than he can give, but has given, all the same, less than he might have done. Like *The Rector* and *The Doctor's Family*, *Salem Chapel* points forward to the future without exactly defining it. As the story ends, Arthur knows what it is to mistake one's calling, and to be misunderstood, and to suffer. He still has to learn what it is to be happy.

Penelope Fitzgerald, London, 1985

CHAPTER I.

Towards the west end of Grove Street, in Carlingford, on the shabby side of the street, stood a red brick building, presenting a pinched gable terminated by a curious little belfry, not intended for any bell, and looking not unlike a handle to lift up the edifice by to the public observation. This was Salem Chapel, the only Dissenting place of worship in Carlingford. It stood in a narrow strip of ground, just as the little houses which flanked it on either side stood in their gardens, except that the enclosure of the chapel was flowerless and sombre, and showed at the farther end of a few sparsely-scattered tombstones – unmeaning slabs, such as the English mourner loves to inscribe his sorrow on. On either side of this little tabernacle were the humble houses – little detached boxes, each two storeys high, each fronted by a little flower-plot – clean, respectable, meagre, little habitations, which contributed most largely to the ranks of the congregation in the chapel. The big houses opposite, which turned their backs and staircase windows to the street, took little notice of the humble Dissenting community. Twice in the winter, perhaps, the Miss Hemmings, mild Evangelical women, on whom the late rector – the Low-Church rector, who reigned before the brief and exceptional incumbency of the Rev. Mr Proctor – had bestowed much of his confidence, would cross the street, when other profitable occupations failed them, to hear a special sermon on a Sunday evening. But the Miss Hemmings were the only representatives of anything which could, by the utmost stretch, be called Society, who ever patronised the

Dissenting interest in the town of Carlingford. Nobody from Grange Lane had ever been seen so much as in Grove Street on a Sunday, far less in the chapel. Green-grocers, dealers in cheese and bacon, milkmen, with some dress-makers of inferior pretensions, and teachers of day-schools of similar humble character, formed the *élite* of the congregation. It is not to be supposed, however, on this account, that a prevailing aspect of shabbiness was upon this little community; on the contrary, the grim pews of Salem Chapel blushed with bright colours, and contained both dresses and faces on the summer Sundays which the Church itself could scarcely have surpassed. Nor did those unadorned walls form a centre of asceticism and gloomy religiousness in the cheerful little town. Tea-meetings were not uncommon occurrences in Salem – tea-meetings which made the little tabernacle festive, in which cakes and oranges were diffused among the pews, and funny speeches made from the little platform underneath the pulpit, which woke the unconsecrated echoes with hearty outbreaks of laughter. Then the young people had their singing-class, at which they practised hymns, and did not despise a little flirtation; and charitable societies and missionary auxiliaries diversified the congregational routine, and kept up a brisk succession of "Chapel busi-ness," mightily like the Church business which occupied Mr Wentworth and his Sisters of Mercy at St Roque's. To name the two communities, however, in the same breath, would have been accounted little short of sacrilege in Carlingford. The names which figured highest in the benevolent lists of Salem Chapel, were known to society only as appearing, in gold letters, upon the backs of those mystic tradesmen's books which were deposited every Monday in little heaps at every house in Grange Lane. The Dissenters, on their part, aspired to no conquests in the unattainable territory of high life, as it existed in Carlingford. They were content to keep their privileges among themselves, and to enjoy their superior preaching and purity with a compassionate complacence. While Mr Proctor was rector, indeed, Mr Tozer, the butterman, who was senior deacon, found it difficult to refrain from an audible expression of pity for the "Church folks" who knew no better; but, as a general rule, the congregation of Salem kept by itself, gleaning new adherents by times at an "anniversary" or the coming of a new minister, but knowing and keeping "its own place" in a manner edifying to behold.

Such was the state of affairs when old Mr Tufton declined in popularity, and impressed upon the minds of his hearers those now-established principles about the unfitness of old men for any important post, and the urgent necessity and duty incumbent upon old clergymen, old generals, old admirals, &c. – every aged functionary, indeed, except old statesmen – to resign in favour of younger men, which have been, within recent years, so much enforced upon the world. To communicate this opinion to the old minister was perhaps less difficult to Mr Tozer and his brethren than it might have been to men more refined and less practical; but it was an undeniable relief to the managers of the chapel when grim Paralysis came mildly in and gave the intimation in the manner least calculated to wound the sufferer's feelings. Mild but distinct was that undeniable warning. The poor old minister retired, accordingly, with a purse and a presentation, and young Arthur Vincent, fresh from Homerton, in the bloom of hope and intellectualism, a young man of the newest school, was recognised as pastor in his stead.

A greater change could not have possibly happened. When the interesting figure of the young minister went up the homely pulpit-stairs, and appeared, white-browed, white-handed, in snowy linen and glossy clerical apparel, where old Mr Tufton, spiritual but homely, had been wont to impend over the desk and exhort his beloved brethren, it was natural that a slight rustle of expectation should run audibly through the audience. Mr Tozer looked round

4 CHRONICLES OF CARLINGFORD

him proudly to note the sensation, and see if the Miss Hemmings, sole representatives of a cold and unfeeling aristocracy, were there. The fact was, that few of the auditors were more impressed than the Miss Hemmings, who *were* there, and who talked all the evening after about the young minister. What a sermon it was! not much in it about the beloved brethren; nothing very stimulating, indeed, to the sentiments and affections, except in the youth and good looks of the preacher, which naturally made a more distinct impression upon the female portion of his hearers than on the stronger sex. But then what eloquence! what an amount of thought! what an honest entrance into all the difficulties of the subject! Mr Tozer remarked afterwards that such preaching was food for *men*. It was too closely reasoned out, said the excellent butterman, to please women or weak-minded persons; but he did not doubt, for his part, that soon the young men of Carlingford, the hope of the country, would find their way to Salem. Under such prognostications, it was fortunate that the young minister possessed something else besides close reasoning and Homerton eloquence to propitiate the women too.

Mr Vincent arrived at Carlingford in the beginning of winter, when society in that town was reassembling, or at least reappearing, after the temporary summer seclusion. The young man knew very little of the community which he had assumed the spiritual charge of. He was almost as particular as the Rev. Mr Wentworth of St Roque's about the cut of his coat and the precision of his costume, and decidedly preferred the word clergyman to the word minister, which latter was universally used by his flock; but notwithstanding these trifling predilections, Mr Vincent, who had been brought up upon the 'Nonconformist' and the 'Eclectic Review,' was strongly impressed with the idea that the Church Establishment, though outwardly prosperous, was in reality a profoundly rotten institution; that the Nonconforming portion of the English public was

the party of progress; that the eyes of the world were
turned upon the Dissenting interest; and that his own
youthful eloquence and the Voluntary principle were
quite enough to counterbalance all the ecclesiastical
advantages on the other side, and make for himself a
position of the highest influence in his new sphere. As he
walked about Carlingford making acquaintance with the
place, it occurred to the young man, with a thrill of not
ungenerous ambition, that the time might shortly come
when Salem Chapel would be all too insignificant for the
Nonconformists of this hitherto torpid place. He pictured
to himself how, by-and-by, those jealous doors in Grange
Lane would fly open at his touch, and how the dormant
minds within would awake under his influence. It was a
blissful dream to the young pastor. Even the fact that Mr
Tozer was a butterman, and the other managers of the
chapel equally humble in their pretensions, did not dis-
concert him in that flush of early confidence. All he
wanted – all any man worthy of his post wanted – was a
spot of standing-ground, and an opportunity of making the
Truth – and himself – known. Such, at least, was the teaching
of Homerton and the Dissenting organs. Young Vincent,
well educated and enlightened according to his fashion,
was yet so entirely unacquainted with any world but that
contracted one in which he had been brought up, that he
believed all this as devoutly as Mr Wentworth believed in
Anglicanism, and would have smiled with calm scorn at
any sceptic who ventured to doubt. Thus it will be seen he
came to Carlingford with elevated expectations – by no
means prepared to circulate among his flock, and say
grace at Mrs Tozer's "teas," and get up soirees to amuse
the congregation, as Mr Tufton had been accustomed to
do. These secondary circumstances of his charge had little
share in the new minister's thoughts. Somehow the tone of
public writing has changed of late days. Scarcely a newspaper writer condescends now to address men who are not
free of "society," and learned in all its ways. The 'Times'

and the Magazines take it for granted that all their readers
dine out at splendid tables, and are used to a solemn
attendant behind their chair. Young Vincent was one of
those who accept the flattering implication. It is true, he
saw few enough of such celestial scenes in his college-
days. But now that life was opening upon him, he doubted
nothing of the society that must follow; and with a swell of
gratification listened when the advantages of Carlingford
were discussed by some chance fellow-travellers on the
railway; its pleasant parties – its nice people – Mr Wodehouse's capital dinners, and the charming breakfasts – such
a delightful novelty! – so easy and agreeable! – of the
pretty Lady Western, the young Dowager. In imagination
Mr Vincent saw himself admitted to all these social pleasures; not that he cared for capital dinners more than
became a young man, or had any special tendencies
towards tuft-hunting, but because fancy and hope, and
ignorance of the real world, made him naturally project
himself into the highest sphere within his reach, in the
simple conviction that such was his natural place.

With these thoughts, to be asked to Mrs Tozer's to tea
at six o'clock, was the most wonderful cold plunge for the
young man. He shrugged his shoulders, smiled to himself
over the note of invitation, which, however, was very
prettily written by Phoebe, Mrs Tozer's blooming daughter,
on paper as pink as Lady Western's, and consented, as he
could not help himself. He went out from his nice lodgings
a little after six, still smiling, and persuading himself that
this would be quite a pleasant study of manners, and that
of course he could not do less than patronise the good
homely people in their own way, whatever that might be.
Mr Vincent's rooms were in George Street, at what the
Grange Lane people called *the other end*, in an imposing
house with a large door, and iron extinguishers fixed in the
railing, which had in their day quenched the links of the
last century. To cross the street in his evening coat, and
walk into the butter-shop, where the two white-aproned

lads behind the counter stared, and a humble member of
the congregation turned sharply round, and held out the
hand, which had just clutched a piece of bacon, for her
minister to shake, was a sufficiently trying introduction
to the evening's pleasure; but when the young pastor
had been ushered up-stairs, the first aspect of the
company there rather took away his breath, as he
emerged from the dark staircase. Tozer himself, who
awaited the minister at the door, was fully habited in the
overwhelming black suit and white tie, which produced
so solemnising an effect every Sunday at chapel; and the
other men of the party were, with a few varieties, similarly
attired. But the brilliancy of the female portion of the
company overpowered Mr Vincent. Mrs Tozer herself sat
at the end of her hospitable table, with all her best china
tea-service set out before her, in a gown and cap which
Grange Lane could not have furnished any rivals to. The
brilliant hue of the one, and the flowers and feathers of the
other, would require a more elaborate description than
this chronicle has space for. Nor indeed in the particular of
dress did Mrs Tozer do more than hold her own among the
guests who surrounded her. It was scarcely dark, and the
twilight softened down the splendours of the company,
and saved the dazzled eyes of the young pastor. He felt
the grandeur vaguely as he came in with a sense of
reproof, seeing that he had evidently been waited for. He
said grace devoutly when the tea arrived and the gas was
lighted, and with dumb amaze gazed round him. Could
these be the veritable womankind of Salem Chapel? Mr
Vincent saw bare shoulders and flower-wreathed heads
bending over the laden tea-table. He saw pretty faces
and figures not inelegant, remarkable among which was
Miss Phoebe's, who had written him that pink note, and
who herself was pink all over – dress, shoulders, elbows,
cheeks, and all. Pink – not red – a softened youthful flush,
which had not an angle anywhere. As for the men, the
lawful owners of all this feminine display, they huddled

all together, indisputable cheese-mongers as they were, quite transcended and extinguished by their wives and daughters. The pastor was young and totally inexperienced. In his heart he asserted his own claim to an entirely different sphere; but, suddenly cast into this little crowd, Mr Vincent's inclination was to join the dark group of husbands and fathers whom he knew, and who had made no false pretences. He was shy of venturing upon those fine women who surely never could be Mrs Brown of the Devonshire Dairy, and Mrs Pigeon, the poulterer's wife; whereas Pigeon and Brown themselves were exactly like what they always were on Sundays, if not perhaps a trifle graver and more depressed in their minds.

"Here's a nice place for you, Mr Vincent – quite the place for you, where you can hear all the music, and see all the young ladies. For I do suppose ministers, bein' young, are like other young men," said Mrs Tozer, drawing aside her brilliant skirts to make room for him on the sofa. "I have a son myself as is at college, and feel motherlike to those as go in the same line. Sit you down comfortable, Mr Vincent. There ain't one here, sir, I'm proud to say, as grudges you the best seat."

"Oh mamma, how could you think of saying such a thing?" said Phoebe, under her breath; "to be sure, Mr Vincent never could think there was anybody anywhere that would be so wicked – and he the minister."

"Indeed, my dear," said Mrs Pigeon, who was close by, "not to affront Mr Vincent, as is deserving of our best respects, I've seen many and many's the minister I wouldn't have given up my seat to; and I don't misdoubt, sir, you've heard of such as well as we. There was Mr Bailey at Parson's Green, now. He went and married a poor bit of a governess, as common a looking creature as you could see, that set herself up above the people, Mr Vincent, and was too grand, sir, if you'll believe me, to visit the deacons' wives. Nobody cares less than me about them vain shows. What's visiting, if you know the vally of your time? Nothing but a laying up of judgment. But I wouldn't be put upon neither by a chit that got her bread out of me and my husband's hard earnins; and so I told my sister, Mrs Tozer, as lives at Parson's Green."

"Poor thing!" said the gentler Mrs Tozer, "it's hard lines on a minister's wife to please the congregation. Mr Vincent here, he'll have to take a lesson. That Mrs Bailey was pretty-looking, I must allow—"

"Sweetly pretty!" whispered Phoebe, clasping her plump pink hands.

"Pretty-looking! I don't say anything against it," continued her mother; "but it's hard upon a minister when his wife won't take no pains to please his flock. To have people turn up their noses at you ain't pleasant—"

"And them getting their livin' off you all the time," cried Mrs Pigeon, clinching the milder speech.

"But it seems to me," said poor Vincent, "that a minister can no more be said to get his living off you than any other man. He works hard enough generally for what little he has. And really, Mrs Tozer, I'd rather not hear all these unfortunate particulars about one of my brethren—"

"He ain't one of the brethren now," broke in the poulterer's wife. "He's been gone out o' Parson's Green this twelve-months. Them stuck-up ways may do with the Church folks as can't help themselves, but they'll never do with us Dissenters. Not that we ain't as glad as can be to see you, Mr Vincent, and I hope you'll favour my poor house another night like you're favouring Mrs Tozer's. Mr Tufton always said that was the beauty of Carlingford in our connection. Cheerful folks and no display. No display, you know – nothing but a hearty meetin', sorry to part, and happy to meet again. Them's our ways. And the better you know us, the better you'll like us, I'll be bound to say. We don't put it all on the surface, Mr Vincent," continued Mrs Pigeon, shaking out her skirts and expanding herself on her chair, "but it's all real and solid; what we say we mean – and we don't say no more than we mean – and them's the kind of folks to trust to wherever you go."

Poor Vincent made answer by an inarticulate murmur, whether an assent or dissent it was impossible to say; and, inwardly appalled, turned his eyes towards his deacons, who, more fortunate than himself, were standing all in a group together discussing chapel matters, and wisely leaving general conversation to the fairer portion of the company. The unlucky minister's secret looks of distress awoke the interest and sympathy of Phoebe, who sat in an interesting manner on a stool at her mother's side. "Oh, mamma," said that young lady, too bashful to address himself directly, "I wonder if Mr Vincent plays or sings? There are some such nice singers here. Perhaps we might have some music, if Mr Vincent—"

"I don't perform at all," said that victim, – "not in any way; but I am an exemplary listener. Let me take you to the piano."

The plump Phoebe rose after many hesitations, and with a simper and a blush and pretty air of fright, took the minister's arm. After all, even when the whole company is beneath a man's level, it is easier to play the victim under the *supplice* inflicted by a pretty girl than by two mature matrons. Phoebe understood pretty well about her *h*'s, and did not use the double negative; and when she rose up rustling from her low seat, the round, pink creature, with dimples all about her, was not an unpleasant object of contemplation. Mr Vincent listened to her song with decorous interest. Perhaps it was just as well sung as Lucy Wodehouse, in Grange Lane, would have sung it. When Phoebe had concluded, the minister was called to the side of Mrs Brown of the Devonshire Dairy, who had been fidgeting to secure him from the moment he approached the piano. She was fat and roundabout, good woman, and had the aspect of sitting upon the very edge of her chair. She held out to the distressed pastor a hand covered with a rumpled white glove, which did not fit, and had never been intended to fit, and beckoned to him anxiously. With the calmness of despair Mr Vincent obeyed the call.

"I have been looking so anxiously to catch your eye, Mr Vincent," said Mrs Brown; "do sit down, now there's a chance, and let me talk to you a minnit. Bless the girl! there's Miss Polly Pigeon going to play, and everybody can use their freedom in talking. For my part," said Mrs Brown, securing the vacant chair of the performer for her captive, "that's why I like instrumental music best. When a girl sings, why, to be sure, it's only civil to listen – ain't it now, Mr Vincent? but nobody expects it of you, don't you see, when she only plays. Now do you sit down. What I wanted to speak to you was about that poor creetur in Back Grove Street – that's the lane right behind the chapel. She do maunder on so to see the minister. Mr Tozer he's been to see her, and I sent Brown, but it wasn't a bit of use. It's you, Mr Vincent, she's awanting of. If you'll call in to-morrow, I'll show you the place myself, as you're a stranger; for if you'll excuse me saying it, I am as curious as can be to hear what she's got to say."

"If she has got anything to say, she might prefer that it was not heard," said Vincent, with an attempt to smile. "Is she ill – and who is she? I have never heard of her before."

"Well, you see, sir, she doesn't belong rightly to Salem. She's a stranger here, and not a joined member; and she ain't ill either, as I can see – only something on her mind. You ministers," said Mrs Brown, with a look of awe, "must have a deal of secrets confided to you. Folks may stand out against religion as long as things go on straight with them, but they're sure to want the minister as soon as they've got something on their mind; and a deal better to have it out, and get a little comfort, than to bottle it all up till their latter end, like old Mrs Thompson, and let it out in their will, to drive them as was expecting different distracted. It's a year or two since that happened. I don't suppose you've heerd tell of it yet. But that's what makes old Mrs Christian – I dare say you've seen her at chapel – so uncomfortable in her feelings. She's never got over it, sir, and never will to her dying day."

"Some disappointment about money?" said Mr Vincent.

"Poor old folks! their daughter did very well for herself –
and very well for them too," said Mrs Brown: "but it don't
make no difference in Mrs Christian's feelins: they're
living, like, on Mr Brown the solicitor's charity, you see,
sir, instead of their own fortin, which makes a deal o'
difference. It would have been a fine thing for Salem,
too," added Mrs Brown, reflectively, "if they had had the
old lady's money; for Mrs Christian was always one that
liked to be first, and stanch to her chapel, and would
never have been wanting when the collecting-books went
round. But it wasn't to be, Mr Vincent – that's the long of
it; and we never have had nobody in our connection worth
speaking of in Carlingford but's been in trade. And a very
good thing too, as I tell Brown. For if there's one thing I
can't abear in a chapel, it's one set setting up above the
rest. But bein' all in the way of business, except just the
poor folks, as is all very well in their place, and never
interferes with nothing, and don't count, there's nothing
but brotherly love here, which is a deal more than most
ministers can say for their flocks. I've asked a few friends
to tea, Mr Vincent, on next Thursday, at six. As I haven't
got no daughters just out of boarding-school to write notes
for me, will you take us in a friendly way, and just come
without another invitation? All our own folks, sir, and a
comfortable evening; and prayers, if you'll *be* so good, at
the end. I don't like the new fashion," said Mrs Brown,
with a significant glance towards Mrs Tozer, "of separatin',
like heathens, when all's of one connection. We might
never meet again, Mr Vincent. In the midst of life, you
know, sir. You'll not forget Thursday, at six."

"But, my dear Mrs Brown, I am very sorry: Thursday
is one of the days I have specially devoted to study,"
stammered forth the unhappy pastor. "What with the
Wednesday meeting and the Friday committee—"

Mrs Brown drew herself up as well as the peculiarities of
her form permitted, and her roseate countenance assumed a

deeper glow. "We've been in the chapel longer than Tozer," said the offended deaconess. "We've never been backward in takin' trouble, nor spendin' our substance, nor puttin' our hands to every good work; and as for makin' a difference between one member and another, it's what we ain't been accustomed to, Mr Vincent. I'm a plain woman, and speak my mind. Old Mr Tufton was very particular to show no preference. He always said, it never answered in a flock to show more friendship to one nor another; and if it had been put to me, I wouldn't have said, I assure you, sir, that it was us as was to be made the first example of. If I haven't a daughter fresh out of a boarding-school, I've been a member of Salem five-and-twenty year, and had ministers in my house many's the day, and as friendly as if I were a duchess; and for charities and such things, we've never been known to fail, though I say it; and as for trouble——"

"But I spoke of my study," said the poor minister, as she paused, her indignation growing too eloquent for words: "you want me to preach on Sunday, don't you? and I must have some time, you know, to do my work."

"Sir," said Mrs Brown, severely, "I know it for a fact that Mr Wentworth of St Roque's dines out five days in the week, and it don't do *his* sermons no injury; and when you go out to dinner, it stands to reason it's a different thing from a friendly tea."

"Ah, yes, most likely!" said Mr Vincent, with a heavy sigh. "I'll come, since you wish it so much; but," added the unlucky young man, with a melancholy attempt at a smile, "you must not be too kind to me. Too much of this kind of thing, you know, might have an effect——" Here he paused, inclined to laugh at his own powers of sarcasm. As chance would have it, as he pointed generally to the scene before them, the little wave of his hand seemed to Mrs Brown to indicate the group round the piano, foremost in which was Phoebe, plump and pink, and full of dimples. The good mistress of the Devonshire Dairy gave her head a little toss.

"Ah!" said Mrs Brown, with a sigh, "you don't know, you young men, the half of the tricks of them girls that look so innocent. But I don't deny it's a pleasant party," added the deaconess, looking round on the company in general with some complacency. "But just you come along our way on Thursday, at six, and judge for yourself if mine ain't quite as good; though I have not got no daughters, Mr Vincent," she concluded, with severe irony, elevating her double chin and nodding her flowery head.

The subdued minister made no reply; only deeper and deeper humiliation seemed in store for him. Was it he, the first-prize man of Homerton, who was supposed to be already smitten by the pink charms of Phoebe Tozer? The unfortunate young man groaned in spirit, and, seizing a sudden opportunity, plunged into the black group of deacons, and tried to immerse himself in chapel business. But vain was the attempt. He was recaptured and led back in triumph to Mrs Tozer's sofa. He had to listen to more singing, and accept another invitation to tea. When he got off at last, it was with a sensation of dreadful dwindlement that poor Vincent crossed the street again to his lonely abode. He knocked quite humbly at the big door, and, with a sensation of unclerical rage, wondered to himself whether the policeman who met him knew he had been out to tea. Ah, blessed Mr Wentworth of St Roque's! The young Nonconformist sighed as he put on his slippers, and kicked his boots into a corner of his sitting-room. Somehow he had come down in the world all at once, and without expecting it. Such was Salem Chapel and its requirements; and such was Mr Vincent's first experience of social life in Carlingford.

CHAPTER II.

It was with a somewhat clouded aspect that the young
pastor rose from his solitary breakfast-table next morning
to devote himself to the needful work of visiting his flock.
The minister's breakfast, though lonely, had not been
without alleviations. He had the 'Carlingford Gazette' at
his elbow, if that was any comfort, and he had two letters
which were more interesting; one was from his mother,
a minister's widow, humbly enough off, but who had
brought up her son in painful gentility, and had done
much to give him that taste for good society which was to
come to so little fruition in Carlingford. Mr Vincent smiled
sardonically as he read his good mother's questions about
his "dear people," and her anxious inquiry whether he
had found a "pleasant circle" in Salem. Remembering the
dainty little household which it took her so much pains and
pinching to maintain, the contrast made present affairs
still more and more distasteful to her son. He could fancy
her trim little figure in that traditionary black silk gown
which never wore out, and the whitest of caps, gazing
aghast at Mrs Brown and Mrs Tozer. But, nevertheless,
Mrs Vincent understood all about Mrs Brown and Mrs
Tozer, and had been very civil to such, and found them
very serviceable in her day, though her son, who knew
her only in that widowed cottage where she had her own
way, could not have realised it. The other letter was from
a Homerton chum, a young intellectual and ambitious
Nonconformist like himself, whose epistle was full of
confidence and hope, triumph in the cause, and its perpetual advance. "We are the priests of the poor," said the

Homerton enthusiast, encouraging his friend to the sacrifices and struggles which he presumed to be already
surrounding him. Mr Vincent bundled up this letter with a
sigh. Alas! there were no grand struggles or sacrifices in
Carlingford. "The poor" were mostly church-goers, as he
had already discovered. It was a tolerably comfortable
class of the community, that dreadful "connection" of
Browns, Pigeons, and Tozers. Amid their rude luxuries
and commonplace plenty, life could have no heroic circumstances. The young man sighed, and did not feel so
sure as he once did of the grand generalities in which his
friend was still confident. If Dissenters led the van of
progress generally, there was certainly an exception to
be made in respect to Carlingford. And the previous
evening's entertainment had depressed the young minister's
expectations even of what he himself could do – a sad blow
to a young man. He was less convinced that opportunity of
utterance was all that was necessary to give him influence
in the general community. He was not half so sure of
success in opening the closed doors and sealed hearts of
Grange Lane. On the whole, matters looked somewhat
discouraging that particular morning, which was a morning
in October, not otherwise depressing or disagreeable. He
took his hat and went down-stairs with a kind of despairing
determination to do his duty. There an encounter occurred
which did not raise his spirits. The door was open, and his
landlady, who was a member of Salem Chapel, stood
there in full relief against the daylight outside, taking
from the hands of Miss Phoebe Tozer a little basket,
the destination of which she was volubly indicating. Mr
Vincent appearing before Phoebe had half-concluded her
speech, that young lady grew blushingly embarrassed,
and made haste to relinquish her hold of the basket. Her
conscious looks filled the unwitting minister with ignorant
amaze.

"Oh, to think Mr Vincent should catch me here! What
ever will he think? and what ever will Ma say?" cried Miss

Phoebe. "Oh, Mr Vincent, Ma thought, please, you might perhaps like some jelly, and I said I would run over with it myself, as it's so near, and the servant might have made a mistake, and Ma hopes you'll enjoy it, and that you liked the party last night!"

"Mrs Tozer is very kind," said the minister, with cloudy looks. "Some what, did you say, Miss Phoebe?"

"La! only some jelly – nothing worth mentioning – only a shape that was over supper last night, and Ma thought you wouldn't mind," cried the messenger, half alarmed by the unusual reception of her offering. Mr Vincent turned very red, and looked at the basket as if he would like nothing better than to pitch it into the street; but prudence for once restrained the young man. He bit his lips and bowed, and went upon his way, without waiting, as she intended he should, to escort Miss Phoebe back again to her paternal shop. Carrying his head higher than usual, and thrilling with offence and indignation, the young pastor made his way along George Street. It was a very trifling circumstance, certainly; but just when an enthusiastic companion writes to you about the advance of the glorious cause, and your own high vocation as a soldier of the Cross, and the undoubted fact that the hope of England is in you, to have a shape of jelly, left over from the last night's tea-party, sent across the street with complacent kindness, for your refreshment—! It *was* trying. To old Mrs Tufton, indeed, who had an invalid daughter, it might have seemed a Christian bounty; but to Arthur Vincent, five-and-twenty, a scholar and a gentleman – ah me! if he had been a Christchurch man, or even a Fellow of Trinity, the chances are he would have taken it much more graciously, for then he would have had the internal consciousness of his own dignity to support him; whereas the sting of it all was, that poor young Vincent had no special right to his own pretensions, but had come to them he could not tell how, and in reality, had his mind been on a level with his fortunes, ought to have found the Tozers and Pigeons sufficiently congenial company. He went along George Street with troubled haste, pondering his sorrows – those sorrows which he could confide to nobody. Was he actually to live among these people for years – to have no other society – to circulate among their tea-parties, and grow accustomed to their finery, and perhaps "pay attention" to Phoebe Tozer; or, at least, suffer that young lady's attentions to him? And what would become of him at the end? To drop into a shuffling old gossip, like good old Mr Tufton, seemed the best thing he could hope for; and who could wonder at the mild stupor of paralysis – disease not tragical, only drivelling – which was the last chapter of all?

The poor young man accordingly marched along George Street deeply disconsolate. When he met the perpetual curate of St Roque's at the door of Masters's bookshop – where, to be sure, at that hour in the morning, it was natural to encounter Mr Wentworth – the young Non-conformist gazed at him with a certain wistfulness. They looked at each other, in fact, being much of an age, and not unsimilar in worldly means just at the present moment. There were various points of resemblance between them. Mr Vincent, too, wore an Anglican coat, and assumed a high clerical aspect – sumptuary laws forbidding such presumption being clearly impracticable in England; and the Dissenter was as fully endowed with natural good looks as the young priest. How was it, then, that so vast a world of difference and separation lay between them? For one compensating moment Mr Vincent decided that it was because of his more enlightened faith, and felt himself persecuted. But even that pretence did not serve the purpose. He began to divine faintly, and with a certain soreness, that external circumstances do stand for some-thing, if not in the great realities of a man's career, at least in the comforts of his life. A poor widow's son, educated at Homerton, and an English squire's son, public school and university bred, cannot begin on the same level. To compensate that disadvantage requires something more

than a talent for preaching. Perhaps genius would scarcely
do it without the aid of time and labour. The conviction
fell sadly upon poor Arthur Vincent as he went down the
principal street of Carlingford in the October sunshine.
He was rapidly becoming disenchanted, and neither the
'Noncomformist' nor the 'Patriot,' nor Exeter Hall itself,
could set him up again.

With these feelings the young pastor pursued his way
to see the poor woman who, according to Mrs Brown's
account, was so anxious to see the minister. He found this
person, whose desire was at present shared by most of the
female members of Salem without the intervention of the
Devonshire Dairy, in a mean little house in the close lane
dignified by the name of Back Grove Street. She was a
thin, dark, vivacious-looking woman, with a face from
which some forty years of energetic living had withdrawn
all the colour and fulness which might once have rendered
it agreeable, but which was, nevertheless, a remarkable
face, not to be lightly passed over. Extreme thinness of
outline and sharpness of line made the contrast between
this educated countenance and the faces which had lately
surrounded the young minister still more remarkable.
It was not a profound or elevated kind of education,
perhaps, but it was very different from the thin superficial
lacker with which Miss Phoebe was coated. Eager dark
eyes, with dark lines under them – thin eloquent lips, the
upper jaw projecting slightly, the mouth closing fast and
firm – a well-shaped small head, with a light black lace
handkerchief fastened under the chin – no complexion or
softening of tint – a dark, sallow, colourless face, thrilling
with expression, energy, and thought, was that on which
the young man suddenly lighted as he went in, somewhat
indifferent, it must be confessed, and expecting to find
nothing that could interest him. She was seated in a
shabby room, only half-carpeted, up two pair of stairs,
which looked out upon no more lively view than the back
of Salem Chapel itself, with its few dismal scattered

graves – and was working busily at men's clothing of the coarsest kind, blue stuff which had transferred its colour to her thin fingers. Meagre as were her surroundings, however, Mr Vincent, stumbling listlessly up the narrow bare stair of the poor lodging-house, suddenly came to himself as he stood within this humble apartment. If this was to be his penitent, the story she had to tell might be not unworthy of serious listening. He stammered forth a half apology and explanation of his errand, as he gazed surprised at so unexpected a figure, wondering within himself what intense strain and wear of life could have worn to so thin a tissue the outer garment of this keen and sharp-edged soul.

"Come in," said the stranger; "I am glad to see you. I know you, Mr Vincent, though I can't suppose you've observed me. Take a seat. I have heard you preach ever since you came – so, knowing in a manner how your thoughts run, I've a kind of acquaintance with you: which, to be sure, isn't the same on your side. I daresay the woman at the Dairy sent you to me?"

"I understood – from Mrs Brown certainly – that you wanted to see me," said the puzzled pastor.

"Yes, it was quite true. I have resources in myself, to be sure, as much as most people," said his new acquaintance, whom he had been directed to ask for as Mrs Hilyard, "but still human relations are necessary; and as I don't know anybody here, I thought I'd join the Chapel. Queer set of people, rather, don't you think?" she continued, glancing up from her rapid stitching to catch Vincent's conscious eye; "they thought I was in spiritual distress, I suppose, and sent me the butterman. Lord bless us! if I had been, what could he have done for me, does anybody imagine? and when he didn't succeed, there came the Dairy person, who, I daresay, would have understood what I wanted had I been a cow. Now I can make out what I'm doing when I have you, Mr Vincent. I know your line a little from your sermons. That was wonderfully clever on Sunday morning

about confirmation. I belong to the Church myself by
rights, and was confirmed, of course, at the proper time,
like other people, but I am a person of impartial mind. That
was a famous downright blow. I liked you there."

"I am glad to have your approbation," said the young
minister, rather stiffly; "but excuse me – I was quite in
earnest in my argument."

"Yes, yes; that was the beauty of it," said his eager interlocutor, who went on without ever raising her eyes, intent
upon the rough work which he could not help observing
sometimes made her scarred fingers bleed as it passed
rapidly through them. "No argument is ever worth listening
to if it isn't used in earnest. I've led a wandering life, and
heard an infinity of sermons of late years. When there are
any brains in them at all, you know, they are about the only
kind of mental stimulant a poor woman in my position can
come by, for I've no time for reading lately. Down here, in
these regions, where the butterman comes to inquire after
your spiritual interests, and is a superior being," added this
singular new adherent of Salem, looking full for a single
moment in her visitor's eyes, with a slight movement of the
muscles of her thin face, and making a significant pause,
"the air's a trifle heavy. It isn't pure oxygen we breathe in
Back Grove Street, by any means."

"I assure you it surprises me more than I can explain, to
find," said Vincent, hesitating for a proper expression, "to
find—"

"Such a person as I am in Back Grove Street," interrupted his companion, quickly; "yes – and thereby hangs a
tale. But I did not send for you to tell it. I sent for you for
no particular reason, but a kind of yearning to talk to
somebody. I beg your pardon sincerely – but you know,"
she said, once more with a direct sudden glance and that
half-visible movement in her face which meant mischief,
"you are a minister, and are bound to have no inclinations
of your own, but to give yourself up to the comfort of the
poor."

"Without any irony, that is the aim I propose to myself," said Vincent; "but I fear you are disposed to take rather a satirical view of such matters. It is fashionable to talk lightly on those subjects; but I find life and its affairs sufficiently serious, I assure you—"

Here she stopped her work suddenly, and looked up at him, her dark sharp eyes lighting up her thin sallow face with an expression which it was beyond his powers to fathom. The black eyelashes widened, the dark eyebrows rose, with a full gaze of the profoundest tragic sadness, on the surface of which a certain gleam of amusement seemed to hover. The worn woman looked over the dark world of her own experience, of which she was conscious in every nerve, but of which he knew nothing, and smiled at his youth out of the abysses of her own life, where volcanoes had been, and earthquakes. He perceived it dimly, without understanding how, and faltered and blushed, yet grew angry with all the self-assertion of youth.

"I don't doubt you know that as well as I do – perhaps better; but notwithstanding, I find my life leaves little room for laughter," said the young pastor, not without a slight touch of heroics.

"Mr Vincent," said Mrs Hilyard, with a gleam of mirth in her eye, "in inferring that I perhaps know better, you infer also that I am older than you, which is uncivil to a lady. But for my part, I don't object to laughter. Generally it's better than crying, which in a great many cases I find the only alternative. I doubt, however, much whether life, from the butterman's point of view, wears the same aspect. I should be inclined to say not; and I daresay your views will brighten with your company," added the aggravating woman, again resuming, with eyes fixed upon it, her laborious work.

"I perceive you see already what is likely to be my great trial in Carlingford," said young Vincent. "I confess that the society of my office-bearers, which I suppose I must always consider myself bound to—"

"That was a very sad sigh," said the rapid observer beside him; "but don't confide in me, lest I should be tempted to tell somebody. I can speak my mind without prejudice to anybody; and if you agree with me, it may be a partial relief to your feelings. I shall be glad to see you when you can spare me half an hour. I can't look at you while I talk, for that would lose me so much time, but at my age it doesn't matter. Come and see me. It's your business to do me good – and it's possible I might even do some good to you."

"Thank you. I shall certainly come," said the minister, rising with the feeling that he had received his dismissal for today. She rose, too, quickly, and but for a moment, and held out her hand to him.

"Be sure you don't betray to the dairywoman what I had on my mind, and wanted to tell you, though she is dying to know," said his singular new acquaintance, without a smile, but with again a momentary movement in her thin cheeks. When she had shaken hands with him, she seated herself again immediately, and without a moment's pause proceeded with her work, apparently concentrating all her faculties upon it, and neither hearing nor seeing more of her visitor, though he still stood within two steps of her, overshadowing the table. The young man turned and left the room with involuntary quietness, as if he had been dismissed from the presence of a princess. He went straight down-stairs without ever pausing, and hastened through the narrow back-street with still the impulse communicated by that dismissal upon him. When he drew breath, it was with a curious mixture of feelings. Who she was or what she was – how she came there, working at those "slops" till the colour came off upon her hands, and her poor thin fingers bled – she so strangely superior to her surroundings, yet not despising or quarrelling with them, or even complaining of them, so far as he could make out – infinitely perplexed the inexperienced minister. He came away excited and bewildered from the interview, which had turned out so different from his expectations. Whether she had done him good, was extremely doubtful; but she had changed the current of his thoughts, which was in its way an immediate benefit. Marvelling over such a mysterious apparition, and not so sure as in the morning that nothing out of the most vulgar routine ever could occur in Carlingford, Mr Vincent turned with meditative steps towards the little house at the extreme end of Grove Street, where his predecessor still lingered. A visit to old Mr Tufton was a periodical once-a-week duty, to be performed with the utmost regularity. Tozer and Pigeon had agreed that it would be the making of the young minister to draw thus from the experience of the old one. Whether Mr Vincent agreed with them, may be apprehended from the scene which follows.

CHAPTER III.

Mr Tufton's house was at the extremity of Grove Street – at the extremity, consequently, in that direction, of Carlingford, lying parallel with the end of Grange Lane, and within distant view of St Roque's. It was a little old-fashioned house, with a small garden in front and a large garden behind, in which the family cabbages, much less prosperous since the old minister became unable to tend them, flourished. The room into which Mr Vincent, as an intimate of the house, was shown, was a low parlour with two small windows, overshadowed outside by ivy, and inside by two large geraniums, expanded upon a Jacob's ladder of props, which were the pride of Mrs Tufton's heart, and made it almost impossible to see anything clearly within, even at the height of day. Some prints, of which one represented Mr Tufton himself, and the rest other ministers of "the connection," in mahogany frames, hung upon the green walls. The furniture, though it was not unduly abundant, filled up the tiny apartment, so that quite a dislocation and rearrangement of everything was necessary before a chair could be got for the visitor, and he got into it. Though it was rather warm for October out of doors, a fire, large for the size of the room, was burning in the fireplace, on either side of which was an easy-chair and an invalid. The one fronting the light, and conse-quently fronting the visitor, was Adelaide Tufton, the old minister's daughter, who had been confined to that chair longer than Phoebe Tozer could remember; and who, during that long seclusion, had knitted, as all Salem Chapel believed, without intermission, nobody having ever yet succeeded in discovering where the mysterious results of her labour went to. She was knitting now, reclining back in the cushioned chair which had been made for her, and was her shell and habitation. A very pale, emaciated, eager-looking woman, not much above thirty, but looking, after half a lifetime spent in that chair, any age that imagination might suggest; a creature altogether separated from the world – separated from life, it would be more proper to say – for nobody more interested in the world and other people's share of it than Adelaide Tufton existed in Carlingford. She had light-blue eyes, rather prominent, which lightened without giving much expression to her perfectly colourless face. Her very hair was pale, and lay in braids of a clayey yellow, too listless and dull to be called brown, upon the thin temples, over which the thin white skin seemed to be strained like an overtight bandage. Somehow, however, people who were used to seeing her, were not so sorry as they might have been for Adelaide Tufton. No one could exactly say why; but she somehow appeared, in the opinion of Salem

Chapel, to indemnify herself for her privations, and was
treated, if without much sympathy, at least without that
ostentatious pity which is so galling to the helpless. Few
people could afford to be sorry for so quick-sighted and
all-remembering an observer; and the consequence was,
that Adelaide, almost without knowing it, had managed to
neutralise her own disabilities, and to be acknowledged as
an equal in the general conflict, which she could enter
only with her sharp tongue and her quick eye.

It was Mr Tufton himself who sat opposite – his large
expanse of face, with the white hair which had been
apostrophised as venerable at so many Salem tea-parties,
and which Vincent himself had offered homage to, looming
dimly through the green shade of the geraniums, as he sat
with his back to the window. He had a green shade over
his eyes besides, and his head moved with a slight palsied
tremor, which was now the only remnant of that "visitation" which had saved his feelings, and dismissed more
benignly than Tozer and his brother deacons the old
pastor from his old pulpit. He sat very contentedly doing
nothing, with his large feet in large loose slippers, and
his elbows supported on the arms of his chair. By the
evidence of Mrs Tufton's spectacles, and the newspaper
lying on the table, it was apparent that she had been
reading the 'Carlingford Gazette' to her helpless companions; and that humble journal, which young Vincent
had kicked to the other end of his room before coming out,
had made the morning pass very pleasantly to the three
secluded inmates of Siloam Cottage, which was the name
of the old minister's humble home. Mr Tufton said "'umble
'ome," and so did his wife. They came from storied
Islington, both of them, and were of highly respectable
connections, not to say that Mrs Tufton had a little property
as well; and, acting in laudable opposition to the general
practice of poor ministers' wives, had brought many divi-
dends and few children to the limited but comfortable
fireside. Mr Vincent could not deny that it was comfortable

in its way, and quite satisfied its owners, as he sat down in the shade of the geraniums in front of the fire, between Adelaide Tufton and her father; but, oh heavens! to think of such a home as all that, after Homerton and high Nonconformist hopes, could come to himself! The idea, however, was one which did not occur to the young minister. He sat down compassionately, seeing no analogy whatever between his own position and theirs; scarcely even seeing the superficial contrast, which might have struck anybody, between his active youth and their help-lessness and suffering. He was neither hard-hearted nor unsympathetic, but somehow the easy moral of that con-trast never occurred to him. Adelaide Tufton's bloodless countenance conveyed an idea of age to Arthur Vincent; her father was really old. The young man saw no grounds on which to form any comparison. It was natural enough for the old man and ailing woman to be as they were, just as it was natural for him, in the height of his early manhood, to rejoice in his strength and youth.

"So there was a party at Mr Tozer's last night – and you were there, Mr Vincent," said old Mrs Tufton, a cheerful active old lady, with pink ribbons in her cap, which asserted their superiority over the doubtful light and the green shade of the geraniums. "Who did you have? The Browns and the Pigeons, and – everybody else, of course. Now tell me, did Mrs Tozer make tea herself, or did she leave it to Phoebe?"

"As well as I can remember, she did it herself," said the young pastor.

"Exactly what I told you, mamma," said Adelaide, from her chair. "Mrs Tozer doesn't mean Phoebe to make tea this many a year. I daresay she wants her to marry somebody, the little flirting thing. I suppose she wore her pink, Mr Vincent – and Mrs Brown that dreadful red-and-green silk of hers; and didn't they send you over a shape of jelly this morning? Ha, Ha! I told you so, mamma; that was why it never came to me."

"Pray let me send it to you," cried Vincent, eagerly.

The offer was not rejected, though coquetted with for a few minutes. Then Mr Tufton broke in, in solemn bass.

"Adelaide, we shouldn't talk, my dear, of pinks and green silks. Providence has laid you aside, my love, from temptations; and you remember how often I used to say in early days, no doubt it was a blessing, Jemima, coming when it did, to wean our girl from the world; she might have been as fond of dress as other girls, and brought us to ruin, but for her misfortune. Everything is for the best."

"Oh, bother!" said Adelaide, sharply – "I don't complain, and never did; but everybody else finds my misfortune, as they call it, very easy to be borne, Mr Vincent – even papa, you see. There is a reason for everything, to be sure; but how things that are hard and disagreeable are always to be called for the best, I can't conceive. However, let us return to Phoebe Tozer's pink dress. Weren't you rather stunned with all their grandeur? You did not think we could do as much in Salem, did you? Now tell me, who has Mrs Brown taken in hand to do good to now? I am sure she sent you to somebody; and you've been to see somebody this morning," added the quick-witted invalid, "who has turned out different from your expectations. Tell me all about it, please."

"Dear Adelaide does love to hear what's going on. It is almost the only pleasure she has – and we oughtn't to grudge it, ought we?" said Adelaide's mother.

"Stuff!" muttered Adelaide, in a perfectly audible aside. "Now I think of it, I'll tell you who you've been to see. That woman in Back Grove Street – there! What do you think of that for a production of Salem, Mr Vincent? But she does not really belong to Carlingford. She married somebody who turned out badly, and now she's in hiding that he mayn't find her; though most likely, if all be true, he does not want to find her. That's her history. I never pretend to tell more than I know. Who she was to begin

with, or who he is, or whether Hilyard may be her real
name, or why she lives there and comes to Salem Chapel,
I can't tell; but that's the bones of her story, you know. If
I were a clever romancer like some people, I could have
made it all perfect for you, but I prefer the truth. Clever
and queer, isn't she? So I have guessed by what people
say."

"Indeed, you seem to know a great deal more about her
than I do," said the astonished pastor.

"I daresay," assented Adelaide, calmly. "I have never
seen her, however, though I can form an idea of what she
might be like, all the same. I put things together, you see;
and it is astonishing the number of scraps of news I get. I
shake them well down, and then the broken pieces come
together; and I never forget anything, Mr Vincent," she
continued, pausing for a moment to give him a distinct
look out of the pale-blue eyes, which for the moment
seemed to take a vindictive feline gleam. "She's rather
above the Browns and the Tozers, you understand. Somehow or other, she's mixed up with Lady Western, whom
they call the young Dowager, you know. I have not made
that out yet, though I partly guess. My lady goes to see
her up two pairs of stairs in Back Grove Street. I hope it
does her ladyship good to see how the rest of the world
manage to live and get on."

"I am afraid, Adelaide, my dear," said Mr Tufton, in
his bass tones, "that my young brother will not think this
very improving conversation. Dear Tozer was speaking to
me yesterday about the sermon to the children. I always
preached them a sermon to themselves about this time of
the year. My plan has been to take the congregation in
classes; the young men – ah, and they're specially important, are the young men! Dear Tozer suggested that some
popular lectures now would not come amiss. After a long
pastorate like mine," said the good man, blandly, unconscious that dear Tozer had already begun to suggest a
severance of that tie before gentle sickness did it for him,

"a congregation may be supposed to be a little unsettled, – without any offence to you, my dear brother. If I could appear myself and show my respect to your ministry, it would have a good effect, no doubt; but I am laid aside, laid aside, brother Vincent! I can only help you with my prayers."

"But dear, dear Mr Tufton!" cried his wife, "bless you, the chapel is twice as full as it was six months ago – and natural too, with a nice young man."

"My dear!" said the old minister in reproof. "Yes, quite natural – curiosity about a stranger; but my young brother must not be elated; nor discouraged when they drop off. A young pastor's start in life is attended by many trials. There is always a little excitement at first, and an appearance of seats letting and the ladies very polite to you. Take it easily, my dear brother! Don't expect too much. In a year or two – by-and-by, when things settle down – then you can see how it's going to be."

"But don't you think it possible that things may never settle down, but continue rising up instead?" said Mr Vincent, making a little venture in the inspiration of the moment.

Mr Tufton shook his head and raised his large hands slowly, with a deprecating regretful motion, to hold them over the fire. "Alas! he's got the fever already," said the old minister. "My dear young brother, you shall have my experience to refer to always. You're always welcome to my advice. Dear Tozer said to me just yesterday, 'You point out the pitfalls to him, Mr Tufton, and give him your advice, and I'll take care that he shan't go wrong outside,' says dear Tozer. Ah, an invaluable man!"

"But a little disposed to interfere, I think," said Vincent with an irrestrainable inclination to show his profound disrelish of all the advice which was about to be given him.

Mr Tufton raised his heavy forefinger and shook it slowly. "No – no. Be careful, my dear brother. You must keep well with your deacons. You must not take up prejudices against them. Dear Tozer is a man of a thousand – a man of a thousand! Dear Tozer, if you listen to him, will keep you out of trouble. The trouble he takes and the money he spends for Salem Chapel is, mark my words, unknown – and," added the old pastor, awfully syllabling the long word in his solemn bass, "in-con-ceiv-able."

"He is a bore and an ass for all that," said the daring invalid opposite, with perfect equanimity, as if uttering the most patent and apparent of truths. "Don't you give in to him, Mr Vincent. A pretty business you will have with them all," she continued, dropping her knitting-needles and lifting her pale-blue eyes, with their sudden green gleam, to the face of the newcomer with a rapid perception of his character, which, having no sympathy in it, but rather a certain mischievous and pleased satisfaction in his probable discomfiture, gave anything but comfort to the object of her observation. "You are something new for them to pet and badger. I wonder how long they'll be of killing Mr Vincent. Papa's tough; but you remember, mamma, they finished off the other man before us in two years."

"Oh, hush, Adelaide, hush! you'll frighten Mr Vincent," cried the kind little mother, with uneasy looks: "when he comes to see us and cheer us up – as I am sure is very kind of him – it is a shame to put all sorts of things in his head, as papa and you do. Never mind Adelaide, Mr Vincent, dear. Do your duty, and never fear anybody: that's always been my maxim, and I've always found it answer. Not going away, are you? Dear, dear! and we've had no wise talk at all, and never once asked for your poor dear mother – quite well, I hope? – and Miss Susan? You should have them come and see you, and cheer you up. Well, good morning, if you must go; don't be long before you come again."

"And, my dear young brother, don't take up any preju-dices," interposed Mr Tufton, in tremulous bass, as he pressed Vincent's half-reluctant fingers in that large soft

flabby ministerial hand. Adelaide added nothing to
these valedictions; but when she too had received his
leave-taking, and he had emerged from the shadow of
the geraniums, the observer paused once more in her
knitting. "This one will *not* hold out two years," said
Adelaide, calmly, to herself, no one else paying any
attention; and she returned to her work with the zest of a
spectator at the commencement of an exciting drama. She
did double work all the afternoon under the influence of
this refreshing stimulant. It was quite a new interest in her
life.

Meanwhile young Vincent left the green gates of
Siloam Cottage with no very comfortable feelings –
with feelings, indeed, the reverse of comfortable,
yet conscious of a certain swell and elevation in his
mind at the same moment. It was for him to show the
entire community of Carlingford the difference between
his reign and the old *régime*. It was for him to change
the face of affairs – to reduce Tozer into his due place
of subordination, and to bring in an influx of new life,
intelligence, and enlightenment over the prostrate
butterman. The very sordidness and contraction of
the little world into which he had just received so
distinct a view, promoted the revulsion of feeling
which now cheered him. The aspiring young man could
as soon have consented to lose his individuality
altogether as to acknowledge the most distant possibility
of accepting Tozer as his guide, philosopher, and friend.
He went back again through Grove Street, heated and
hastened on his way by those impatient thoughts.
When he came as far as Salem, he could not but pause
to look at it with its pinched gable and mean little belfry,
innocent of a bell. The day was overclouded, and no
clearness of atmosphere relieved the aspect of the
shabby chapel, with its black railing, and locked gates,
and dank flowerless grass inside. To see anything venerable or sacred in the aspect of such a place, required

an amount of illusion and glamour which the young
minister could not summon into his eyes. It was not the
centre of light in a dark place, the simple tribune from
which the people's preacher should proclaim, to the awe
and conviction of the multitude, that Gospel once preached
to the poor, of which he flattered himself he should be the
truest messenger in Carlingford. Such had been the young
man's dreams in Homerton – dreams mingled, it is true,
with personal ambition, but full notwithstanding of generous enthusiasm. No – nothing of the kind. Only Salem
Chapel, with so many pews let, and so many still to be
disposed of, and Tozer a guardian angel at the door. Mr
Vincent was so far left to himself as to give vent to an
impatient exclamation as he turned away. But still matters
were not hopeless. He himself was a very different man
from Mr Tufton. Kindred spirits there must surely be in
Carlingford to answer to the call of his. Another day might
dawn for the Nonconformists, who were not aware of their
own dignity. With this thought he retraced his steps a
little, and, with an impulse which he did not explain to
himself, threaded his way up a narrow lane and emerged
into Back Grove Street, about the spot where he had
lately paid his pastoral visit, and made so unexpected an
acquaintance. This woman – or should he not say lady? –
was a kind of first-fruits of his mission. The young man
looked up with a certain wistful interest at the house in
which she lived. She was neither young nor fair, it is true,
but she interested the youthful Nonconformist, who was
not too old for impulses of chivalry, and who could not
forget her poor fingers scarred with her rough work. He
had no other motive for passing the house but that of
sympathy and compassion for the forlorn brave creature
who was so unlike her surroundings; and no throbbing
pulse or trembling nerve forewarned Arthur Vincent of
the approach of fate.

    At that moment, however, fate was approaching in the
shape of a handsome carriage, which made quite an

exaggeration of echo in this narrow back street, which rang back every jingle of the harness and dint of the hoofs from every court and opening. It drew up before Mrs Hilyard's door – at the door of the house, at least, in which Mrs Hilyard was a humble lodger; and while Vincent slowly approached, a brilliant vision suddenly appeared before him, rustling forth upon the crowded pavement, where the dirty children stood still to gape at her. A woman – a lady – a beautiful dazzling creature, resplendent in the sweetest English roses, the most delicate bewildering bloom. Though it was but for a moment, the bewildered young minister had time to note the dainty foot, the daintier hand, the smiling sunshiny eyes, the air of conscious supremacy, which was half command and half entreaty – an ineffable combination. That vision descended out of the heavenly chariot upon the mean pavement just as Mr Vincent came up; and at the same moment a ragged boy, struck speechless, like the young minister, by the apparition, planted himself full in her way with open mouth and staring eyes, too much overpowered by sudden admiration to perceive that he stopped the path. Scarcely aware what he was doing, as much beauty-struck as his victim, Vincent, with a certain unconscious fury, seized the boy by the collar, and swung him impatiently off the pavement with a feeling of positive resentment against the imp, whose rags were actually touching those sacred splendid draperies. The lady made a momentary pause, turned half round, smiled with a gracious inclination of her head, and entered at the open door, leaving the young pastor in an incomprehensible ecstasy, with his hat off, and all his pulses beating loud in his ears, riveted, as the romancers say, to the pavement. When the door shut he came to himself, stared wildly into the face of the next passenger who came along the narrow street, and then, becoming aware that he still stood uncovered, grew violently red, put on his hat, and went off at a great pace. But what was the use of going off? The deed was done. The world on the other side of these prancing horses was a different world from that on this side. Those other matters, of which he had been thinking so hotly, had suddenly faded into a background and accessories to the one triumphant figure which occupied all the scene. He scarcely asked himself who was that beautiful vision? The fact of her existence was at the moment too overpowering for any secondary inquiries. He had seen her – and lo! the universe was changed. The air tingled softly with the sound of prancing horses and rolling wheels, the air breathed an irresistible soft perfume, which could nevermore die out of it, the air rustled with the silken thrill of those womanly robes. There she had enthroned herself – not in his startled heart, but in the palpitating world, which formed in a moment's time into one great background and framework for that beatific form.

What the poor young man had done to be suddenly assailed and carried off his feet by this wonderful and unexpected apparition, we are unable to say. He seemed to have done nothing to provoke it: approaching quietly as any man might do, pondering grave thoughts of Salem Chapel, and how he was to make his post tenable, to be transfixed all at once and unawares by that fairy lance, was a spite of fortune which nobody could have predicted. But the thing was done. He went home to hide his stricken head, as was natural; tried to lay plans for his campaign and heroic desperate attempts to resuscitate the shopkeeping Dissenterism of Carlingford into a lofty Nonconformist ideal. But vain were the efforts. Wherever he lifted his eyes, was not She there, all-conquering and glorious? when he did not lift his eyes, was not she everywhere Lady Paramount of the conscious world? Womankind in general, which had never, so to speak, entered his thoughts before, had produced much trouble to poor Arthur Vincent since his arrival in Carlingford. But Phoebe Tozer, pink and blooming – Mrs Hilyard, sharp and strange – Adelaide Tufton, pale spectator of a life with which she had nothing to do – died off like shadows, and left no sign of their presence. Who was She?

CHAPTER IV.

AFTER the remarkable encounter which had thus happened
to the young minister, life went on with him in the dullest
routine for some days. Thursday came, and he had to go
to Mrs Brown's tea-party, where, in the drawing-room up-
stairs, over the Devonshire Dairy, after tea, and music,
and the diversions of the evening, he conducted prayers to
the great secret satisfaction of the hostess, who felt that
the superior piety of her entertainment entirely made up
for any little advantage in point of gentility which Mrs
Tozer, with a grown-up daughter fresh from a boarding-
school, might have over her. On Friday evening there was
the singing-class at the chapel, which Mr Vincent was
expected to look in upon, and from which he had the
privilege of walking home with Miss Tozer. When he
arrived with his blooming charge at the private door, the
existence of which he had not hitherto been aware of,
Tozer himself appeared, to invite the young pastor to
enter. This time it was the butterman's unadorned domestic hearth to which Mr Vincent was introduced. This
happy privacy was in a little parlour, which, being on the
same floor with the butter-shop, naturally was not without
a reminiscence of the near vicinity of all those hams and
cheeses – a room nearly blocked up by the large family-
table, at which, to the disgust of Phoebe, the apprentices
sat at meal-times along with the family. One little boy,
distinguished out of doors by a red worsted comforter,
was, besides Phoebe, the only member of the family itself
now at home; the others being two sons, one in Australia,
and the other studying for a minister, as Mrs Tozer had

already informed her pastor, with motherly pride. Mrs
Tozer sat in an easy-chair by the fire darning stockings on
this October night; her husband, opposite to her, had been
looking over his greasy books, one of which lay open upon
a little writing-desk, where a bundle of smaller ones in red
leather, with "Tozer, Cheesemonger," stamped on them
in gilt letters, lay waiting Phoebe's arrival to be made up.
The Benjamin of the house sat half-way down the long
table with his slate working at his lessons. The margin of
space round this long table scarcely counted in the aspect
of the room. There was space enough for chairs to be set
round it, and that was all: the table with its red-and-blue
cover and the faces appearing above it, constituted the
entire scene. Mr Vincent stood uneasily at a corner when
he was brought into the apartment, and distinctly placed
himself at table, as if at a meal, when he sat down.

"Do you now take off your greatcoat, and make yourself comfortable," said Mrs Tozer; "there's a bit of supper
coming presently. This is just what I like, is this. A party
is very well in its way, Mr Vincent, sir; but when a
gen'leman comes in familiar, and takes us just as we are,
that's what I like. We never can be took wrong of an
evening, Tozer and me; there's always a bit of something
comfortable for supper; and after the shop's shut in them
long evenings, time's free. Phoebe, make haste and take
off your things. What a colour you've got, to be sure, with
the night air! I declare, Pa, somebody must have been
saying something to her, or she'd never look so bright."

"I daresay there's more things than music gets talked of
at the singing," said Tozer, thus appealed to. "But she'd
do a deal better if she'd try to improve her mind than take
notice what the young fellows says."

"Oh, Pa, the idea! and before Mr Vincent too," cried
Phoebe – "to think I should ever dream of listening to
anything that *anybody* might choose to say!"

Vincent, to whom the eyes of the whole family turned,
grinned a feeble smile, but, groaning in his mind, was

totally unequal to the effort of saying anything. After a
moment's pause of half-disappointed expectation, Phoebe
disappeared to take off her bonnet; and Mrs Tozer, bestir-
ring herself, cleared away the desk and books, and went
into the kitchen to inquire into the supper. The minister
and the deacon were accordingly left alone.

"Three more pews applied for this week – fifteen sittings
in all," said Mr Tozer; "that's what I call satisfactory, that
is. We mustn't let the steam go down – not on no account.
You keep well at them of Sundays, Mr Vincent, and trust
to the managers, sir, to keep 'em up to their dooty. Me
and Mr Tufton was consulting the other day. He says as
we oughtn't to spare you, and you oughtn't to spare
yourself. There hasn't been such an opening not in our
connection for fifteen year. We all look to you to go into it,
Mr Vincent. If all goes as I expect, and you keep up as
you're doing, I see no reason why we shouldn't be able to
put another fifty to the salary next year."

"Oh!" said poor Vincent, with a miserable face. He
had been rather pleased to hear about the "opening" but
this matter-of-fact encouragement and stimulus threw
him back into dismay and disgust.

"Yes," said the deacon, "though I wouldn't advise you,
as a young man settin' out in life, to calculate upon it, yet
we all think it more than likely; but if you was to ask my
advice, I'd say to give it 'em a little more plain – meaning
the Church folks. It's expected of a new man. I'd touch
'em up in the State-Church line, Mr Vincent, if I was you.
Give us a coorse upon the anomalies, and that sort of
thing – the bishops in their palaces, and the fisherman as
was the start of it all; there's a deal to be done in that way.
It always tells; and my opinion is as you might secure the
most part of the young men and thinkers, and them as can
see what's what, if you lay it on pretty strong. Not,"
added the deacon, remembering in time to add that necessary salve to the conscience – "not as I would have you
neglect what's more important; but, after all, what *is* more

important, Mr Vincent, than freedom of opinion and choosing your own religious teacher? You can't put gospel truth in a man's mind till you've freed him out of them bonds. It stands to reason – as long as he believes just what he's told, and has it all made out for him the very words he's to pray, there may be feelin', sir, but there can't be no spiritual understandin' in that man."

"Well, one can't deny that there have been enlightened men in the Church of England," said the young Nonconformist, with lofty candour. "The inconsistencies of the human mind are wonderful; and it is coming to be pretty clearly understood in the intellectual world, that a man may show the most penetrating genius, and even the widest liberality, and yet be led a willing slave in the bonds of religious rite and ceremony. One cannot understand it, it is true; but in our clearer atmosphere we are bound to exercise Christian charity. Great as the advantages are on our side of the question, I would not willingly hurt the feelings of a sincere Churchman, who, for anything I know, may be the best of men."

Mr Tozer paused with a "humph!" of uncertainty; rather dazzled with the fine language, but doubtful of the sentiment. At length light seemed to dawn upon the excellent butterman. "Bless my soul! that's a new view," said Tozer; "that's taking the superior line over them! My impression is as that would tell beautiful. Eh! it's famous, that is! I've heard a many gentlemen attacking the Church, like, from down below, and giving it her about her money and her greatness, and all that; but our clearer atmosphere – there's the point! I always knew as you was a clever young man, Mr Vincent, and expected a deal from you; but that's a new view, that is!"

"Oh, Pa, dear! don't be always talking about chapel business," said Miss Phoebe, coming in. "I am sure Mr Vincent is sick to death of Salem. I am sure his heart is in some other place now; and if you bore him always about the chapel, he'll never, *never* take to Carlingford. Oh, Mr Vincent, I am sure you know it is quite true!"

"Indeed," said the young minister, with a sudden recollection, "I can vouch for my heart being in Carlingford, and nowhere else;" and as he spoke his colour rose. Phoebe clapped her hands with a little semblance of confusion.

"Oh, la!" cried that young lady, "that is *quite* as good as a confession that you have lost it, Mr Vincent. Oh, I *am* so interested! I wonder who it can be!"

"Hush, child; I daresay we shall know before long," said Mrs Tozer, who had also rejoined the domestic party; "and don't you colour up or look ashamed, Mr Vincent. Take my word, it's the very best a young minister can do. To be sure, where there's a quantity of young ladies in a congregation, it sometimes makes a little dispeace; but there ain't to say many to choose from in Salem."

"La, mamma, how *can* you think it's a lady in Salem?" cried Phoebe, in a flutter of consciousness.

"Oh, you curious thing!" cried Mrs Tozer: "she'll never rest, Mr Vincent, till she's found it all out. She always was from a child, a dreadful one for finding out a secret. But don't you trouble yourself; it's the very best thing a young minister can do."

Poor Vincent made a hasty effort to exculpate himself from the soft impeachment, but with no effect. Smiles, innuendoes, a succession of questions asked by Phoebe, who retired, whenever she had made her remark, with conscious looks and pink blushes, perpetually renewed this delightful subject. The unlucky young man retired upon Tozer. In desperation he laid himself open to the less troublesome infliction of the butterman's advice. In the mean time the table was spread, and supper appeared in most substantial and savoury shape; the only drawback being, that whenever the door was opened, the odours of bacon and cheese from the shop came in like a musty shadow of the boiled ham and hot sausages within.

"I am very partial to your style, Mr Vincent," said the

deacon; "there's just one thing I'd like to observe, sir, if
you'll excuse *me*. I'd give 'em a coorse; there's nothing
takes like a coorse in our connection. Whether it's on a
chapter or a book of Scripture, or on a perticklar doctrine,
I'd make a pint of giving 'em a coorse if it was me. There
was Mr Bailey, of Parson's Green, as was so popular
before he married – he had a historical coorse in the evenings, and a coorse upon the eighth of Romans in the
morning; and it was astonishing to see how they took.
I walked over many and many's the summer evening
myself, he kep' up the interest so. There ain't a cleverer
man in our body, nor wasn't a better liked as he was
then."

"And now I understand he's gone away – what was the
reason?" asked Mr Vincent.

Tozer shrugged his shoulders and shook his head. "All
along of the women: they didn't like his wife; and my own
opinion is, he fell off dreadful. Last time I heard him, I
made up my mind I'd never go back again – me that was
such an admirer of his; and the managers found the chapel
was falling off, and a deputation waited on him; and, to be
sure, he saw it his duty to go."

"And, oh, she was sweetly pretty!" cried Miss Phoebe:
"but pray, pray, Mr Vincent, don't look so pale. If you
marry a pretty lady, we'll all be so kind to her! We shan't
grudge her our minister; we shall—"

Here Miss Phoebe paused, overcome by her emotions.

"I do declare there never was such a child," said Mrs
Tozer: "it's none of your business, Phoebe. She's a great
deal too feelin', Mr Vincent. But I don't approve, for my
part, of a minister marrying a lady as is too grand for her
place, whatever Phoebe may say. It's her that should
teach suchlike as us humility and simple ways; and a fine
lady isn't no way suitable. Not to discourage you, Mr
Vincent, I haven't a doubt, for my part, that you'll make a
nice choice."

"I have not the least intention of trying the experiment,"

said poor Vincent, with a faint smile; then, turning to his
deacon, he plunged into the first subject that occurred to
him. "Do you know a Mrs Hilyard in Back Grove Street?"
asked the young minister. "I went to see her the other
day. Who is she, or where does she belong to, can you tell
me? – and which of your great ladies in Carlingford is it,"
he added, with a little catching of his breath after a
momentary pause, "who visits that poor lady? I saw a
carriage at her door."

"Meaning the poor woman at the back of the chapel?"
said Tozer – "I don't know nothing of her, except that I
visited there, sir, as you might do, in the way of dooty.
Ah! I fear she's in the gall of bitterness, Mr Vincent; she
didn't take my 'umble advice, sir, not as a Christian
ought. But she comes to the chapel regular enough; and
you may be the means of putting better thoughts into
her mind; and as for our great ladies in Carlingford,"
continued Mr Tozer, with the air of an authority, "never a
one of them, I give you my word, would go out of her way
a-visiting to one of the Chapel folks. They're a deal too
bigoted for that, especially them at St Roque's."

"Oh, Pa, how can you say so," cried Phoebe, "when it's
very well known the ladies go everywhere, where the
people are very, very poor? but then Mr Vincent said a
poor *lady*. Was it a nice carriage? The Miss Wodehouses
always walk, and so does Mrs Glen, and all the Strange-
ways. Oh, I know! it was the young Dowager – that pretty,
pretty lady, you know, mamma, that gives the grand
parties, and lives in Grange Lane. I saw her carriage going
up the lane by the chapel once. Oh, Mr Vincent, wasn't
she very, *very* pretty, with blue eyes and brown hair?"

"I could not tell you what kind of eyes and hair they
were," said Mr Vincent, trying hard to speak indifferently,
and quite succeeding so far as Phoebe Tozer was concerned;
for who could venture to associate the minister of Salem,
even as a victim, with the bright eyes of Lady Western? "I
thought it strange to see her there, whoever she was."

"Oh, how insensible you are!" murmured Phoebe, across the table. Perhaps, considering all things, it was not strange that Phoebe should imagine her own pink bloom to have dimmed the young pastor's appreciation of other beauty.

"But it was Mrs Hilyard I inquired about, and not this Lady – Lady what, Miss Phoebe?" asked the reverend hypocrite; "I don't profess to be learned in titles, but hers is surely a strange one. I thought dowager was another word for an old woman."

"She's a beautiful young creature," broke in the butterman. "I mayn't approve of such goings-on, but I can't shut my eyes. She deals with me regular, and I can tell you the shop looks like a different place when them eyes of hers are in it. She's out of our line, and she's out of your line, Mr Vincent," added Tozer, apologetically, coming down from his sudden enthusiasm, "or I mightn't say as much as I do say; for she's gay, and always a-giving parties, and spending her life in company, as I don't approve of; but to look in her face, you couldn't say a word against her – nor I couldn't. She might lead a man out of his wits, and I wouldn't not to say blame him. If the angels are nicer to look at, it's a wonder to me!" Having reached to this pitch of admiration, the alarmed butterman came to a sudden pause, looked round him somewhat dismayed, wiped his forehead, rubbed his hands, and evidently felt that he had committed himself, and was at the mercy of his audience. Little did the guilty Tozer imagine that never before – not when giving counsel upon chapel business in the height of wisdom, or complimenting the sermon as only a chapel-manager, feeling in his heart that the seats were letting, could – had he spoken so much to the purpose in young Vincent's hearing, or won so much sympathy from the minister. As for the female part of the company, they were at first too much amazed for speech. "Upon my word, Papa!" burst from the lips of the half-laughing, half-angry Phoebe. Mrs Tozer, who had been cutting bread

with a large knife, hewed at her great loaf in silence, and
not till that occupation was over divulged her sentiments.

"Some bread, Mr Vincent?" said at last that injured
woman: "that's how it is with all you men. Niver a one,
however you may have been brought up, nor whatever
pious ways you may have been used to, can stand out
against a pretty face. Thank goodness, *we* know better.
Beauty's but skin-deep, Mr Vincent; and, for my part, I
can't see the difference between one pair o' eyes and
another. I daresay I see as well out of mine as Lady
Western does out o' hers, though Tozer goes on about 'em.
It's a mercy for the world, women ain't carried away so;
and to hear a man as is the father of a family, and ought to
set an example, a-talking like this in his own house! What
is the minister to think, Tozer? and Phoebe, a girl as is as
likely to take up notions about her looks as most? It's what
I didn't expect from you."

"La, mamma! as if there was any likeness between Lady
Western and me!" cried Phoebe, lifting a not-unexpectant
face across the table. But Mr Vincent was not equal to the
occasion. In that *locale*, and under these circumstances, a
tolerable breadth of compliment would not have shocked
anybody's feelings; but the pastor neglected his opportunities. He sat silent and made no reply to Phoebe's look.
He even at this moment, if truth must be told, devoted
himself to the well-filled plate which Mrs Tozer's hospitality
had set before him. He would fain have made a diversion
in poor Tozer's favour had anything occurred to him in the
thrill of sudden excitement which Tozer's declaration had
surprised him into. As it was, tingling with anxiety to hear
more of that unknown enchantress, whose presence made
sunshine even in the butterman's shop, no indifferent
words would find their way to Vincent's lips. So he bestowed his attentions instead upon the comfortable supper
to which everybody around him, quite unexcited by this
little interlude, was doing full justice, and, not venturing
to ask, listened with a palpitating heart.

"You see, Mr Vincent," resumed Mrs Tozer, "that title of 'the young Dowager' has been given to Lady Western by them as is her chief friends in Carlingford. Such little things comes to our knowledge as they mightn't come to other folks in our situation, by us serving the best families. There's but two families in Grange Lane as don't deal with Tozer, and one of them's a new-comer as knows no better, and the other a stingy old bachelor, as we wouldn't go across the road to get his custom. A well-kept house must have its butter, and its cheese, and its ham regular; but when there's but a man and a maid, and them nigh as bilious as the master, and picking bits of cheese as one never heard the name of, and as has to be sent to town for or to the Italian shop, it stands to reason neither me nor Tozer cares for a customer like that."

"Oh, Ma, what *does* Mr Vincent care about the customers?" cried Phoebe, in despair.

"He might, then, before all's done," said the deaconess. "We couldn't be as good friends to the chapel, nor as serviceable, nor as well thought on in our connection, if it wasn't for the customers. So you see, sir, Lady Western, she's a young lady not a deal older than my Phoebe, but by reason of having married an old man, she has a step-son twice as old as herself, and he's married; and so this gay pretty creature here, she's the Dowager Lady Western. I've seen her with *young* Lady Western, her step-daughter-in-law, and young Lady Western was a deal older, and more serious-looking, and knew twenty times more of life than the Dowager – and you may be sure she don't lose the opportunity to laugh at it neither – and so that's how the name arose."

"Thank you for the explanation; and I suppose, of course, she lives in Grange Lane," said the pastor, still bending with devotion over his plate.

"Dear, dear, you don't eat nothink, Mr Vincent," cried his benevolent hostess; "that comes of study, as I'm always a-telling Tozer. A deal better, says I, to root the minister out, and get him to move about for the good of his health, than to put him up to sermons and coorses, when we're all as pleased as Punch to start with. She lives in Grange Lane, to be sure, as they most all do as is anything in Carlingford. Fashion's all – but I like a bit of stir and life myself, and couldn't a-bear them close walls. But it would be news in Salem that we was spending our precious time a-talking over a lady like Lady Western; and as for the woman at the back of the chapel, don't you be led away to go to everybody as Mrs Brown sends you to, Mr Vincent. She's a good soul, but she's always a-picking up somebody. Tozer's been called up at twelve o'clock, when we were all a-bed, to see somebody as was dying; and there was no dying about it, but only Mrs Brown's way. My son, being at his eddication for a minister, makes me feel motherlike to a young pastor, Mr Vincent. I'd be grateful to anybody as would give my boy warning when it comes to be his time."

"I almost wonder," said Vincent, with a little natural impatience, "that you did not struggle on with Mr Tufton for a little longer, till your son's education was finished."

Mrs Tozer held up her head with gratified pride. "He'll be two years before he's ready, and there's never no telling what may happen in that time," said the pleased mother, forgetting how little favourable to her guest was any anticipated contingency. The words were very innocently spoken, but they had their effect upon Vincent. He made haste to extricate himself from the urgent hospitality which surrounded him. He was deafer than ever to Miss Phoebe's remarks, and listened with a little impatience to Tozer's wisdom. As soon as he could manage it, he left them, with abundant material for his thoughts. "There's never no telling what may happen in that time," rang in his ears as he crossed George Street to his lodging, and the young minister could scarcely check the disgust and impatience which were rising in his mind. In all the pride of his young intellect, to be advised by Tozer – to have

warning stories told him of that unfortunate brother in
Parson's Green, whose pretty wife made herself obnoxious
to the deacons' wives – to have the support afforded by the
butterman to the chapel thrown in his face with such an
undisguised claim upon his gratitude – oh heaven, was this
what Homerton was to come to? Perhaps he had been
brought here, in all the young flush of his hopes, only to
have the life crushed out of him by those remorseless
chapel-managers, and room made over his tarnished fame
and mortified expectations – over his body, as the young
man said to himself in unconscious heroics – for young
Tozer's triumphant entrance. On the whole, it was not to
be supposed that to see himself at the mercy of such a
limited and jealous coterie – people proud of their liberality
to the chapel, and altogether unable to comprehend the
feelings of a sensitive and cultivated mind – could be an
agreeable prospect to the young man. Their very approbation chafed him; and if he went beyond their level, or
exceeded their narrow limit, what mercy was he to expect,
what justice, what measure of comprehension? He went
home with a bitterness of disgust in his mind far more
intense and tragical than appeared to be at all necessary in
the circumstances, and which only the fact that this was
his first beginning in real life, and that his imagination had
never contemplated the prominent position of the butter-
shop and the Devonshire Dairy, in what he fondly called
his new sphere, could have justified. Perhaps no new
sphere ever came up to the expectations of the neophyte;
but to come, if not with too much gospel, yet with an
intellectual Christian mission, an evangelist of refined
Nonconformity, an apostle of thought and religious opinion,
and to sink suddenly into "coorses" of sermons and statis-
tics of seat-letting in Salem – into tea-parties of deacons'
wives, and singing-classes – into the complacent society of
those good people who were conscious of doing so much
for the chapel and supporting the minister – that was a
downfall not to be lightly thought of. Salem itself, and the

new pulpit, which had a short time ago represented to poor Vincent that tribune from which he was to influence the world, that point of vantage which was all a true man needed for the making of his career, dwindled into a miserable scene of trade before his disenchanted eyes – a preaching shop, where his success was to be measured by the seat-letting, and his soul decanted out into periodical issue under the seal of Tozer & Co. Such, alas! were the indignant thoughts with which, the old Adam rising bitter and strong within him, the young Nonconformist hastened home.

And She was Lady Western – the gayest and brightest and highest luminary in all the society of Carlingford. As well love the moon, who no longer descends to Endymion, as lift presumptuous eyes to that sweeter planet which was as much out of reach of the Dissenting minister. Poor fellow! his room did not receive a very cheerful inmate when he shut the door upon the world and sat down with his thoughts.

CHAPTER V.

It was about this time, when Mr Vincent was deeply cast down about his prospects, and saw little comfort before or around him, and when, consequently, an interest apart from itself, and which could detach his thoughts from Salem and its leading members, was of importance, that his mother's letters began to grow specially interesting. Vincent could not quite explain how it was, but unquestionably those female epistles had expanded all at once; and instead of the limited household atmosphere hitherto breathing in them – an atmosphere confined by the strait cottage walls, shutting in the little picture which the absent son knew so well, and in which usually no figure appeared but those of his pretty sister Susan, and their little servant, and a feminine neighbour or two – instead of those strict household limits, the world, as we have said, had expanded round the widow's pen; the cottage walls or windows seemed to have opened out to disclose the universe beyond: life itself, and words the symbols of life, seemed quickened and running in a fuller current; and the only apparent reason for all this revolution was that one new acquaintance had interrupted Mrs Vincent's seclusion, – one only visitor, who, from an unexpected call, recorded with some wonderment a month or two before, had gained possession of the house apparently, and was perpetually referred to – by Susan, in her gradually shortening letters, with a certain timidity and reluctance to pronounce his name; by the mother with growing frequency and confidence. Vincent, a little jealous of this new influence, had out of the depths of his own depression written with some impatience to ask who this Mr Fordham was, and how he had managed to establish himself so confidentially in the cottage, when his mother's letter astounded him with the following piece of news: –

"My dearest Boy, – Mr Fordham is, or at least will be – or, if I must be cautious, as your poor dear papa always warned me I should – wishes very much, and I hope will succeed in being – your brother, my own Arthur. This is sudden news, but you know, and I have often told you, that a crisis always does seem to arrive suddenly; however much you may have been looking for it, or making up your mind to it, it does come like a blow at the time; and no doubt there is something in human nature to account for it, if I was a philosopher, like your dear papa and you. Yes, my dear boy, that is how it is. Of course, I have known for some time past that he must have had a motive – no mother could long remain ignorant of that; and I can't say but what, liking Mr Fordham so much, and seeing him *every way so unexceptionable*, except, perhaps, in the way of means, which we know nothing about, and which I have always thought a secondary consideration to character, as I always brought up my children to think, I was very much pleased. For you know, my dear boy, life is uncertain with the strongest; and I am becoming an old woman, and you will marry no doubt, and what is to become of Susan unless she does the same? So I confess I was pleased to see Mr Fordham's inclinations showing themselves. And now, dear Arthur, I've given them my blessing, and they are as happy as ever they can be, and nothing is wanting to Susan's joy but your sympathy. I need not suggest to my dear boy to write a few words to his sister to make her feel that he shares our happiness; for Providence has blessed me in affectionate children, and I can trust the instincts of my Arthur's heart; and oh! my dear son, how thankful I ought to be, and how deeply I ought to feel God's blessings! He has been a father to the fatherless, and the strength of the widow. To think that before old age comes upon me, and while I am still able to enjoy the sight of your prosperity, I should have the happiness of seeing you comfortably settled, and in the way to do your Master's work, and make yourself a good position, and Susan so happily provided for, and instead of losing her, a new son to love – indeed, I am overpowered, and can scarcely hold up my head under my blessings.

"Write immediately, my dearest boy, that we may have the comfort of your concurrence and sympathy, and I am always, with much love,

"My Arthur's loving mother,   "E.S. VINCENT.

"*P.S.* – Mr Fordham's account of his circumstances seems quite satisfactory. He is not in any profession, but has enough he says, to live on very comfortably, and is to give me more particulars afterwards; which, indeed, I am ashamed to think he could imagine necessary, as it looks like want of trust, and as if Susan's happiness was not the first thing with us – but indeed I must learn to be prudent and *self-interested* for your sakes."

It was with no such joyful feelings as his mother's that
Vincent read this letter. Perhaps it was the jealousy with
which he had heard of this unknown Mr Fordham suddenly
jumping into the friendship of the cottage, which made him
contemplate with a most glum and suspicious aspect the
stranger's promotion into the love of Susan, and the
motherly regard of Mrs Vincent. Hang the fellow! who was
he? the young minister murmured over his spoiled breakfast:
and there appeared to him in a halo of sweet memories, as
he had never seen them in reality, the simple graces of his
pretty sister, who was as much above the region of the
Phoebe Tozers as that ineffable beauty herself who had
seized with a glance the vacant throne of poor Arthur
Vincent's heart. There was nothing ineffable about Susan –
but her brother had seen no man even in Homerton whom
he would willingly see master of her affections; and he was
equally startled, dissatisfied, and alarmed by this information. Perhaps his mother's unworldliness was excessive.
He imagined that *he* would have exacted more positive
information about the fortunes of a stranger who had
suddenly appeared without any special business there, who
had no profession, and who might disappear lightly as he
came, breaking poor Susan's heart. Mr Vincent forgot
entirely the natural process by which, doubtless, his mother's
affections had been wooed and won as well as Susan's. To
him it was a stranger who had crept into the house, and
gained ascendancy there. Half in concern for Susan, half in
jealousy for Susan's brother eclipsed, but believing himself
to be entirely actuated by the former sentiment, the young
minister wrote his mother a hurried, anxious, not too good-
tempered note, begging her to think how important a
matter this was, and not to come to too rapid a conclusion;
and after he had thus relieved his feelings, went out to his
day's work in a more than usually uncomfortable frame of
mind. Mrs Vincent congratulated herself upon her son's
happy settlement, as well as upon her daughter's engagement. What if Mr Fordham should turn out as unsatisfactory

as Salem Chapel? His day's work was a round of visits, which were not very particularly to Mr Vincent's mind. It was the day for his weekly call upon Mr Tufton and various other members of the congregation not more attractive; and at Siloam Cottage he was reminded of Mrs Hilyard, whom he had not seen again. Here at least was something to be found different from the ordinary level. He went up to Back Grove Street, not without a vague expectation in his mind, wondering if that singular stranger would look as unlike the rest of his flock to-day as she had done on the former occasion. But when Vincent emerged into the narrow street, what was that unexpected object which threw the young man into such sudden agitation? His step quickened unconsciously into the rapid silent stride of excitement. He was at the shabby door before any of the onlookers had so much as perceived him in the street. For once more the narrow pavement owned a little tattered crowd gazing at the pawing horses, the big footman, the heavenly chariot; and doubtless the celestial visitor must be within.

Mr Vincent did not pause to think whether he ought to disturb the interview which, no doubt, was going on up-stairs. He left himself no time to consider punctilios, or even to think what was right in the matter. He went up with that swell of excitement somehow winging his feet and making his footsteps light. How sweet that low mur-mur of conversation within as he reached the door! Another moment, and Mrs Hilyard herself opened it, looking out with some surprise, her dark thin head, in its black lace kerchief, standing out against the bit of shabby drab-coloured wall visible through the opening of the door. A look of surprise for one moment, then a gleam of something like mirth lighted in the dark eyes, and the thin lines about her mouth moved, though no smile came. "It is you, Mr Vincent? – come in," she said, "I should not have admitted any other visitor, but you shall come in, as you are my ghostly adviser. Sit down. My dear, this gentle-man is my minister and spiritual guide."

And She, sitting there in all her splendour, casting extraordinary lights of beauty round her upon the mean apartment, perfuming the air and making it musical with that rustle of woman's robes which had never been out of poor Vincent's ears since he saw her first; – She lifted her lovely face, smiled, and bowed her beautiful head to the young man, who would have liked to go down on his knees, not to ask anything, but simply to worship. As he dared not do that, he sat down awkwardly upon the chair Mrs Hilyard pointed to, and said with embarrassment, that he feared he had chosen a wrong time for his visit, and would return again – but nevertheless did not move from where he was.

"No, indeed; I am very glad to see you. My visitors are not so many, nowadays, that I can afford to turn one from the door because another chooses to come the same day. My dear, you understand Mr Vincent has had the goodness to take charge of my spiritual affairs," said the mistress of the room, sitting down, in her dark poor dress, beside her beautiful visitor, and laying her thin hands, still marked with traces of the coarse blue colour which rubbed off her work, and of the scars of the needle, upon the table where that work lay. "Thank heaven that's a luxury the poorest of us needs not deny herself. I liked your sermon last Sunday, Mr Vincent. That about the fashion of treating serious things with levity, was meant for me. Oh, I didn't dislike it, thank you! One is pleased to think one's self of so much consequence. There are more ways of keeping up one's *amour propre* than *your* way, my lady. Now, don't you mean to go? You see I cannot possibly unburden my mind to Mr Vincent while you are here."

"Did you ever hear anything so rude?" said the beauty, turning graciously to the young minister. "You call me a great lady, and all sorts of things, Rachel; but I never could be as rude as you are, and as you always were as long as I remember."

"My dear, the height of good-breeding is to be perfectly ill-bred when one pleases," said Mrs Hilyard, taking her work upon her knee and putting on her thimble: "but though you are wonderfully pretty, you never had the makings of a thorough fine lady in you. You can't help trying to please everybody – which, indeed, if there were no women in the world," added that sharp observer, with a sudden glance at Vincent, who saw the thin lines again move about her mouth, "you might easily do without giving yourself much trouble. Mr Vincent, if this lady won't leave us, might I trouble you to talk? For two strains of thought, carried on at the same moment, now that I'm out of society, are too exhausting for me."

With which speech she gravely pinned her work to her knee, threaded her needle with a long thread of blue cotton, and began her work with the utmost composure, leaving her two visitors in the awkward *tête-à-tête* position which the presence of a third person, entirely absorbed in her own employment, with eyes and face abstracted, naturally produces. Never in his life had Vincent been so anxious to appear to advantage – never had he been so totally deprived of the use of his faculties. His eager looks, his changing colour, perhaps interceded for him with the beautiful stranger, who was not ignorant of those signs of subjugation which she saw so often.

"I think it was you that were so good as to clear the way for me the last time I was here," she said, with the sweetest grace, raising those lovely eyes, which put even Tozer beside himself, to the unfortunate pastor's face. "I remember fancying you must be a stranger here, as I had not seen you anywhere in society. Those wonderful little wretches never seem to come to any harm. They always appear to me to be scrambling among the horses' feet. Fancy, Rachel, one of those boys who flourish in the back streets, with such rags – oh, such rags – you could not possibly *make* them, if you were to try, with scissors – such perfection must come of itself; – had just pushed in before me, and I don't know what I should have done, if Mr — (I beg your pardon) — if *you* had not cleared the way."

"Mr Vincent," said Mrs Hilyard, breaking in upon Vincent's deprecation. "I am glad to hear you had some-body to help you in such a delicate distress. We poor women can't afford to be so squeamish. What! are you going away? My dear, be sure you say down-stairs that you brought that poor creature some tea and sugar, and how grateful she was. That explains everything, you know, and does my lady credit at the same time. Good-bye. Well, I'll kiss you if you insist upon it; but what can Mr Vincent think to see such an operation performed between us? There! my love, you can make the men do what you like, but you know of old you never could conquer me."

"Then you will refuse over and over again — and you don't mind what I say — and you know he's in Lonsdale, and why he's there, and all about him— "

"Hush," said the dark woman, looking all the darker as she stood in that bright creature's shadow. "I know, and always will know, wherever he goes, and that he is after evil wherever he goes; and I refuse, and always will refuse — and my darling pretty Alice," she cried, suddenly going up with rapid vehemence to the beautiful young woman beside her, and kissing once more the delicate rose-cheek to which her own made so great a contrast, "I *don't* mind in the least what you say."

"Ah, Rachel, I don't understand you," said Lady Western, looking at her wistfully.

"You never did, my dear; but don't forget to mention about the tea and sugar as you go down-stairs," said Mrs Hilyard, subsiding immediately, not without the usual gleam in her eyes and movement of her mouth, "else it might be supposed you came to have your fortune told, or something like that; and I wish your ladyship *bon voyage*, and no encounter with ragged boys in your way. Mr Vincent," she continued, with great gravity, standing in the middle of the room, when Vincent, trembling with excitement, afraid, with the embarrassing timidity of inferior position, to offer his services, yet chafing in his heart to be obliged to stay, reluctantly closed the door, which he had opened for Lady Western's exit, "tell me why a young man of your spirit loses such an opportunity of conducting the greatest beauty in Carlingford to her carriage? Suppose she should come across another ragged boy, and faint on the stairs?"

"I should have been only too happy; but as I am not so fortunate as to know Lady Western," said the young minister, hesitating, "I feared to presume—"

With an entirely changed aspect his strange companion interrupted him. "Lady Western could not think that any man whom she met in *my* house presumed in offering her a common civility," said Mrs Hilyard, with the air of a duchess, and an imperious gleam out of her dark eyes. Then she recollected herself, gave her startled visitor a comical look, and dropped into her chair, before which that coarsest of poor needlewoman's work was lying. "*My* house! it does look like a place to inspire respect, to be sure," she continued, with a hearty perception of the ludicrous, which Vincent was much too preoccupied to notice. "What fools we all are! but, my dear Mr Vincent, you are too modest. My Lady Western could not frown upon anybody who honoured her with such a rapt observation. Don't fall in love with her, I beg of you. If she were merely a flirt, I shouldn't mind, but out of her very goodness she's dangerous. She can't bear to give pain to anybody, which of course implies that she gives double and treble pain when the time comes. There! I've warned you; for of course you'll meet again."

"Small chance of that," said Vincent, who had been compelling himself to remain quiet, and restraining his impulse, now that the vision had departed, to rush away out of the impoverished place. "Small chance of that," he repeated, drawing a long breath, as he listened with intent ears to the roll of the carriage which carried Her away; "society in Carlingford has no room for a poor Dissenting minister."

"All the better for him," said Mrs Hilyard, regarding him with curious looks, and discerning with female acuteness the haze of excitement and incipient passion which surrounded him. "Society's all very well for people who have been brought up in it; but for a young recluse like you, that don't know the world, it's murder. Don't look affronted. The reason is, you expect too much – twenty times more than anybody ever finds. But you don't attend to my philosophy. Thinking of your sermon, Mr Vincent? And how is our friend the butterman? I trust life begins to look more cheerful to you under his advice."

"Life?" said the preoccupied minister, who was gazing at the spot where that lovely apparition had been; "I find it change its aspects perpetually. You spoke of Lonsdale just now, did you not? Is it possible that you know that little place? My mother and sister live there."

"I am much interested to know that you have a mother and sister,"said the poor needlewoman before him, looking up with calm, fine-lady impertinence in his face. "But you did not hear me speak of Lonsdale; it was her ladyship who mentioned it. As for me, I interest myself in what is going on close by, Mr Vincent. I am quite absorbed in the chapel; I want to know how you get on, and all about it. I took that you said on Sunday about levity deeply to heart. I entertain a fond hope that you will see me improve under your ministrations, even though I may never come up to the butterman's standard. Some people have too high an ideal. If you are as much of an optimist as your respected deacon, I fear it will be ages before I can manage to make you approve of me."

Vincent's wandering thoughts were recalled a little by this attack. "I hope," he said, rousing himself, "that you don't think me so inexperienced as not to know that you are laughing at me? But indeed I should be glad to believe that the services at the chapel might sometimes perhaps be some *comfort* to you," added the young pastor, assuming the dignity of his office. He met his penitent's eyes at the moment, and faltered, moonstruck as he was, wondering if she saw through and through him, and knew that he was neither thinking of consolation nor of clerical duties, but only of those lingering echoes which, to any ears but his own, were out of hearing. There was little reason to doubt the acute perceptions of that half-amused, half-malicious glance.

"Comfort!" she cried; "what a very strange suggestion to make! Why, all the old churches in all the old ages have offered comfort. I thought you new people had something better to give us; enlightenment," she said, with a gleam of secret mockery, throwing the word like a stone – "religious freedom, private judgment. Depend upon it, that is the *rôle* expected from you by the butterman. Comfort! one has that in Rome."

"You never can have that but in conjunction with truth, and truth is not to be found in Rome," said Vincent, pricking up his ears at so familiar a challenge.

"We'll not argue, though you do commit yourself by an assertion," said Mrs Hilyard; "but oh, you innocent young man, where is the comfort to come from? Comfort will not let your seats and fill your chapel, even granting that you knew how to communicate it. I prefer to be instructed, for my part. You are just at the age, and in the circumstances, to do that."

"I fear you still speak in jest," said the minister, with some doubt, yet a little gratification; "but I shall be only too happy to have been the means of throwing any light to you upon the doctrines of our faith."

For a moment the dark eyes gleamed with something like laughter. But there was nothing ill-natured in the amusement with which his strange new friend contemplated the young pastor in the depressions and confidences of his youth. She answered with a mock gravity which, at that moment, he was by no means clear-sighted enough to see through.

"Yes," she said, demurely, "be sure you take advantage of your opportunities, and instruct us as long as you have any faith in instruction. Leave consolation to another time: but you don't attend to me, Mr Vincent; come another day: come on Monday, when I shall be able to criticise your sermons, and we shall have no Lady Western to put us out. These beauties are confusing, don't you think? Only, I entreat you, whatever you do, don't fall in love with her; and now, since I know you wish it, you may go away."

Vincent stammered a faint protest as he accepted his dismissal, but rose promptly, glad to be released. Another thought, however, seemed to strike Mrs Hilyard as she shook hands with him.

"Do your mother and sister in Lonsdale keep a school?" she said. "Nay, pray don't look affronted. Clergymen's widows and daughters very often do in the Church. I meant no impertinence in this case. They don't? well, that is all I wanted to know. I daresay they are not likely to be in the way of dangerous strangers. Good-bye; and you must come again on Monday, when I shall be alone."

"But – dangerous strangers – may I ask you to explain?" said Vincent, with a little alarm, instinctively recurring to his threatened brother-in-law, and the news which had disturbed his composure that morning before he came out.

"I can't explain; and you would not be any the wiser," said Mrs Hilyard, peremptorily. "Now, good morning. I am glad they don't keep a school; because, you know," she added, looking full into his eyes, as if defying him to make any meaning out of her words, "it is very tiresome, tedious work, and wears poor ladies out. There! – good-bye; next day you come I shall be very glad to see you, and we'll have no fine ladies to put us out."

Vincent had no resource but to let himself out of the shabby little room which this strange woman inhabited as

if it had been a palace. The momentary alarm roused by
her last words, and the state of half offence, half interest,
into which, notwithstanding his preoccupation, she had
managed to rouse him, died away, however, as he re-
entered the poor little street, which was now a road in
Fairyland instead of a lane in Carlingford, to his rapt eyes.
Golden traces of those celestial wheels surely lingered still
upon the way; they still went rolling and echoing over the
poor young minister's heart, which he voluntarily threw
down before that heavenly car of Juggernaut. Every other
impression faded out of his mind, and the infatuated
young man made no effort of resistance, but hugged the
enchanted chain. He had seen Her – spoken with Her –
henceforward was of her acquaintance. He cast reason to
the winds, and probability, and every convention of life.
Did anybody suppose that all the world leagued against
him could prevent him from seeing her again? He went
home with an unspeakable elation, longing, and excitement,
and at the same time with a vain floating idea in his mind
that, thus inspired, no height of eloquence was impossible
to him, and that triumph of every kind was inevitable.
He went home, and got his writing-desk, and plunged into
his lecture, nothing doubting that he could transfer to
his work that glorious tumult of his thoughts; and, with
his paper before him, wrote three words, and sat three
hours staring into the roseate air, and dreaming dreams
as wild as any Arabian tale. Such was the first effort of that
chance encounter, in which the personages were not Lady
Western and the poor Dissenting minister, but Beauty
and Love, perennial hero and heroine of the romance
that never ends.

CHAPTER VI.

IT was only two days after this eventful meeting that Vincent, idling and meditative as was natural in such a condition of mind, strayed into Masters's shop to buy some books. It would have been difficult for him to have explained why he went there, except, perhaps, because it was the last place in the world which his masters at the chapel would have advised him to enter. For there was another bookseller in the town, an Evangelical man, patronised by Mr Bury, the whilom rector, where all the Tract Society's publications were to be had, not to speak of a general range of literature quite wide enough for the minister of Salem. Masters's was a branch of the London Masters, and, as might be supposed, was equally amazed and indignant at the intrusion of a Dissenter among its consecrated book-shelves. He was allowed to turn over all the varieties of the 'Christian Year' on a side-table before any of the attendants condescended to notice his presence; and it proved so difficult to find the books he wanted, and so much more difficult to find anybody who would take the trouble of looking for them, that the young Nonconformist, who was sufficiently ready to take offence, began to get hot and impatient, and had all but strode out of the shop, with a new mortification to record to the disadvantage of Carlingford. But just as he began to get very angry, the door swung softly open, and a voice became audible, lingering, talking to somebody before entering. Vincent stopped speaking, and stared in the shopman's astonished face when these tones came to his ear. He fell back instantly upon the side-table and the

Christian Year', forgetting his own business, and what he had been saying – forgetting everything except that She was there, and that in another moment they would stand again within the same walls. He bent over the much-multiplied volume with a beating heart, poising in one hand a tiny miniature copy just made to slip within the pocket of an Anglican waistcoat, and in the other the big red-leaved and morocco-bound edition, as if weighing their respective merits – put beside himself, in fact, if the truth must be told, oblivious of his errand, his position – of everything but the fact that She was at the door. She came in with a sweet flutter and rustle of sound, a perfumed air entering with her, as the unsuspected enthusiast thought, and began to lavish smiles, for which he would have given half his life, upon the people of the place, who flew to serve her. She had her tablets in her hand, with a list of what she wanted, and help up a dainty forefinger as she stood reading the items. As one thing after another was mentioned, Masters and his men darted off in search of it. There was fortunately enough to give each of them a separate errand, and the principal ranged his shining wares upon the counter before her, and bathed in her smiles, while all his satellites kept close at hand, listening with all their ears for another commission. Blessed Masters! happy shopmen! that one who looked so blank when Vincent stopped short at the sound of her voice and stared at him, had forgotten all about Vincent. *She* was there; and if a little impromptu litany would have pleased her ladyship, it is probable that it could have been got up on the spot after the best models, and that even the Nonconformist would have waived his objections to liturgical worship and led the responses. But Masters's establishment offered practical homage – only the poor Dissenting minister, divided between eagerness and fear, stood silent, flushed with excitement, turning wistful looks upon her, waiting till perhaps she might turn round and see him, and letting fall out of his trembling fingers those unregarded editions of the Anglican lyre.

"And two copies of the 'Christian Year'," said Lady Western, suddenly. "Oh, thank you *so* much! but I know they are all on the side-table, and I shall go and look at them. Not the very smallest copy, Mr Masters, and not that solemn one with the red edges; something pretty, with a little ornament and gilding; they are for two little *protégées* of mine. Oh, here is exactly what I want! another one like this, please. How very obliging all your people are," said her ladyship, benignly, as the nearest man dashed off headlong to bring what she wanted – "but I think it is universal in Carlingford; and indeed the manners of our country people in general have improved very much of late. Don't you think so? oh, there can't be a question about it!"

"I beg your ladyship's pardon, I am sure; but perhaps, my lady, it is not safe to judge the general question from your ladyship's point of view," said the polite bookseller, with a bow.

"Oh, pray don't say so; I should be wretched if I thought you took more trouble for me than for other people," said the young Dowager, with a sweetness which filled Vincent's heart with jealous pangs. She was close by his side – so close that those sacred robes rustled in his very ear, and her shawl brushed his sleeve. The poor young man took off his hat in a kind of ecstacy. If she did not notice him, what did it matter? – silent adoration, speechless homage, could not affront a queen.

And it was happily very far from affronting Lady Western. She turned round with a little curiosity, and looked up in his face. "Oh, Mr – Mr Vincent," cried the beautiful creature, brightening in recognition. "How do you do? I suppose you are a resident in Carlingford now, are not you? Pardon me, that I did not see you when I came in. How very, very good it is of you to go and see my – my friend! Did you ever see anything so dreadful as the place where she lives? and isn't she an extraordinary creature? Thank you, Mr Masters; that's exactly what I want. I do believe she might have been Lord Chancellor, or something, if she had not been a woman," said the enchantress, once more lifting her lovely eyes with an expression of awe to Vincent's face.

"She seems a very remarkable person," said Vincent. "To see her where she is, makes one feel how insignificant are the circumstances of life."

"Really! now, how do you make out that?" said Lady Western; "for, to tell the truth, I think, when I see her, oh, how important they are! and that I'd a great deal rather die than live so. But you clever people take such strange views of things. Now tell me how you make that out."

"Nay," said Vincent, lowering his voice with a delicious sense of having a subject to be confidential upon, "you know what conditions of existence all her surroundings imply; yet the most ignorant could not doubt for a moment her perfect superiority to them – a superiority so perfect," he added, with a sudden insight which puzzled even himself, "that it is not necessary to assert it."

"Oh, to be sure," said Lady Western, colouring a little, and with a momentary hauteur, "of course a Russell – I mean a gentlewoman – must always look the same to a certain extent; but, alas! I am only a very commonplace little woman," continued the beauty, brightening into those smiles which perhaps might be distributed too liberally, but which intoxicated for the moment every man on whom they fell. "I think those circumstances which you speak of so disrespectfully are everything! I have not a great soul to triumph over them. I should break down, or they would overcome me – oh, you need not shake your head! I know I am right so far as I myself am concerned."

"Indeed I cannot think so," said the intoxicated young man; "you would make any circumstances—"

"What?"

But the bewildered youth made no direct reply. He only gazed at her, grew very red, and said, suddenly, "I beg your pardon," stepping back in confusion, like the guilty man he was. The lady blushed too, as her inquiring eyes met that unexpected response. Used as she was to adoration, she felt the silent force of the compliment withheld – it was a thousand times sweeter in its delicate suggestiveness and reserve of incense than any effusion of words. They were both a little confused for the moment, poor Vincent's momentary betrayal of himself having somehow suddenly dissipated the array of circumstances which surrounded and separated two persons so far apart from each other in every conventional aspect. The first to regain her place and composure was of course Lady Western, who made him a pretty playful curtsy, and broke into a low, sweet ring of laughter.

"Now I shall never know whether you meant to be complimentary or contemptuous," cried the young Dowager, "which is hard upon a creature with such a love of approbation as our friend says I have. However, I forgive you, if you meant to be very cutting, for her sake. It is so very kind of you to go to see her, and I am sure she enjoys your visits. Thank you, Mr Masters, that is all. Have you got the two copies of the 'Christian Year'? Put them into the carriage, please. Mr Vincent, I am going to have the last of my summer-parties next Thursday – twelve o'clock; will you come? – only a cup of coffee, you know, or tea if you prefer it, and talk *au discretion*. I shall be happy to see you, and I have some nice friends and one or two good pictures; so there you have an account of all the attractions my house can boast of. Do come: it will be my last party this season, and I rather want it to be a great success," said the syren, looking up with her sweet eyes.

Vincent could not tell what answer he made in his rapture; but the next thing he was properly conscious of was the light touch of her hand upon his arm as he led her to her carriage, some sudden courageous impulse having prompted him to secure for himself that momentary blessedness. He walked forth in a dream, conducting that heavenly vision: and there, outside, stood the celestial chariot with those pawing horses, and the children standing round with open mouth to watch the lovely lady's progress. It was he who put her in

with such pride and humbleness as perhaps only a generous
but inexperienced young man, suddenly surprised into
passion, could be capable of – ready to kiss the hem of her
garment, or do any other preposterous act of homage – and
just as apt to blaze up into violent self-assertion should any
man attempt to humble him who had been thus honoured.
While he stood watching the carriage out of sight, Masters
himself came out to tell the young Nonconformist, whose
presence that dignified tradesman had been loftily unconscious of a few minutes before, that they had found the
book he wanted; and Vincent, thrilling in every pulse with
the unlooked-for blessedness which had befallen him, was
not sorry, when he dropped out of the clouds at the bookseller's accost, to re-enter that place where this enchantment
still hovered, by way of calming himself down ere he
returned to those prose regions which were his own lawful
habitation. He saw vaguely the books that were placed on
the counter before him – heard vaguely the polite purling of
Masters's voice, all-solicitous to make up for the momentary
incivility with which he had treated a friend of Lady
Western's – and was conscious of taking out his purse and
paying something for the volume, which he carried away
with him. But the book might have been Sanscrit for
anything Mr Vincent cared – and he would have paid any
fabulous price for it with the meekest resignation. His
attempt to appear moderately interested, and to conduct
this common transaction as if he had all his wits about him,
was sufficient occupation just at this moment. His head was
turned. There should have been roses blossoming all along
the bare pavement of George Street to account for the
sweet gleams of light which warmed the entire atmosphere
as he traversed that commonplace way. Not only the
interview just passed, but the meeting to come, bewildered
him with an intoxicating delight. Here, then, was the
society he had dreamed of, opening its perfumed doors to
receive him. From Mrs Tozer's supper-table to the bowery
gates of Grange Lane was a jump which, ten days ago,

would have itself made the young minister giddy with satisfaction and pleasure. Now these calm emotions had ceased to move him; for not society, but a sweeter syren, had thrown chains of gold round the unsuspecting Non-conformist. With Her, Back Grove Street was Paradise. Where her habitation was, or what he should see there, was indifferent to Vincent. He was again to meet Herself.

CHAPTER VII.

THE days which intervened between this meeting and Lady Western's party were spent in a way which the managers of Salem would have been far from approving of. Mr Vincent, indeed, was rapt out of himself, out of his work, out of all the ordinary regions of life and thought. When he sat down to his sermons, his pen hung idly in his hand, and his mind, wilfully cheating itself by that sem-blance of study, went off into long delicious reveries, indescribable, intangible – a secret sweet intoxication which forbade labour, yet nourished thought. Though he sometimes did not write a word in an hour, so deep was the aspect of studiousness displayed by the young pastor at his writing-desk, and so entire the silence he maintained in his room, shut up in that world of dreams which nobody knew anything of, that his landlady, who was one of his hearers, communicated the fact to Tozer, and expatiated everywhere upon the extreme devotion to study displayed by the new minister. Old Mr Tufton, who had been in the habit of putting together the disjointed palaver which he called a sermon on the Saturday morning, shook his head over the information, and doubted that his young brother was resorting more to carnal than to spiritual means of filling his chapel; but the members of Salem generally heard the rumour with pride, and felt a certain distinction accrue to themselves from the possibility that their pastor might ruin his health by over-study. It was a new sensation in Salem; and the news, as it was whispered about, certainly came to the ears of a few of those young men and thinkers, principally poor lawyers' clerks and drapers' assistants, whom Tozer was so anxious to reach, and drew two or three doubtful, genteel hearers to the chapel, where Mr Vincent's sermon, though no better than usual, and in reality dashed off at the last moment in sheer desperation, when necessity momentarily thrust the dreams away, was listened to with a certain awe and devout attention, solely due to the toil it was reported to have cost. The young minister himself came out of the pulpit remorseful and ashamed, feeling that he had neglected his duty, and thoroughly disgusted with the superficial production, just lighted up with a few fiery sentences of that eloquence which belongs to excitement and passion, which he had just delivered. But Tozer and all the deacons buzzed approbation. They were penetrated with the conviction that he had worked hard at his sermon, and given them his best, and were not to be undeceived by the quality of the work itself, which was a secondary matter. More deeply disgusted and contemptuous than ever was the young pastor at the end of that Sunday – disgusted with himself to have done his work so poorly – contemptuous of those who were pleased with it – his heart swelling with mortified pride to think that what he thought so unworthy of him was more appreciated than his best efforts. For he did not know the report that had gone abroad; he did not know that, while brooding over his own rising passion, and absorbed in dreams with which Salem had nothing to do, the little world around him was complacently giving him credit for a purpose of wearing himself out in its behalf. The sermons so hastily written, thrust into a corner by the overpowering enchantment of those reveries, were not the only sin he had to charge against himself. He could not bring himself to bear the irksome society that surrounded him, in the state of elevation and excitement he was in. Tozer was unendurable, and Phoebe to be avoided at all costs. He did not even pay his promised visit to Mrs Hilyard, nor go to Siloam Cottage as usual. In short, he spent the days in a kind of dream, avoiding all his duties, paying no visits, doing no pastoral work, neglecting the very sermon over which his landlady saw him hanging so many silent hours, without knowing that all the vacant atmosphere between him and that blank sheet of paper, in which she saw nothing, was peopled with fairy visitants and unreal scenes to the dreamy eyes of her lodger. Such were the first effects of Circe's cup upon the young minister. He indulged himself consciously, with apologetic self-remonstrances, as Thursday approached. After that day, life was to go on as usual. No – not as usual – with a loftier aim and a higher inspiration; but the season of dreams was to be over when he had real admittance into that Eden garden, where the woman of all women wandered among her flowers. He thought what he was to say to her on that eventful day – how he should charm her into interest in his difficulties, and beautify his office, and the barren spot in which he exercised it, with her sympathy. He imagined himself possessed of her ear, certain of a place by her side, a special guest of her own election. He was not vain, nor deeply persuaded of his own importance; yet all this seemed only natural to his excited imagination. He saw himself by her side in that garden of beatitudes, disclosing to her all that was in his heart; instinctively he recalled all that the poets have said of woman the consoler – woman the inspirer. When he had gained that priceless sympathy, what glorious amends he should make for the few days' indolence to which he now gave way! Thus in his inexperience he went on, preparing for himself, as any one a little wiser could have seen at a glance, one of the bitterest disappointments of early life.

Thursday came, a day of days – such a day as people

reckon by, months after; a soft and bright autumnal morning, breathing like spring. As Vincent issued from his own door and took his way along George Street to Grange Lane, he saw the curate of St Roque's walking before him in the same direction; but Mr Wentworth himself was not more orthodoxly clerical in every detail of his costume than was the young Nonconformist, who was going, not to Lady Western's breakfast-party, but into the Bower of Bliss, the fool's paradise of his youth. Mr Wentworth, it is true, was to see Lucy Wodehouse there, and was a true lover; but he walked without excitement to the green gate which concealed from him no enchanted world of delights, but only a familiar garden, with every turn of which he was perfectly acquainted, and which, even when Lucy was by his side, contained nothing ineffable or ecstatic. It was, to tell the truth, an autumnal garden, bright enough still with scarlet gleams of geranium and verbena, with a lawn of velvet smoothness, and no great diminution as yet in the shade of the acacias and lime trees, and everything in the most perfect order in the trim shrubberies, through the skilful mazes of which some bright groups were already wandering, when Vincent passed through to the sunny open door. At the open windows within he could see other figures in a pleasant flutter of gay colour and light drapery, as he advanced breathless to take his own place in the unknown world. He heard his own name announced, and went in, with a chill of momentary doubt upon his high expectations into the airy sunshiny room, with its gay, brilliant, rustling crowd, the ladies all bright and fresh in their pretty morning dresses, and the din of talk and laughter confusing his unaccustomed ears. For a moment the stranger stood embarrassed, looking round him, eagerly investigating the crowd for that one face, which was not only the sole face of woman in the world so far as he was concerned, but in reality the only face he knew in the gay party, where everybody except himself knew everybody else. Then he saw her, and his doubts were over. When she perceived him, she made a few steps forward to meet him and held out her hand.

"I am so glad to see you – how kind of you to come!" said Lady Western; "and such a beautiful day – just what I wanted for my last *fête*. Have you seen my friend again since I saw you, Mr Vincent – quite well, I hope? Now, do have some coffee – How do you do, Mr Wentworth? You have been here full five minutes, and you have never paid your respects to me. Even under the circumstances, you know, one cannot overlook such neglect."

"I am too deeply flattered that your ladyship should have observed my entrance to be able to make any defence," said the curate of St Roque's, who could speak to her as to any ordinary woman; "but as for circumstances—"

"Oh dear, yes, we all know," cried Lady Western, with her sweet laugh. "Was it you, Mr Vincent, who were saying that circumstances were everything in life? – oh, no, I beg your pardon, quite the reverse. I remember it struck me as odd and clever. Now, I daresay, you two could quite settle that question. I am such an ignoramus. So kind of you to come!"

Vincent was about to protest his delight in coming, and to deprecate the imputation of kindness, but ere he had spoken three words, he suddenly came to a stop, perceiving that not only Lady Western's attention but her ear was lost, and that already another candidate for her favour had possession of the field. He stepped back into the gay assembly, disturbing one group, the members of which all turned to look at him with well-bred curiosity. He stood quite alone and silent for some time, waiting if, perhaps, he could catch the eye of Lady Western. But she was surrounded, swept away, carried off even from his neighbourhood, while he stood gazing. And here was he left, out of the sunshine of her presence in the midst of Carlingford society, knowing nobody, while every face smiled and every tongue was busy but his own: talk *au discretion!* such there certainly was – but Vincent had never in his life felt so preposterously alone, so dismally silent, so shut up in himself. If he had come to woo society, doubtless he could have plucked up a spirit, and made a little effort for his object. But he had come to see Her, flattering himself with vain dreams of securing her to himself – of wandering by her side through those garden-paths, of keeping near her whenever she moved – and the dream had intoxicated him more deeply than even he himself was aware of. Now he woke to his sober wits with a chill of mortification and disappointment not to be expressed. He stood silent, following her with his eyes as she glided about from one corner to the other of the crowded room. He had neither eyes nor ears for anything else. Beautiful as she had always been, she was lovelier than ever to-day, with her fair head uncovered and un-adorned, her beautiful hair glancing in the gleams of sunshine, her tiny hands ungloved. Poor Vincent drew near a window, when it dawned upon his troubled percep-tion that he was standing amidst all those chattering, laughing people, a silent statue of disappointment and dismay, and from that little refuge watched her as she made her progress. And, alas! Lady Western assured everybody that they were "*so* kind" to come – she dis-tributed her smiles, her kind words, everywhere. She beamed upon the old men and the young, the handsome and the stupid, with equal sweetness. After a while, as he stood watching, Vincent began to melt in his heart. She was hostess – she had the party's pleasure to think of, not her own. If he could but help her, bring himself to her notice again in some other way! Vincent made another step out of his window, and looked out eagerly with shy scrutiny. Nobody wanted his help. They stared at him, and whispered questions who he was. When he at length nerved himself to speak to his next neighbour, he met with a courteous response and no more. Society was not cruel, or repulsive, or severely exclusive, but simply did not know him, could not make out who he was, and was busy talking that conversation of a limited sphere full of personal

allusions into which no stranger could enter. Instead of the
ineffable hour he expected, an embarrassing, unbearable
tedium was the lot of the poor Dissenting minister by
himself among the beauty, wit, and fashion of Carlingford.
He would have stolen away but for the forlorn hope that
things might mend – that Lady Western might return, and
that the sunshine he had dreamed of would yet fall upon
him. But no such happiness came to the unfortunate young
minister. After a while, a perfectly undistinguished middle-
aged individual charitably engaged Mr Vincent in conversation; and as they talked, and while the young man's eager
wistful eyes followed into every new combination of the
little crowd that one fair figure which had bewitched him, it
became apparent that the company was flowing forth into
the garden. At last Vincent stopped short in the languid
answer he was making to his respectable interlocutor with a
sudden start and access of impatience. The brilliant room
had suddenly clouded over. She had joined her guests
outside. With bitterness, and a sharp pang at his heart,
Vincent looked round and wondered to find himself in the
house, in the company, from which she had gone. What
business had he there? No link of connection existed
between him and this little world of unknown people except
herself. She had brought him here; she alone knew even so
much of him as his name. He had not an inch of ground to
stand on in the little alien assembly when she was not there.
He broke off his conversation with his unknown sympathiser
abruptly, and rushed out, meaning to leave the place. But
somehow, fascinated still, in a hundred different moods a
minute, when he got outside, he too lingered about the
paths, where he continually met with groups and stray
couples who stared at him, and wondered again, sometimes
not inaudibly, who he was. He met her at last under the
shadow of the lime-trees with a train of girls about her,
and a following of eager male attendants. When he came
forward lonely to make his farewell, with a look in which
he meant to unite a certain indignation and reproach with

still chivalrous devotion, the unconscious beauty met him with unabated sweetness, held out her hand as before, and smiled the most radiant of smiles.

"Are you going to leave us already?" she said, in a tone which half persuaded the unlucky youth to stay till the last moment, and swallow all his mortifications. "So sorry you must go away so soon! and I wanted to show you my pictures too. Another time, I hope, we may have better fortune. When you come to me again, you must really be at leisure, and have no other engagements. Good-bye! It was *so* kind of you to come, and I am so sorry you can't stay!"

In another minute the green door had opened and closed, the fairy vision was gone, and poor Vincent stood in Grange Lane between the two blank lines of garden-wall, come back to the common daylight after a week's vain wandering in the enchanted grounds, half stupified, half maddened by the disappointment and downfall. He made a momentary pause at the door, gulped down the big indignant sigh that rose in his throat, and, with a quickened step and a heightened colour, retraced his steps along a road which no longer gleamed with any rosy reflections, but was harder, more real, more matter-of-fact than ever it had looked before. What a fool he had been, to be led into such a false position! – to be cheated of his peace, and seduced from his duty, and intoxicated into such absurdities of hope, all by the gleam of a bright eye, and the sound of a sweet voice! He who had never known the weakness before, to cover himself with ridicule, and compromise his dignity so entirely for the sake of the first beautiful woman who smiled upon him! Poor Vincent! He hurried to his rooms thrilling with projects, schemes, and sudden vindictive ambition. That fair creature should learn that the young Nonconformist was worthy of her notice. Those self-engrossed simperers should yet be startled out of their follies by the new fame rising up amongst them. Who was he, did they ask? One day they should know.

That the young man should despise himself for this outbreak of injured feeling, as soon as he had cooled down, was inevitable; but it took some considerable time to cool down; and in the mean time his resolution rose and swelled into the heroic region which youth always attains so easily. He thought himself disenchanted for ever. That night, in bitter earnest, he burned the midnight oil – that night his pen flew over the paper with outbreaks, sometimes indignant, sometimes pathetic, on subjects as remote as possible from Lady Western's breakfast-party; and with a sudden revulsion he bethought himself of Salem and its oligarchy, which just now prophesied so much good of their new minister. He accepted Salem with all the heat of passion at that moment. His be the task to raise it and its pastor into a common fame!

CHAPTER VIII.

THE events above narrated were all prefatory of the great success accomplished by Mr Vincent in Carlingford. Indeed, the date of the young minister's fame – fame which, as everybody acquainted with that town must be aware, was widely diffused beyond Carlingford itself, and even reached the metropolis, and gladdened his *Alma Mater* at Homerton – might almost be fixed by a reference to Lady Western's housekeeping-book, if she kept any, and the date of her last summer-party. That event threw the young Nonconformist into just the state of mind which was wanted to quicken all the prejudices of his education, and give individual force to all the hereditary limits of thought in which he had been born. An attempt on the part of the

Government to repeal the Toleration Act, or reinstate the
Test, could scarcely have produced a more permanent
and rapid effect than Lady Western's neglect, and the
total ignorance of Mr Vincent displayed by polite society
in Carlingford. No shame to him. It was precisely the
same thing in private life which the other would have been
in public. Repeal of the Toleration Act, or re-enactment of
the Test, are things totally impossible; and when per-
secution is not to be apprehended or hoped for, where but
in the wrongs of a privileged class can the true zest of
dissidence be found? Mr Vincent, who had received his
Dissenting principles as matters of doctrine, took up the
familiar instruments now with a rush of private feeling.
He was not conscious of the power of that sentiment of
injury and indignation which possessed him. He believed
in his heart that he was but returning, after a temporary
hallucination, to the true duties of his post; but the fact
was, that this wound in the tenderest point – this general
slight and indifference – pricked him forward in all that
force of personal complaint which gives warmth and
piquancy to a public grievance. The young man said
nothing of Lady Western even to his dearest friend – tried
not to think of her except by way of imagining how she
should one day hear of him, and know his name when it
possessed a distinction which neither the perpetual curate
of St Roque's, nor any other figure in that local world,
dared hope for. But with fiery zeal he flew to the question
of Church and State, and set forth the wrongs which
Christianity sustained from endowment, and the heinous
evils of rich livings, episcopal palaces, and spiritual lords.
It was no mean or ungenerous argument which the young
Nonconformist pursued in his fervour of youth and
wounded self-regard. It was the natural cry of a man who
had entered life at disadvantage, and chafed, without
knowing it, at all the phalanx of orders and classes above
him, standing close in order to prevent his entrance. With
eloquent fervour he expatiated upon the kingdom that was

not of this world. If these words were true, what had the
Church to do with worldly possessions, rank, dignities,
power? Was his Grace of Lambeth more like Paul the
tentmaker than his Holiness of Rome? Mr Vincent went
into the whole matter with genuine conviction, and confidence in his own statements. He believed and had been
trained in it. In his heart he was persuaded that he himself,
oft disgusted and much misunderstood in his elected place
at Salem Chapel, ministered the gospel more closely to his
Master's appointment than the rector of Carlingford, who
was nominated by a College; or the curate of St Roque's,
who had his forty pounds a-year from a tiny ancient
endowment, and was spending his own little fortune on
his church and district. These men had joined God and
mammon – they were in the pay of the State. Mr Vincent
thundered forth the lofty censures of an evangelist whom
the State did not recognise, and with whom mammon had
little enough to do. He brought forth all the weapons out of
the Homerton armoury, new, bright, and dazzling and he
did not know any more than his audience that he never
would have wielded them so heartily – perhaps would
scarcely have taken them off the wall – but for the sudden
sting with which his own inferior place, and the existence of
a privileged class doubly shut against his entrance, had
quickened his personal consciousness. Such, however, was
the stimulus which woke the minister of Salem Chapel into
action, and produced that series of lectures on Church and
State which, as everybody knows, shook society in Carlingford to its very foundation.

"Now we've got a young man as is a credit to us," said
Tozer; "and now he's warming to his work, as I was a little
afraid of at first; for somehow I can't say as I could see to
my satisfaction, when he first come, that his heart was in
it, – I say, now as we've got a pastor as does us credit, I am
not the man to consider a bit of expense. My opinion is as
we should take the Music Hall for them lectures. There's
folk might go to the Music Hall as would never come to

Salem, and we're responsible for our advantages. A clever young man like Mr Vincent ain't to be named along with Mr Tufton; we're the teachers of the community, that's what we are. I am for being public-spirited – I always was; and I don't mind standing my share. My opinion is as we should take the Music Hall."

"If we was charging sixpence a-head or so—" said prudent Pigeon, the poulterer.

"That's what I'll never give my consent to – never!" said Tozer. "If we was amusin' the people, we might charge sixpence a-head; but mark my words," continued the butterman, "there ain't twenty men in Carlingford, nor in no other place, as would give sixpence to have their minds enlightened. No sir, we're conferring of a boon; and let's do it handsomely, I say – let's do it handsomely; and here's my name down for five pound to clear expenses: and if every man in Salem does as well, there ain't no reason for hesitating. I'm a plain man, but I don't make no account of a little bit of money when a principle's at stake."

This statement was conclusive. When it came to the sacrifice of a little bit of money, neither Mrs Pigeon nor Mrs Brown could have endured life had their husbands yielded the palm to Tozer. And the Music Hall was accordingly taken; and there, every Wednesday for six weeks, the young Nonconformist mounted his *cheval de bataille*, and broke his impetuous spear against the Church. Perhaps Carlingford was in want of a sensation at the moment; and the town was virgin soil, and had never yet been invaded by sight or sound of heresy. Anyhow, the fact was, that this fresh new voice attracted the ear of the public. That personal impetuosity and sense of wrong which gave fire to the discourse, roused the interest of the entire community. Mr Vincent's lectures became the fashion in Carlingford, where nobody in the higher levels of society had ever heard before of the amazing evils of a Church Establishment. Some of the weaker or more candid minds among the audience were even upset by the

young minister's arguments. Two or three young people
of both sexes declared themselves converted, and were
persecuted to their heart's desire when they intimated
their intention of henceforward joining the congregation of
Salem. The two Miss Hemmings were thrown into a state
of great distress and perplexity, and wrung their hands,
and looked at each other, as each new enormity was
brought forth. A very animated interested audience filled
the benches in the Music Hall for the three last lectures.
It was Mr Tozer's conviction, whispered in confidence to
all the functionaries at Salem, that the rector himself,
in a muffler and blue spectacles, listened in a corner
to the voice of rebellion; but no proof of this monstrous
supposition ever came before the public. Notwithstanding,
the excitement was evident. Miss Wodehouse took tremulous notes, her fingers quivering with anger, with the
intention of calling upon Mr Wentworth to answer and
deny these assertions. Dr Marjoribanks, the old Scotchman,
who in his heart enjoyed a hit at the Episcopate, cried
"Hear, hear," with his sturdy northern *r* rattling through
the hall, and clapped his large brown hands, with a broad
grin at his daughter, who was "High," and one of Mr
Wentworth's Sisters of Mercy. But poor little Rose Lake,
the drawing-master's daughter, who was going up for
confirmation next time the bishop came to Carlingford,
turned very pale under Mr Vincent's teaching. All the
different phases of conviction appeared in her eager
little face – first indignation, then doubt, lastly horror
and intense determination to flee out from Babylon. Her
father laughed, and told her to attend to her needlework,
when Rose confided to him her troubles. Her needlework!
She who had just heard that the Church was rotten, and
tottering on its foundations; that it was choked with filthy
lucre and State support; that Church to which she had
been about to give in her personal adhesion! Rose put
away her catechism and confirmation good-books, and
crossed to the other side of the street that she might

not pass Masters's, that emporium of evil. She looked
wistfully after the young Nonconformist as he passed her
on the streets, wondering what high martyr-thoughts must
be in the apostolic mind which entertained so high a
contempt for all the honours and distinctions of this world.
Meanwhile Mr Vincent pursued his own way, entirely
convinced, as was natural for a young man, that he was
"doing a great work" in Carlingford. He was still in that
stage of life when people imagine that you have only to
state the truth clearly to have it believed, and that to
convince a man of what is right is all that is necessary to
his immediate reformation. But it was not with any very
distinct hopes or wishes of emptying the church in Carlingford, and crowding Salem Chapel, that the young man
proceeded. Such expectations, high visions of a day to
come when not a sitting could be had in Salem for love or
money, did indeed glance into the souls of Tozer and his
brother deacons; but the minister did not stand up and
deliver his blow at the world – his outcry against things in
general – his warm youthful assertion that he too had a
right to all the joys and privileges of humanity, – as, by
means of sermons, lectures, poems, or what not, youth
and poverty, wherever they have a chance, do proclaim
their protest against the world.

On the last night of the lectures, just as Vincent had
taken his place upon his platform, a rustle as of some one
of importance entering, thrilled the audience. Looking
over the sea of heads before him, the breath almost left
the young minister's lips when he saw the young Dowager,
in all her glory of full-dress, threading her way through the
crowd, which opened to let her pass. Mr Vincent stood
watching her progress, unaware that it was time for him to
begin, and that his hearers, less absorbed than he, were
asking each other what it was which had so suddenly paled
his face and checked his utterance. He watched Lady
Western and her companion come slowly forward; he saw
Tozer, in a delighted bustle, leading the way to one of the

raised seats of the orchestra close to the platform. When
they were seated, and not till then, the lecturer, drawing a
long gasping breath, turned to his audience. But the crowd
was hazy to his eyes. He began, half mechanically, to
speak – then made a sudden pause, his mind occupied with
other things. On the very skirts of the crowd, far back at
the door, stood his friend of Back Grove Street. In that
momentary pause, he saw her standing alone, with the air
of a person who had risen up unconsciously in sudden
surprise and consternation. Her pale dark face looked
not less confused and startled than Vincent himself was
conscious of looking, and her eyes were turned in the same
direction as his had been the previous moment. The crowd
of Carlingford hearers died off from the scene for the
instant, so far as the young Nonconformist was concerned.
He knew but of that fair creature in all her sweet bloom
and blush of beauty – the man who accompanied her – Mrs
Hilyard, a thin, dark, eager shadow in the distance – and
himself standing, as it were, between them, connecting
all together. What could that visionary link be which
distinguished and separated these four, so unlike each
other, from all the rest of the world? But Mr Vincent had
no leisure to follow out the question, even had his mind
been sufficiently clear to do it. He saw the pale woman at
the end of the hall suddenly drop into her seat, and draw a
thick black veil over her face; and the confused murmur of
impatience in the crowd before him roused the young man
to his own position. He opened the eyes which had been
hazing over with clouds of imagination and excitement.
He delivered his lecture. Though he never was himself
aware what he had said, it was received with just as much
attention and applause as usual. He got through it somehow; and, sitting down at last, with parched lips and
a helpless feeling of excitement, watched the audience
dispersing, as if they were so many enemies from whom
he had escaped. Who was this man with Her? Why did
She come to bewilder him in the midst of his work? It did

not occur to the poor young fellow that Lady Western came to his lecture simply as to a "distraction." He thought she had a purpose in it. He pretended not to look as she descended daintily from her seat in the orchestra, drawing her white cloak with a pretty shiver over her white shoulders. He pretended to start when her voice sounded in his expectant ear.

"Oh, Mr Vincent, how very clever and wicked of you!" cried Lady Western. "I am so horrified, and charmed. To think of you attacking the poor dear old Church, that we all ought to support through everything! And I am such a stanch Churchwoman, and so shocked to hear all this; but you won't do it any more."

Saying this, Lady Western leaned her beautiful hand upon Mr Vincent's table, and looked in his face with a beseeching insinuating smile. The poor minister did all he could to preserve his virtue. He looked aside at Lady Western's companion to fortify himself, and escape the enervating influence of that smile.

"I cannot pretend to yield the matter to your ladyship," said Vincent, "for it had been previously arranged that this was to be the last of my lectures at present. I am sorry it did not please you."

"But it did please me," said the young Dowager; "only that it was so very wicked and wrong. Where did you learn such dreadful sentiments? I am so sorry I shan't hear you again, and so glad you are finished. You never came to see me after my little *fête*. I am afraid you thought us stupid. Goodnight: but you really must come to me, and I shall convert you. I am sure you never can have looked at the Church in the right way: why, what would become of us if we were all Dissenters? What a frightful idea! Thank you for such a charming evening. Good-night."

And Lady Western held out that "treasured splendour, her hand," to the bewildered Nonconformist, who only dared touch it, and let it fall, drawing back from the smile with which the syren beguiled him back again into her toils. But Mr Vincent turned round hastily as he heard a muttered exclamation, "By Jove!" behind him, and fixed the gaze of angry and instinctive repugnance upon the tall figure which brushed past. "Make haste, Alice – do you mean to stay here all night?" said this wrathful individual, fixing his eyes with a defiant stare upon the minister; and he drew the beauty's arm almost roughly into his own, and hurried her away, evidently remonstrating in the freest and boldest manner upon her civility. "By Jove! the fellow will think you are in love with him," Vincent, with his quickened and suspicious ears, could hear the stranger say, with that delightful indifference to being overheard which characterises some Englishmen of the exalted classes; and the strain of reproof evidently continued as they made their way to the door. Vincent, for his part, when he had watched them out of sight, dropped into his chair, and sat there in the empty hall, looking over the vacant benches with the strangest mixture of feelings. Was it possible that his eager fervour and revolutionary warmth were diminished by these few words and that smile? – that the wrongs of Church and State looked less grievous all at once, and that it was an effort to return to the lofty state of feeling with which he had entered the place two hours ago? As he sat there in his reverie of discomfiture, he could see Tozer, a single black figure, come slowly up the hall, an emissary from the group at the door of "Chapel people," who had been enjoying the defeat of the enemy, and were now waiting for the conqueror. "Mr Vincent," shouted Tozer, "shall we turn off the gas, and leave you to think it all over till the morning, sir? They're all as pleased as Punch and as curious as women down below here, and my Phoebe will have it you're tired. I must say it is peculiar to see you a-sitting up there all by yourself, and the lights going out, and not another soul in the place," added the butterman, looking round with a sober grin; and in reality the lights diminished every moment as Mr Vincent rose and stumbled down from his platform into the great empty hall with its skeleton benches. If they *had* left him there till the morning, it would have been a blessed exchange from that walk home with the party, that invitation to supper, and all the applauses and inquiries that followed. They had the Pigeons to supper that night at the butter-shop, and the whole matter was discussed in all its bearings – the flutter of the "Church folks," the new sittings let during the week, the triumphant conviction of the two deacons that Salem would soon be overflowing.

> "Oh, why were 'deacons' made so coarse,
>   Or parsons made so fine?"

Mr Vincent did not bethink himself of that touching ditty. He could not see the serio-comic lights in which the whole business abounded. It was all the saddest earnest to the young pastor, who found so little encouragement or support even in the enthusiasm of his flock.

"And, oh, Mr Vincent," said the engaging Phoebe, in a half-whisper aside, "how *did* you come to be *so* friendly with Lady Western? How she did listen, to be sure! and smiled at you *so* sweetly. Ah, I don't wonder now that you can't see anything in the Carlingford young ladies; but do tell us, please, how you came to know her so well?"

Insensibly to himself, a gleam of gratification lighted up Mr Vincent's face. He was gracious to Phoebe. "I can't pretend to know her *well*," he said, with a little mock humility; whereupon the matrons of the party took up their weapons immediately.

"And all the better, Mr Vincent – all the better!" cried Mrs Tozer; "she didn't come there for no good, you may be sure. Them great ladies, when they're pretty-looking, as I don't deny she's pretty-looking—"

"Oh, mamma, beautiful!" exclaimed Phoebe.

"When they're pretty-looking, as I say," continued Mrs Tozer, "they're no better nor evil spirits – that's what I tell you Phoebe. They'll go out o' their way, they will, for to lay hold on a poor silly young man (which was not meaning you, Mr Vincent, that knows better, being a minister), and when they've got him fast, they'll laugh at him – that's their sport. A minister of our connection as was well acquainted among them sort of folks would be out o' nature. My boy shall never make no such acquaintances as long as I'm here."

"I saw her a-speaking to the minister," said Mrs Pigeon, "and the thought crossed my mind as it wasn't just what I expected of Mr Vincent. Painted ladies, that come out of a night with low necks and flowers in their hair, to have all Carlingford a-staring at them, ain't fit company for a good pastor. *Them*'s not the lambs of the flock – not so far as I understand; they're not friends as Salem folks would approve of, Mr Vincent. I'm always known for a plain speaker, and I don't deceive you. It's a deal better to draw back in time."

"I have not the least reason to believe that Lady Western means to honour me with her friendship," said Vincent, haughtily – "so it is premature to discuss the matter. As I feel rather tired, perhaps you'll excuse me to-night. Come over to my rooms, Mr Tozer, to-morrow, if you can spare a little time and we will discuss our business there. I hope Mrs Tozer will pardon me withdrawing so early, but I am not very well – rather tired – out of sorts a little to-night."

So saying, the young pastor extricated himself from the table, shook hands, regardless of all remonstrances, and made his way out with some difficulty from the little room, which was choke-full, and scarcely permitted egress. When he was gone, the three ladies looked at each other in dumb amazement. Phoebe, who felt herself aggrieved, was the first to break silence.

"Ma and Mrs Pigeon," cried the aggravated girl, "you've been and hurt his feelings. I knew you would. He's gone home angry and disappointed; he thinks none of us understand him; he thinks we're trying to humble him and keep him down, when, to tell the truth—"

Here Phoebe burst into tears.

"Upon *my* word," said Mrs Pigeon, "dear, deary me! It's just what I said whenever I knew you had made up your minds to a *young* minister. He'll come a-dangling after our girls, says I, and a-trifling with their affections. Bless my heart, Phoebe! if it had been my Maria now that's always a-crying about something – but you! Don't take on, dear – fretting's no good – it'll spoil your colour and take away your appetite, and that ain't the way to mend matters: and to think of his lifting his eyes to my Lady Dowager! Upon *my* word! but there ain't no accounting for young men's ways no more than for girls – and being a minister don't make a bit of difference, so far as I can see."

"Why, what's the matter?" cried Tozer: "the pastor's gone off in a huff, and Phoebe crying. What's wrong? You've been saying somethin' – you women with your sharp tongues."

"It's Phoebe and Mr Vincent have had some words. Be quiet, Tozer – don't you see the child's hurt in her feelings?" said his wife.

Mr and Mrs Pigeon exchanged looks. "I'll tell you what it is," said the latter lady, solemnly. "It's turned his head. I never approved of the Music Hall myself. It's a deal of money to throw away, and it's not like as if it was mercy to poor souls. And such a crush, and the cheering, and my Lady Western to shake hands with him, has turned the minister's head. Now, just you mark my words. He hasn't been here three month yet, and he's a-getting high already. You men'll have your own adoes with him. Afore a year's over our heads, he'll be a deal too high for Salem. His head's turned – that's what it is."

"Oh, Mrs Pigeon, how unkind of you!" cried Phoebe, "when he's as good as good – and not a bit proud, nor ever was – and always such a gentleman! – and never neglects the very poorest whenever he's sent for – oh, it's *so* unkind of you."

"I can't see as his head isn't straight enough on his shoulders," said Tozer himself, with authority. "He's tired, that's what it is – and excited a bit, I shouldn't

wonder: a man can't study like he does, and make hisself
agreeable at the same time – no, no – by a year's time he'll
be settling down, and we'll know where we are; and as for
Salem and our connection, they never had a chance, I can
tell you, like what they're a-going to have now."

But Mrs Pigeon shook her head. It was the first cloud
that had risen on the firmament of Salem Chapel, so far as
Mr Vincent was concerned.

CHAPTER IX.

It was a January night on which Vincent emerged abruptly
from Tozer's door, the evening of that lecture – a winter
night, not very cold, but very dark, the skies looking not
blue, but black overhead, and the light of the lamps
gleaming dismally on the pavement, which had received a
certain squalid power of reflection from the recent rain;
for a sharp, sudden shower had fallen while Vincent had
been seated at the hospitable table of the butterman,
which had chased everybody from the darkling streets. All
the shops were closed, a policeman marched along with
heavy tread, and the wet pavement glimmered round his
solitary figure. Nothing more uncomfortable could be
supposed after the warmth and light of a snug interior,
however humble; and the minister turned his face hastily
in the direction of his lodging. But the next moment he
turned back again, and looked wistfully in the other
direction. It was not to gaze along the dark length of street
to where the garden-walls of Grange Lane, undiscernible
in the darkness, added a far-withdrawing perspective of
gentility and aristocratic seclusion to the vulgar pretensions
of George Street; it was to look at a female figure which

came slowly up, dimming out the reflection on the wet stones as it crossed one streak of lamplight after another. Vincent was excited and curious, and had enough in his own mind to make him wistful for sympathy, if it were to be had from any understanding heart. He recognised Mrs Hilyard instinctively as she came forward, not conscious of him, walking, strange woman as she was, with the air of a person walking by choice at that melancholy hour in that dismal night. She was evidently not going anywhere: her step was firm and distinct, like the step of a person thoroughly self-possessed and afraid of nothing – but it lingered with a certain meditative sound in the steady firm footfall. Vincent felt a kind of conviction that she had come out here to think over some problem of that mysterious life into which he could not penetrate, and he connected this strange walk involuntarily with the appearance of Lady Western and her careless companion. To his roused fancy, some incomprehensible link existed between himself and the equally incomprehensible woman before him. He turned back almost in spite of himself, and went to meet her. Mrs Hilyard looked up when she heard his step. She recognised him also on the spot. They approached each other much as if they had arranged a meeting at eleven o'clock of that wet January night in the gleaming, deserted streets.

"It is you, Mr Vincent!" she said. "I wonder why I happen to meet you, of all persons in the world, to-night. It is very odd. What, I wonder, can have brought us both together at such an hour and in such a place? You never came to see me that Monday – nor any Monday. You went to see my beauty instead, and you were so lucky as to be affronted with the syren at the first glance. Had you been less fortunate, I think I might have partly taken you into my confidence to-night."

"Perhaps I *am* less fortunate, if that is all that hinders," said Vincent; "but it is strange to see you out here so late in such a dismal night. Let me go with you, and see you safe home."

"Thank you. I am perfectly safe – nobody can possibly be safer than such a woman as I am, in poverty and middle age," said his strange acquaintance. "It is an immunity that women don't often prize, Mr Vincent, but it is very valuable in its way. If anybody saw you talking to an equivocal female figure at eleven o'clock in George Street, think what the butterman would say; but a single glimpse of my face would explain matters better than a volume. I am going down towards Grange Lane, principally because I am restless to-night, and don't know what to do with myself. I shall tell you what I thought of your lecture if you will walk with me to the end of the street."

"Ah, my lecture! – never mind," said the hapless young minister; "I forget all about that. What is it that brings you here, and me to your side? – what is there in the dark-veiled house yonder that draws your steps and mine to it? It is not accidental, our meeting here."

"You are talking romance and nonsense, quite inconceivable in a man who has just come from the society of deacons," said Mrs Hilyard, glancing up at him with that habitual gleam of her eyes. "We have met, my dear Mr Vincent, because, after refreshing my mind with your lecture, I thought of refreshing my body by a walk this fresh night. One saves candles, you know, when one does one's exercise at night: whereas walking by day one wastes everything – time, tissue, daylight, invaluable treasures: the only light that hurts nobody's eyes, and costs nobody money, is the light of day. That illustration of yours about the clouds and the sun was very pretty. I assure you I thought the whole exceedingly effective. I should not wonder if it made a revolution in Carlingford."

"Why do you speak to me so? I know you did not go to listen to my lecture," said the young minister, to whom sundry gleams of enlightenment had come since his last interview with the poor needlewoman of Back Grove Street.

"Ah! how can you tell that?" she said, sharply, looking at him in the streak of lamplight. "But to tell the truth," she continued, "I did actually go to hear you, and to look at other people's faces, just to see whether the world at large – so far as that exists in Carlingford – was like what it used to be; and if I confess I saw something there more interesting than the lecture, I say no more than the lecturer could agree in, Mr Vincent. You, too saw something that made you forget the vexed question of Church and State."

"Tell me," said Vincent, with an earnestness he was himself surprised at, "who was that man?"

His companion started as if she had received a blow, turned round upon him with a glance in her dark eyes such as he had never seen there before, and in a sudden momentary passion drew her breath hard, and stopped short on the way. But the spark of intense and passionate emotion was as shortlived as it was vivid. "I do not suppose he is anything to interest you," she answered the next moment, with a movement of her thin mouth, letting the hands that she had clasped together drop to her side. "Nay, make yourself quite easy; he is not a lover of my lady's. He is only a near relation: – and," she continued, lingering on the words with a force of subdued scorn and rage, which Vincent dimly apprehended, but could not understand, "a very fascinating fine gentleman – a man who can twist a woman round his fingers when he likes, and break all her heartstrings – if she has any – so daintily afterwards, that it would be a pleasure to see him do it. Ah, a wonderful man!"

"You know him then? I saw you knew him," said the young man, surprised and disturbed, thrusting the first commonplace words he could think of into the silence, which seemed to tingle with the restrained meaning of this brief speech.

"I don't think we are lucky in choosing our subjects to-night," said the strange woman. "How about the ladies in

Lonsdale, Mr Vincent? They don't keep a school? I am glad they don't keep a school. Teaching, you know, unless when one has a vocation for it, as you had a few weeks ago, is uphill work. I am sorry to see you are not so sure about your work as you were then. Your sister is pretty, I suppose? and does your mother take great care of her and keep her out of harm's way? Lambs have a silly faculty of running directly in the wolf's road. Why don't you take a holiday and go to see them, or have them here to live with you?"

"You know something about them," said Vincent, alarmed. "What has happened? – tell me. It will be the greatest kindness to say it out at once."

"Hush," said Mrs Hilyard: "now you are absurd. I speak out of my thoughts, as most persons do, and you, like all young people, make personal applications. How can I possibly know about them? I am not a fanciful woman, but there are some things that wake one's imagination. In such a dark night as this, with such wet gleams about the streets, when I think of people at a distance, I always think of something uncomfortable happening. Misfortune seems to lie in wait about those black corners. I think of women wandering along dismal solitary roads with babies in their shameful arms – and of dreadful messengers of evil approaching unconscious houses, and looking in at peaceful windows upon the comfort they are about to destroy; and I think," she continued, crossing the road so rapidly (they were now opposite Lady Western's house) that Vincent, who had not anticipated the movement, had to quicken his pace suddenly to keep up with her, "of evil creatures pondering in the dark vile schemes against the innocent—" Here she broke off all at once, and, looking up in Vincent's face with that gleam of secret mockery in her eyes and movement of her mouth to which he was accustomed, added, suddenly changing her tone, "Or of fine gentlemen, Mr Vincent, profoundly bored with their own society, promenading in a dreary garden and smoking a disconsolate cigar. Look there!"

The young minister, much startled and rather nervous, mechanically looked, as she bade him, through the little grated loophole in Lady Western's garden-door. He saw the lights shining in the windows, and a red spark moving about before the house, as, with a little shame for his undignified position, he withdrew his eyes from that point of vantage. But Mrs Hilyard was moved by no such sentiment. She planted herself opposite the door, and, bending her head to the little grating, gazed long and steadfastly. In the deep silence of the night, standing with some uneasiness at her side, and not insensible to the fact that his position, if he were seen by anybody who knew him, would be rather absurd and slightly equivocal, Vincent heard the footsteps of the man inside, the fragrance of whose cigar faintly penetrated the damp air. The stranger was evidently walking up and down before the house in enjoyment of that luxury which the feminine arrangements of the young Dowager's household would not permit indoors; but the steady eagerness with which this strange woman gazed – the way in which she had managed to interweave Mrs Vincent and pretty Susan at Lonsdale into the conversation – the suggestions of coming danger and the evil with which her words had invested the very night, all heightened by the instinctive repugnance and alarm of which the young man had himself been conscious whenever he met the eye of Lady Western's companion – filled him with discomfort and dread. His mind, which had been lately too much occupied in his own concerns to think much of Susan, reverted now with sudden uneasiness to his mother's cottage, from which Susan's betrothed had lately departed to arrange matters for their speedy marriage. But how Lady Western's "near relation" – this man whom Mrs Hilyard watched with an intense regard which looked like hatred, but might be dead love – could be connected with Lonsdale, or Susan, or himself, or the poor needlewoman in Back Grove Street, Vincent could not form the remotest idea. He stood

growing more and more impatient by that dark closed door,
which had once looked a gate of paradise – which, he felt in
his heart, half-a-dozen words or a single smile could any
day make again a gate of the paradise of fools to his
bewildered feet – the steps of the unseen stranger within,
and the quick breath of agitation from the watcher by his
side, being the only sounds audible in the silence of the
night. At last some restless movement he made disturbed
Mrs Hilyard in her watch. She left the door noiselessly and
rapidly, and turned to recross the wet road. Vincent accompanied her without saying a word. The two walked along
together half the length of Grange Lane without breaking
silence, without even looking at each other, till they came
to the large placid white lamp at Dr Marjoribanks's gate,
which cleared a little oasis of light out of the heart of the
gloom. There she looked up at him with a face full of
agitated life and motion – kindled eyes, elevated head,
nostril and lips swelling with feelings which were totally
undecipherable to Vincent; her whole aspect changed by an
indescribable inspiration which awoke remnants of what
might have been beauty in that thin, dark, middle-aged face.

"You are surprised at me and my curiosity," she said,
"and indeed you have good reason; but it is astonishing,
when one is shut up in one's self and knows nobody,
how excited one gets over the sudden apparition of a
person one has known in the other world. Some people
die two or three times in a lifetime, Mr Vincent. There
is a real transmigration of souls, or bodies, or both if
you please. This is my third life I am going through at
present. I knew that man, as I was saying, in the other
world."

"The world *does* change strangely," said Vincent, who
could not tell what to say; "but you put it very strongly –
more strongly than I—"

"More strongly than you can understand; I know that
very well," said Mrs Hilyard; "but you perceive you are
speaking to a woman who has died twice. Coming to life is

a bitter process, but one gets over it. If you ever should have such a thing to go through with – and survive it," she added, giving him a wistful glance, "I should like to tell you my experiences. However, I hope better things. You are very well looked after at Salem Chapel, Mr Vincent. I think of you sometimes when I look out of my window and see your tabernacle. It is not so pretty as Mr Wentworth's at St Roque's, but you have the advantage of the curate otherwise. So far as I can see, he never occupies himself with anything higher than his prayer-book and his poor people. I doubt much whether he would ever dream of replying to what you told us to-night."

"Probably he holds a Dissenting minister in too much contempt," said Vincent, with an uncomfortable smile on his lips.

"Don't sneer – never sneer – no gentleman does," said his companion. "I like you, though you are only a Dissenting minister. You know me to be very poor, and you have seen me in very odd circumstances to-night; yet you walk home with me – I perceive you are steering towards Back Grove Street, Mr Vincent – without an allusion which could make me feel myself an equivocal person, and just as if this was the most reasonable thing in the world which I have been doing to-night. Thank you. You are a Paladin in some things, though in others only a Dissenting minister. If I were a fairy, the gift I would endow you with would be just that same unconsciousness of your own disadvantages, which courtesy makes you show of mine."

"Indeed," said Vincent, with natural gratification, "it required no discrimination on my part to recognise at once that I was addressing—"

"Hush! you have never even insinuated that an explanation was necessary, which is the very height and climax of fine manners," said Mrs Hilyard; "and I speak who am, or used to be, an authority in such matters. I don't mean to give you any explanation either. Now, you must turn back and go home. Good-night. One thing I may tell you, however," she continued, with a little warmth; "don't mistake me. There is no reason in this world why you might not introduce me to the ladies in Lonsdale, if any accident brought it about that we should meet. I say this to make your mind easy about your penitent; and now, my good young father in the faith, good-night."

"Let me see you to your door first," said the wondering young man.

"No – no farther. Good-night," she said hastily, shaking hands, and leaving him. The parting was so sudden that it took Vincent a minute to stop short, under way and walking quickly as he was. When she had made one or two rapid steps in advance, Mrs Hilyard turned back, as if with a sudden impulse.

"Do you know I have an uneasiness about these ladies in Lonsdale?" she said; "I know nothing whatever about them – not so much as their names; but you are their natural protector; and it does not do for women to be as magnanimous and generous in their reception of strangers as you are. There! don't be alarmed. I told you I knew nothing. They may be as safe, and as middle-aged, and as ugly as I am; instead of a guileless widow and a pretty little girl, they may be hardened old campaigners like myself; but they come into my mind, I cannot tell why. Have them here to live beside you, and they will do you good."

"My sister is about to be married," said Vincent, more and more surprised, and looking very sharply into her face in the lamplight, to see whether she really did not know anything more than she said.

A certain expression of relief came over her face.

"Then all is well," she said, with strange cordiality, and again held out her hand to him. Then they parted, and pursued their several ways through the perfectly silent and dimly-lighted streets. Vincent walked home with the most singular agitation in his mind. Whether to give any weight to such vague but alarming suggestions – whether to act immediately upon the indefinite terror thus insinuated into his thoughts – or to write, and wait till he heard whether any real danger existed – or to cast it from him altogether as a fantastic trick of imagination, he could not tell. Eventful and exciting as the evening had been, he postponed the other matters to this. If any danger threatened Susan, his simple mother could suffer with her, but was ill qualified to protect her: but what danger could threaten Susan? He consoled himself with the thought that these were not the days of abductions or violent love-making. To think of an innocent English girl in her mother's house as threatened with mysterious danger, such as might have surrounded a heroine of the last century, was impossible. If there are Squire Thornhills nowadays, their operations are of a different character. Walking rapidly home, with now and then a blast of chill rain in his face, and the lamplight gleaming in the wet streets, Vincent found less and less reason for attaching any importance to Mrs Hilyard's hints and alarms. It was the sentiment of the night and her own thoughts, which had suggested such fears to her mind – a mind evidently experienced in paths more crooked than any which Vincent himself, much less simple Susan, had ever known. When he reached home, he found his little fire burning brightly, his room arranged with careful nicety, which was his landlady's appropriate and sensible manner of showing her appreciation of the night's lecture, and her devotion to the minister; and, lastly, on the table a letter from that little house in Lonsdale, round which such fanciful fears had gathered. Never was there a letter which breathed more of the peaceful security and tranquillity of home. Mrs Vincent wrote to her Arthur in mingled rejoicing and admonition, curious and delighted to hear of his lectures, but no more anxious about his fame and success than about his flannels and precautions against wet feet; while Susan's postscript – a half longer than the letter to which it was appended – furnished her affectionate brother with sundry details, totally incomprehensible to him, of her

wedding preparations, and, more shyly, of her perfect
girlish happiness. Vincent laughed aloud as he folded up
that woman's letter. No mysterious horror, no whispering
doubtful gloom, surrounded that house from which the
pure, full daylight atmosphere, untouched by any darkness, breathed fresh upon him out of these simple pages.
Here, in this humble virtuous world, were no mysteries. It
was a deliverance to a heart which had begun to falter.
Wherever fate might be lingering in the wild darkness of
that January night, it was not on the threshold of his
mother's house.

CHAPTER X.

ON the next evening after this there was a tea-meeting in
Salem Chapel. In the back premises behind the chapel
were all needful accommodations for the provisions of that
popular refreshment – boilers, tea-urns, unlimited crockery
and pewter. In fact, it was one of Mr Tozer's boasts, that
owing to the liberality of the "connection" in Carlingford,
Salem was fully equipped in this respect, and did not need
to borrow so much as a spoon or teapot, a very important
matter under the circumstances. This, however, was the
first tea-meeting which had taken place since that one at
which Mr Tufton's purse had been presented to him, and
the old pastor had taken leave of his flock. The young
pastor, indeed, had set his face against tea-meetings. He
was so far behind his age as to doubt their utility, and
declared himself totally unqualified to preside over such
assemblies; but, in the heat of his recent disappointment,
when, stung by other people's neglect, he had taken up
Salem and all belonging to it into his bosom, a cruel use

had been made of the young minister's compliance. They had wrung a reluctant consent from him in that unguarded moment, and the walls of Carlingford had been for some days blazing with placards of the tea-meeting, at which the now famous (in Carlingford) lecturer on Church and State was to speak. Not Tozer, with all his eloquence, had been able to persuade the pastor to preside; but at least he was to appear, to take tea at that table elevated on the platform, where Phoebe Tozer, under the matronly care of Mrs Brown (for it was necessary to divide these honours, and guard against jealousy), dispensed the fragrant lymph, and to address the meeting. There had been thoughts of a grand celebration in the Music Hall to do more honour to the occasion; but as that might have neutralised the advantages of having all the needful utensils within themselves, convenience and economy carried the day, and the scene of these festivities, as of all the previous festivities of Salem, was the large low room underneath the chapel, once intended for a school, but never used, except on Sundays, in that capacity. Thither for two or three days all the "young ladies" of the chapel had streamed to and fro, engaged in decorations. Some manufactured festoons of evergreens, some concocted pink and white roses in paper to embellish the same. The printed texts of the Sunday school were framed, and in some cases obliterated, in Christmas garlands. Christmas, indeed, was past, but there were still holly and red berries and green smooth laurel leaves. The Pigeon girls, Phoebe Tozer, Mrs Brown's niece from the country, and the other young people in Salem who were of sufficiently advanced position, enjoyed the preparations greatly – entering into them with even greater heartiness than Lucy Wodehouse exhibited in the adornment of St Roque's, and taking as much pleasure in the task as if they had been picturesque Italians adorning the shrine of their favourite saint. Catterina and Francesca with their flower-garlands are figures worthy of any picture, and so is Lucy Wodehouse under the chancel arch at St Roque's; but

how shall we venture to ask anybody's sympathy for
Phoebe and Maria Pigeon as they put up their festoons
round the four square walls of the low schoolroom in
preparation for the Salem tea-party? Nevertheless it is a
fact that the two last mentioned had very much the same
intentions and sen- sations, and amid the coils of fresh ivy
and laurel did not look amiss in their cheerful labour – a fact
which, before the work was completed, had become per-
ceptible to various individuals of the Carlingford public.
But Mr Vincent was, on this point, as on several others,
unequal to the requirements of his position. When he did
glance in for a moment on the afternoon of the eventful
day, it was in company with Tozer and the Rev. Mr Raffles
of Shoebury, who was to take the chair. Mr Raffles was
very popular in Carlingford, as everywhere. To secure him
for a tea-meeting was to secure its success. He examined
into all the preparations, tasted the cake, pricked his
fingers with the garlands to the immense delight of the
young ladies, and complimented them on their skill with
beaming cheerfulness; while the minister of Salem, on the
contrary, stalked about by his side pale and preoccupied,
with difficulty keeping himself from that contempt of the
actual things around to which youth is so often tempted.
His mind wandered off to the companion of his last night's
walk – to the stranger pacing up and down that damp
garden with inscrutable unknown thoughts – to the beautiful
creature within those lighted windows, so near and yet so
overwhelmingly distant – as if somehow they had abstracted
life and got it among themselves. Mr Vincent had little
patience for what he considered the mean details of existence near at hand. As soon as he could possibly manage it,
he escaped, regarding with a certain hopeless disgust the
appearance he had to make in the evening, and without
finding a single civil thing to say to the fair decorators.
"My young brother looks sadly low and out of spirits,"
said jolly Mr Raffles. "What do you mean by being so
unkind to the minister, Miss Phoebe, eh? " Poor Phoebe

blushed pinker than ever, while the rest laughed. It was
pleasant to be supposed "unkind" to the minister; and
Phoebe resolved to do what she could to cheer him when
she sat by his elbow at the platform table making tea for
the visitors of the evening.

The evening came, and there was not a ticket to
be had anywhere in Carlingford: the schoolroom, with
its blazing gas, its festoons, and its mottoes, its tables
groaning with dark-complexioned plumcake and heavy
buns, was crowded quite beyond its accommodation; and
the edifying sight might be seen of Tozer and his brother
deacons, and indeed all who were sufficiently interested in
the success of Salem to sacrifice themselves on its behalf,
making an erratic but not unsubstantial tea in corners,
to make room for the crowd. And in the highest good-
humour was the crowd which surrounded all the narrow
tables. The urns were well filled, the cake abundant, the
company in its best attire. The ladies had bonnets, it is
true, but these bonnets were worthy the occasion. At the
table on the platform sat Mr Raffles, in the chair, beaming
upon the assembled party, with cheerful little Mrs Tufton
and Mrs Brown at one side of him, and Phoebe looking
very pink and pretty, shaded from the too enthusiastic
admiration of the crowd below by the tea-urn at which she
officiated. Next to her, the minister cast abstracted looks
upon the assembly. He was, oh, so interesting in his
silence and pallor! – he spoke little; and when any one
addressed him, he had to come back as if from a distance
to hear. If anybody could imagine that Mr Raffles con-
trasted dangerously with Mr Vincent in that reserve and
quietness, it would be a mistake unworthy a philosophic
observer. On the contrary, the Salem people were all
doubly proud of their pastor. It was not to be expected
that such a man as he should unbend as the reverend
chairman did. They preferred that he should continue on
his stilts. It would have been a personal humiliation to the
real partisans of the chapel, had he really woke up and

come down from that elevation. The more commonplace
the ordinary "connection" was, the more proud they felt
of their student and scholar. So Mr Vincent leaned his
head upon his hands and gazed unmolested over the lively
company, taking in all the particulars of the scene, the
busy group engaged in mere tea-making and tea-consuming
– the flutter of enjoyment among humble girls and womankind who knew no pleasure more exciting – the whispers
which pointed out himself to strangers among the party –
the triumphant face of Tozer at the end of the room,
jammed against the wall, drinking tea out of an empty
sugar-basin. If the scene woke any movement of human
sympathy in the bosom of the young Nonconformist, he
was half ashamed of himself for it. What had the high
mission of an evangelist – the lofty ambition of a man
trained to enlighten his country – the warm assurance of
talent which felt itself entitled to the highest sphere, –
what had these great things to do in a Salem Chapel tea-
meeting? So the lofty spirit held apart, gazing down from a
mental elevation much higher than the platform; and all
the people who had heard his lectures pointed him out to
each other, and congratulated themselves on that studious
and separated aspect which was so unlike other men. In
fact, the fine superiority of Mr Vincent was at the present
moment the very thing that was wanted to rivet their
chains. Even Mrs Pigeon looked on with silent admiration.
He was "high" – never before had Salem known a minister
who did not condescend to be gracious at a tea-meeting –
and the leader of the opposition honoured him in her
heart.

And even when at last the social meal was over, when
the urns were cleared away, and with a rustle and flutter
the assembly composed itself to the intellectual regale
about to follow, Mr Vincent did not change his position.
Mr Raffles made quite one of his best speeches; he kept
his audience in a perpetual flutter of laughter and applause;
he set forth all the excellencies of the new minister with

such detail and fulness as only the vainest could have
swallowed. But the pleased congregation still applauded.
He praised Mr Tufton, the venerable father of the community; he praised the admirable deacons; he praised the
arrangements. In short, Mr Raffles applauded everybody,
and everybody applauded Mr Raffles. After the chairman
had concluded his speech, the hero of the evening gathered
himself up dreamily, and rose from Phoebe Tozer's side.
He told them he had been gazing at them this hour past,
studying the scene before him; how strangely they appeared
to him, standing on this little bright gaslighted perch amid
the dark sea of life that surged round them; that now he
and they were face to face with each other, it was not their
social pleasure he was thinking of, but that dark unknown
existence that throbbed and echoed around: he bade them
remember the dark night which enclosed that town of
Carlingford, without betraying the secret of its existence
even to the nearest village; of those dark streets and
houses which hid so many lives and hearts and tragic
histories; he enlarged upon Mrs Hilyard's idea of the
sentiment of "such a night," till timid people threw
glances behind them, and some sensitive mothers paused
to wonder whether the minister could have heard that
Tommy had fallen into the fire, or Mary scalded herself,
and took this way to break the news. The speech was the
strangest that ever was listened to at a tea-party. It was the
wayward capricious pouring forth of a fanciful young mind
under an unquiet influence, having no connection whatever with the "object," the place, or the listeners. The
consequence was, that it was listened to with breathless
interest – that the faces grew pale and the eyes bright, and
shivers of restrained emotion ran through the astonished
audience. Mr Vincent perceived the effect of his eloquence,
as a nursery story-teller perceives the rising sob of her
little hearers. When he saw it, he awoke, as the same
nursery minstrel does sometimes, to feel how unreal was
the sentiment in his own breast which had produced this

genuine feeling in others, and with a sudden amusement
proceeded to deepen his colours and make bolder strokes of
effect. His success was perfect; before he concluded, he
had in imagination dismissed the harmless Salem people
out of their very innocent recreation to the dark streets
which thrilled round them – to the world of unknown life,
of which each man for himself had some knowledge – to
the tragedies that might be going on side by side with
them, for aught they knew. His hearers drew a long
breath when it was over. They were startled, frightened,
enchanted. If they had been witnessing a melodrama,
they scarcely could have been more excited. He had put
the most dreadful suggestions in their mind of all sorts of
possible trouble; he sat down with the consciousness of
having done his duty by Salem for this night at least.

But when Tozer got up after him to tell about the
prosperity of the congregation, the anticlimax was felt
even by the people of Salem. Some said, "No, no," audibly,
some laughed, not a few rose up and went away. Vincent
himself, feeling the room very hot, and not disliking the
little commotion of interest which arose on his departure,
withdrew himself from the platform, and made his way to
the little vestry, where a breath of air was to be had; for,
January night as it was, the crowd and the tea had
established a very high temperature in the under-regions
of Salem. He opened the window in the vestry, which
looked out upon the damp ground behind the chapel and
the few gravestones, and threw himself down on the little
sofa with a sensation of mingled self-reproach and amusement. Somehow, even when one disapproves of one's self
for doing it, one has a certain enjoyment in bewildering
the world. Mr Vincent was rather pleased with his success,
although it was only a variety of "humbug." He entertained
with Christian satisfaction the thought that he had
succeeded in introducing a certain visionary uneasiness
into the lively atmosphere of the tea-meeting – and he was
delighted with his own cleverness in spite of himself.

While he lay back on his sofa, and pondered this gratifying thought, he heard a subdued sound of voices outside
– voices and steps that fell with but little sound upon the
damp grass. A languid momentary wonder touched the
mind of the minister: who could have chosen so doleful a
retirement? It was about the last place in the world for a
lovers' interview, which was the first thing that suggested
itself to the young man; the next moment he started bolt
upright, and listened with undisguised curiosity. That
voice so different from the careless voices of Salem,
the delicate refined intonations which had startled him in
the shabby little room in Back Grove Street, awoke an
interest in his mind which no youthful accents in Carlingford could have excited. He sat upright on the instant, and
edged towards the open window. The gas burned low in
the little vestry, which nobody had been expected to
enter, and the illumination from all the schoolroom
windows, and sounds of cheering and commotion there,
had doubtless made the absolute darkness and silence
behind seem perfectly safe to the two invisible people now
meeting under the cloud of night. Mr Vincent was not
startled into eavesdropping unawares, nor did he engage
in any sophistical argument to justify himself for listening.
On the contrary, he listened honestly, with the full intention of hearing all he could – suddenly changed from the
languid sentimentalist, painful and self-conscious, which
the influences of the evening had made him, into a spectator
very wide awake and anxious, straining his ear to catch
some knowledge of a history, in which a crowd of pre-
sentiments warned him that he himself should yet be
concerned.

"If you must speak, speak here," said the voice which
Vincent had recognised: "it is scarcely the atmosphere for
a man of your fine taste, to be sure; but considering the
subject of the conference, it will do. What do you want
with me?"

"By Jove, it looks dangerous! – what do you mean to

suggest by this sweet rendezvous – murder?" said the man, whoever he was, who had accompanied Mrs Hilyard to the damp yard of Salem Chapel, with its scattered graves.

"My nerves are strong," she answered. "It is a pity you should take the trouble to be melodramatic. Do you think I am vain enough to imagine that you could subject yourself to all the unpleasant accessories of being hanged on my account? Fancy a rough hempen rope, and the dirty fingers that would adjust it. Pah! you would not risk it for me."

Her companion swore a muttered oath. "By Jove! I believe you'd be content to be murdered, to make such an end of me," he answered, in the baffled tone of rage which a man naturally sinks into when engaged in unequal conflict of recrimination with a woman.

"This is too conjugal," said Mrs Hilyard; "it reminds me of former experiences: come to the point, I beg of you. You did not come here and seek me out that we might have an amusing conversation – what do you want with me?"

"Don't tempt me too far with your confounded impertinence," exclaimed the man, "or there is no telling what may happen. I want to know where that child is; you know I do. I mean to reclaim my rights so far as she is concerned. If she had been a ward in Chancery, a man might have submitted. But I am a reformed individual – my life is of the most exemplary description – no court in Christendom would keep her from my custody now. I want the girl for her own good – she shall marry brilliantly, which she never could do with you. I know she's grown up as lovely as I expected—"

"How do you know?" interrupted Mrs Hilyard, with a certain hoarseness in her voice.

"Ah! I have touched you at last. Remembering what her mother was," he went on, in a mocking tone, "though I am grieved to see how much you have gone off in late years – and having a humble consciousness of her father's personal advantages, and, in short, of her relatives in general, I know she's a little beauty – and, by Jove, she shall be a duchess yet."

There was a pause – something like a hard sob thrilled in the air, rather a vibration than a sound; and Vincent, making a desperate gesture of rage towards the schoolroom, from which a burst of applause at that moment sounded, approached closer to the window. Then the woman's voice burst forth passionate, but subdued.

"You have seen her! – you that blasted her life before she was born, and confused her sweet mind for ever – how did you dare to look at my child? And I," cried the passionate voice, forgetting even caution – "*I*, that would give my life drop by drop to restore what never can be restored to that victim of your sin and my weakness – I do not see her. I refuse myself that comfort. I leave it to others to do all that love and pity can do for my baby. You speak of murder – man! if I had a knife, I could find it in my heart to put an end to your horrid career; and, look you, I will – Coward! I will! I will kill you before you shall lay your vile hands on my child."

"She-wolf!" cried the man, grinding his teeth, "do you know how much it would be to my advantage if you never left this lonely spot you have brought me to? By Jove, I have the greatest mind—"

Another momentary silence. Vincent, wound up to a high state of excitement, sprang noiselessly to his feet, and was rushing to the window to proclaim his presence, when Mrs Hilyard's voice, perfectly calm, and in its usual tone, brought him back to himself.

"Second thoughts are best. It would compromise you horribly, and put a stop to many pleasures – not to speak of those dreadful dirty fingers arranging that rough rope round your neck, which, pardon me, I can't help thinking of when you associate your own name with such a vulgar suggestion as murder. *I* should not mind these little details, but *you!* However, I excited myself unreasonably;

you have not seen her. That skilful inference of yours was only a lie. She was not at Lonsdale, you know."

"How the devil do you know I was at Lonsdale?" said her companion.

"I keep myself informed of the movements of so interesting a person. She was not there."

"No," replied the man, "she was not there; but I need not suggest to your clear wits that there are other Lonsdales in England. What if Miss Mildmay were in her father's lawful guardianship now!"

Here the air palpitated with a cry, the cry as of a wild creature in sudden blind anguish. It was echoed by a laugh of mockery and exultation. "Should you like me to tell you which of the Lonsdales you honoured with your patronage?" continued the mocking voice: "that in Derbyshire, or that in Devonshire, or that in Cumberland? I am afflicted to have defeated your skilful scheme so easily. Now that you see I am a match for you, perhaps you will perceive that it is better to yield peaceably, and unite with me in securing the girl's good. She needs only to be seen to—"

"Who do you imagine you are addressing, Colonel Mildmay?" said Mrs Hilyard, haughtily; "there has been enough of this: you are mistaken if you think you can deceive me for more than a moment: my child is not in your hands, and never will be, please God. But mark what I say," she continued, drawing a fierce, hard breath, "if you should ever succeed in tracing her – if you should ever be able to snatch her from me – then confess your sins, and say your last prayers, for as sure as I live you will die in a week."

"She-devil! murderess!" cried her companion, not without a certain shade of alarm in his voice; "if your power were equal to your will—"

"In that case my power should be equal to my will," said the steady, delicate woman's voice, as clear in very fine articulation as if it were some peaceful arrangement of daily life for which she declared herself capable: "you should not escape if you surrounded yourself with a king's guards. I swear to you, if you do what you say, that I will kill you somehow, by whatever means I can attain – and I have never yet broken my word."

An unsteady defiant laugh was the only reply. The man was evidently more impressed with the sincerity, and power to execute her intentions, of the woman than she with his. Apparently they stood regarding each other for another momentary interval in silence. Again Mrs Hilyard was the first to speak.

"I presume our conference is over now," she said, calmly; "how you could think of seeking it is more than I can understand. I suppose poor pretty Alice, who thinks every woman can be persuaded, induced you to attempt this. Don't let me keep you any longer in a place so repugnant to your taste. I am going to the tea-meeting at Salem Chapel to hear my young friend the minister speak: perhaps this unprofitable discussion has lost me that advantage. You heard him the other night, and were pleased, I trust. Good-night. I suppose, before leaving you, I should thank you for having spared my life."

Vincent heard the curse upon her and her stinging tongue, which burst in a growl of rage from the lips of the other, but he did not see the satirical curtsy with which this strange woman swept past, nor the scarcely controllable impulse which made the man lift his stick and clench it in his hand as she turned away from him those keen eyes, out of which even the gloom of night could not quench the light. But even Mrs Hilyard herself never knew how near, how very near, she was at that moment to the unseen world. Had her step been less habitually firm and rapid – had she lingered on her way – the temptation might have been too strong for the man, maddened by many memories. He made one stride after her, clenching his stick. It was perfectly dark in that narrow passage which led out to the front of the chapel. She might have been stunned in a moment, and left there to die, without any man being the wiser. It was not virtue, nor hatred of bloodshed, nor repugnance to harm her, which restrained Colonel Mildmay's hand: it was half the rapidity of her movements, and half the instinct of a gentleman, which vice itself could not entirely obliterate. Perhaps he was glad when he saw her disppear from before him down the lighted steps into the Salem schoolroom. He stood in the darkness and watched her out of sight, himself unseen by any one, and then departed on his way, a splendid figure, all unlike the population of Grove Street. Some of the Salem people, dispersing at the moment, saw him saunter-ing down the street grand and leisurely, and recognised the gentleman who had been seen in the Music Hall with Lady Western. They thought he must have come privately once more to listen to their minister's eloquence. Probably Lady Western herself, the leader of fashion in Carlingford, would appear next Sunday to do Mr Vincent honour. The sight of this very fine gentleman picking his leisurely way along the dark pavement of Grove Street, leaning con-fidingly upon that stick over which his tall person swayed with fashionable languor, gave a climax to the evening in the excited imaginations of Mr Vincent's admirers. Nobody but the minister and one utterly unnoted individual in the crowd knew what had brought the Colonel and his stick to such a place. Nobody but the Colonel himself, and the watchful heavens above, knew how little had prevented him from leaving a silent, awful witness of that secret interview upon the chapel steps.

When Mr Vincent returned to the platform, which he did hurriedly, Mr Pigeon was addressing the meeting. In the flutter of inquiries whether he was better, and gentle hopes from Phoebe that his studies had not been too much for him, nobody appeared to mark the eagerness of his eyes, and the curiosity in his face. He sat down in his old place, and pretended to listen to Mr Pigeon. Anxiously from under the shadow of his hands he inspected the

crowd before him, who had recovered their spirits. In a
corner close to the door he at last found the face he was in
search of. Mrs Hilyard sat at the end of the table, leaning
her face on her hand. She had her eyes fixed upon the
speaker, and there passed now and then across the corners
of her close-shut mouth that momentary movement which
was her symbol for a smile. She was not *pretending* to
listen, but giving her entire attention to the honest poulterer.
Now and then she turned her eyes from Pigeon, and
perused the room and the company with rapid glances
of amusement and keen observation. Perhaps her eyes
gleamed keener, and her dark cheek owned a slight flush –
that was all. Out of her mysterious life – out of that
interview, so full of violence and passion – the strange
woman came, without a moment's interval, to amuse
herself by looking at and listening to all those homely
innocent people. Could it be that she was taking notes of
Pigeon's speech? Suddenly, all at once, she had taken a
pencil out of her pocket and began to write, glancing up
now and then towards the speaker. Mr Vincent's head
swam with the wonder he was contemplating – was she
flesh and blood after all, or some wonderful skeleton living
a galvanic life? But when he asked himself the question,
her cry of sudden anguish, her wild, wicked promise to kill
the man who stole her daughter, came over his mind, and
arrested his thoughts. He, dallying as he was on the verge
of life, full of fantastic hopes and disappointment, could
only pretend to listen to Pigeon; but the good poulterer
turned gratified eyes towards Mrs Hilyard. He recognised
her real attention and interest; was it the height of voluntary sham and deception – or was she really taking notes?
     The mystery was solved after the meeting was over.
There was some music, in the first place – anthems in
which all the strength of Salem united, Tozer taking
a heavy bass, while Phoebe exerted herself so in the
soprano that Mr Vincent's attention was forcibly called off
his own meditations, in terror lest something should break

in the throat so hardly strained. Then there were some
oranges, another speech, a hymn, and a benediction; and
then Mr Raffles sprang joyfully up, and leaned over the
platform to shake hands with his friends. This last process
was trying. Mr Vincent, who could no longer take refuge
in silence, descended into the retiring throng. He was
complimented on his speech, and even by some superior
people, who had a mind to be fashionable, upon the
delightful evening they had enjoyed. When they were
all gone, there were still the Tozers, the Browns, the
Pigeons, Mrs Tufton, and Mr Raffles. He was turning
back to them disconsolate, when he was suddenly confronted by Mrs Hilyard out of her corner with the flyleaf
of the hymn-book the unscrupulous woman had been
writing in, torn out in her hand.

"Stop a minute!" she cried; "I want to speak to you. I
want your help, if you will give it me. Don't be surprised
at what I ask. Is your mother a good woman – was it she
that trained you to act to the forlorn as you did to me last
night? I have been too hasty – I take away your breath; –
never mind, there is no time to choose one's words. The
butterman is looking at us, Mr Vincent. The ladies are
alarmed; they think I want spiritual consolation at this
unsuitable moment. Make haste – answer my question.
Would she do an act of Christian charity to a woman in
distress?"

"My mother is – yes, I know she would; what do you
want of her? – my mother is the best and tenderest of
women," cried Vincent, in utter amazement.

"I want to send a child to her – a persecuted, helpless
child, whom it is the object of my life to keep out of evil
hands," said Mrs Hilyard, her dark thin face growing
darker and more pallid, her eyes softening with tears.
"She will be safe at Lonsdale now, and I cannot go in my
own person at present to take her anywhere. Here is a
message for the telegraph," she added, holding up the
paper which Vincent had supposed to be notes of Mr

Pigeon's speech; "take it for me – send it off to-night – you will? and write to your mother; she shall suffer no loss, and I will thank her on my knees. It is life or death."

"I know – I am aware!" cried Vincent, not knowing what he said. "There is no time to be lost."

She put the paper into his hand, and clasped it tight between both of hers, not knowing, in the excitement which she was so well trained to repress, that he had betrayed any special knowledge of her distress. It seemed natural, in that strain of desperation, that everybody should understand her. "Come to-morrow and tell me," she said, hurriedly, and then hastened away, leaving him with the paper folded close into his hand as her hard grasp had left it. He turned away from the group which awaited his coming with some curiosity and impatience, and read the message by the light of one of the garlanded and festive lamps. "Rachel Russell to Miss Smith, Lonsdale, Devonshire. Immediately on receiving this, take the child to Lonsdale, near Peterborough – to Mrs Vincent's; leave the train at some station near town, and drive to a corresponding station on the Great Northern; don't enter London. Blue veil – care – not to be left for an instant. I trust all to you." Mr Vincent put the message in his pocket-book, took it out again – tried it in his purse, his waistcoat pocket, everywhere he could think of – finally, closed his hand over it as at first, and in a high state of excitement went up to the chattering group at the little platform, the only thought in his mind being how to get rid of them, that he might hasten upon his mission before the telegraph office was closed for the night.

And, as was to be expected, Mr Vincent found it no easy matter to get rid of the Tozers and Pigeons, who were all overflowing about the tea-party, its provisions, its speeches, and its success. He stood with that bit of paper clenched in his hand, and endured the jokes of his reverend brother, the remarks of Mrs Tufton, the blushes of Phoebe. He stood for half an hour at least perforce in unwilling and constrained civility – at last he became desperate; – with a wild promise to return presently, he rushed out into the night. The station was about half a mile out of Carlingford, at the new end, a long way past Dr Rider's. When Vincent reached it, the telegraph clerk was putting on his hat to go away, and did not relish the momentary detention; when the message was received and despatched, the young minister drew breath – he went out of the office, wiping his hot forehead, to the railway platform, where the last train for town was just starting. As Vincent stood recovering himself and regaining his breath, the sudden flash of a match struck in one of the carriages attracted his attention. He looked, and saw by the light of the lamp inside a man stooping to light his cigar. The action brought the face, bending down close to the window, clearly out against the dark-blue background of the empty carriage; hair light, fine and thin, in long but scanty locks – a high-featured eagle-face, too sharp for beauty now, but bearing all the traces of superior good looks departed – a light beard, so light that it did not count for its due in the aspect of that remarkable countenance – a figure full of ease and haughty grace: all these particulars Vincent noted with a keen rapid inspection. In another moment the long leash of carriages had plunged into the darkness. With a strange flush of triumph he watched them disappear, and turned away with a smile on his lips. The message of warning was already tingling along the sensitive wires, and must out-speed the slow human traveller. This face, which so stamped itself upon his memory, which he fancied he could see pictured on the air as he returned along the dark road, was the face of the man who had been Lady Western's companion at the lecture. That it was the same face which had confronted Mrs Hilyard in the dark graveyard behind Salem Chapel he never doubted. With a thrill of active hatred and fierce enmity which it was difficult to account for, and still more difficult for a man of his profession to excuse, the young man looked forward to the unknown future with a certainty of meeting that face again.

We drop a charitable veil over the conclusion of the night. Mr Raffles and Mr Vincent supped at Pigeon's, along with the Browns and Tozers; and Phoebe's testimony is on record that it was a feast of reason and a flow of soul.

CHAPTER XI.

THE next morning Vincent awoke with a sense of personal occupation and business, which perhaps is only possible to a man engaged with the actual occurrences of individual life. Professional duties and the general necessities of existing, do not give that thrill of sensible importance and use which a man feels who is busy with affairs which concern his own or other people's very heart and being. The young Nonconformist was no longer the sentimentalist who had made the gaping assembly at Salem Chapel uneasy over their tea-drinking. That dark and secret ocean of life which he had apostrophised, opened up to him immediately thereafter one of its most mysterious scenes. This had shaken Vincent rudely out of his own youthful vagaries. Perhaps the most true of philosophers, contemplating, however profoundly, the secrets of nature or thought, would come to a sudden standstill over a visible abyss of human guilt, wretchedness, heroic self-restraint, and courage, yawning apparent in the meditative way. What, then, were the poor dialectics of Church and State controversy, or the fluctuations of an uncertain young mind feeling itself superior to its work, to such a spectacle of passionate life, full of evil and of noble qualities – of guilt and suffering more intense than anything philosophy dreams of?

The thin veil which youthful ignorance, believing in the supremacy of thought and superior charm of intellectual concerns, lays over the world, shrivelled up under the fiery lurid light of that passionate scene. Two people clearly, who had once loved each other, hating each other to the death, struggling desperately over a lesser thread of life proceeding from them both – the mother, driven to the lowest extremities of existence, standing up like a wild creature to defend her offspring – what could philosophy say to such phenomena? A wild circle of passion sprang into conscious being under the young man's half-frightened eyes – wild figures that filled the world, leaving small space for the calm suggestions of thought, and even to truth itself so little vantage-ground. Love, Hatred, Anger, Jealousy, Revenge – how many more? Vincent, who was no longer the lofty reasoning Vincent of Homerton, found life look different under the light of those torch-bearers. But he had no leisure on this particular morning to survey the subject. He had to carry his report and explanation to the strange woman who had so seized upon and involved him in her concerns.

Mrs Hilyard was seated in her room, just as he had seen her before, working with flying needle and nervous fingers at her coarsest needlework. She said, "Come in," and did not rise when he entered. She gave him an eager, inquiring look, more importunate and commanding than any words, but never stopped working, moving her thin fingers as if there was some spell in the continuance of her labour. She was impatient of his silence before he had closed the door – desperate when he said the usual greeting. She opened her pale lips and spoke, but Vincent heard nothing. She was beyond speech.

"The message went off last night, and I wrote to my mother," said Vincent; "don't fear. She will do what you wish, and everything will be well."

It was some time before Mrs Hilyard quite conquered

her agitation; when she succeeded, she spoke so entirely
in her usual tone that Vincent started, being inexperienced
in such changes. He contemplated her with tragic eyes
in her living martyrdom; she, on the contrary, more
conscious of her own powers, her own strength of resistance
and activity of life, than of any sacrifice, had nothing
about her the least tragical, and spoke according to nature.
Instead of any passionate burst of self-relevation, this is
what she said –

"Thank you. I am very much obliged to you. How
everything is to be well, does not appear to me; but
I will take your word for it. I hope I may take your
word for your mother also, Mr Vincent. You have a right
to know how this is. Do you claim it, and must I tell you
now?"

Here for the first time Vincent recollected in what
an unjustifiable way he had obtained his information.
Strangely enough, it had never struck him before. He
had felt himself somehow identified with the woman
in the strange interview he had overheard. The man
was a personal enemy. His interest in the matter was
so honest and simple, amid all the complication of his
youthful superficial insincerities, that this equivocal
action was one of the very few which Vincent had
actually never questioned even to himself. He was confounded now when he saw how the matter stood. His face
became suddenly crimson; – shame took possession of his
soul.

"Good heavens, I have done the most dishonourable
action!" cried Vincent, betrayed into sudden exclamation
by the horror of the discovery. Then he paused, turning
an alarmed look upon his new friend. She took it very
calmly. She glanced up at him with a comic glance in
her eyes, and a twitch at the corners of her mouth.
Notwithstanding last night – notwithstanding the anxiety
which she dared not move in her own person to alleviate –
she was still capable of being amused. Her eyes said,

"What now?" with no very alarming apprehensions. The situation was a frightful one for poor Vincent.

"You will be quite justified in turning me out of your house," he said, clearing his throat, and in great confusion; "but if you will believe it, I never till this moment saw how atrocious – Mrs Hilyard, I was in the vestry; the window was open; I heard your conversation last night."

For a moment Vincent had all the punishment he expected, and greater. Her eyes blazed upon him out of that pale dark face with a certain contempt and lofty indifference. There was a pause. Mr Vincent crushed his best hat in his hands, and sat speechless doing penance. He was dismayed with the discovery of his own meanness. Nobody could deliver such a cutting sentence as he was pronouncing on himself.

"All the world might have listened, so far as I am concerned," she said, after a while, quietly enough. "I am sorry you did it; but the discovery is worse for yourself than for me." Then, after another pause, "I don't mean to quarrel. I am glad for my own sake, though sorry for yours. Now you know better than I can tell you. There were some pleasant flowers of speech to be gathered in that dark garden," she continued, with another odd upward gleam in her eyes. "We must have startled your clerical ideas rather. At the moment, however, Mr Vincent, people like Colonel Mildmay and myself mean what we say."

"If I had gained my knowledge in a legitimate way," said the shame-stricken minister, not venturing to look her in the face, "I should have said that I hoped it was only for the moment."

Mrs Hilyard laid down her work, and looked across at him with undisguised amusement. "I am sorry there is nobody here to perceive this beautiful situation," she said. "Who would not have their ghostly father commit himself, if he repented after this fashion? Thank you, Mr Vincent, for what you don't say. And now we shall drop the subject, don't you think? Were the deacons all charmed with the tea-meeting last night?"

"You want me to go now," said Vincent, rising, with disconcerted looks.

"Not because I am angry. I am not angry," she said, rising and holding out her hand to him. "It was a pity, but it was an inadvertence, and no dishonourable action. Yes, go. I am best to be avoided till I hear how this journey has been managed, and what your mother says. It was a sudden thought, that sending them to Lonsdale. I know that, even if he has not already found the right one, he will search all the others now. And your Lonsdale has been examined and exhausted; all is safe there. Yes, go. I am glad you know; but don't say anything to Alice, if you see her, as she is sure to seek you out. You know who I mean by Alice? Lady Western – yes. Goodbye. I trust you, notwithstanding the vestry window; but close it after this on January nights."

She had sunk into her seat again, and was absorbed in her needlework, before Vincent left the room. He looked back upon her before he shut the door, but she had no look to spare from that all-engrossing work; her thin fingers were more scarred than ever, and stained with the coarse blue stuff. All his life after the young man never saw that colour without thinking of the stains on those poor hands.

He went about his work assiduously all that day, visiting sick people, poor people, men and women, "which were sinners." That dark ocean of life with which he had frightened the Salem people last night, Mr Vincent made deeper investigations into this day than he had made before during all the time he had been in Carlingford. He kept clear of the smug comfort of the leading people of "the connection." Absolute want, suffering and sorrow, were comparatively new to him; and being as yet a stranger to philanthropic schemes, and not at all scientific in the distribution of his sympathies, the minister of Salem conducted himself in a way which would have called forth

the profoundest contempt and pity of the curate of St
Roque's. He believed everybody's story, and emptied his
purse with the wildest liberality; for, indeed, visitation of
the poor had not been a branch of study at Homerton.
Tired and all but penniless, he did not turn his steps
homeward till the wintry afternoon was sinking into the
night, and the lamps began to be lighted about the cheerful
streets. As he came into George Street, he saw Lady
Western's carriage waiting at the door of Masters's. Alice!
that was the name they called her. He looked at the
celestial chariot wistfully. He had nothing to do with it or
its beautiful mistress – never, as anything but a stranger,
worshipping afar off, could the Dissenting minister of
Carlingford approach that lovely vision – never think of
her but as of a planet, ineffably distant – never—

"My lady's compliments," said a tall voice on a level
with Vincent's eyebrows: "will you please to step over and
speak to her ladyship?" The startled Nonconformist raised
his eyes. The big footman, whose happy privilege it was to
wait upon that lady of his dreams, stood respectful by his
side, and from the carriage opposite the fairest face in the
world was beaming, the prettiest of hands waving to him.
Vincent believed afterwards that he crossed the entire
breadth of George Street in a single stride.

"I am so glad to see you, Mr Vincent," said Lady
Western, giving him her hand; "I did so want to see you
after the other night. Oh, how could you be *so* clever and
wicked – so wicked to your friends! Indeed, I shall never
be pleased till you recant, and confess how wrong you
were. I must tell you why I went that night. I could not
tell what on earth to do with my brother, and I took him to
amuse him: or else, you know, I never could have gone to
hear the poor dear old Church attacked. And how violent
you were too! Indeed I must not say how clever I thought
it, or I should feel I was an enemy to the Church. Now I
want you to dine with me, and I shall have somebody to
come who will be a match for you. I am very fond of

clever society, though there is so little of it in Carlingford.
Tell me, will you come to-morrow? I am disengaged. Oh,
pray, do! and Mr Wentworth shall come too, and you shall
fight."

Lady Western clapped her pretty hands together with
the greatest animation. As for Vincent, all the superior
thoughts in which he would probably have indulged – the
contrast he would have drawn between the desperate
brother and this butterfly creature, fluttering on the edge
of mysteries so dark and evil, had she been anybody else –
deserted him totally in the present crisis. She was not
anybody else – she was herself. The words that fell from
those sweetest lips were of a half-divine simplicity to the
bewildered young man. He would have gone off straight-
way to the end of the world, if she had chosen to command
him. All unwarned by his previous failure, paradise opened
again to his delighted eyes.

"And I want to consult you about our friend," said Lady
Western; "it will be so kind of you to come. I am so
pleased you have no engagement. I am sure you thought
us very stupid last time; and I am stupid, I confess,"
added the beauty, turning those sweet eyes, which were
more eloquent than genius, upon the slave who was re-
conquered by a glance; "but I like clever people dearly.
Good-bye till to-morrow. I shall quite reckon upon to-
morrow. Oh, there is Mr Wentworth! John, call Mr Wentworth to speak to me. Good-morning – remember, half-
past six – now, you must not forget."

Spite of the fact that Mr Wentworth took his place
immediately by the side of the carriage, Vincent passed
on, a changed man. Forget! He smiled to himself at the
possibility, and as he walked on to his lodging a wonderful
maze of expectation fell upon the young man's mind.
Why, he asked, was he brought into this strange connection
with Her relations and their story? what could be, he said
to himself with a little awe, the purpose of that Providence
which shapes men's ends, in interweaving his life with

Hers by these links of common interest? The skies throbbed
with wonder and miracle as soon as they were lighted up
by her smile. Who could predict what might be coming,
through all the impossibilities of fact and circumstance?
He would not dissipate that delicious haze by any definite
expectations like those which brought him to sudden grief
on a former occasion. He was content to believe it was not
for nothing that all these strange circles of fate were
weaving round his charmed feet.

In this elevated frame of mind, scarcely aware of the
prosaic ground he trod, Vincent reached home. The little
maid at the door said something about a lady, to which he
paid no attention, being occupied with his own thoughts.
With an unconscious illumination on his face he mounted
the stair lightly, three steps at a time, to his own rooms.
The lamp was lighted in his little sitting-room, and some
one rose nervously from the table as he went in at the
door. What was this sudden terror which fell upon the
young man in the renewed glory of his youthful hopes? It
was his mother, pale and faint, with sleepless tearful
eyes, who, with the cry of an aching heart, worn out by
fatigue and suspense, came forward, holding out anxious
hands to him, and dropped in an utter *abandon* of weariness
and distress into his astonished arms.

CHAPTER XII.

"WHAT has happened? For heaven's sake tell me, mother,"
cried Vincent, as she sank back, wiping her eyes, and
altogether overpowered, half with the trouble which he
did not know, half with the joy of seeing him again –
"say it out at once, and don't keep me in this dreadful
suspense. Susan? She is not married? What is wrong?"

"Oh, my dear boy!" said Mrs Vincent, recovering herself, but still trembling in her agitation – "oh, my affectionate boy, always thinking of us in his good heart! No, dear. It's – it's nothing particular happened. Let me compose myself a little, Arthur, and take breath."

"But, Susan?" cried the excited young man.

"Susan, poor dear! – she is very well; and very happy up to this moment, my darling boy," said Mrs Vincent, "though whether she ought to be happy under the circumstances – or whether it's only a cruel trick – or whether I haven't been foolish and precipitate – but, my dear, what could I do but come to you, Arthur? I could not have kept it from her if I had stayed an hour longer at home. And to put such a dreadful suspicion into her head, when it might be all a falsehood, would have only been killing her; and, my dear boy, now I see your face again, I'm not so frightened – and surely it can be cleared up, and all will be well."

Vincent, whose anxiety conquered his impatience, even while exciting it, kneeled down by his mother's side and took her hands, which still trembled, into his own. "Mother, think that I am very anxious; that I don't know what you are referring to; and that the sudden sight of you has filled me with all sort of terrors – for I know you would not lightly take such a journey all by yourself," said the young man, growing still more anxious as he thought of it – "and try to collect your thoughts and tell me what is wrong."

His mother drew one of her hands out of his, laid it on his head, and fondly smoothed back his hair. "My dear good son! you were always so sensible – I wish you had never left us," she said, with a little groan; "and indeed it was a great thought to undertake such a journey; and since I came here, Arthur, I have felt so flurried and strange, that I have not, as you see, even taken off my bonnet; but I think now you've come, dear, if you would ring the bell and order up the tea? When I see you, and see you looking so well, Arthur, it seems as if things could never be so bad, you know. My dear," she said at last, with a little quiver in her voice, stopping and looking at him with a kind of nervous alarm, "it was about Mr Fordham, you may be sure."

"Tea directly," said Vincent to the little maid, who appeared just at this crisis, and who was in her turn alarmed by the brief and peremptory order. "What about Mr Fordham?" he said, helping his mother to take off the cloak and warm wraps in which she had been sitting, in her nervous tremor and agitation, while she waited his return.

"Oh, my dear, my dear," cried poor Mrs Vincent, wringing her hands, "if he should not turn out as he ought, how can I ever forgive myself? I had a kind of warning in my mind the first time he came to the house, and I have always dreamt such uncomfortable dreams of him, Arthur. Oh! if *you* only could have seen him, my dear boy! But he was such a gentleman, and had such ways. I am sure he must have mixed in the very highest society – and he seemed so to *appreciate* Susan – not only to be in love with her, you know, my dear, as any young man might, but to really appreciate my sweet girl. Oh, Arthur, Arthur, if he should turn out badly, it will kill me, for my Susan will break her heart."

"Mother, you drive me frantic. What has he done?" cried poor Vincent.

"He has done nothing, my dear, that I know of. It is not him, Arthur, for he has been gone for a month, arranging his affairs, you know, before the wedding, and writes Susan regularly, and beautiful letters. It is a dreadful scrawl I got last night. I have it in my pocket-book. It came by the last post when Susan was out, thank heaven. I'll show it you presently, my dear, as soon as I can find it, but I have so many papers in my pocket-book. She saw directly when she came in that something had happened, and oh, Arthur, it was so hard to keep it from her. I don't know when I have kept anything from her before. I can't tell how we got through the night. But this morning I made up the most artful story I could – here is the dreadful letter, my dear, at last – about being determined to see you, and making sure that you were taking care of yourself; for she knew as well as I did how negligent you always are about wet feet. Are you sure your feet are dry now, Arthur? Yes, my dear boy, it makes me very uncomfortable. You don't wonder to see your poor mother here, now, after that?"

The letter which Vincent got meanwhile, and anxiously read, was as follows – the handwriting very mean, with a little tremor in it, which seemed to infer that the writer was an old man: –

"MADAM, – Though I am but a poor man, I can't abear to see wrong going on, and do nothink to stop it. Madam, I beg of you to excuse me, as am unknown to you, and as can't sign my honest name to it like a man. This is the only way as I can give you a word of warning. Don't let the young lady marry him as she's agoing to, not if her heart should break first. Don't have nothink to do with Mr Fordham. That's not his right name, as he has got a wife living – and this I say is true, as sure as I have to answer at the judgment; – and I say to you as a friend, Stop it, stop it! Don't let it go on a step, if you vally the young lady's charackter and her life. I don't add no more, because that's all I dare say, being only a servant; but I hope it's enough to save the poor young lady out of his clutches, as is a man that goeth about seeking whom he may devour. – From a well-wisher, though   A STRANGER."

Mrs Vincent's mind was easier when this epistle was out of her hands. She stood up before the mirror to take off her bonnet, and put her cap tidy; she glided across the room to take up the shawl and cloak which her son had flung upon the little sofa anyhow, and to fold them and lay

them together on a chair. Then the trim little figure
approached the table, on which stood a dimly burning
lamp, which smoked as lamps will when they have it all
their own way. Mrs Vincent turned down the light a little,
and then proceeded to remove the globe and chimney by
way of seeing what was wrong – bringing her own anxious
patient face, still retaining many traces of the sweet
comeliness which had almost reached the length of beauty
in her daughter, into the full illumination of the smoky
blaze. Notwithstanding the smoke, the presence of the
little woman made the strangest difference in the room.
She took note of various evidences of litter and untidiness
with her mind's eye as she examined the lamp. She had
drawn a long breath of relief when she put the letter
into Arthur's hand. The sense of lightened responsibility
seemed almost to relieve her anxiety as well. She held the
chimney of the lamp in her hand, when an exclamation
from her son called her back to the consideration of
that grievous question. She turned to him with a sudden
deepening of all the lines in her face.

"Oh, Arthur dear! don't you think it may be an enemy?
don't you think it looks like some cruel trick? You don't
believe it's true?"

"Mother, have you an enemy in the world?" cried
Vincent, with an almost bitter affectionateness. "Is there
anybody living that would take pleasure in wounding
you?"

"No, dear; but Mr Fordham might have one," said the
widow. "He is not like you or your dear father, Arthur. He
looks as if he might have been in the army, and had seen a
great deal of life. That is what has been a great consolation
to me. A man like that, you know, dear, is sure to have
enemies; so very different from our quiet way of life," said
Mrs Vincent, holding up the chimney of the lamp, and
standing a little higher than her natural five feet, with
a simple consciousness of that grandeur of experience:
"some one that wished him ill might have got some one

else to write the letter. Hush, Arthur, here is the maid with the tea."

The maid with the tea pushed in, bearing her tray into a scene which looked very strange to her awakened curiosity. The minister stood before the fire with the letter in his hand, narrowly examining it, seal, post-mark, handwriting, even paper. He did not look like the same man who had come upstairs three steps at a time, in the glow and exhilaration of hope, scarcely half an hour ago. His teeth were set, and his face pale. On the table the smoky lamp blazed into the dim air, unregulated by the chimney, which Mrs Vincent was nervously rubbing with her handkerchief before she put it on. The little maid, with her round eyes, set down the tray upon the table with an answering thrill of excitement and curiosity. There was "somethink to do" with the minister and his unexpected visitor. Vincent himself took no notice of the girl; but his mother, with feminine instinct, proceeded to disarm this possible observer. Mrs Vincent knew well, by long experience, that when the landlady happens to be one of the flock, it is as well that the pastor should keep the little shocks and crises of his existence studiously to himself.

"Does it always smoke?" said the gentle Jesuit, addressing the little maid.

The effect of so sudden and discomposing a question, at a moment when the person addressed was staring with all her soul at the minister, open-mouthed and open-eyed, may be better imagined than described. The girl gave a start and stifled exclamation, and made all the cups rattle on the tray as she set it down. Did what smoke? – the chimney, or the minister, or the landlady's husband down-stairs?

"Does it always smoke?" repeated Mrs Vincent, calmly putting on the chimney. "I don't think it would if you were very exact in putting this on. Look here: always at this height, don't you see? and now it burns perfectly well."

"Yes, ma'am; I'll tell missis, ma'am," said the girl, backing out with some alarm. Mrs Vincent sat down at the

table with all the satisfaction of success and conscious
virtue. Her son, for his part, flung himself into the easy-
chair which she had given up, and stared at her with an
impatience and wonder which he could not restrain.

"To think you should talk about the lamp at such a
time, or notice it all, indeed, if it smoked like fifty
chimneys!" he exclaimed, with a tone of annoyance;
"why, mother, this is life or death."

"Yes, yes, my dear!" said the mother, a little mortified
in her turn; "but it does not do to let strangers see when
you are in trouble. Oh, Arthur, my own boy, you must not
get into any difficulty here. I know what gossip is in a
congregation; you never would bear half of what your poor
dear papa did," said the widow, with tears in her eyes,
laying her soft old fingers upon the young man's impatient
hand. "You have more of my quick temper, Arthur; and
whatever you do, dear, you must not expose yourself to be
talked of. You are all we have in the world. You must be
your sister's protector; for oh, if this should be true, what a
poor protector her mother has been! And, dear boy, tell me,
what are we to do?"

"Had he any friends?" asked Vincent, half sullenly; for
he did feel an instinctive desire to blame somebody, and
nobody seemed so blamable as the mother, who had
admitted a doubtful person into her house. "Did he know
anybody – in Lonsdale, or anywhere? Did he never speak
of his friends?"

"He had been living abroad," said Mrs Vincent, slowly.
"He talked of gentlemen sometimes, at Baden, and
Homburg, and such places. I am afraid you would think
it very silly, and – and perhaps wrong, Arthur; but he
seemed to know so much of the world – so different from
our quiet way of life – that being so nice and good and
refined himself with it all – I am afraid it was rather an
attraction to Susan. It was so different to what she was
used with, my dear. We used to think a man who had seen
so much, and known so many temptations, and kept his

nice simple tastes through it all – oh, dear, dear! If it is
true, I was never so deceived in all my life."

"But you have not told me," said Arthur, morosely, "if
he had any friends?"

"Nobody in Lonsdale," said Mrs Vincent. "He came to
see some young relative at school in the neighbourhood—"

At this point Mrs Vincent broke off with a half scream,
interrupted by a violent start and exclamation from her
son, who jumped off his seat, and began to pace up and
down the room in an agitation which she could not comprehend. This start entirely overpowered his mother. Her
overwrought nerves and feelings relieved themselves in
tears. She got up, trembling, approached the young man,
put her hand, which shook, through his arm, and implored
him, crying softly all the time, to tell her what he feared,
what he thought, what was the matter? Poor Vincent's
momentary ill-humour deserted him: he began to realise
all the complications of the position; but he could not resist
the sight of his mother's tears. He led her back gently to
the easy-chair, poured out for her a cup of the neglected
tea, and restrained himself for her sake. It was while she
took this much-needed refreshment that he unfolded to
her the story of the helpless stranger whom, only the night
before, he had committed to her care.

"The mother you shall see for yourself to-morrow.
I can't tell what she is, except a lady, though in the
strangest circumstances," said Vincent. "She has some
reason – I cannot tell what – for keeping her child out of
the father's hands. She appealed to me to let her send it to
you, because he had been at Lonsdale already, and I
could not refuse. His name is Colonel Mildmay; he has
been at Lonsdale; did you hear of such a man?"

Mrs Vincent shook her head – her face grew more and
more troubled.

"I don't know about reasons for keeping a child from its
father," she said, still shaking her head. "My dear, dear
boy, I hope no designing woman has got a hold upon you.

Why did you start so, Arthur? what had Mr Fordham to do with the child? Susan would open my letters, of course, and I daresay she will make them very comfortable; but, Arthur dear, though I don't blame you, it was very imprudent. Is Colonel Mildmay the lady's husband? or – or what? Dear boy, you should have thought of Susan: Susan, a young girl, must not be mixed up with anybody of doubtful character. It was all your good heart, I know, but it was very imprudent, to be sure."

Vincent laughed, in a kind of agony of mingled distress, anxiety, and strange momentary amusement. His mother and he were both blaming each other for the same fault. Both of them had equally yielded to kind feelings, and the natural impulse of generous hearts, without any consideration of prudence. But his mistake could not be attended by any consequence a hundredth part so serious as hers.

"In the mean time, we must do something," he said. "If he has no friends, he has at least an address, I suppose. Susan" – and a flush of indignation and affectionate anger crossed the young man's face – "Susan, no doubt, writes to the rascal. Susan! my sister! Good heaven!"

"Arthur!" said Mrs Vincent. "Your dear papa always disapproved of such exclamations: he said they were just a kind of oath, though people did not think so. And you ought not to call him a rascal without proof – indeed, it is very sinful to come to such hasty judgments. Yes, I have got the address written down – it is in my pocket-book. But what shall you do? Will you write to himself, Arthur? or what? To be sure, it would be best to go to him and settle it at once."

"Oh, mother, have a little prudence now," cried the afflicted minister; "if he were base enough to propose marriage to Susan – confound him! (that's not an oath – my father himself would have said as much) under such circumstances, don't you think he has the courage to tell a lie as well? I shall go up to town, and to his address to-morrow, and see what is to be found there. You must rest

in the mean time. Writing is out of the question; what is to
be done, I must *do* – and without a moment's loss of time."

The mother took his hand again, and put her handkerchief to her eyes – "God bless my dear boy," she said,
with a mother's tearful admiration – "Oh, what a thing for
me, Arthur, that you are grown up and a man, and able to
do what is right in such a dreadful difficulty at this! You
put me in mind more and more of your dear father when
you settle so clearly what is to be done. He was always
ready to act when I used to be in a flutter, which was best.
And oh, how good has the Father of the fatherless been to
me in giving me such a son!"

"Ah, mother," said the young minister, "you gave
premature thanks before, when you thought the Father of
the fatherless had brought poor Susan a happy lot. Do you
say the same now?"

"Always the same, Arthur dear," cried his mother, with
tears – "always the same. If it is even so, is it me, do you
think, or is it *Him* that knows best?"

After this the agitation and distress of the first meeting
gradually subsided. That mother, with all her generous
imprudence and innocence of heart, was, her son well
knew, the tenderest, the most indulgent, the most sympathetic of all his friends. Though the little – the very little
insight he had obtained into life and the world had made
him think himself wiser than she was in some respects,
nothing had ever come between them to disturb the boy's
half-adoring, half-protecting love. He bethought himself
of providing for her comfort, as she sat looking at him in the
easy-chair, with her eyes smiling on him through their
tears, patiently sipping the tea, which was a cold and
doubtful infusion, nothing like the fragrant lymph of home.
He poked the fire till it blazed, and drew her chair towards
it, and hunted up a footstool which he had himself kicked
out of the way under the sofa, a month before. When he
looked at the dear tender fresh old face opposite him, in
that close white cap which even now, after the long
fatiguing journey, looked fresher and purer than other

people's caps and faces look at their best, a thaw came upon the young man's heart. Nature awoke and yearned in him. A momentary glimpse crossed his vision of a humble happiness long within his reach, which never till now, when it was about to become impossible for ever, had seemed real or practicable, or even desirable before.

"Mother, dear," said Vincent, with a tremulous smile, "you shall come here, Susan and you, to me; and we shall all be together again – and comfort each other," he added, with a deeper gravity still, thinking of his own lot.

His mother did not answer in many words. She said, "My own boy!" softly, following him with her eyes. It was hard, even with Susan's dreadful danger before her, to help being tearfully happy in seeing him again – in being his guest – in realising the full strength of his manhood and independence. She gave herself up to that feeling of maternal pride and consolation as she once more dried the tears which would come, notwithstanding all her efforts. Then he sat down beside her, and resigned himself to that confidential talk which can rarely be but between members of the same family. He had unburdened his mind unconsciously in his letters about Tozer and the deacons; and it cannot be told what a refreshment it was to be able to utter roundly in words his sentiments on all those subjects. The power of saying it out with no greater hindrance than her mild remonstrances, mingled, as they were, with questions which enabled him to complete his sketches, and smiles of amusement at his descriptive powers, put him actually in better humour with Salem. He felt remorseful and charitable after he had said his worst.

"And you are sure, dear," said Mrs Vincent, at last resuming the subject nearest her heart, "that you can go away tomorrow without neglecting any duty? You must not neglect a duty, Arthur – not even for Susan's sake. Whatever happens to us, you must keep right."

"I have no duty to detain me," said Vincent, hastily. Then a sudden glow came over the young man, a flush of happiness which stole upon him like a thief, and brightened his own personal firmament with a secret acknowledgable delight; "but I must return early," he added, with a momentary hesitation – "for if you won't think it unkind to leave you, mother, I am engaged to dinner. I should scarcely like to miss it," he concluded, after another pause, tying knots in his handkerchief, and taking care not to look at her as he spoke.

"To dinner, Arthur? I thought your people only gave teas," said Mrs Vincent, with a smile.

"The Salem people do; but this – is not one of the Salem people," said the minister, still hesitating. "In fact, it would be ungracious of me not to go, and cowardly, too – for *that* curate, I believe, is to meet me – and Lady Western would naturally think—"

"Lady Western!" said Mrs Vincent, with irrestrainable pleasure; "is that one of the great people in Carlingford?" The good woman wiped her eyes again with the very tenderest and purest demonstration of that adoration of rank which is said to be an English instinct. "I don't mean to be foolish, dear," she said, apologetically; "I know these distinctions of society are not worth your caring about; but to see my Arthur appreciated as he should be, is—" She could not find words to say what it was – she wound up with a little sob. What with trouble and anxiety, and pride and delight, and bodily fatigue added to all, tears came easiest that night.

Vincent did not say whether or not these distinctions of society were worth caring about. He sat abstractedly, untying the knots in his handkerchief, with a faint smile on his face. Then, while that pleasurable glow remained, he escorted his mother to his own sleeping-room, which he had given up to her, and saw that her fire burned brightly, and that all was comfortable. When he returned to poke his solitary fire, it was some time before he took out the letter which had disturbed his peace. The smile died away first by imperceptible degrees from his face. He gradually erected himself out of the meditative lounge into which he had fallen; then, with a little start, as if throwing dreams away, he took out and examined the letter. The more he looked at it, the graver and deeper became the anxiety in his face. It had every appearance of being genuine in its bad writing and doubtful spelling. And Vincent started again with an unexplainable thrill of alarm when he thought how utterly unprotected his mother's sudden journey had left that little house in Lonsdale. Susan had no warning, no safeguard. He started up in momentary fright, but as suddenly sat down again with a certain indignation at his own thoughts. Nobody could carry her off, or do any act of violence; and as for taking advantage of her solitude, Susan, a straight-forward, simple-minded English girl, was safe in her own pure sense of right.

CHAPTER XIII.

NEXT morning Mr Vincent got up early, with an indescrib-able commotion in all his thoughts. He was to institute inquiries which might be life or death to his sister, but yet could not keep his mind to the contemplation of that grave necessity. A flicker of private hope and expectation kept gleaming with uncertain light over the dark weight of anxiety in his heart. He could not help, in the very deepest of his thoughts about Susan, breaking off now and then into a momentary digression, which suddenly carried him into Lady Western's drawing-room, and startled his heart with a thrill of conscious delight, secret and exquisite, which he could neither banish nor deny. In and out, and round about that grievous doubt which had suddenly disturbed the quiet history of his family, the capricious fairy played, touching all his anxious thoughts with thrills of sweetness. It seemed an action involuntary to himself, and over which he had no power; but it gave the young man an equally involuntary and careless cheer and comfort. It did not seem possible that any dreadful discovery could be made that day, in face of the fact that he was to meet Her that night.

When he met his mother at breakfast, the recollection of Mrs Hilyard and the charge she had committed to him came to his mind again. No doubt Susan would take the wanderers in – no doubt they were as safe in the cottage as it was possible to be in a humble inviolable English home, surrounded by all the strength of neighbours and friends, and the protection of a spotless life which everybody knew; but yet – That was not what his strange acquaintance had expected or bargained for. He felt as if he had broken faith with her when he realised his mother's absence from her own house. Yet somehow he felt a certain hesitation in broaching the subject, and unconsciously prepared himself for doubts and reluctance. The certainty of this gave a forced character to the assumed easiness with which he spoke.

"You will go to see Mrs Hilyard," he said; "I owe it to her to explain that you were absent before her child went there. They will be safe enough at home, no doubt, with Susan; but still, you know, it would have been different had you been there."

"Yes, Arthur," said Mrs Vincent, with an indescribable dryness in her voice.

"You will find her a very interesting woman," said her son, instinctively contending against that unexpressed doubt – "the strangest contrast to her surroundings. The very sound of her voice carries one a thousand miles from Salem. Had I seen her in a palace, I doubt whether I should have been equally impressed by her. You will be interested in spite of yourself."

"It is, as you say, very strange, Arthur," said Mrs Vincent – the dryness in her voice increasing to the extent of a short cough, "when does your train start?"

"Not till eleven," said Vincent, looking at his watch; "but you must please me, and go to see her, mother."

"That reminds me, dear," said Mrs Vincent, hurriedly, "that now I am here, little as it suits my feelings, you must take me to see some of your people, Arthur. Mrs Tufton, and perhaps the Tozers, you know. They might not like to hear that your mother had been in Carlingford, and had not gone to see them. It will be hard work visiting strangers while I am in this dreadful anxiety, but I must not be the means of bringing you into any trouble with your flock."

"Oh, never mind my flock," said Vincent, with some impatience; "put on your bonnet, and come and see her, mother."

"Arthur, you are going by the first train," said his mother.

"There is abundant time, and it is not too early for *her*," persisted the minister.

But it was not so easy to conquer that meek little woman. "I feel very much fatigued to-day," she said, turning her eyes, mild but invincible, with the most distinct contradiction of her words to her son's face; "if it had not been my anxiety to have all I could of you, Arthur, I should not have got up to-day. A journey is a very serious matter, dear, for an old woman. One does not feel it so much at first," continued this plausible defendant, still with her mild eyes on her son's face, secure in the perfect reasonableness of her plea, yet not unwilling that he should perceive it was a pretence; "it is the next day one feels it. I shall lie down on the sofa and rest when you are gone."

And, looking into his mother's soft eyes, the young Nonconformist retreated, and made no more attempts to shake her. Not the invulnerability of the fortress alone discouraged him – though that was mildly obdurate, and proof to argument – but a certain uneasiness in the thought of that meeting, an inclination to postpone it,

and stave off the thought of all that might follow, surprised
himself in his own mind. Why he should be afraid of the
encounter, or how any complication could arise out of it,
he could not by any means imagine, but such was the
instinctive sentiment in his heart.

Accordingly he went up to London by the train, leaving
Mrs Hilyard unwarned, and his mother reposing on
the sofa, from which, it is sad to say, she rose a few
minutes after he was gone, to refresh herself by tidying
his bookcase and looking over all his linen and stockings,
in which last she found a very wholesome subject of
contemplation, which relieved the pressure of her thoughts
much more effectually than could have been done by
the rest which she originally proposed. Arthur, for his
part, went up to London with a certain nervous thrill
of anxiety rising in his breast, as he approached the
scene and the moment of his inquiries; though it was
still only by intervals that he realised the momentous
nature of those inquiries, on the result of which poor
Susan's harmless girlish life, all unconscious of the
danger that threatened it, hung in the balance. Poor
Susan! just then going on with a bride's preparations
for the approaching climax of her youthful existence.
Was she, indeed, really a bride, with nothing but truth
and sweet honour in the contract that bound her, or
was she the sport of a villanous pastime that would
break her heart, and might have shipwrecked her fair
fame and innocent existence? Her brother set his
teeth hard as he asked himself that question. Minister
as he was, it might have been a dangerous chance for
Fordham, had he come at that moment without ample
proofs of guiltlessness in the Nonconformist's way.

When he got to town, he whirled, as fast as it was
possible to go, to the address where Susan's guileless
letters were sent almost daily. It was in a street of Piccadilly, full of lodging-houses, and all manner of hangers-on
and ministrants to the world of fashion. He found the

house directly, and was somewhat comforted to find it really an actual house, and not a myth or Doubtful Castle, or a post-office window. He knocked with the real knocker, and heard the bell peal through the comparative silence in the street, and insensibly cheered up, and began to look forward to the appearance of a real Mr Fordham, with unquestionable private history and troops of friends. A quiet house, scrupulously clean, entirely respectable, yet distinct in all its features of lodging-house; a groom in the area below, talking to an invisible somebody, also a man, who seemed to be cleaning somebody else's boots; up-stairs, at the first-floor balcony, a smart little tiger making a fashion of watering plants, and actually doing his best to sprinkle the conversational groom below; altogether a superabundance of male attendants, quite incompatible with the integrity of the small dwelling-place as a private house. Another man, who evidently belonged to the place, opened the door, interrupting Vincent suddenly in his observations – an elderly man, half servant, half master, in reality the proprietor of the place, ready either to wait or be waited on as occasion might require. Turning with a little start from his inspection of the attendant circumstances, Vincent asked, Did Mr Fordham live there?

The man made a momentary but visible pause; whatever it might betoken, it was not ignorance. He did not answer with the alacrity of frank knowledge or simple non-information. He paused, then said, "Mr Fordham, sir?" looking intently at Vincent, and taking in every particular of his appearance, dress and professional looks, with one rapid glance.

"Mr Fordham," repeated Vincent, "does he live here?"

Once more the man perused him, swiftly and cautiously. "No sir; he does not live here," was the second response.

"I was told this was his address," said Vincent. "I perceive you are not ignorant of him; where does he live? I know his letters come here."

"There are a many gentlemen in the house in the course of the season," answered the man, still on the alert to find out Vincent's meaning by his looks – "sometimes letters keep on coming months after they are gone. When we knows their home address, sir, we sends them; when we don't, we keeps them by us till we see if any owner turns up. Gen'leman of the name of Fordham? – do you happen to know sir, what part o' the country *he* comes from? There's the Lincolnshire Fordhams, as you know, sir, and the Northumberland Fordhams; but there's no gen'leman of that name lives here."

"I am sure you know perfectly whom I mean," said Vincent in his heat of impatience. "I don't mean Mr Fordham any harm – I only want to see him, or to get some information about him, if he is not to be seen. Tell me where he does live, or tell me which of his friends is in town, that I may ask them. I tell you I don't mean Mr Fordham any harm."

"No, sir? – nor I don't know as anybody means any harm," said the man, once more examining Vincent's appearance. "What was it as you were wishing to know? Though I ain't acquainted with the gen'leman myself, the missis or some of the people may be. We have a many coming and going, and I might confuse a name. – What was it you were wishful to know?"

"I wish to see Mr Fordham," said Vincent, impatiently.

"I have told you sir, he don't live here," said the guardian of the house.

"Then, look here; you don't deceive me, remember. I can see you know all about him," said Vincent; "and, as I can tell you, I mean him no harm; answer me one or two simple questions, and I will either thank or reward you as you like best. In the first place, Is this Mr Fordham a married man? and, Has he ever gone by another name?"

As he asked these questions the man grinned in his face. "Lord bless you, sir, we don't ask no such questions here. A gen'leman comes and has his rooms, and pays, and goes away, and gives such name as he pleases. I don't ask a certificate of baptism, not if all's right in the pay department. We don't take ladies in, being troublesome; but if a man was to have a dozen wives, what could we know about it? Sorry to disoblige a clergyman, sir; but as I don't know nothing about Mr Fordham, perhaps you'll excuse me, as it's the busiest time of day."

"Well, then, my good man," said Vincent, taking out his purse, "tell me what friend he has that I can apply to; you will do me the greatest service, and I—"

"Sorry to disoblige a clergyman, as I say," said the man, angrily; "but, begging your pardon, I can't stand jabbering here. I never was a spy on a gen'leman, and never will be. If you want to know, you'll have to find out. Time's money to me."

With which the landlord of No.10 Nameless Street, Piccadilly, shut the door abruptly in Vincent's face. A postman was audibly approaching at the moment. Could that have anything to do with the sudden breaking off of the conference? The minister, exasperated, yet, becoming more anxious, stood for a moment in doubt, facing the blank closed door. Then, desperate, turned round suddenly, and faced the advancing Mercury. He had no letters for No.10; he was hastening past, altogether regardless of Vincent's look of inquiry. When he was addressed, however, the postman responded with immediate directness. "Fordham, sir – yes – a gentleman of that name lives at No.10 – leastways he has his letters there – No.10 – where you have just been, sir."

"But they say he doesn't live there," said Vincent.

"Can't tell, sir – has his letters there," said the public servant, decidedly.

More than ever perplexed, Vincent followed the postman to pursue his inquiries. "What sort of a house is it?" he asked.

"Highly respectable house, sir," answered the terse and decisive functionary, performing an astounding rap next door.

In an agony of impatience and uncertainty, the young man lingered opposite the house, conscious of a helplessness and impotence which made him furious with himself. That he ought to be able to get to the bottom of it was clear; but that he was as far as possible from knowing how to do that same, or where to pursue his inquiries, was indisputable. One thing was certain, that Mr Fordham did not choose to be visible at this address to which his letters were sent, and that it was hopeless to attempt to extract any information on the subject by such frank inquiries as the minister had already made. He took a half-hour's walk, and thought it over with no great enlightenment on the subject. Then, coming back, applied once more at the highly respectable uncommunicative door. He had entertained hopes that another and more manageable adherant of the house might possibly appear this time – a maid, or impressionable servitor of some description, and had a little piece of gold ready for the propitiatory tip in his hand. His hopes were, however, put to flight by the appearance of the same face, increased in respectability and composure by the fact that the owner had thrown off the jacket in which he had formerly been invested, and now appeared in a solemn black coat, the essence of respectable and dignified servitude. He fixed his eyes severely upon Vincent as soon as he opened the door. He was evidently disgusted by this return to the charge.

"Look here," said Vincent, somewhat startled and annoyed to find himself confronted by the same face which had formerly defied him; "could you get a note conveyed from me to Mr Fordham? – the postman says he has his letters here."

"If he gets his letters here they come by the post," said the man, insolently. "There's a post-office round the corner, but I don't keep one here. If one reaches him, another will. It ain't nothing to me."

"But it is a great deal to me," said Vincent, with involuntary earnestness. "You have preserved his secret faithfully, whatever it may be; but it surely can't be any harm to convey a note to Mr Fordham. Most likely, when he hears my name," said the young man, with a little consciousness that what he said was more than he believed, "he will see me; and I have to leave town this evening. You will do me a great service if you will save me the delay of the post, and get it delivered at once. And you may do Mr Fordham a service too."

The man looked with less certainty in Vincent's face. – "Seems to me some people don't know what 'No' means, when it's said," he replied, with a certain relenting in his voice. "There's things as a gen'leman ought to know, sure enough – something happened in the family or so; but you see, he don't live here; and since you stand it out so, I don't mind saying that he's a gen'leman as can't be seen in town to-day, seeing he's in the country, as I'm informed, on urgent private affairs. It's uncommon kind of a clergyman, and a stranger, to take such an interest in my house," continued the fellow, grinning spitefully; "but what I say first I say last – he don't live here."

"And he is not in town?" asked Vincent eagerly, without noticing the insolence of the speech. The man gradually closed the door upon himself till he had shut it, and stood outside, facing his persistent visitor.

"In town or out of town," he said, folding his arms upon his chest, and surveying Vincent with all the indolence of a lackey who knows he has to deal with a man debarred by public opinion from the gratifying privilege of knocking him down, "there ain't no more information to be got here."

Such was the conclusion of Vincent's attempted investigation. He went away at once, scarcely pausing to hear this speech out, to take the only means that presented themselves now; and, going into the first stationer's shop in his way, wrote a note entreating Mr Fordham to meet him, and giving a friend's address in London, as well as his own in Carlingford, that he might be communicated with instantly. When he had written and posted this note, Vincent proceeded to investigate the Directory and all the red and blue books he could lay his hands upon, for the name of Fordham. It was not a plentiful name, but still it occurred sufficiently often to perplex and confuse him utterly. When he had looked over the list of Fordhams in London, sufficiently long to give himself an intense headache, and to feel his undertaking entirely hopeless, he came to a standstill. What was to be done? He had no clue, nor the hope of any, to guide him through this labyrinth; but he had no longer any trust in the honour of the man whom his mother had so rashly received, and to whom Susan had given her heart. By way of the only precaution which occurred to him, he wrote a short note to Susan, begging her not to send any more letters to Mr Fordham until her mother's return; and desiring her not to be alarmed by this prohibition, but to be very careful of herself, and wait for an explanation when Mrs Vincent should return. He thought he himself would accompany his mother home. The note was written, as Vincent thought, in the most guarded terms; but in reality was such an abrupt, alarming performance, as was sure to drive a sensitive girl into the wildest fright and uncertainty. Having eased his conscience by this, he went back to the railway, and returned to Carlingford. Night had fallen before he reached home. Under any other circumstances, he would have encountered his mother after such an ineffectual enterprise, conscious as he was of carrying back nothing but heightened suspicion, with very uncomfortable feelings, and would have been in his own person too profoundly concerned about this dreadful danger which menaced his only sister, to be able to rest or occupy himself about other things. But the fact was, that whenever he relapsed into the solitary carriage in which he travelled to Carlingford, and when utterly quiet and alone, wrapped in the haze of din and smoke and speed which abstracts railway travellers from all the world, – gave himself up to thought, the rosy hue of his own hopes came stealing over him unawares. Now and then he woke up, as men wake up from a doze, and made a passing snatch at his fears. But again and again they eluded his grasp, and the indefinite brightness which had no foundation in reason, swallowed up everything which interfered with its power. The effect of this was to make the young man preternaturally solemn when he entered the room where his mother awaited him. He felt the reality of the fear so much less than he ought to do, that it was necessary to put on twice the appearance. Had he really been as deeply anxious and alarmed as he should have been, he would naturally have tried to ease and lighten the burden of the discovery to his mother; feeling it so hazily as he did, no such precautions occurred to him. She rose up when he came in, with a face which gradually paled out of all its colour as he approached. When he was near enough to hold out his hand to her, Mrs Vincent was nearly fainting. "Arthur," she cried, in a scarcely audible voice, "God have pity upon us; it is true: I can see it in your face."

"Mother, compose yourself. I have no evidence that it is true. I have discovered nothing," cried Vincent, in alarm.

The widow dropped heavily into her chair, and sobbed aloud. "I can read it in your face," she said. "Oh! my dear boy, have you seen that – that villain? Does he confess it? Oh, my Susan, my Susan! I will never forgive myself; I have killed my child."

From this passion it was difficult to recover her, and Vincent had to represent so strongly the fact that he had ascertained nothing certain, and that, for anything he could tell, Fordham might still prove himself innocent, that he almost persuaded his own mind in persuading hers.

"His letters might be taken in at a place where he did not live, for convenience sake," said Vincent. "The man might think me a dun, or something disagreeable. Fordham himself, for anything we can tell, may be very angry about it. Cheer up, mother; things are no worse than they were last night. I give you my word I have made no discovery, and perhaps tomorrow may bring us a letter clearing it all up."

"Ah! Arthur, you are so young and hopeful. It is different with me, who have seen so many terrors come true," said the mother, who notwithstanding was comforted. As for Vincent, he felt neither the danger nor the suspense. His whole soul was engrossed with the fact that it was time to dress; and it was with a little conscious sophistry that he himself made the best of it, and excused himself for his indifference.

"I can't bear to leave you, mother, in such suspense and distress," he said, looking at his watch; "but – I have to be at Lady Western's at half-past six."

Mrs Vincent looked up with an expression of stupified surprise and pain for a moment, then brightened all at once. "My dear, I have laid out all your things," she said, with animation. Do you think I would let you miss it, Arthur? Never mind talking to me. I shall hear all about it when you come home to-night. Now go, dear, or you will be late. I will come and talk to you when you are dressing, if you don't mind your mother? Well, perhaps not. I will stay here, and you can call me when you are ready, and I will bring you a cup of tea. I am sure you are tired, what with the fatigue and what with the anxiety. But you must try to put it off your mind, and enjoy yourself to-night."

"Yes, mother," said Vincent, hastening away; the tears were in her gentle eyes when she gave him that unnecessary advice. She pressed his hands fast in hers when he left her at last, repeating it, afraid in her own heart that this trouble had spoilt all the brightness of the opening hopes which she perceived with so much pride and joy. When he was gone, she sat down by the solitary fire, and cried over her Susan in an utter forlornness and helplessness, which only a woman so gentle, timid, and unable to struggle for herself, could feel. Her son, in the mean time, walked down Grange Lane, first with a momentary shame at his own want of feeling, but soon, with an entire forgetfulness

both of the shame and the subject of it, absorbed in
thoughts of his reception there. With a palpitating heart
he entered the dark garden, now noiseless and chill in
winterly decay, and gazed at the lighted windows which
had looked like distant planets to him the last time he saw
them. He lingered looking at them, now that the moment
approached so near. A remembrance of his former disappointment went to his heart with a momentary pang as
he hesitated on the edge of his present happiness. Another
moment and he had thrown himself again, with a degree
of suppressed excitement wonderful to think of, upon the
chance of his fate.

Not alarming chances, so far as could be predicated
from the scene. A small room, the smaller half of that
room which he had seen full of the pretty crowd of the
summer-party, the folding-doors closed, and a curtain
drawn across them; a fire burning brightly; groups of
candles softly lighting the room in clusters upon the
wall, and throwing a colourless soft illumination upon the
pictures of which Lady Western was so proud. She herself,
dropped amid billows of dark blue silk and clouds of black
lace in a low easy-chair by the side of the fire, smiled at
Vincent, and held out her hand to him without rising, with
a sweet cordiality and friendliness which rapt the young
man into paradise. Though Lucy Wodehouse was scarcely
less pretty than the young Dowager, Mr Vincent saw her
as if he saw her not, and still less did he realise the
presence of Miss Wodehouse, who was the shadow to all
this brightness. He took the chair which Lady Western
pointed to him by her side. He did not want anybody to
speak, or anything to happen. The welcome was not given
as to a stranger, but made him at once an intimate and
familiar friend of the house. At once all his dreams
were realised. The sweet atmosphere was tinged with the
perfumy breath which always surrounded Her; the room,
which was so fanciful and yet so home-like, seemed a
reflection of her to his bewildered eyes; and the murmur

of soft sound, as these two lovely creatures spoke to each other, made the most delicious climax to the scene; although the moment before he had been afraid lest the sound of a voice should break the spell. But the spell was not to be broken that night. Mr Wentworth came in a few minutes after him, and was received with equal sweetness; but still the young Nonconformist was not jealous. It was he whose arm Lady Western appropriated, almost without looking at him as she did so, when they went to dinner. She had put aside the forms which were intended to keep the outer world at arm's length. It was as her own closest personal friends that the little party gathered around the little table, just large enough for them, which was placed before the fire in the great dining-room. Lady Western was not a brilliant talker, but Mr Vincent thought her smallest observation more precious than any utterance of genius. He listened to her with a fervour which few people showed when listening to *him*, notwithstanding his natural eloquence; but as to what he himself said in reply, he was entirely oblivious, and spoke like a man in a dream. When she clapped her pretty hands, and adjured the Churchman and the Nonconformist to fight out their quarrel, it was well for Vincent that Mr Wentworth declined the controversy. The lecturer on Church and State was *hors de combat*; he was in charity with all men. The curate of St Roque's, who – blind and infatuated man! – thought Lucy Wodehouse the flower of Grange Lane, did not come in his way. He might pity him, but it was a sympathetic pity. Mr Vincent took no notice when Miss Wodehouse launched tiny arrows of argument at him. She was the only member of the party who seemed to recollect his heresies in respect to Church and State – which, indeed, he had forgotten himself, and the state of mind which led to them. No such world existed now as that cold and lofty world which the young man of genius had seen glooming down upon his life, and shutting jealous barriers against his progress. The barriers were opened, the coldness gone – and he himself

raised high on the sunshiny heights, where love and
beauty had their perennial abode. He had gained nothing
– changed in nothing – from his former condition: not even
the golden gates of society had opened to the Dissenting
minister; but glorious enfranchisement had come to the
young man's heart. It was not Lady Western who had
asked him to dinner – a distinction of which his mother
was proud. It was the woman of all women who had
brought him to her side, whose sweet eyes were sunning
him over, whose voice thrilled to his heart. By her side he
forgot all social distinctions, and all the stings contained
in them. No prince could have reached more completely
the ideal elevation and summit of youthful existence.
Ambition and its success were vulgar in comparison.
It was a poetic triumph amid the prose tumults and
downfalls of life.

When the two young men were left over their wine, a
somewhat grim shadow fell upon the evening. The curate
of St Roque's and the minister of Salem found it wonderfully hard to get up a conversation. They discussed the
advantages of retiring with the ladies as they sat glum and
reserved opposite each other – not by any means unlike,
and, by consequence, natural enemies. Mr Wentworth
thought it an admirable plan, much more sensible than the
absurd custom which kept men listening to a parcel of old
fogies, who retained the habits of the last generation; and
he proposed that they should join the ladies – a proposal to
which Vincent gladly acceded. When they returned to the
drawing-room, Lucy Wodehouse was at the piano; her
sister sat at table with a pattern-book before her, doing
some impossible pattern in knitting; and Lady Western
again sat languid and lovely by the fire, with her beautiful
hands in her lap, relieved from the dark background of the
billowy blue dress by the delicate cambric and lace of her
handkerchief. She was not doing anything, or looking as if
she could do anything. She was leaning back in the low
chair, with the rich folds of her dress sweeping the carpet,

and her beautiful ungloved hands lying lightly across each other. She did not move when the gentlemen entered. She turned her eyes to them, and smiled those sweet welcoming smiles, which Vincent knew well enough were for both alike, yet which made his heart thrill and beat. Wentworth (insensible prig!) went to Lucy's side, and began to talk to her over her music, now and then appealing to Miss Wodehouse. Vincent, whom no man hindered, and for whose happiness all the fates had conspired, invited by those smiling eyes, approached Lady Western with the surprised delight of a man miraculously blessed. He could not understand why he was permitted to be so happy. He drew a chair between her and the table, and, shutting out the other group by turning his back upon them, had her all to himself. She never changed her position, nor disturbed her sweet indolence, by the least movement. The fire blazed no longer. The candles, softly burning against the wall, threw no very brilliant light upon this scene. To Vincent's consciousness, bewildered as he was by the supreme delight of his position, they were but two in a new world, and neither thing nor person disturbed the unimaginable bliss. But Miss Wodehouse, when she raised her eyes from her knitting, only saw the young Dowager leaning back in her chair, smiling the natural smiles of her sweet temper and kind heart upon the young stranger whom she had chosen to make a *protégé* of. Miss Wodehouse silently concluded that perhaps it might be dangerous for the young man, who knew no better, and that Lady Western always looked well in a blue dress. Such was the outside world's interpretation of that triumphant hour of Vincent's life.

How it went on he never could tell. Soft questions, spoken in that voice which made everything eloquent, gently drew from him the particulars of his life; and sweet laughter, more musical than that song of Lucy's to which the curate (dull clod!) gave all his attention, rang silvery peals over the name of Tozer and the economics of Salem.

Perhaps Lady Western enjoyed the conversation almost half as much as her worshipper did. She was amused, most delicate and difficult of all successes. She was pleased with the reverential devotion which had a freshness and tender humility conjoined with sensitive pride, which was novel to her, and more flattering than ordinary adoration. When he saw it amused her, the young man exerted himself to set forth his miseries with their ludicrous element fully developed. They were no longer miseries, they were happinesses which brought him those smiles. He said twice enough to turn him out of Salem, and make him shunned by all the connection. He forgot everything in life but the lovely creature beside him, and the means by which he could arouse her interest, and keep her ear a little longer. Such was the position of affairs, when Miss Wodehouse came to the plain part of her pattern, where she could go on without counting; and seeing Lady Western so much amused, became interested and set herself to listen too. By this time Vincent had come to more private concerns.

"I have been inquiring to-day after some one whom my mother knows, and whom I am anxious to hear about," said Vincent. "I cannot discover anything about him. It is a wild question to ask if you know him, but it is just possible; there are such curious encounters in life."

"What is his name?" said Lady Western, with a smile as radiant as a sunbeam.

"His name is Fordham – Herbert Fordham: I do not know where he comes from, nor whether he is of any profession; nor, indeed, anything but his name. I have been in town to-day—"

Here Vincent came to a sudden stop. He had withdrawn his eyes from that smile of hers for the moment. When he raised them again, the beautiful picture was changed as if by magic. Her eyes were fixed upon him dilated and almost wild. Her face was deadly pale. Her hands, which had been lying lightly crossed, grasped each other in a grasp of sudden anguish and self-control. He stopped short with a pang too bitter and strange for utterance. At that touch all his fancies dispersed into the air. He came to himself strangely, with a sense of chill and desolation. In one instant, from the height of momentary bliss down to the miserable flat of conscious unimportance. Such a downfall was too much for man to endure without showing it. He stopped short at the aspect of her face.

"You have been in town to-day?" she repeated, pointedly, with white and trembling lips.

"And could hear nothing of him," said Vincent, with a little bitterness. "He was not to be heard of at his address."

"Where was that?" asked Lady Western again, with the same intent and anxious gaze.

Vincent, who was sinking down, down in hopeless circles of jealousy, miserable fierce rage and disappointment, answered, "10 Nameless Street, Piccadilly," without an unnecessary word.

Lady Western uttered a little cry of excitement and wonder. She knew nothing of the black abyss into which her companion had fallen any more than she knew the splendid heights to which her favour had raised him; but the sound of her own voice recalled her to herself. She turned away from Vincent and pulled the bell which was within her reach – pulled it once and again with a nervous twitch, and entangled her bracelet in the bell-pull, so that she had to bend over to unfasten it. Vincent sat gloomily by and looked on, without offering any assistance. He knew it was to hide her troubled face and gain a moment to compose herself; but he was scarcely prepared for her total avoidance of the subject when she next spoke.

"They are always so late of giving us tea," she said, rising from her chair, and going up to Miss Wodehouse: "I can see you have finished your pattern; let me see how it looks. That is pretty; but I think it is too elaborate. How many things has Mary done for this bazaar, Mr Wentworth? – and do tell us when is it to be?"

What did Vincent care for the answer? He sat disenchanted in the same place which had been his bower of
bliss all the evening, watching her as she moved about the
room; her beautiful figure went and came with a certain
restlessness, surely not usual to her, from one corner to
another. She brought Miss Wodehouse something to look
at from the work-table, and fetched some music for Lucy
from the window. She had the tea placed in a remote
corner, and made it there; and insisted on bringing it
to the Miss Wodehouses with her own hands. She was
disturbed; her sweet composure was gone. Vincent sat and
watched her under the shade of his hands, with feelings as
miserable as ever moved man. It was not sorrow for having
disturbed her; – feelings much more personal, mortification
and disappointment, and, above all, jealousy, raged in his
heart. Warmer and stronger than ever was his interest in
Mr Fordham now.

After a miserable interval, he rose to take his leave.
When he came up to her, Lady Western's kind heart once
more awoke in his behalf. She drew him aside after a
momentary struggle with herself.

"I know that gentleman," she said, quickly, with a
momentary flush of colour, and shortening of breath; "at
least I knew him once; and the address you mention is my
brother's address. If you will tell me what you want to
know, I will ask for you. My brother and he used not to be
friends, but I suppose—. What did you want to know?"

"Only," said Vincent, with involuntary bitterness, "if
he was a man of honour, and could be trusted; nothing
else."

The young Dowager paused and sighed; her beautiful
eyes softened with tears. "Oh, yes – yes; with life – to
death!" she said, with a low accompaniment of sighing,
and a wistful, melancholy smile upon her lovely face.

Vincent hastened out of the house. He ventured to say
nothing to himself as he went up Grange Lane in the
starless night, with all the silence and swiftness of passion.

He dared not trust himself to think. His very heart, the physical organ itself, seemed throbbing and bursting with conscious pain. Had she loved this mysterious stranger whose undecipherable shadow hung over the minister's path? To Vincent's fancy, nothing else could account for her agitation; and was he so true, and to be trusted? Poor gentle Susan, whom such a fate and doom was approaching as might have softened her brother's heart, had but little place in his thoughts. He was not glad of that favourable verdict. He was overpowered with jealous rage and passion. Alas for his dreams! Once more, what downfall and over-throw had come of it! once more he had come down to his own position, and the second awakening was harder than the first. When he got home, and found his mother, affectionately proud, waiting to hear all about the great lady he had been visiting, it is impossible to express in words the intolerable impatience and disgust with himself and his fate which overpowered the young man. He had a bad headache, Mrs Vincent said, she was sure, and he did not contradict her. It was an unspeakable relief to him when she went to her own room, and delivered him from the tender scrutiny of her eyes – those eyes full of nothing but love, which, in the irritation of his spirit, drove him desperate. He did not tell her about the unexpected discovery he had made. The very name of Fordham would have choked him that night.

CHAPTER XIV.

The next morning brought no letters except from Susan. Fordham, if so true as Lady Western called him, was not, Vincent thought with bitterness, acting as an honourable man should in this emergency. But perhaps he might come to Carlingford in the course of the day, to see Susan's brother. The aspect of the young minister was changed when he made his appearance at the breakfast table. Mrs Vincent made the most alarmed inquiries about his health, but – stopped abruptly in making them by his short and ungracious answer – came to a dead pause; and with a pang of fright and mortification, acknowledged to herself that her son was no longer her boy, whose entire heart she knew, but a man with a life and concerns of his own, possibly not patent to his mother. That breakfast was not a cheerful meal. There had been a long silence, broken only by those anxious attentions to each other's personal comfort, with which people endeavour to smooth down the embarrassment of an intercourse apparently confidential, into which some sudden unexplainable shadow has fallen. At last Vincent got up from the table, with a little outbreak of impatience.

"I can't eat this morning; don't ask me. Mother, get your bonnet on," said the young man; "we must go to see Mrs Hilyard to-day."

"Yes, Arthur," said Mrs Vincent, meekly; she had determined *not* to see Mrs Hilyard, of whom her gentle respectability was suspicious; but, startled by her son's looks, and by the evident arrival of that period, instinctively perceived by most women, at which a man snatches the reins out of his adviser's hand, and has his way, the alarmed and anxious mother let her arms fall, and gave in without a struggle.

"The fact is, I heard of Mr Fordham last night," said Vincent, walking about the room, lifting up and setting down again abstractedly the things on the table. "Lady Western knows him, it appears; perhaps Mrs Hilyard does too."

"Lady Western knows him? Oh, Arthur, tell me – what did she say? " cried his mother, clasping her hands.

"She said he could be trusted – with life – to death,"

said Vincent, very low, with an inaudible groan in his heart. He was prepared for the joy and the tears and the thanksgiving with which his words were received; but he could not have believed how sharply his mother's exclamation, "God bless my Susan! now I am happy about her, Arthur. I could be content to die," would go to his heart. Susan, yes; – it was right to be happy about her; and as for himself, who cared? He shut up his heart in that bitterness; but it filled him with an irritation and restlessness which he could not subdue.

"We must go to Mrs Hilyard; probably she can tell us more," he said, abruptly; "and there is her child to speak of. I blame myself," he added, with impatience, "for not telling her before. Let us go now directly – never mind ringing the bell; all that can be done when we are out. Dinner? oh, for heaven's sake, let *them* manage that! Where is your bonnet, mother? the air will do me good after a bad night."

"Yes, dear," said Mrs Vincent, moved by this last argument. It must be his headache, no doubt, she tried to persuade herself. Stimulated by the sound of his footstep in the next room, she lost very little time over her toilette. Perhaps the chill January air, sharp with frost, air full of natural exhilaration and refreshment, did bring a certain relief to the young Nonconformist's aching temples and exasperated temper. It was with difficulty his mother kept time with his long strides, as he hurried her along the street, not leaving her time to look at Salem, which was naturally the most interesting point in Carlingford to the minister's mother. Before she had half prepared herself for this interview, he had hurried her up the narrow bare staircase which led to Mrs Hilyard's lodgings. On the landing, with the door half open, stood Lady Western's big footman, fully occupying the narrow standing-ground, and shedding a radiance of plush over the whole shabby house. The result upon Mrs Vincent was an immediate increase of comfort, for surely the woman must be respect-

able to whom people sent messages by so grand a functionary. The sight of the man struck Vincent like another
pang. She had sent to take counsel, no doubt, on the
evidently unlooked-for-information which had startled her
so last night.

"Come in," said the inhabitant of the room. She was
folding a note for which the footman waited. Things were
just as usual in that shabby place. The coarse stuff at
which she had been working lay on the table beside her.
Seeing a woman with Vincent, she got up quickly, and
turned her keen eyes upon the new-comer. The timid
doubtful mother, the young man, somewhat arbitrary and
self-willed, who had brought his companion there against
her will, the very look, half fright, half suspicion, which
Mrs Vincent threw round the room, explained matters to
this quick observer. She was mistress of the position at
once.

"Take this to Lady Western, John," said Mrs Hilyard.
"She may come when she pleases – I shall be at home all
day; but tell her to send a maid next time, for you are
much too magnificent for Back Grove Street. This is Mrs
Vincent, I know. Your son has brought you to see me,
and I hope you have not come to say that I was too rash
in asking a Christian kindness from this young man's
mother. If he had not behaved like a paladin, I should not
have ventured upon it; but when a young man conducts
himself so, I think his mother is a good woman. You have
taken in my child?"

She had taken Mrs Vincent by both hands, and placed
her in a chair, and sat down beside her. The widow had
not a word to say. What with the praise of her son, which
was music to her ears – what with the confusion of her own
position, she was painfully embarrassed and at a loss, and
anxiously full of explanations. "Susan has, I have no
doubt; but I am sorry I left home on Wednesday morning,
and we did not know then they were expected; but we
have a spare room, and Susan, I don't doubt—"

"The fact is, my mother had left home before they could have reached Lonsdale," interposed Vincent; "but my sister would take care of them equally well. They are all safe. A note came this morning, announcing their arrival. My mother," said the young man, hastily, "returns almost immediately. It will make no difference to the strangers."

"I am sure Susan will make them comfortable, and the beds will be well aired," said Mrs Vincent; "but I had sudden occasion to leave home, and did not even know of it till the night before. My dear," she said, with hesitation, "did you think Mrs Hilyard would know? I brought Susan's note to show you," she added, laying down that simple performance in which Susan announced the receipt of Arthur's letter, and the subsequent arrival of "a governess-lady, and the most beautiful girl that ever was seen." The latter part of Susan's hurried note, in which she declared this beautiful girl to be "very odd – a sort of grown-up baby," was carefully abstracted by the prudent mother.

The strange woman before them took up the note in both her hands and drank it in, with an almost trembling eagerness. She seemed to read over the words to herself again and again with moving lips. Then she drew a long breath of relief.

"Miss Smith is the model of a governess-lady," she said, turning with a composure wonderfully unlike that eagerness of anxiety to Mrs Vincent again – "she never writes but on her day, whatever may happen; and yesterday did not happen to be her day. Thank you; it is Christian charity. You must not be any loser meantime, and we must arrange these matters before you go away. This is not a very imposing habitation," she said, glancing round with a movement of her thin mouth, and comic gleam in her eye – "but that makes no difference, so far as they are concerned. Mr Vincent knows more about me than he has any right to know," continued the strange woman, turning her head towards him for the moment with an amused glance – "a man takes one on trust sometimes, but a woman must always explain herself to a woman: perhaps, Mr Vincent, you will leave us together while I explain my circumstances to your mother?"

"Oh, I am sure it – it is not necessary," said Mrs Vincent, half alarmed; "but, Arthur, you were to ask—"

"What were you to ask?" said Mrs Hilyard, laying her hand with an involuntary movement upon a tiny note lying open on the table, to which Vincent's eyes had already wandered.

"The fact is," he said, following her hand with his eyes, "that my mother came up to inquire about some one called Fordham, in whom she is interested. Lady Western knows him," said Vincent, abruptly, looking in Mrs Hilyard's face.

"Lady Western knows him. You perceive that she has written to ask me about him this morning. Yes," said Mrs Hilyard, looking at the young man, not without a shade of compassion. "You are quite right in your conclusions; poor Alice and he *were* in love with each other before she married Sir Joseph. He has not been heard of for a long time. What do you want to know, and how is it he has showed himself now?"

"It is for Susan's sake," cried Mrs Vincent, interposing; "oh, Mrs Hilyard, you will feel for me better than any one – my only daughter! I got an anonymous letter the night before I left. I am so flurried, I almost forget what night it was – Tuesday night – which arrived when my dear child was out. I never kept anything from her in all her life, and to conceal it was dreadful – and how we got through that night—"

"Mother, the details are surely not necessary now," said her impatient son. "We want to know what are this man's antecedents and his character – that is all," he added, with irrestrainable bitterness.

Mrs Hilyard took up her work, and pinned the long coarse seam to her knee. "Mrs Vincent will tell me herself,"

she said, looking straight at him with her amused look. Of
all her strange peculiarities, this faculty of amusement
was the strangest. Intense restrained passion, anxiety of
the most desperate kind, a wild will which would pause at
nothing, all blended with and left room for this unfail-
ing perception of any ludicrous possibility. Vincent got up
hastily, and, going to the window, looked out upon the
dismal prospect of Salem, throwing its shabby shadow
upon those dreary graves. Instinctively he looked for the
spot where that conversation must have been held which
he had overheard from the vestry window; it came most
strongly to his mind at that moment. As his mother went
through her story, how Mr Fordham had come accidentally
to the house – how gradually they had admitted him to
their friendship – how, at last, Susan and he had become
engaged to each other – her son stood at the window,
following in his mind all the events of that evening, which
looked so long ago, yet was only two or three evenings
back. He recalled to himself his rush to the telegraph
office; and again, with a sharp stir of opposition and
enmity, recalled, clear as a picture, the railway-carriage
just starting, the flash of light inside, the face so clearly
evident against the vacant cushions. What had he to do
with that face, with its eagle outline and scanty long locks?
Somehow, in the meshes of fate he felt himself so involved
that it was impossible to forget this man. He came and
took his seat again with his mind full of that recollection.
The story had come to a pause, and Mrs Hilyard sat silent,
taking in with her keen eyes every particular of the
gentle widow's character, evidently, as Vincent could see,
following her conduct back to those springs of gentle but
imprudent generosity and confidence in what people said
to her, from which her present difficulties sprang.

"And you admitted him first?" said Mrs Hilyard,
interrogatively, "because—?" She paused. Mrs Vincent
became embarrassed and nervous.

"It was very foolish, very foolish," said the widow,

wringing her hands; "but he came to make inquiries, you know. I answered him civilly the first time, and he came again and again. It looked so natural. He had come down to see a young relation at school in the neighbourhood."

Mrs Hilyard uttered a sudden exclamation – very slight, low, scarcely audible; but it attracted Vincent's attention. He could see her thin lips were closed, her figure slightly erected, a sudden keen gleam of interest in her face. "Did he find his relation?" she asked, in a voice so ringing and distant that the young minister started, and sat upright, bracing himself for something about to happen. It did not flash upon him yet what that meaning might be; but his pulses leapt with a prescient thrill of some tempest or earthquake about to fall.

"No; he never could find her – it did not turn out to be our Lonsdale, I think – what is the matter?" cried Mrs Vincent; "you both know something I don't know – what has happened? Arthur, have I said anything dreadful? – oh, what does it mean?"

"Describe him if you can," said Mrs Hilyard, in a tone which, sharp and calm, tingled through the room with a passionate clearness which nothing but extreme excitement could give. She had taken Mrs Vincent's hand, and held it tightly with a certain compassionate compulsion, forcing her to speak. As for Vincent, the horrible suspicion which stole upon him unmanned him utterly. He had sprung to his feet, and stood with his eyes fixed on his mother's face with an indescribable horror and suspense. It was not her he saw. With hot eyes that blazed in their sockets, he was fixing the gaze of desperation upon a picture in his mind, which he felt but too certain would correspond with the faltering words which fell from her lips. Mrs Vincent, for her part, would have thrown herself wildly upon him, and lost her head altogether in a frightened attempt to find out what this sudden commotion meant, had she not been fixed and supported by that strong yet gentle grasp upon her hand. "Describe him – take time," said her strange companion again – not looking at her, but waiting in an indescribable calm of passion for the words which she could frame in her mind before they were said.

"Tall," said the widow's faltering alarmed voice, falling with a strange uncertainty through the intense stillness, in single words, with gasps between; "not – a very young man – aquiline – with a sort of eagle-look – light hair – long and thin, and as fine as silk – very light in his beard, so that it scarcely showed. Oh, God help us! what is it? what is it? – You both know whom I mean."

Neither of them spoke; but the eyes of the two met in a single look, from which both withdrew, as if the communication was a crime. With a shudder Vincent approached his mother; and, speechless though he was, took hold of her, and drew her to him abruptly. Was it murder he read in those eyes, with their desperate concentration of will and power? The sight of them, and recollection of their dreadful splendour, drove even Susan out of his mind. Susan, poor gentle soul! – what if she broke her tender heart, in which no devils lurked? "Mother, come – come," he said hoarsely, raising her up in his arm, and releasing the hand which the extraordinary woman beside her still clasped fast. The movement roused Mrs Hilyard as well as Mrs Vincent. She rose up promptly from the side of the visitor who had brought her such news.

"I need not suggest to you that this must be acted on at once," she said to Vincent, who, in his agitation, saw how the hand, with which she leant on the table, clenched hard till it grew white with the pressure. "The man we have to deal with spares nothing." She stopped, and then, with an effort, went up to the half-fainting mother, who hung upon Vincent's arm, and took her hands and pressed them close. "We have both thrust our children into the lion's mouth," she cried, with a momentary softening. "Go, poor woman, and save your child if you can, and so will I – we are companions in misfortune. And you are a priest, why cannot you curse him?" she exclaimed, with a bitter cry.

The next moment she had taken down a travelling-bag from a shelf, and, kneeling down by a trunk, began to transfer some things to it. Vincent left his mother, and went up to her with a sudden impulse. "I am a priest, let me bless you," said the young man, touching with a compassionate hand the dark head bending before him. Then he took his mother away. He could not speak as he supported her down-stairs; she, clinging to him with double weakness could scarcely support herself at all in her agitation and wonder when they got into the street. She kept looking in his face with a pitiful appeal that went to his heart.

"Tell me, Arthur, tell me!" She sobbed it out unawares, and over and over before he knew what she was saying. And what could he tell her? "We must go to Susan – poor Susan!" was all the young man could say.

CHAPTER XV.

MRS VINCENT came to a dead stop as they passed the doors of Salem, which were ajar, taking resolution in the desperateness of her uncertainty; for the feelings in the widow's mind were not confined to one burning impulse of terror for Susan, but complicated by a wonderful amount of flying anxieties about other matters as well. *She* knew, by many teachings of experience, what would be said by all the connection, when it was known that the minister's mother had been in Carlingford without going to see anybody – not even Mrs Tufton, the late minister's wife, or Mrs Tozer, who was so close at hand. Though her heart was racked, Mrs Vincent knew her duty. She stopped short in her fright and distress with the mild obduracy of which she

was capable. Before rushing away out of Carlingford to
protect her daughter, the mother, notwithstanding her
anxiety, could not forget the injury which she might
possibly do by this means to the credit of her son.

"Arthur, the chapel is open – I should like to go in and
rest," she said, with a gasp; "and oh, my dear boy, take a
little pity upon me! To see the state you are in, and not to
know anything, is dreadful. You must have a vestry,
where one could sit down a little – let us go in."

"A vestry – yes; it will be a fit place," cried Vincent,
scarcely knowing what he was saying, and indeed worn
out with the violence of his own emotions. This little
persistent pause of the widow, who was not absorbed by
any one passionate feeling, but took all the common cares
of life with her into her severest trouble, awoke the young
man to himself. He, too, recollected that this enemy who
had stolen into his house was not to be reached by one wild
rush, and that everything could not be suffered to plunge
after Susan's happiness into an indiscriminate gulf of
ruin. All his own duties pricked at his heart with bitter
reminders in that moment when he stood by the door of
Salem, where two poor women were busy inside, with
pails and brushes, preparing for Sunday. The minister,
too, had to prepare for Sunday. He could not dart forth,
breathing fire and flame at a moment's notice, upon the
serpent who had entered his Eden. Even at this dreadful
moment, in all the fever of such a discovery, the thought of
his mother's hand upon his arm brought him back to his
lot. He pushed open the mean door, and led her into the
scene of his weekly labours with a certain sickening disgust
in his heart which would have appalled his companion. *She*
was a dutiful woman, subdued by long experience of that
inevitable necessity against which all resistance fails; and
he a passionate young man, naturally a rebel against
every such bond. They could not understand each other;
but the mother's troubled face, all conscious of Tufton and
Tozer, and what the connection would say, brought all the

weight of his own particular burden back upon Vincent's mind. He pushed in past the pails with a certain impatience which grieved Mrs Vincent. She followed him with a pained and disapproving look, nodding, with a faint little smile, to the women, who no doubt were members of the flock, and might spread an evil report of the pastor, who took no notice of them. As she followed him to the vestry, she could not help thinking, with a certain strange mixture of pain, vexation, and tender pride, how different his dear father would have been. "But Arthur, dear boy, has my quick temper," sighed the troubled woman. After all, it was her fault rather than her son's.

"This is a very nice room," said Mrs Vincent, sitting down with an air of relief; "but I think it would be better to close the window, as there is no fire. You were always very susceptible to cold, Arthur, from a child. And now, my dear boy, we are undisturbed, and out of those dreadful glaring streets where everybody knows you. I have not troubled you, Arthur, for I saw you were very much troubled; but, oh! don't keep me anxious now."

"Keep you anxious! You ask me to make you anxious beyond anything you can think of," said the young man, closing the window with a hasty and fierce impatience, which she could not understand. "Good heavens, mother! why did you let that man into your innocent house?"

"Who is he, Arthur?" asked Mrs Vincent, with a balanced face.

"He is—" Vincent stopped with his hand upon the window where he had overheard that conversation, a certain awe coming over him. Even Susan went out of his mind when he thought of the dreadful calmness with which his strange acquaintance had promised to kill her companion of that night. Had she started already on this mission of vengeance? A cold thrill came over him where he stood. "I can't tell who he is," he exclaimed, abruptly, throwing himself down upon the little sofa; "but it was to

be in safety from him that Mrs Hilyard sent her daughter to
Lonsdale. It was he whom she vowed to kill if he found the
child. Ah! – he is," cried the young man, springing to his
feet again with a sudden pang and smothered exclamation
as the truth dawned upon him, "Lady Western's brother.
What other worse thing he is I cannot tell. Ruin, misery,
and horror at the least – death to Susan – not much less to
me."

"To you? Oh, Arthur, have pity upon me, my heart is
breaking," said Mrs Vincent. "Oh, my boy, my boy, whom
I would die to save from any trouble! don't tell me I have
destroyed you. That cannot be, Arthur – *that* cannot be!"

The poor minister did not say anything – his heart was
bitter within him. He paced up and down the vestry with
dreadful thoughts. What was She to him if she had a
hundred brothers? Nothing in the world could raise the
young Nonconformist to the sweet height which she made
beautiful; and far beyond that difference came the
cruel recollection of those smiles and tears – pathetic,
involuntary confessions. If there was another man in the
world whom she could trust "with life – to death!" what
did it matter though a thousand frightful combinations
involved poor Vincent with her kindred? He tried to
remind himself of all this, but did not succeed. In the mean
time, the fact glared upon him that it was her brother who
had aimed this deadly blow at the honour and peace of his
own humble house; and his heart grew sad with the
thought that, however indifferent she might be to him,
however unattainable, here was a distinct obstacle which
must cut off all that bewildering tantalising intercourse
which at present was still possible, notwithstanding every
other hindrance. He thought of this, and not of Susan, as
the floor of the little vestry thrilled under his feet. He was
bitter, aggrieved, indignant. His troubled mother, who sat
by there, half afraid to cry, watching him with frightened,
anxious, uncomprehending eyes, had done him a sharp
and personal injury. *She* could not fancy how it was,

nor what she could have done. She followed him with
mild tearful glances, waiting with a woman's compelled
patience till he should come to himself, and revolving
thoughts of Salem, and supply for the pulpit there, with an
anxious pertinacity. But in her way Mrs Vincent was a
wise woman. She did not speak – she let him wear himself
out first in that sudden apprehension of the misfortune
personal to himself, which was at the moment so much
more poignant and bitter than any other dread. When he
had subsided a little – and first of all he threw up the
window, leaning out, to his mother's great vexation, with a
total disregard of the draught, and receiving the chill of
the January breeze upon his heated brow – she ventured
to say, gently, "Arthur, what are we to do?"

"To go to Lonsdale," said Vincent. "When we came in
here, I thought we could rush off directly; but these
women outside there, and this place, remind me that I am
not a free man, who can go at once and do his duty. I am
in fetters to Salem, mother. Heaven knows when I may be
able to get away. Sunday must be provided for first. No
natural immediate action is possible to me."

"Hush, Arthur dear – oh, hush! Your duty to your flock
is above your duty even to your sister," said the widow,
with a tremulous voice, timid of saying anything to him
whose mood she could not comprehend. "You must find
out when the first train starts, and I will go. I have been
very foolish," faltered the poor mother, "as you say,
Arthur; but if my poor child is to bear such a dreadful
blow, I am the only one to take care of her. Susan" – here
she made a pause, her lip trembled, and she had all but
broken into tears – "will not upbraid me, dear. You must
not neglect your duty, whatever happens; and now let us
go and inquire about the train, Arthur, and you can come
on Monday, after your work is over; and, oh! my dear
boy, we must not repine, but accept the arrangements of
Providence. It was what your dear father always said to
his dying day."

Her face all trembling and pale, her eyes full of tears which were not shed, her tender humility, which never attempted a defence, and those motherly, tremulous, wistful advices which it now for the first time dawned upon Mrs Vincent her son was not certain to take, moved the young Nonconformist out of his personal vexation and misery.

"This will not do," he said. "I must go with you; and we must go directly. Susan may be less patient, less believing, less ready to take our word for it, than you imagine, mother. Come; if there is anybody to be got to do this preaching, the thing will be easy. Tozer will help me, perhaps. We will waste no more time here."

"I am quite rested, Arthur dear," said Mrs Vincent; "and it will be right for me to call at Mrs Tozer's too. I wish I could have gone to Mrs Tufton's, and perhaps some others of your people. But you must tell them, dear, that I was very hurried – and – and not very well; and that it was family business that brought me here."

"I do not see they have any business with the matter," said the rebellious minister.

"My dear, it will of course be known that I was in Carlingford; and I know how things are spoken of in a flock," said Mrs Vincent, rising; "but you must tell them all I wanted to come, and could not – which, indeed, will be quite true. A minister's family ought to be very careful, Arthur," added the much-experienced woman. "I know how little a thing makes mischief in a congregation. Perhaps, on the whole, I ought not to call at Mrs Tozer's, as there is no time to go elsewhere. But still I should like to do it. One good friend is often everything to a young pastor. And, my dear, you should just say a word in passing to the women outside."

"By way of improving the occasion?" said Vincent, with a little scorn. "Mother, don't torture yourself about me. I shall get on very well; and we have plenty on our hands just now without thinking of Salem. Come, come; with this horrible cloud overhanging Susan, how can you spare a thought for such trifles as these?"

"Oh, Arthur, my dear boy, must not we keep you right?" said his mother; "are not you our only hope? If this dreadful news you tell me is true, my child will break her heart, and I will be the cause of it; and Susan has no protector or guardian, Arthur dear, that can take care of her, but you."

Wiping her eyes, and walking with a feeble step, Mrs Vincent followed her son out of Salem; but she looked up with gentle interest to his pulpit as she passed, and said it was a cold day to the cleaners, with anxious carefulness. She was not carried away from her palpable standing-ground by any wild tempest of anxiety. Susan, whose heart would be broken by this blow, was her mother's special object in life; but the thought of that coming sorrow which was to crush the girl's heart, made Mrs Vincent only the more anxiously concerned to conciliate and please everybody whose influence could be of any importance to her son.

So they came out into the street together, and went on to Tozer's shop. She, tremulous, watchful, noting everything; now lost in thought as to how the dreadful truth was to be broken to Susan; now in anxious plans for impressing upon Arthur the necessity of considering his people – he, stinging with personal wounds and bitterness, much more deeply alarmed than his mother, and burning with consciousness of all the complications which she was totally ignorant of. Fury against the villain himself, bitter vexation that he was Lady Western's brother, anger at his mother for admitting, at Susan for giving him her heart, at Mrs Hilyard for he could not tell what, because she had added a climax to all, burned in Vincent's mind as he went on to George Street with his mother leaning on his arm, who asked him after every wayfarer who passed them, Who was that? It was not wonderful that the young man gradually grew into a fever of excitement and restless misery.

Everything conspired to exasperate him, – even the fact that Sunday came so near, and could not be escaped. The whirl of his brain came to a climax when Lady Western's carriage drove past, and through the mist of his wretchedness he saw the smile and the beautiful hand waved to him in sweet recognition. Oh heaven! to bring tears to those eyes, or a pang to that heart! – to have her turn from him shuddering, or pass him with cold looks, because her brother was a villain, and *he* the avenger of that crime! His mother, almost running to keep up with his unconsciously quickened pace, cast pitiful looks at him, inquiring what it was. The poor young fellow could not have told even if he would. It was a combination of miseries, sharply stimulated to the intolerable point by the mission on which he had now to enter Tozer's shop.

"We heard you was come, ma'am," said Tozer, graciously, "and in course was looking for a call. I hope you are going to stay awhile and help us take care of the pastor. He don't take that care of himself as his friends would wish," said the butterman. "Mr Vincent, sir, I've a deal to say to you when you're at leisure. Old Mr Tufton, he has a deal to say to you. We are as anxious as ever we can be, us as are old stagers, to keep the minister straight, ma'am. He's but a young man, and he's come into a deal of popularity, and any one more thought on in our connection, I don't know as I would wish to see; but it wouldn't do to let him have his head turned. Them lectures on Church and State couldn't but be remarked, being delivered, as you may say, in the world, all on us making a sacrifice to do our duty by our fellow-creatures, seein' what we had in our power. But man is but mortal; and us Salem folks don't like to see no signs of *that* weakness in a pastor; it's our duty to see as his head's not turned."

"Indeed, I trust there is very little fear of that," said Mrs Vincent, roused, and set on the defensive. "My dear boy has been used to be appreciated, and to have people round him who could understand him. As for having his

head turned, that might happen to a man who did not
know what intelligent approbation was; but after doing so
well as he did at college, and having his dear father's
approval, I must say I don't see any cause to apprehend
that, Mr Tozer. I am not surprised at all, for my part, – I
always knew what my Arthur could do."

"No more of this," said Vincent, impatiently. "Look
here, I have come on a special business. Can any one be
got, do you think, to preach on Sunday? I must go home
with my mother to-day."

"To-day!" Tozer opened his eyes, with a blank stare, as
he slowly took off his apron. "You was intimated to begin
that course on the Miracles, Mr Vincent, if you'll excuse
me, on Sunday. Salem folks is a little sharp, I don't deny.
It would be a great disappointment, and I can't say I think
as it would be took well if you was to go away."

"I can't help that," said the unfortunate minister, to
whom opposition at this moment was doubly intolerable.
"The Salem people, I presume, will hear reason. My
mother has come upon—"

"Family business," interrupted Mrs Vincent, with the
deepest trembling anxiety. "Arthur dear, let me explain
it, for you are too susceptible. My son is all the comfort we
have in the world, Mr Tozer," said the anxious widow. "I
ought not to have told him how much his sister wanted
him, but I was rash, and did so; and now I ought to bear
the penalty. I have made him anxious about Susan; but,
Arthur dear, never mind; you must let me go by myself,
and on Monday you can come. Your dear father always
said his flock was his first duty, and if Sunday is a special
day, as Mr Tozer says—"

"Oh, Pa, is it Mrs Vincent? and you keep her in the
shop, when we are all as anxious as ever we can be to see
her," said Phoebe, who suddenly came upon the scene.
"Oh, please to come up-stairs to the drawing-room. Oh, I
am so glad to see you! and it was so unkind of Mr Vincent
not to let us know you were coming. Mamma wanted to

ask you to come here, for she thought it would be more
comfortable than a bachelor's rooms; and we did think the
minister would have told *us*," said Phoebe, with reproachful
looks; "but now that you have come back again, after such
a long time, please, Mr Vincent, let your mother come up-
stairs. They say you don't think us good enough to be
trusted now; but oh, I don't think you could ever be like
that!" continued Phoebe, pausing by the door as she
ushered Mrs Vincent into the drawing-room, and giving
the minister an appealing remonstrative glance before she
dropped her eyelids in virginal humility. Poor Vincent
paused too, disgusted and angry, but with a certain confusion. To fling out of the house, dash off to his rooms,
make his hasty preparations for the journey, was the
impulse which possessed him; but his mother was looking
back with wistful curiosity, wondering what the two could
mean by pausing behind her at the door.

"I am exactly as I was the last time I saw you, which
was on Tuesday," he said, with some indignation. "I will
follow you, please. My mother has no time to spare, as she
leaves to-day – can Mrs Tozer see her? She has been
agitated and worn out, and we have not really a moment
to spare."

"Appearingly not – not for your own friends, Mr
Vincent," said Mrs Tozer, who now presented herself.
"I hope I see you well, ma'am, and proud to see you
in my house, though I will say the minister don't show
himself not so kind as was to be wished. Phoebe, don't
put on none o' your pleading looks – for shame of yourself,
Miss! If Mr Vincent has them in Carlingford as he likes
better than any in his own flock, it ain't no concern of ours.
It's a thing well known as the Salem folks are all in
trade, and don't drive their carriages, nor give themselves
up to this world and vanity. I never saw no good come,
for my part, of folks sacrificing theirselves and their good
money as Tozer and the rest set their hearts on, with
that Music Hall and them advertising and things –

not as I was meaning to upbraid you, Mr Vincent,
particular not before your mother, as is a stranger –
but we was a deal comfortabler before them lectures
and things, and taking off your attention from your own
flock."

Before this speech was finished, the whole party had
assembled in the drawing-room, where a newly-lighted
fire, hastily set light to on the spur of the moment by
Phoebe, was sputtering drearily. Mrs Vincent had been
placed in an arm-chair at one side, and Mrs Tozer, spreading out her black silk apron and arranging her cap, set
herself doggedly on the other, with a little toss of her head
and careful averting of her eyes from the accused pastor.
Tozer, without his apron, had drawn a chair to the table,
and was drumming on it with the blunt round ends of his
fingers; while Phoebe, in a slightly pathetic attitude,
ready for general conciliation, hovered near the minister,
who grew red all over, and clenched his hand with an
emphasis most intelligible to his frightened mother. The
dreadful pause was broken by Phoebe, who rushed to the
rescue.

"Oh, Ma, how can you!" cried the young lady – "you
were all worrying and teasing Mr Vincent, you know you
were; and if he does know that beautiful lady," said
Phoebe, with her head pathetically on one side, and
another glance at him, still more appealing and tenderly
reproachful – "and – and likes to go to see her – it's – it's
the naturalest thing that ever was. Oh, I knew he never
could think anything of anybody else in Carlingford after
Lady Western! and I am sure, whatever other people may
say, I – I – never can think Mr Vincent was to blame."

Phoebe's words were interrupted by her feelings – she
sank back into a seat when she had concluded, and put a
handkerchief to her eyes. As for Tozer, he still drummed
on the table. A certain human sympathy was in the mind
of the butterman, but he deferred to the readier utterance
of his indignant wife.

"I never said it was any concern of ours," said Mrs Tozer. "It ain't our way to court nobody as doesn't seek our company; but a minister as we've all done a deal to make comfortable, and took an interest in equal to a son, and has been made such a fuss about as I never see in our connection – it's disappointing, I will say, to see him a-going off after worldly folks that don't care no more about religion than I do about playing the piano. Not as Phoebe doesn't play the piano better than most – but such things ain't in my thoughts. I do say it's disappointing, and gives folks a turn. If she's pretty-lookin' – as she may be, for what I can tell – it ain't none of the pastor's business. Them designing ladies is the ruin of a young man; and when he deserts his flock, as are making sacrifices, and goes off after strangers, I don't say if it's right or wrong, but I say it's disappointin', and what wasn't looked for at Mr Vincent's hand."

Vincent had listened up to this point with moderate self-restraint – partially, perhaps, subdued by the alarmed expression of his mother's face, who had fixed her anxious eyes upon him, and vainly tried to convey telegraphic warnings; but the name of Lady Western stung him. "What is all this about?" he asked with assumed coldness. "Nobody supposes, surely, that I am to render an account of my private friends to the managers of the chapel. It is a mistake, if it has entered any imagination. I shall do nothing of the kind. There is enough of this. When I neglect my duties, I presume I shall hear of it more seriously. In the mean time, I have real business in hand."

"But, Arthur dear, I daresay some one has misunderstood you," said his mother; "it always turns out so. I came the day before yesterday, Mrs Tozer. I left home very suddenly in great anxiety, and I was very much fatigued by the journey, and I must go back to-day. I have been very selfish, taking my son away from his usual occupations. Never mind me, Arthur dear; if you have any business, leave me to rest a little with Mrs Tozer. I can take such a liberty here, because I know she is such a friend of yours. Don't keep Mr Tozer away from his business on my account. I know what it is when time is valuable. I will just stay a little with Mrs Tozer, and you can let me know when it is time for the train. Yes, I came up very hurriedly," said the gentle diplomatist, veiling her anxiety as she watched the gloomy countenances round her. "We had heard some bad news; I had to ask my son to go to town yesterday for me, and – and I must go home to-day without much comfort. I feel a good deal shaken, but I dare not stay away any longer from my dear child at home."

"Dear, dear; I hope it's nothing serious as has happened?" said Mrs Tozer, slightly mollified.

"It is some bad news about the gentleman Susan was going to marry," said Mrs Vincent, with a rapid calculation of the necessities of the position; "and she does not know yet. Arthur, my dear boy, it would be a comfort to my mind to know about the train."

"Oh, and you will be so fatigued!" said Phoebe. "I do so hope it's nothing bad. I *am* so interested about Miss Vincent. Oh, Pa, do go down-stairs and look at the railway bill. Won't you lie down on the sofa a little and rest? Fancy, mamma, taking two journeys in three days! – it would kill you; and, oh, I do so hope it is nothing very bad. I have so longed to see you and Mr Vincent's sister. He told me all about her one evening. Is the gentleman ill? But do lie down and rest after all your fatigue. Mamma, don't you think it would do Mrs Vincent good?"

"We'll have a bit of dinner presently," said Mrs Tozer. "Phoebe, go and fetch the wine. There is one thing in trouble, that it makes folks find out their real friends. It wouldn't be to Lady Western the minister would think of taking his mother. I ain't saying anything. If I speak my mind a bit, I don't bear malice. Phoebe's a deal too feelin', Mrs Vincent – she's overcome, that's what she is;

and if I must speak the truth, it's disappointing to see our pastor, as we've all made sacrifices for, following after the ungodly. I am a mother myself," continued Mrs Tozer, changing her seat, as her husband, followed by the indignant Vincent, went down-stairs, "and I know a mother's feelings: but after what I heard from Mrs Pigeon, and how it's going through all the connection in Carlingford—"

Mrs Vincent roused herself to listen. Her son's cause was safe in her hands.

Meantime Vincent went angry and impetuous down-stairs. "I will not submit to any inquisition," cried the young man. "I have done nothing I am ashamed of. If I dine with a friend, I will suffer no questioning on the subject. What do you mean? What right has any man in any connection to interfere with my actions? Why, you would not venture to attack your servant so! Am I the servant of this congregation? Am I their slave? Must I account to them for every accident of my life? Nobody in the world has a right to make such a demand upon me."

"If a minister ain't a servant, we pays him his salary at the least, and expects him to please us," said Tozer, sulkily. "If it weren't for that, I don't give a sixpence for the Dissenting connection. Them as likes to please themselves would be far better in a State Church, where it wouldn't disappoint nobody; not meaning to be hard on you as has given great satisfaction, them's my views; but if the Chapel folks is a little particular, it's no more nor a pastor's duty to bear with them, and return a soft answer. I don't say as I'm dead again' you, like the women," added the butterman, softening; "they're jealous, that's what they are; but I couldn't find it in my heart, not for my own part, to be hard on a man as was led away after a beautiful creature like that. But there can't no good come of it, Mr Vincent; take my advice, sir, as have seen a deal of the world – there can't no good come of it. A man as goes dining with Lady Western, and thinking as she means to make a friend of him, ain't the man for Salem.

We're different sort of folks, and we can't go on together.
Old Mr Tufton will tell you just the same, as has gone
through it all – and that's why I said both him and me had
a deal to say to you, as are a young man, and should take
good advice."

It was well for Vincent that the worthy butterman was
lengthy in his address. The sharp impression of resentment
and indignation which possessed him calmed down under
this outpouring of words. He bethought himself of his
dignity, his character. A squabble of self-defence, in
which the sweet name of the lady of his dreams must be
involved – an angry encounter of words about her, down
here in this mean world to which the very thought of her
was alien, wound up her young worshipper into supernatural self-restraint. He edged past the table in the back-
parlour to the window, and stood there looking out with a
suppressed fever in his veins, biting his lip, and bearing
his lecture. On the whole, the best way, perhaps, would
have been to leave Carlingford at once, as another man
would have done, and leave the Sunday to take care of
itself. But though he groaned under his bonds, the young
Nonconformist was instinctively confined by them, and
had the habits of a man trained in necessary subjection
to circumstances. He turned round abruptly when the
butterman at last came to a pause.

"I will write to one of my friends in Homerton," he said,
"if you will make an apology for me in the chapel. I
daresay I could get Beecher to come down, who is a very
clever fellow; and as for the beginning of that course of
sermons—"

He stopped short with a certain suppressed disgust.
Good heavens! what mockery it seemed. Amid these
agonies of life, a man overwhelmed with deadly fear,
hatred, and grief might indeed pause to snatch a burning
lesson, or appropriate with trembling hands a consolatory
promise; but with the whole solemn future of his sister's
life hanging on a touch, with all the happiness and peace

of his own involved in a feverish uncertainty, with dark unsuspected depths of injury and wretchedness opening at his feet – to think of courses of sermons and elaborate preachments, ineffectual words, and pretences of teaching! For the first time in the commotion of his soul, in the resentments and forebodings to which he gave no utterance, in the bitter conviction of uncertainty in everything which consumed his heart, a doubt of his own ability to teach came to Vincent's mind. He stopped short with an intolerable pang of impatience and self-disgust.

"And what of that, Mr Vincent?" said Tozer. "I can't say as I think it'll be well took to see a stranger in the pulpit after them intimations. I made it my business to send the notices out last night; and after saying everywhere as you were to begin a coorse, as I always advised, if you had took my advice, it ain't a way to stop talk to put them off now. Old Mr Tufton, you know, he was a different man; it was experience as was his line; and I don't mean to say nothing against experience," said the worthy deacon. "There ain't much true godliness, take my word, where there's a shrinking from disclosin' the state of your soul; but for keeping up a congregation there's nothing I know on like a coorse – and a clever young man as has studied his subjects, and knows the manners of them old times, and can give a bit of a description as takes the interest, that's what I'd set my heart on for Salem. There's but three whole pews in the chapel as isn't engaged," said the butterman, with a softening glance at the pastor; "and the Miss Hemmings sent over this morning to say as they meant to come regular the time you was on the Miracles; and but for this cackle of the women, as you'll soon get over, there ain't a thing as I can see to stop us filling up to the most influential chapel in the connection, – I mean in our parts."

The subdued swell of expectation with which the ambitious butterman concluded, somehow made Vincent more tolerant even in his undiminished excitement. He gave a subdued groan over all this that was expected of him, but not without a little answering thrill in his own troubled and impatient heart.

"A week can't make much difference, if I am ever to do any good," said the young man. "I must go now; but if you explain the matter for me, you will smooth the way. I will bring my mother and sister here," he went on, giving himself over for a moment to a little gleam of comfort, "and everything will go on better. I am worried and anxious now, and don't know what I am about. Give me some paper, and I will write to Beecher. You will like him. He is a good fellow, and preaches much better than I do," added poor Vincent with a sigh, sitting wearily down by the big table. He was subdued to his condition at that moment, and Tozer appreciated the momentary humbleness.

"I am not the man to desert my minister when he's in trouble," said the brave butterman. "Look you here, Mr Vincent; don't fret yourself about it. I'll take it in hand; and I'd like to see the man in Salem as would say to the contrary again' me and the pastor both. Make your mind easy; I'll manage 'em. As for the women," said Tozer, scratching his head, "I don't pretend not be equal to that; but my missis is as reasonable as most; and Phoebe, she'll stand up for you, whatever you do. If you'll take my advice, and be a bit prudent, and don't go after no more vanities, things ain't so far wrong but a week or two will make them right."

With this consolatory assurance Vincent began to write his letter. Before he had concluded it, the maid came to lay the cloth for dinner, thrusting him into a corner, where he accomplished his writing painfully on his knee with his ink on the widow-sill, a position in which Phoebe found him when she ventured down-stairs. It was she who took his letter from him, and ran with it to the shop to despatch it at once; and Phoebe came back to tell him that Mrs Vincent was resting, and that it was *so* pleasant to see him back again after such a time. "I never expected you would

have any patience for us when I saw you knew Lady
Western *so* well. Oh, she is so sweetly pretty! and if I were
a gentleman, I know I should fall *deep* in love with her,"
said Phoebe, with a sidelong glance, and not without
hopes of calling forth a disclaimer from the minister; but
the poor minister, jammed up in the corner, whence it was
now necessary to extricate his chair preparatory to sitting
down to a family dinner with the Tozers, was, as usual,
unequal to the occasion, and had nothing to say. Phoebe's
chair was by the minister's side during that substantial
meal; and the large fire which burned behind Mrs Tozer at
the head of the table, and the steaming viands on the
hospitable board, and the prevailing atmosphere of cheese
and bacon which entered when the door was opened,
made even Mrs Vincent pale and flush a little in the heroic
patience and friendliness with which she bent all her
powers to secure the support of these adherents to her son.
"I could have wished, Arthur, they were a little more
refined," she said, faintly, when the dinner was over, and
they were at last on their way to the train; "but I am sure
they are very *genuine,* my dear; and one good friend is
often everything to a pastor; and I am so glad we went at
such a time." So glad! The young Nonconformist heaved a
tempestuous sigh, and turned away not without a reflection
upon the superficial emotions of women who at such a time
could be glad. But Mrs Vincent, for her part, with a
fatigue and sickness of heart which she concealed from
herself as much as she could, let down her veil, and cried
quietly behind it. Perhaps her share of the day's exhaustion
had not been the mildest or least hard.

CHAPTER XVI.

THE journey was troublesome and tedious, involving a change from one railway to another, and a troubled glimpse into the most noisy streets of London by the way. Vincent had left his mother, as he thought, safe in the cab which carried them to the second railway station, and was disposing of the little luggage they had with them, that he might not require to leave her again, when he heard an anxious voice calling him, and found her close behind him, afloat in the bustle and confusion of the crowd, dreadfully agitated and helpless, calling upon her Arthur with impatient accents and distress. His annoyance to find her there increased her confusion and trembling. "Arthur," she gasped out, "I saw him – I saw him – not a minute ago – in a cab – with some ladies; oh, my dear, run after him. That was the way it went. Arthur, Arthur, why don't you go? Never mind me – I can take care of myself."

"Who was it – how did he go? – why didn't you stop him, mother?" cried the young man, rushing back to the spot she had left. Nothing was to be seen there but the usual attendant group of railway porters, and the alarmed cabman who had been keeping his eye on Mrs Vincent. The poor widow gasped as she gazed and saw no traces of the enemy who had eluded them.

"Oh, Arthur, my dear boy, I thought, in such a case, it ought to be a man to speak to him," faltered Mrs Vincent. "He went that way – that way, look! – in a cab, with somebody in a blue veil."

Vincent rushed away in the direction she indicated, at a pace which he was totally unused to, and of course quite unable to keep up beyond the first heat; but few things could be more hopeless than to dash into the whirl of vehicles in the crowded current of the New Road, with any vain hope of identifying one which had ten minutes' start, and no more distinctive mark of identity than the spectrum of a blue veil. He rushed back again, angry with himself for losing breath in so vain an attempt, just in time to place his mother in a carriage and jump in beside her before the train started. Mrs Vincent's anxiety, her questions which he could not hear, her doubts whether it might not have been best to have missed the train and followed Mr Fordham, aggravated the much-tried patience of her son beyond endurance. They set off upon their sad journey with a degree of injured feeling on both sides, such as often gives a miserable complication to a mutual anxiety. But the mother, wounded and timid, feeling more than ever the difference between the boy who was all her own and the man who had thoughts and impulses of which she knew nothing, was naturally the first to recover and to make wistful overtures of peace.

"Well, Arthur," she said, after a while, leaning forward to him, her mild voice making a gentle murmur through the din of the journey, "though it was very foolish of me not to speak to him when I saw him, still, dear, he is gone and out of the way; that is a great comfort – we will never, never let him come near Susan again. That is just what I was afraid of; I have been saying to myself all day, 'What if he should go to Lonsdale too, and deny it all?' but Providence, you see, dear, has ordered it for us, and now he shall never come near my poor child again."

"Do you think he has been to Lonsdale?" asked Vincent.

"My poor Susan!" said his simple mother, "she will be happier than ever when we come to her with this dreadful news. Yes; I suppose he must have been seeing her, Arthur – and I am glad it has happened while I was away, and before we knew; and now he is gone," said the widow, looking out of the carriage with a sigh of relief, as if she

could still see the road by which he had disappeared – "now
he is gone, there will be no need for any dreadful strife or
arguments. God always arranges things for us so much
better than we can arrange them for ourselves. Fancy if he
had come to-morrow to tear her dear heart to pieces! – Oh,
Arthur, I am very thankful! There will be nothing to do now
but to think best how to break it to her. He had ladies with
him; it is dreadful to think of such villany. Oh, Arthur, do you
imagine it could be his wife? – and somebody in a blue veil."

"A blue veil!" – Mrs Hilyard's message suddenly occurred
to Vincent's mind, with its special mention of that article of
disguise. "If this man is the man we suppose, he has
accomplished one of his wishes," said the minister, slowly;
"and she will kill him as sure as he lives."

"Who will kill him? – I hope nothing has occurred about
your friend's child to agitate my Susan," said his mother.
"It was all the kindness of your heart, my dear boy; but it
was very imprudent of you to let Susan's name be connected
with anybody of doubtful character. Oh, Arthur dear, we
have both been very imprudent! – you have so much of my
quick temper. It was a punishment to me to see how
impatient you were to-day; but Susan takes after your dear
father. Oh, my own boy, pray – pray for her, that her heart
may not be broken by this dreadful news."

And Mrs Vincent leant back in her corner, and once more
put down her veil. Pray! – who was he to pray for? Susan,
forlorn and innocent, disappointed in her first love, but
unharmed by any worldly soil or evil passion? – or the other
sufferers involved in more deadly sort, himself palpitating
with feverish impulses, broken loose from all his peaceful
youthful moorings, burning with discontents and aspirations,
not spiritual, but of the world? Vincent prayed none as he
asked himself that bitter question. He drew back in his seat
opposite his mother, and pondered in his heart the wonderful
difference between the objects of compassion to whom the
world gives ready tears, and those of whom the world
knows and suspects nothing. Susan! he could see her

mother weeping over her in her white and tender innocence. What if, perhaps, she broke her young heart? the shock would only send the girl with more clinging devotion to the feet of the great Father; but as for himself, all astray from duty and sober life, devoured with a consuming fancy, loathing the way and the work to which he had been trained to believe that Father had called him – who thought of weeping? – or for Her, whom his alarmed imagination could not but follow, going forth remorseless and silent to fulfil her promise, and kill the man who had wronged her? Oh, the cheat of tears! – falling sweet over the young sufferers whom sorrow blessed – drying up from the horrible complex pathways where other souls, in undisclosed anguish, went farther and farther from God!

With such thoughts the mother and son hurried on upon their darkling journey. It was the middle of the night when they arrived in Lonsdale – a night starless, but piercing with cold. They were the only passengers who got out at the little station, where two or three lamps glared wildly on the night, and two pale porters made a faint bustle to forward the long convey of carriages upon its way. One of these men looked anxiously at the widow, as if with the sudden impulse of asking a question, or communicating some news, but was called off by his superior before he could speak. Vincent unconsciously observed the look, and was surprised and even alarmed by it, without knowing why. It returned to his mind, as he gave his mother his arm to walk the remaining distance home. Why did the man put on that face of curiosity and wonder? But, to be sure, to see the mild widow arrive in this unexpected way in the middle of the icy January night, must have been surprising enough to any one who knew her, and her gentle decorous life. He tried to think no more of it, as they set out upon the windy road, where a few sparsely-scattered lamps blinked wildly, and made the surrounding darkness all the darker. The station was half a mile from the town, and Mrs Vincent's cottage was on the other side of Lonsdale, across the river,

which stole sighing and gleaming through the heart of the
little place. Somehow the sudden black shine of that water
as they caught it, crossing the bridge, brought a shiver and
flash of wild imagination to the mind of the Nonconformist.
He thought of suicides, murders, ghastly concealment and
misery; and again the face of the porter returned upon him.
What if something had happened while the watchful mother
had been out of the way? The wind came sighing round the
corners with an ineffectual gasp, as if it too had some
warning, some message to deliver. Instinctively he drew
his mother's arm closer, and hurried her on. Suggestions of
horrible unthought-of evil seemed lurking everywhere in
the noiseless blackness of the night.

Mrs Vincent shivered too, but it was with cold and
natural agitation. In her heart she was putting tender words
together, framing tender phrases – consulting with herself
how she was to look, and how to speak. Already she could
see the half-awakened girl, starting up all glowing and
sweet from her safe rest, unforeboding of evil, and sent
back with an effort the unshed tears from her eyes, that
Susan might not see any traces in her face, till she had
"prepared her" a little for that dreadful, inevitable blow.

The cottage was all dark, as was natural – doubly dark to-
night, for there was no light in the skies, and the wind had
extinguished the lamp which stood nearest, and on ordinary
occasions threw a doubtful flicker on the little house.
"Susan will soon hear us, she is such a light sleeper," said
Mrs Vincent. "Ring the bell, Arthur. I don't like using the
knocker, to disturb the neighbours. Everybody would
think it so surprising to hear a noise in the middle of the
night from our house. There – wait a moment. That was a
very loud ring; Susan must be sleeping very soundly if that
does not wake her up."

There was a little pause; not a sound, except the tinkling
of the bell, which they could hear inside as the peal
gradually subsided, was in the air; breathless silence,
darkness, cold, an inhuman preternatural chill and watch-

fulness, no welcome sound of awakening sleepers, only their own dark shadows in the darkness, listening like all the hushed surrounding world at that closed door.

"Poor dear! Oh, Arthur it is dreadful to come and break her sleep," sighed Mrs Vincent, whose strain of suspense and expectation heightened the effect of the cold: "when will she sleep as sound again? Give another ring, dear. How terribly dark and quiet it is! Ring again, again, Arthur! – dear, dear me, to think of Susan in such a sound sleep! – and generally she starts at any noise. It is to give her strength to bear what is coming, poor child, poor child!"

The bell seemed to echo out into the silent road, it pealed so clearly and loudly through the shut-up house, but not another sound disturbed the air without or within. Mrs Vincent began to grow restless and alarmed. She went out into the road, and gazed up at the closed windows; her very teeth chattered with anxiety and cold.

"It is very odd she does not wake," said the widow; "she must be rousing now, surely. Arthur, don't look as if we had bad news. Try to command your countenance, dear. Hush! don't you hear them stirring? Now, Arthur, Arthur, oh remember not to look so dreadful as you did in Carlingford! I am sure I hear her coming down-stairs. Hark! what is it? Ring again, Arthur – again!"

The words broke confused and half-articulate from her lips; a vague dread took possession of her, as of her son. For his part, he rang the bell wildly without pausing, and applied the knocker to the echoing door with a sound which seemed to reverberate back and back through the darkness. It was not the sleep of youth Vincent thought of, as, without a word to say, he thundered his summons on the cottage door. He was not himself aware what he was afraid of; but in his mind he saw the porter's alarmed and curious look, and felt the ominous silence thrilling with the loud clangour of his own vain appeals through the deserted house.

At length a sound – the mother and son both rushed speechless towards the side-window, from which it came.

The window creaked slowly open, and a head, which was not Susan's, looked cautiously out. "Who is there?" cried a strange voice; "it's some mistake. This is Mrs Vincent's, this is, and nobody's at home. If you don't go away I'll spring the rattle, and call Thieves, thieves – Fire! What do you mean coming rousing folks like this in the dead of night?"

"Oh, Williams, are you there? Thank God! – then all is well," said Mrs Vincent, clasping her hands. "It is I – you need not be afraid – I and my son: don't disturb Miss Susan, since she has not heard us – but come down, and let us in; – don't disturb my daughter. It is I – don't you know my voice?"

"Good Lord!" cried the speaker at the window; then in a different tone, "I'm coming, ma'am – I'm coming." Instinctively, without knowing why, Vincent drew his mother's arm within his own, and held her fast. Instinctively the widow clung to him, and kept herself erect by his aid. They did not say a word – no advices now about composing his countenance. Mrs Vincent's face was ghastly, had there been any light to see it. She went sheer forward when the door was open, as though neither her eyes nor person were susceptible of any other motion. An inexpressible air of desolation upon the cottage parlour, where everything looked far too trim and orderly for recent domestic occupation, brought to a climax all the fanciful suggestions which had been tormenting Vincent. He called out his sister's name in an involuntary outburst of dread and excitement, "Susan! Susan!" The words pealed into the midnight echoes – but there was no Susan to answer to the call.

"It is God that keeps her asleep to keep her happy," said his mother, with her white lips. She dropt from his arm upon the sofa in a dreadful pause of determination, facing them with wide-open eyes – daring them to undeceive her – resolute not to hear the terrible truth, which already in her heart she knew. "Susan is asleep, asleep!" she cried, in a terrible idiocy of despair, always facing the frightened woman before her with those eyes which knew better, but would not be undeceived. The shivering midnight, the mother's dreadful looks, the sudden waking to all this fright and wonder, were too much for the terrified guardian of the house. She fell on her knees at the widow's feet.

"Oh, Lord! Miss Susan's gone! I'd have kep her if I had been here. I'd have said her mamma would never send no gentleman but Mr Arthur to fetch her away. But she's gone. Good Lord! it's killed my missis – I knew it would kill my missis. Oh, good Lord! good Lord! Run for a doctor, Mr Arthur; if the missis is gone, what shall we do?"

Vincent threw the frightened creature off with a savage carelessness of which he was quite unconscious, and raised his mother in his arms. She had fallen back in a dreary momentary fit which was not fainting – her eyes fluttering under their half-closed lids, her lips moving with sounds that did not come. The shock had struck her as such shocks strike the mortal frame when it grows old. When sound burst at last from the moving lips, it was in a babble that mocked all her efforts to speak. But she was not unconscious of the sudden misery. Her eyes wandered about, taking in everything around her, and at last fixed upon a letter lying half-open on Susan's work-table, almost the only token of disorder or agitation in the trim little room. The first sign of revival she showed was pointing at it with a doubtful but impatient gesture. Before she could make them understand what she meant, that "quick temper" of which Mrs Vincent accused herself blazed up in the widow's eyes. She raised herself erect out of her son's arms, and seized the paper. It was Vincent's letter to his sister, written from London after he had failed in his inquiries about Mr Fordham. In the light of this dreadful midnight the young man himself perceived how alarming and peremptory were its brief injunctions. "Don't write to Mr Fordham again till my mother's return; probably I shall bring her home: we have something to say to you on this subject,

and in the mean time be sure you do as I tell you." Mrs
Vincent gradually recovered herself as she read this; she
said it over under her breath, getting back the use of her
speech. There was not much explanation in it, yet it seemed
to take the place, in the mother's confused faculties, of an
apology for Susan. "She was frightened," said Mrs Vincent,
slowly, with strange twitches about her lips – "she was
frightened." That was all her mind could take in at once.
Afterwards, minute by minute, she raised herself up, and
came to self-command and composure. Only as she recovered did the truth reveal itself clearly even to Vincent,
who, after the first shock, had been occupied entirely by
his mother. The young man's head throbbed and tingled
as if with blows. As she sat up and gazed at him with her
own recovered looks, through the dim ice-cold atmosphere,
lighted faintly with one candle, they both woke up to the
reality of their position. The shock of the discovery was
over – Susan was gone; but where, and with whom? There
was still something to hope, if everything to fear.

"She is gone to her aunt Alice," said Mrs Vincent, once
more looking full in the eyes of the woman who had been
left in charge of the house, and who stood shivering with
cold and agitation, winding and unwinding round her a
thin shawl in which she had wrapped up her arms. "She
has gone to her aunt Alice – she was frightened, and
thought something had happened. To-morrow we can go
and bring her home."

"Oh, good Lord! No; she ain't there," cried the frightened
witness, half inaudible with her chattering teeth.

"Or to Mrs Hastings at the farm. Susan knows what
friends I can trust her to. Arthur dear, let us go to bed. It's
uncomfortable, but you won't mind for one night," said
the widow, with a gasp, rising up and sitting down again.
She dared not trust herself to hear any explanation, yet all
the time fixed with devouring eyes upon the face of the
woman whom she would not suffer to speak.

"Mother, for Heaven's sake let us understand it; let her

speak – let us know. Where has Susan gone? Speak out;
never mind interruptions. Where is my sister?" cried
Vincent, grasping the terrified woman by the arm.

"Oh Lord! If the missis wouldn't look at me like that! I
ain't to blame!" cried Williams, piteously. "It was the day
afore yesterday as the ladies came. I come up to help
Mary with the beds. There was the old lady as had on a
brown bonnet and the young miss in the blue veil—"

Vincent uttered a sudden exclamation, and looked at his
mother; but she would not meet his eyes – would not
acknowledge any recognition of that fatal piece of gauze.
She gave a little gasp, sitting bolt upright, holding fast by
the back of a chair, but kept her eyes steadily and sternly
upon the woman's face.

"We tidied the best room for the lady, and Miss Susan's
little closet; and Mary had out the best sheets, for she
says—"

"Mary – where's Mary?" cried Mrs Vincent, suddenly.

"I know no more nor a babe," cried Williams, wringing
her hands. "She's along with Miss Susan – wherever that
may be – and the one in the blue veil."

"Go on, go on!" cried Vincent.

But his mother did not echo his cry. Her strained hand
fell upon her lap with a certain relaxation and relief; her
gaze grew less rigid; incomprehensible moisture came to
her eyes. "Oh, Arthur, there's comfort in it!" said Mrs
Vincent, looking like herself again. "She's taken Mary,
God bless her! she's known what she was doing. Now I'm
more easy; Williams, you can sit down and tell us the rest."

"Go on!" cried Vincent, fiercely. "Good heavens! what
good can a blundering country girl do here? – go on."

The women thought otherwise; they exchanged looks of
sympathy and thankfulness; they excited the impatient
young man beside them, who thought he knew the world,
into the wildest exasperation by that pause of theirs. His
mother even loosed her bonnet off her aching head, and
ventured to lean back under the influence of that visionary

consolation; while Vincent, aggravated to the intolerable pitch, sprang up, and, once more seizing Williams by the arm, shook her unawares in the violence of the anxiety. "Answer me!" cried the young man; "you tell us everything but the most important of all. Besides this girl – and Mary – who was with my sister when she went away?"

"Oh Lord! you shake the breath out of me, Mr Arthur – you do," cried the woman. "Who? why, who should it be, to be sure, but him as had the best right after yourself to take Miss Susan to her mamma? You've crossed her on the road, poor dear," said the adherent of the house, wringing her hands; "but she was going to her ma – that's where she was going. Mr Arthur's letter gave her a turn; and then, to be sure, when Mr Fordham came, the very first thing he thought upon was to take her to her mamma."

Vincent groaned aloud. In his first impulse of fury he seized his hat and rushed to the door to pursue them anyhow, by any means. Then, remembering how vain was the attempt, came back again, dashed down the hat he had put on, and seized upon the railway book in his pocket, to see when he could start upon that desperate mission. Minister as he was, a muttered curse ground through his teeth – villain! coward! destroyer! curse him! His passion was broken in the strangest way by the composed sounds of his mother's voice.

"It was very natural," she said, with dry tones, taking time to form the words as if they choked her; "and of course, as you say, Williams, Mr Fordham had the best right. He will take her to his mother's – or – or leave her in my son's rooms in Carlingford; and as she has Mary with her – Arthur," continued his mother, fixing a warning emphatic look upon him as he raised his astonished eyes to her face, "you know that is quite right: after you – Mr Fordham is – the only person – that could have taken care of her in her journey. There, I am satisfied. Perhaps, Williams, you had better go to bed. My son and I have something to talk of, now I feel myself."

"I'll go light the fire, and get you a cup of tea – oh Lord! what Miss Susan would say if she knew you were here, and had got such a fright!" cried the old servant; "but now you're composed, there's nothing as'll do you good like a cup of tea."

"Thank you – yes; make it strong, and Mr Arthur will have some too," said the widow; "and take care the kettle is boiling; and then, Williams, you must not mind us, but go to bed."

Vincent threw down his book, and stared at her with something of that impatience and half-contempt which had before moved him. "If the world were breaking up, I suppose women could still drink tea!" he said, bitterly.

"Oh, Arthur, my dear boy," cried his mother, "don't you see we must put the best face on it now? Everybody must not know that Susan has been carried away by a—O God, forgive me! don't let *me* curse him, Arthur. Let us get away from Lonsdale, dear, before we say anything. Words will do no good. Oh, my dear boy, till we know better, Mr Fordham is Susan's betrothed husband, and he has gone to take care of her to Carlingford. Hush – don't say any more. I am going to compose myself, Arthur, for my child's sake," cried the mother, with a smile of anguish, looking into her son's face. How did she drive those tears back out of her patient eyes? how did she endure the talk to the old servant about what was to be done to-morrow – and how the sick lady was next door – till the excited and shivering attendant could be despatched upstairs and got out of the way? Woman's weaker nature, that could mingle the common with the great; or woman's strength, that could endure all things – which was it? The young man, sitting by in a sullen, intolerable suspense, waiting till it was practicable to rush away through the creeping gloom of night after the fugitives, could no more understand these phenomena of love and woe, than he could translate the distant mysteries of the spheres.

CHAPTER XVII.

EARLY morning, but black as midnight; bitter cold, if bitterer cold could be, than that to which they entered when they first came to the deserted house; the little parlour, oh, so woefully trim and tidy, with the fire laid ready for lighting, which even the mother, anxious about her son, had not had the heart to light; the candle on the table between them lighting dimly this speechless interval; some shawls laid ready to take with them when they went back again to the earliest train; Mrs Vincent sitting by with her bonnet on, and its veil drooping half over her pale face, sometimes rousing up to cast hidden looks of anxiety at her son, sometimes painfully saying something with a vain effort at smiling – what o'clock was it? when did he think they could reach town? – little ineffectual attempts at the common intercourse, which seemed somehow to deepen the dreadful silence, the shivering cold, the utter desolation of the scene. Such a night! – its minutes were hours as they stole by noiseless in murderous length and tedium – and the climax of its misery was in the little start with which Mrs Vincent now and then woke up out of her own thoughts to make that pitiful effort to talk to her son.

They were sitting thus, waiting, not even venturing to look at each other, when a sudden sound startled them. Nothing more than a footstep outside approaching softly. A footstep – surely two steps. They could hear them far off in this wonderful stillness, making steady progress near – nearer. Mrs Vincent rose up, stretching her little figure into a preternatural hysteric semblance of height. Who

was it? Two people – surely women – and what women
could be abroad at such an hour? One lighter, one heavier,
irregular as female steps are, coming this way – this way!
Her heart fluttered in the widow's ears with a sound that
all but obliterated those steps which still kept advancing.
Hark, sudden silence! A pause, then – O merciful Heaven!
– could it be true – a tinkle at the bell – a summons at the
closed door?

Mrs Vincent had flown forth with open arms – with eyes
blinded. The poor soul thought nothing less than that it
was her child returned. They carried her back speechless,
in a disappointment too cruel and bitter to have expression.
Two women – one sober, sleepy, nervous, and full of
trouble, unknown to either mother or son – the other with
a certain dreadful inspiration in her dark face, and eyes
that gleamed out of it as if they had concentrated into
them all the blackness of the night.

"You are going back, and so am I," Mrs Hilyard said.
"I came to say a word to you before I go away. If I have
been anyhow the cause, forgive me. God knows, of all
things in the world the last I dreamt of was to injure this
good woman or invade her innocent house. Do you know
where they have gone? – did she leave any letters? – Tell
me. She shall be precious to me as my own, if I find them
out."

Mrs Vincent freed herself from her son's arms, and got
up with her blanched face. "My daughter – followed me –
to Carlingford," she said, in broken words, with a determination which sat almost awful on her weakness. "We
have had the great misfortune – to cross each other – on
the way. I am going – after her – directly. I am not afraid
– of my Susan. She is all safe in my son's house."

The others exchanged alarmed looks, as they might
have done had a child suddenly assumed the aspect of a
leader. She, who could scarcely steady her trembling
limbs to stand upright, faced their looks with a dumb
denial of her own anguish. "It is – very unfortunate – but I

am not anxious," she said, slowly, with a ghastly smile. Human nature could do no more. She sank down again on her seat, but still faced them – absolute in her self-restraint, rejecting pity. Not even tears should fall upon Susan's sweet name – not while her mother lived to defend it in life and death.

The Carlingford needlewoman stood opposite her, gazing with eyes that went beyond that figure, and yet dwelt upon it, at so wonderful a spectacle. Many a terrible secret of life unknown to the minister's gentle mother throbbed in her heart; but she stood in a pause of wonder before that weaker woman. The sight of her stayed the passionate current for a moment, and brought the desperate woman to a pause. Then she turned to the young man, who stood speechless by his mother's side –

"You are a priest, and yet you do not curse," she said. "Is God as careless of a curse as of a blessing? *She* thinks He will save the Innocents yet. She does not know that He stands by like a man, and sees them murdered, and shines and rains all the same. God! No – He never interferes. Good-bye," she added, suddenly, holding out to him the thin hand upon which, even in that dreadful moment, his eye still caught the traces of her work, the scars of the needle, and stains of the coarse colour. "If you ever see me again, I shall be a famous woman, Mr Vincent. You will have a little of the trail of my glory, and be able to furnish details of my latter days. This good Miss Smith here will tell you of the life it was before; but if I should make a distinguished end after all, come to see me then – never mind where. I speak madly, to be sure, but you don't understand me. There – not a word. You preach very well, but I am beyond preaching now – Good-bye."

"No," said Vincent, clutching her hand – "never, if you go with that horrible intention in your eyes; I will say no farewell to such an errand as this."

The eyes in their blank brightness paused at him for a moment before they passed to the vacant air on which

they were always fixed – paused with a certain glance of
troubled amusement, the lightning of former days. "You
flatter me," she said, steadily, with the old habitual movement of her mouth. "It is years since anybody has taken
the trouble to read any intention in my eyes. But don't
you understand yet that a woman's intention is the last
thing she is likely to perform in this world? We do have
meanings now and then, we poor creatures, but they
seldom come to much. Good-bye, good-bye!"

"You cannot look at me," said Vincent, with a conscious
incoherence, reason or argument being out of the question.
"What is it you see behind there? Where are you looking
with those dreadful eyes?"

She brought her eyes back as he spoke, with an evident
effort, to fix them upon his face. "I once remarked upon
your high-breeding," said the strange woman. "A prince
could not have shown finer manners than you did in
Carlingford, Mr Vincent. Don't disappoint me now. If I
see ghosts behind you, what then? Most people that have
lived long enough, come to see ghosts before they die. But
this is not exactly the time for conversation, however
interesting it may be. If you and I ever see each other
again, things will have happened before then; you too,
perhaps, may have found the ghosts out. I appoint you to
come to see me after you have come to life again, in the
next world. Good-night. I don't forget that you gave me
your blessing when we parted last."

She was turning away when Mrs Vincent rose, steadying
herself by the chair, and put a timid hand upon the
stranger's arm. "I don't know who you are," said the
widow; "it is all a strange jumble; but I am an older
woman than you, and a – a minister's wife. You have
something on your mind. My son is frightened you will do
something – I cannot tell what. You are much cleverer
than I am; but I am, as I say, an older woman, and a – a
minister's wife. I am not – afraid of anything. Yes! I know
God does not always save the Innocents, as you say – but

He knows why, though we don't. Will you go with me? If
you have gone astray when you were young," said the
mild woman, raising up her little figure with an ineffable
simplicity, "I will never ask any questions, and it will not
matter – for everybody I care for knows me. The dreadful
things you think of will not happen if we go together. I was a
minister's wife thirty years. I know human nature and
God's goodness. Come with me."

"Mother, mother! what are you saying?" cried Vincent,
who had all the time been making vain attempts to interrupt this extraordinary speech. Mrs Hilyard put him away
with a quick gesture. She took hold of the widow's hand
with that firm, supporting, compelling pressure under
which, the day before, Mrs Vincent had yielded up all her
secrets. She turned her eyes out of vacancy to the little
pale woman who offered her this protection. A sudden
mist surprised those gleaming eyes – a sudden thrill ran
through the thin, slight, iron figure, upon which fatigue
and excitement seemed to make no impression. The rock
was stricken at last.

"No – no," she sighed, with a voice that trembled. "No –
no! the lamb and the lion do not go together yet in this poor
world. No – no – no. I wonder what tears have to do in my
eyes; ah, God in the skies! if you ever do miracles, do one
for this woman, and save her child! Praying and crying are
strange fancies for me – I must go away; but first," she said,
still holding Mrs Vincent fast – "a woman is but a woman
after all – if it is more honourable to be a wicked man's wife
than to have gone astray, as you call it, then there is no one
in the world who can breathe suspicion upon me. Ask this
other good woman here, who knows all about me, but fears
me, like you. Fears me! What do you suppose there can be
to fear, Mr Vincent, you who are a scholar, and know better
than these soft women," said Mrs Hilyard, suddenly dropping the widow's hand, and turning round upon the young
minister, with an instant throwing off of all emotion, which
had the strangest horrifying effect upon the little agitated

company, "in a woman who was born to the name of Rachel Russell, the model English wife? Will the world ever believe harm, do you imagine, of such a name? I will take refuge in my ancestress. But we go different ways, and have different ends to accomplish," she continued, with a sudden returning gleam of the subdued horror – "Good-night – good-night!"

"Oh, stop her, Arthur – stop her! – Susan will be at Carlingford when we get there; Susan will go nowhere else but to her mother," cried Mrs Vincent, as the door closed on the nocturnal visitors – "I am as sure – as sure—! Oh, my dear, do you think I can have any doubt of my own child? As for Susan going astray – or being carried off – or falling into wickedness – Arthur," said his mother, putting back her veil from her pale face, "now I have got over this dreadful night, I know better – nobody must breathe such a thing to me. Tell her so, dear – tell her so! – call her back – they will be at Carlingford when we get there!"

Vincent drew his mother's arm through his own, and led her out into the darkness, which was morning and no longer night. "A few hours longer and we shall see," he said, with a hard-drawn breath. Into the darkness Mrs Hilyard and her companion had disappeared. There was another line of railway within a little distance of Lonsdale, but Vincent was at pains not to see his fellow-travellers as he placed his mother once more in a carriage, and once more caught the eye of the man whose curious look had startled him. When the grey morning began to drawn, it revealed two ashen faces, equally speechless and absorbed with thoughts which neither dared communicate to the other. They did not even look at each other, as the merciful noise and motion wrapped them in that little separate sphere of being. One possibility and no more kept a certain coherence in both their thoughts, otherwise lost in wild chaos – horrible suspense – an uncertainty worse than death.

CHAPTER XVIII.

It was the very height of day when the travellers arrived in Carlingford. It would be vain to attempt to describe their transit through London in the bustling sunshine of the winter morning after the vigil of that night, and in the frightful suspense and excitement of their minds. Vincent remembered, for years after, certain cheerful street-corners, round which they turned on their way from one station to another, with shudders of recollection, and an intense consciousness of all the life circulating about them, even to the attitudes of the boys that swept the crossings, and their contrast with each other. His mother made dismal attempts now and then to say something; that he was looking pale; that after all he could yet preach, and begin his course on the Miracles; that it would be such a comfort to rest when they got home; but at last became inaudible, though he knew by her bending across to him, and the motion of those parched lips with which she still tried to smile, that the widow still continued to make those pathetic little speeches without knowing that she had become speechless in the rising tide of her agony. But at last they reached Carlingford, where everything was at its brightest, all the occupations of life, afloat in the streets, and sunshine, lavish though ineffectual, brightening the whole aspect of the town. When they emerged from the railway, Mrs Vincent took her son's arm, and for the last time made some remark with a ghastly smile – but no sound came from her lips. They walked up the sunshiny street together with such silent speed as would have been frightful to look at had anybody known what was in their hearts. Mrs Pigeon, who was

coming along the other side, crossed over on purpose to
accost the minister, and be introduced to his mother, but
was driven frantic by the total blank unconsciousness with
which the two swept past her; "taking no more notice than if
he had never set eyes on me in his born days!" as she
described it afterwards. The door of the house where
Vincent lived was opened to them briskly by the little maid
in holiday attire; everything wore the most sickening,
oppressive brightness within in fresh Saturday cleanliness.
Vincent half carried his mother up the steps, and held fast
in his own to support her the hand which he had drawn
tightly through his arm. "Is there any one here? Has
anybody come for me since I left?" he asked, with the
sound of his own words ringing shrilly into his ears. "Please,
sir, Mr Tozer's been," said the girl, alertly, with smiling
confidence. She could not comprehend the groan with
which the young man startled all the clear and sunshiny
atmosphere, nor the sudden rustle of the little figure beside
him, which moved somehow, swaying with the words as if
they were a wind. "Mother, you are going to faint!" cried
Vincent – and the little maid flew in terror to call her
mistress, and bring a glass of water. But when she came
back, the mother and son were no longer in the bright hall
with its newly-cleaned wainscot and whitened floor. When
she followed them up-stairs with the water,it was the
minister who had dropped into the easy-chair with his face
hidden on the table, and his mother was standing beside
him. Mrs Vincent looked up when the girl came in and said,
"Thank you – that will do," looking in her face, and not at
what she carried. She was of a dreadful paleness, and
looked with eyes that were terrible to that wondering
observer upon the little attendant. "Perhaps there have
been some letters or messages," said Mrs Vincent. "We –
we expected somebody to come; think! a young lady came
here? – and when she found we were gone—"

"Only Miss Phoebe!" said the girl in amazement – "to
say as her Ma—"

"Only Miss Phoebe!" repeated the widow, as if she did not comprehend the words. Then she turned to her son, and smoothed down the ruffled locks on his head; then held out her hand again to arrest the girl as she was going away. "Has your mistress got anything in the house," she asked – "any soup or cold meat, or anything? Would you bring it up, please, directly? – soup would perhaps be best – or a nice chop. Ask what she has got, and bring it up on a tray. You need not lay the cloth – only a tray with a napkin. Yes, I see you know what I mean."

"Mother!" cried Vincent, raising his head in utter fright as the maid left the room. He thought in the shock his mother's gentle wits had gone.

"You have eaten nothing, dear, since we left," she said, with a heartbreaking smile. "I am not going crazy, Arthur. O no, no, my dear boy! I will not go crazy; but you must eat something, and not be killed too. Susan is not here," said Mrs Vincent, with a ghastly, wistful look round the room; "but we are not going to distrust her at the very first moment, far less her Maker, Arthur. Oh, my dear, I must not speak, or something will happen to me; and nothing must happen to you or me till we have found your sister. You must eat when it comes, and then you must go away. Perhaps," said Mrs Vincent, sitting down and looking her son direct in the eyes, as if to read any suggestion that could arise there, "she has lost her way: – perhaps she missed one of these dreadful trains – perhaps she got on the wrong railway, Arthur. Oh, my dear boy, you must take something to eat, and then you must go and bring Susan home. She has nobody to take care of her but you."

Vincent returned his mother's look with a wild inquiring gaze, but with his lips he said "Yes," not daring to put in words the terrible thoughts in his heart. The two said nothing to each other of the horror that possessed them both, or of the dreadful haze of uncertainty in which that Susan whom her brother was to go and bring home as if from an innocent visit, was now enveloped. Their eyes spoke differently as they looked into each other, and silently withdrew again, each from each, not daring to communicate further. Just then a slight noise came below, to the door. Mrs Vincent stood up directly in an agony of listening, trembling all over. To be sure it was nothing. When nothing came of it, the poor mother sank back again with a piteous patience, which it was heartbreaking to look at; and Vincent returned from the window which he had thrown open in time to see Phoebe Tozer disappear from the door. They avoided each other's eyes now; one or two heavy sobs broke forth from Mrs Vincent's breast, and her son walked with a dreadful funereal step from one end of the room to the other. Not even the consolation of consulting together what has to be done, or what might have happened, was left them. They dared not put their position into words – dared not so much as inquire in their thoughts where Susan was, or what had befallen her. She was to be brought home; but whence or from what abyss neither ventured to say.

Upon their misery the little maid entered again with her tray, and the hastily-prepared refreshment which Mrs Vincent had ordered for her son. The girl's eyes were round and staring with wonder and curiosity; but she was aware, with female instinct, that the minister's mother, awful little figure, with lynx eyes, which nothing escaped, was watching her, and her observations were nervous accordingly. "Please, sir, it's a chop," said the girl – "please, sir, missus sent to know was the other gentleman a-coming? – and please, if he is, there ain't nowhere, as missus knows of, as he can sleep – with the lady, and you, and all; and the other lodgers as well" – said the handmaiden with a sigh, as she set down her tray and made a desperate interpretation of all this in the unguarded countenance of the minister; "and please, am I to bring up the Wooster sauce, and would the lady like some tea or anythink? And missus would be par- ticklar obliged if you would say. Miss Phoebe's been to ask the gentleman to tea, but where he's to sleep, missus says—"

"Yes, yes, to be sure," said Vincent, impatiently, "he can have my room, tell your mistress — that will do — we don't want anything more."

"Mr Vincent is going to leave town again this afternoon," said his mother. "Tell your mistress that I shall be glad to have a little conversation with her after my son goes away — and you had better bring the sauce — but it would have saved you trouble and been more sensible, if you had put it on the tray in the first place. Oh, Arthur," cried his mother again, when she had seen the little maid fairly out — "do be a little prudent, my dear! When a minister lodges with one of his flock, he must think of appearances — and if it were only for my dear child's sake, Arthur! Susan must not be spoken of through our anxiety; oh, my child! — Where can she be? — Where can she be?"

"Mother dear, you must keep up, or everything is lost!" cried Vincent, for the first time moved to the depths of his heart by that outcry of despair. He came to her and held her trembling hands, and laid his face upon them without any kiss or caress, that close clinging touch of itself expressing best the fellowship of their wretchedness. But Mrs Vincent put her son away from her, when the door again bounced open. "My dear boy, here is the sauce, and you must eat your chop," she said, getting up and drawing forward a chair for him; her hands, which trembled so, grew steady as she put everything in order, cut the bread, and set his plate before him. "Oh, eat something, Arthur dear — you must, or you cannot go through it," said the widow, with her piteous smile. Then she sat down at the table by him in her defensive armour. The watchful eyes of "the flock" were all around spying upon the dreadful calamity which had overwhelmed them; at any moment the college companion whom Vincent had sent for might come in upon them in all the gaiety of his holiday. What they said had to be said with this conscious-ness — and the mother, in the depth of her suspense and terror, sat like a queen inspected on all sides, and with possible traitors round her, but resolute and self-commanding in her extremity, determined at least to be true to herself.

"Arthur, can you think where to go?" she said, after a little interval, almost under her breath.

"To London first," said Vincent – "to inquire after – *him*, curse him! don't say anything, mother – I am only a man after all. Then, according to the information I get. – God help us! – if I don't get back before another Sunday—"

Mrs Vincent gave a convulsive start, which shook the table against which she was leaning, and fell to shivering as if in a fit of ague. "Oh, Arthur, Arthur, what are you saying? Another Sunday!" she exclaimed, with a cry of despair. To live another day seemed impossible in that horror. But self-restraint was natural to the woman who had been, as she said, a minister's wife for thirty years. She clasped her hands tight, and took up her burden again. "I will see Mr Beecher when he comes, dear, and – and speak to him," she said, with a sigh, "and I will see the Tozers and – and your people, Arthur; and if it should be God's will to keep us so long in suspense, if – if – I can keep alive, dear, I may be of some use. Oh, Arthur, Arthur, the Lord have pity upon us! if my darling comes back, will she come here or will she go home? Don't you think she will come here? If I go back to Lonsdale, I will not be able to rest for thinking she is at Carlingford; and if I stay – oh, Arthur, where do you think Susan will go to? She might be afraid to see you, and think you would be angry, but she never could distrust her poor mother, who was the first to put her in danger; and to think of my dear child going either there or here, and not finding me, Arthur! My dear, you are not eating anything. You can never go through it all without some support. For my sake, try to eat a little, my own boy; and oh, Arthur, what must I do?"

"These Tozers and people will worry you to death if you stay here," said the minister, with an impatient sigh, as he

thought of his own difficulties; "but I must not lose time by
going back with you to Lonsdale, and you must not travel
by yourself, and this is more in the way, whatever happens.
Send word to Lonsdale that you are to have a message by
telegraph immediately – without a moment's loss of time –
if she comes back."

"You might say *when*, Arthur, not *if*," said his mother,
with a little flash of tender resentment – then she gave
way for the moment, and leaned her head against his arm
and held him fast with that pressure and close clasp which
spoke more than any words. When she raised her pale
face again, it was to entreat him once more to eat. "Try to
take something, if it were only a mouthful, for Susan's
sake," pleaded the widow. Her son made a dismal attempt
as she told him. Happy are the houses that have not seen
such dreadful pretences of meals where tears were the
only possible food! When she saw him fairly engaged in
this desperate effort to take "some support," the poor
mother went away and wrote a crafty female letter, which
she brought to him to read. He would have smiled at it
had the occasion been less tragic. It was addressed to the
minister of "the connection" at Lonsdale, and set forth
how she was detained at Carlingford by some family
affairs – how Susan was visiting friends and travelling, and
her mother was not sure where to address her – and how it
would be the greatest favour if he would see Williams
at the cottage, and have a message despatched to Mrs
Vincent the moment her daughter returned. "Do you
think it would be better to confide in him a little, and tell
him what anxiety we are in?" said Vincent, when he read
this letter. His mother took it out of his hands with a little
cry.

"Oh, Arthur, though you are her brother, you are only a
man, and don't understand," cried Mrs Vincent. "Nobody
must have anything to say about my child. If she comes
tonight, she will come here," continued the poor mother,
pausing instinctively once more to listen; "she might have

been detained somewhere; she may come at any moment – at any moment, Arthur dear! Though these telegraphs frighten me, and look as if they must bring bad news, I will send you word directly when my darling girl comes; but oh, my dear, though it is dreadful to send you away, and to think of your travelling to-morrow and breaking the Sunday, and very likely your people hearing it – oh, Arthur, God knows better, and will not blame you: and if you will not take anything more to eat, you should not lose time, my dearest boy! Don't look at me, Arthur – don't say good-bye. Perhaps you may meet her before you leave – perhaps you may not need to go away. Oh, Arthur dear, don't lose any more time!"

"It is scarcely time for the train yet," said the minister, getting up slowly; "the world does not care, though our hearts are breaking; it keeps its own time. Mother, good-bye. God knows what may have happened before I see you again."

"Oh, Arthur, say nothing – say nothing! What can happen but my child to come home?" cried his mother, as he clasped her hands and drew her closer to him. She leaned against her son's breast, which heaved convulsively, for one moment, and no more. She did not look at him as he went slowly out of the room, leaving her to the unspeakable silence and solitude in which every kind of terror started up and crept about. But before Vincent had left the house his mother's anxiety and hope were once more excited to passion. Some one knocked and entered; there was a sound of voices and steps on the stair audibly approaching this room in which she sat with her fears. But it was not Susan; it was a young man of Arthur's own age, with his travelling-bag in his hand, and his sermons in his pocket. He had no suspicion that the sight of him brought the chill of despair to her heart as he went up to shake hands with his friend's mother. "Vincent would not come back to introduce me," said Mr Beecher, "but he said I should find you here. I have known him many years, and it is a great pleasure to make your acquaintance. Sometimes he used to show me your letters years ago. Is Miss Vincent with you? It is pleasant to get out of town for a little, even though one has to preach; and they will all be interested in 'Omerton to hear how Vincent is getting on. Made quite a commotion in the world, they say, with these lectures of his. I always knew he would made an 'it if he had fair-play."

"I am very glad to see you," said Mrs Vincent. "I have just come up from Lonsdale, and everything is in a confusion. When people grow old," said the poor widow, busying herself in collecting the broken pieces of bread which Arthur had crumbled down by way of pretending to eat, "they feel fatigue and being put out of their way more than they ought. What can I get for you? will you have a glass of wine, and dinner as soon as it can be ready? My son had to go away."

"Preaching somewhere?" asked the lively Mr Beecher.

"N-no; he has some – private business to attend to," said Mrs Vincent, with a silent groan in her heart.

"Ah! – going to be married, I suppose?" said the man from 'Omerton; "that's the natural consequence after a man gets a charge. Miss Vincent is not with you, I think you said? I'll take a glass of wine, thank you; and I hear one of the flock has sent over to ask me to tea – Mr Tozer, a leading man, I believe, among our people here," added Mr Beecher, with a little complacence. "It's very pleasant when a congregation is hospitable and friendly. When a pastor's popular, you see, it always reacts upon his brethren. May I ask if you are going to Mr Tozer's to tea to-night?"

"Oh, no," faltered poor Mrs Vincent, whom prudence kept from adding, "heaven forbid!" "They – did not know I was here," she continued, faintly, turning away to ring the bell. Mr Beecher, who flattered himself on his penetration, nodded slightly when her back was turned. "Jealous that they've asked me," said the preacher, with a lively thrill of human satisfaction. How was he to know the

blank of misery, the wretched feverish activity of thought
that possessed that mild little woman, as she gave her
orders about the removal of the tray, and the dinner which
already was being prepared for the stranger? But the lively
young man from 'Omerton perceived that there was something wrong. Vincent's black looks when he met him at the
door, and the exceeding promptitude of that invitation to
tea, were two and two which he could put together. He
concluded directly that the pastor, though he had made "an
'it," was not found to suit the connection in Carlingford; and
that possibly another candidate for Salem might be required
ere long. "I would not injure Vincent for the world," he said
to himself, "but if he does not 'it it, I might." The thought
was not unpleasant. Accordingly, while Vincent's mother
kept her place there in the anguish of her heart, thinking
that perhaps, even in this dreadful extremity, she might be
able to do something for Arthur with his people, and
conciliate the authorities, her guest was thinking, if Vincent
were to leave Carlingford, what a pleasant distance from
town it was, and how very encouraging of the Tozers to ask
him to tea. It might come to something more than preaching
for a friend; and if Vincent did not "'it it," and a change
were desirable, nobody could tell what might happen. All
this smiling fabric the stranger built upon the discomposed
looks of the Vincents and Phoebe's invitation to tea.

To sit by him and keep up a little attempt at conversation
– to superintend his dinner, and tell him what she knew
of Salem and her son's lectures, and his success generally,
as became the minister's mother – was scarcely so hard as to
be left afterwards, when he went out to Tozer's, all alone
once more with the silence, with the sounds outside, with
the steps that seemed to come to the door, and the carriages
that paused in the street, all sending dreadful thrills of hope
through poor Mrs Vincent's worn-out heart. Happily, her
faculties were engaged by those frequent and oft-repeated
tremors. In the fever of her anxiety, she did not enter into
the darker question where Susan might really be, and what

had befallen the unhappy girl. Half an hour after Mr Beecher
left her, Phoebe Tozer came in, affectionate and anxious,
driving the wretched mother almost wild by the sound of
her step and the apparition of her young-womanhood, to
beg and pray that Mrs Vincent would join them at their
"friendly tea." "And so this is Mr Vincent's room," said
Phoebe, with a bashful air; "it feels so strange to be here!
and you must be *so* dull when he is gone. Oh, do come, and
let us try to amuse you a little; though I am sure none of us
could ever be such good company as the minister – oh, not
half, nor quarter!" cried Phoebe. Even in the midst of her
misery, the mother was woman enough to think that Phoebe
showed too much interest in the minister. She declined the
invitation with gentle distinctness. She did not return the
enthusiastic kiss which was bestowed upon her. "I am very
tired, thank you," said Mrs Vincent. "On Monday, if all is
well, I will call to see your mamma. I hope you will not
catch cold coming out in this thin dress. I am sure it was
very kind of you; but I am very tired to-night. On – Monday."
Alas, Monday! could this horror last so long, and she not
die? or would all be well by that time, and Susan in her
longing arms? The light went out of her eyes, and the breath
from her heart, as that dreadful question stared her in the
face. She scarcely saw Phoebe's withdrawal; she lay back in
her chair in a kind of dreadful trance, till those stumbling
steps and passing carriages began again, and roused her
back into agonised life and bootless hope.

CHAPTER XIX.

Vincent had shaken hands with his friend at the door,
and hurried past, saying something about losing the train,
in order to escape conversation; but, with the vivid per-

ceptions of excitement, he heard the delivery of Phoebe's
message, and saw the complacence with which the
Homerton man regarded the invitation which had anticipated his arrival. The young Nonconformist had enough
to think of as he took his way once more to the railway,
and tea at Mrs Tozer's was anything but attractive to
his own fancy; yet in the midst of his wretchedness he
could not overcome the personal sense of annoyance which
this trifling incident produced. It came like a prick of
irritating pain, to aggravate the dull horror which throbbed
through him. He despised himself for being able to think
of it at all, but at the same time it came back to him,
darting unawares again and again into his thoughts.
Little as he cared for the entertainments and attention
of his flock, he was conscious of a certain exasperation
in discovering their eagerness to entertain another.
He was disgusted with Phoebe for bringing the message,
and disgusted with Beecher for looking pleased to receive
it. "Probably he thinks he will supersede me," Vincent
thought, in sudden gusts of disdain now and then, with
a sardonic smile on his lip, waking up afterwards with
a thrill of deeper self-disgust, to think that anything
so insignificant had power to move him. When he plunged
off from Carlingford at last, in the early falling darkness
of the winter afternoon, and looked back upon the few
lights struggling red through the evening mists, it was
with a sense of belonging to the place where he had left
an interloper who might take his post over his head,
which, perhaps, no other possible stimulant could have
given him. He thought with a certain pang of Salem,
and that pulpit which was his own, but in which another
man should stand to-morrow, with a quickened thrill
of something that was almost jealousy; he wondered
what might be the sentiments of the connection about
his deputy – perhaps Brown and Pigeon would prefer
that florid voice to his own – perhaps Phoebe might
find the substitute more practicable than the incumbent.

Nothing before had ever made Salem so interesting to the young pastor as Beecher's complacence over that invitation to tea.

But he had much more serious matters to consider in his rapid journey. Vincent was but a man, though he was Susan's brother. He did not share those desperate hopes which afforded a kind of forlorn comfort and agony of expectation to his mother's heart. No thought that Susan would come home either to Carlingford or Lonsdale was in his mind. In what way soever the accursed villain, whom his face blanched with deadly rage to think of, had managed to get her in his power, Susan's sweet life was lost, her brother knew. He gave her up, and hoped for no deliverance. Shame had taken possession of that image which fancy kept presenting in double tenderness and brightness to him as his heart burned in the darkness. He might find her indeed; he might snatch her out of these polluting arms, and bring home the sullied lily to her mother, but never henceforward could hope or honour blossom about his sister's name. He made up his mind to this in grim misery, with his teeth clenched, and a desperation of rage and horror in his heart. But in proportion to his conviction that Susan would not return, was his eagerness to find her, and snatch her away. To think of her in horror and despair was easier than to think of her deluded and happy, as might be – as most probably was – the case. This latter possibility made Vincent frantic. He could scarcely endure the slowness of the motion which was the highest pitch of speed that skill and steam had yet made possible. No express train could travel so fast as the thoughts which went before him, dismal pioneers penetrating the most dread abysses. To think of Susan happy in her horrible downfall and ruin was more than flesh or blood could bear.

When Vincent reached town, he took his way without a moment's hesitation to the street in Piccadilly where he had once sought Mr Fordham. He approached the place

now with no precautions; he had his cab driven up to the
door, and boldly entered as soon as it was opened. The
house was dark and silent but for the light in the narrow
hall; nobody there at that dead hour, while it was still too
early for dinner. And it was not the vigilant owner of the
place, but a drowsy helper in a striped jacket, who presented
himself at the door, and replied to Vincent's inquiry for
Colonel Mildmay, that the Colonel was not at home –
never was at home at that hour – but was not unwilling to
inquire, if the gentleman would wait. Vincent put up the
collar of his coat about his ears, and stood back with eager
attention, intently alive to everything. Evidently the ruler
of the house was absent as well as the Colonel. The man
lounged to the staircase and shouted down, leaning upon
the bannisters. No aside or concealment was possible in
this perfectly easy method of communication. With an
anxiety strongly at variance with the colloquy thus going
on, and an intensification of all his faculties which only the
height of excitement could give, Vincent stood back and
listened. He heard every step that passed outside; the
pawing of the horse in the cab that waited for him,
the chance voices of the passengers, all chimed in,
without interrupting the conversation between the man
who admitted him and his fellow-servant down-stairs.

"Jim, is the Colonel at home? – he ain't, to be sure, but
we wants to know particklar. Here," in a slightly lowered
voice, "his mother's been took bad, and the parson's sent
for him. When is he agoing to be in to dinner? Ask Cookie;
she'll be sure to know."

"The Colonel ain't coming in to dinner, stoopid,"
answered the unseen interlocutor; "he ain't been here all
day. Out o' town. Couldn't you say so, instead of jabbering?
Out o' town. It's allays safe to say, and this time it's
true."

"What's he adoing of, in case the gen'leman should want
to know?" said the fellow at the head of the stair.

"After mischief," was the brief and emphatic answer.

"You come along down to your work, and let the Colonel alone."

"Any mischief in particklar?" continued the man, tossing a dirty napkin in his hand, and standing in careless contempt, with his back to the minister. "It's a pleasant way the Colonel's got, that is: any more particklars, Jim? – the gen'leman'll stand something if you'll let him know."

"Hold your noise, stoopid – it ain't no concern o'yours – my master's my master, and I ain't agoing to tell his secrets," said the voice below. Vincent had made a step forward, divided between his impulse to kick the impertinent fellow who had admitted him down-stairs, and the equally strong impulse which prompted him to offer any bribe to the witness who knew his master's secrets; but he was suddenly arrested in both by a step on the street outside, and the grating of a latch-key in the door. A long light step, firm and steady, with a certain sentiment of rapid silent progress in it. Vincent could not tell what strange fascination it was that made him turn round to watch this new-comer. The stranger's approach thrilled him vaguely, he could not tell how. Then the door opened, and a man appeared like the footstep – a very tall slight figure, stooping forward a little; a pale oval face, too long to be handsome, adorned with a long brown beard; thoughtful eyes, with a distant gleam in them, now and then flashing into sudden penetrating glances – a loose dress too light for the season, which somehow carried out all the peculiarities of the long light step, the thin sinewy form, the thoughtful softness and keenness of the eye. Even in the height of his own suspense and excitement, Vincent paused to ask himself who this could be. He came in with one sudden glance at the stranger in the hall, passed him, and calling to the man, who became on the moment respectful and attentive, asked if there were any letters. "What name, sir? – beg your pardon – my place ain't up-stairs," said the fellow. What was the name? Vincent rushed forward when he heard it, and seized the new-comer by the shoulder with the fierceness of a tiger. "Fordham!" cried the young man, with boiling rage and hatred. Next moment he had let go his grasp, and was gazing bewildered upon the calm stranger, who looked at him with merely a thoughtful inquiry in his eyes. "Fordham – at your service – do you want anything with me?" he asked, meeting with undiminished calm the young man's excited looks. This composure put a sudden curb on Vincent's passion.

"My name is Vincent," he said, restraining himself with an effort; "do you know now what I want with you? No? Am I to believe your looks or your name? If you are the man," cried the young Nonconformist, with a groan out of his distracted heart, "whom Lady Western could trust with life, to death – or if you are a fiend incarnate, making misery and ruin, you shall not escape me till I know the truth. Where is Susan? Here is where her innocent letters came – they were addressed to your name. Where is she now? Answer me! For you, as well as the rest of us, it is life or death."

"You are raving," said the stranger, keeping his awakened eyes fixed upon Vincent; "but this is easily settled. I returned from the East only yesterday. I don't know you. What was that you said about Lady— Lady— what lady? Come in: and my name? – my name has been unheard in this country, so far as I know, for ten years. Lady—? – come in and explain what you mean."

The two stood together confronting each other in the little parlour of the house, where the striped jacket quickly and humbly lighted the gas. Vincent's face, haggard with misery and want of rest, looked wild in that sudden light. The stranger stood opposite him, leaning forward with a strange eagerness and inquiry. He did not care for Vincent's anxiety, who was a stranger to him; he cared only to hear again that name – Lady—? He had heard it already, or he would have been less curious; he wanted to understand this wonderful message wafted to him out of his old life. What did it matter to Herbert Fordham, used to the danger of the deserts and mountains, whether it was a maniac who brought this chance seed of a new existence to his wondering heart?

"A man called Fordham has gone into my mother's house," said Vincent, fixing his eyes upon those keen but visionary orbs which were fixed on him — "and won the love of my sister. She wrote to him here — to this house; yesterday he carried her away, to her shame and destruction. Answer me," cried the young man, making another fierce step forward, growing hoarse with passion, and clenching his hands in involuntary rage — "was it you?"

"There are other men called Fordham in existence besides me," cried the stranger, with a little irritation; then seizing his loose coat by its pockets, he shook out, with a sudden impatient motion, a cloud of letters from these receptacles. "Because you seem in great excitement and distress, and yet are not, as far as I can judge," said Mr Fordham, with another glance at Vincent, "mad, I will take pains to satisfy you. Look at my letters; their dates and post-marks will convince you that what you say is simply impossible, for that I was not here."

Vincent clutched and took them up with a certain blind eagerness, not knowing what he did. He did not look at them to satisfy himself that what Fordham said was true. A wild, half-conscious idea that there must be something in them about Susan possessed him; he saw neither dates nor post-marks, though he held them up to the light, as if they were proofs of something. "No," he said at last, "it was not you — it was that fiend Mildmay, Rachel Russell's husband. Where is he? he has taken your name, and made you responsible for his devilish deeds. Help me, if you are a Christian! My sister is in his hands, curse him! Help me, for the sake of your name, to find them out. I am a stranger, and they will give me no information; but they will tell you. For God's sake, ask and let me go after them. If ever you were beholden to the help of Christian men, help me! for it is life and death!"

"Mildmay! Rachel Russell's husband? under my name?" said Mr Fordham, slowly. "I *have* been beholden to Christian men, and that for very life. You make a strong appeal: who are you that are so desperate? and what was that you said?"

"I am Susan Vincent's brother," said the young Nonconformist; "that is enough. This devil has taken your name; help me, for heaven's sake, to find him out!"

"Mildmay? – devil? yes, he is a devil! you are right enough: I owe him no love," said Fordham; then he paused and turned away, as if in a momentary perplexity. "To help that villain to his reward would be a man's duty; but," said the stranger, with a heavy sigh, upon which his words came involuntarily, spoken to himself, breathing out of his heart – "he is *her* brother, devil though he is!"

"Yes!" cried Vincent, with passion, "he is *her* brother." When he had said the words, the young man groaned aloud. Partly he forgot that this man, who looked upon him with so much curiosity, was the man who had brought tears and trembling to Her; partly he remembered it, and forgot his jealousy for the moment in a bitter sense of fellow-feeling. In his heart he could see her, waving her hand to him out of her passing carriage, with that smile for which he would have risked his life. Oh, hideous fate! it was *her* brother whom he was bound to pursue to the end of the world. He buried his face in his hands, in a momentary madness of anguish and passion. Susan floated away like a mist from that burning personal horizon. The love and the despair were too much for Vincent. The hope that had always been impossible was frantic now. When he recovered himself, the stranger whom he had thus unawares taken into his confidence was regarding him haughtily from the other side of the table, with a fiery light in his thoughtful eyes. Suspicion, jealousy, resentment, had begun to sparkle in those orbs, which in repose looked so far away and lay so calm. Mr Fordham measured the haggard and worn-out young man with a look of rising dislike and animosity. He was at least ten years older than the young Nonconformist, who stood there in his wretchedness and exhaustion entirely at disadvantage, looking, in his half-clerical dress, which he had not changed for four-and-twenty hours, as different as can be conceived from the scrupulously dressed gentleman in his easy morning habiliments, which would not have been out of place in the rudest scene, yet spoke of personal nicety and high-breeding in every easy fold. Vincent himself felt the contrast with an instant flush of answering jealousy and passion. For a moment the two glanced at each other, conscious rivals, though not a word of explanation had been spoken. It was Mr Fordham who spoke first, and in a somewhat hasty and imperious tone.

"You spoke of a lady – Lady Western, I think. As it was you yourself who sought this interview, I may be pardoned if I stumble on a painful subject," he said, with some bitterness. "I presume you know that lady by your tone – was it she who sent you to me? No? Then I confess your appeal to a total stranger seems to me singular, to say the least of it? Where is your proof that Colonel Mildmay has used my name?"

"Proof is unnecessary," said Vincent, firing with kindred resentment; "I have told you the fact, but I do not press my appeal, though it was made to your honour. Pardon me for intruding on you so long. I have now no time to lose."

He turned away, stung in his hasty youthfulness by the appearance of contempt. He would condescend to ask no farther. When he was once more outside the parlour, he held up the half-sovereign, which he had kept ready in his hand, to the slovenly fellow in the striped jacket. "Twice as much if you will tell where Colonel Mildmay is gone," he said, hurriedly. The man winked and nodded and pointed outside, but before Vincent could leave the room a hasty summons came from the parlour which he had just left. Then Mr Fordham appeared at the door.

"If you will wait I will make what inquiries I can," said the stranger, with distant courtesy and seriousness. "Excuse me – I was taken by surprise: but if you have suffered injury under my name, it is my business to vindicate myself. Come in. If you will take my advice, you will rest and refresh yourself before you pursue a man with all his wits about him. Wait for me here and I will bring you what information I can. You don't suppose I mean to play you false?" he added, with prompt irritation, seeing that Vincent hesitated and did not at once return to the room. It was no relenting of heart that moved him to make this offer. It was with no softening of feeling that the young Nonconformist went back again and accepted it. They met like enemies, each on his honour. Mr Fordham hastened out to acquit himself of that obligation. Vincent threw himself into a chair, and waited for the result.

It was the first moment of rest and quiet he had known since the morning of the previous day, when he and his mother, alarmed but comparatively calm, had gone to see Mrs Hilyard, who was now, like himself, wandering, with superior knowledge and more desperate passion, on the same track. To sit in this house in the suspicious silence, hearing the distant thrill of voices which might guide or foil him in his search; to think who it was whom he had engaged to help him in his terrible mission; to go over again in distracted gleams and snatches the brief little circle of time which had brought all this about, the group of figures into which his life had been absorbed, – rapt the young man into a maze of excited musing, which his exhausted frame at once dulled and intensified. They seemed to stand round him, with their faces so new, yet so familiar – that needlewoman with her emphatic mouth – Mildmay – Lady Western – last of all, this man, who was not Susan's lover – not Susan's destroyer – but a man to be trusted "with life – to death!" Vincent put up his hands to put away from him that wonderful circle of strangers who shut out everything else in the world – even his own life – from his eyes. What were they to him? he asked, with an unspeakable bitterness in his heart. Heaven help him! they were the real creatures for whom life and the world were made – he and his poor Susan the shadows to be absorbed into, and under them; and then, with a wild, bitter, hopeless rivalry, the mind of the poor Dissenting minister came round once more to the immediate contact in which he stood – to Fordham, in whose name his sister's life had been shipwrecked, and by whom, as he divined with cruel foresight, his own hopeless love and dreams were to be made an end of. Well! what better could they come to? but it was hard to think of him, with his patrician looks, his negligent grace, his conscious superiority, and to submit to accept assistance from him even in his sorest need. These thoughts were in his mind when Mr Fordham hastily re-entered the room. A thrill of excitement now was in the long, lightly-falling step, which already Vincent, with the keen ear of rivalry almost as quick as that of love, could recognise as it approached. The stranger was disturbed out of his composure. He shut the door and came up to the young man, who rose to meet him, with a certain excited repugnance and attraction much like Vincent's own feelings.

"You are quite right," he said, hastily; "I find letters have been coming here for some months, addressed as if to me, which Mildmay has had. The man of the house is absent, or I should never have heard of it. I don't know what injury he may have done *you;* but this is an insult I don't forgive. Stop! I have every reason to believe that he has gone," said Fordham, growing darkly red, "to a house of mine, to confirm this slander upon me. To prove that I am innocent of all share of it – I don't mean to you – you believe me, I presume?" he said, with a haughty sudden pause, looking straight in Vincent's face – "I will go——" Here Mr Fordham stopped again, and once more looked at Vincent with that indescribable mixture of curiosity, dislike, resentment, and interest, which the eyes of the young Nonconformist repaid him fully, – "with you – if you choose. At all events, I will go to-night – to Fordham, where the scoundrel is. I cannot permit it to be believed for an hour that it is I who have done this villany. The lady you mentioned, I presume, knows?" – he added, sharply – "knows what has happened, and whom you suspect? This must be set right at once. If you choose, we can go together."

"Where is the place?" asked Vincent, without any answer to this proposition.

Fordham looked at him with a certain haughty offence: he had made the offer as though it were a very disagreeable expedient, but resented instantly the tacit neglect of it shown by his companion.

"In Northumberland – seven miles from the railway," he said, with a kind of gratification. "Once more, I say, you can go with me if you will, which may serve us both. I don't pretend to be disinterested. My object is to have my reputation clear of this, at all events. Your object, I presume, is to get to your journey's end as early as may be. Choose for yourself. Fordham is between Durham and Morpeth – seven miles from Lamington station. You will find difficulty in getting there by yourself, and still greater difficulty in getting admission; and I repeat, if you choose it, you can go with me – or I will accompany you, if that pleases you better. Either way, there is little time to consider. The train goes at eight or nine o'clock – I forget which. I have not dined. What shall you do?"

"Thank you," said Vincent. It was perhaps a greater effort to him to overcome his involuntary repugnance than it was to the stranger beside him, who had all the superior ease of superior rank and age. The Nonconformist turned away his eyes from his new companion, and made a pretence of consulting his watch. "I will take advantage of your offer," he said, coldly, withdrawing a step with instinctive reserve. On these diplomatic terms their engagement was made. Vincent declined to share the dinner which the other offered him, as one duellist might offer hospitality to another. He drove away in his hansom, with a restrained gravity of excitement, intent upon the hour's rest and the meal which were essential to make him anything like a match for this unexpected travelling companion. Every morsel he attempted to swallow when in Carlingford under his mother's anxious eyes, choked the excited young man; but now he ate with a certain stern appetite, and even snatched an hour's sleep and changed his dress, under this novel stimulant. Poor Susan, for whom her mother sat hopelessly watching with many a thrill of agony at home! Poor lost one, far away in the depths of the strange country in the night and darkness! Whether despair and horror enveloped her, or delirious false happiness and delusion, again she stood secondary even in her brother's thoughts. He tried to imagine it was she who occupied his mind, and wrote a hurried note to his mother to that purport; but with guilt and self-disgust, knew in his own mind how often another shadow stood between him and his lost sister – a shadow bitterly veiled from him, turning its sweetness and its smiles upon the man who was about to help him, against whom he gnashed his teeth in the anguish of his heart.

CHAPTER XX.

THEY were but these two in the railway-carriage; no other passenger broke the silent conflict of their companionship. They sat in opposite corners, as far apart as their space would permit, but on opposite sides of the carriage as well, so that one could not move without betraying his every movement to the other's keen observation. Each of them kept possession of a window, out of which he gazed into the visible blackness of the winter night. Two or three times in the course of the long darksome chilly journey, a laconic remark was made by one or the other with a deadly steadiness, and gravity, and facing of each other, as they spoke; but no further intercourse took place between them. When they first met, Fordham had made an attempt to draw his fellow-traveller into some repetition of that first passionate speech which had secured his own attention to Vincent; but the young Nonconformist perceived the attempt, and resented it with sullen offence and gloom. He took the stranger's indifference to *his* trouble, and undisguised and simple purpose of acquitting himself, as somehow an affront, though he could not have explained how it was so; and this notwithstanding his own consciousness of realising this silent conflict and rivalry with Fordham, even more deeply in his own person than he did the special misery which had befallen his house. Through the sullen silent midnight the train dashed on, the faint light flickering in the unsteady carriage, the two speechless figures, with eyes averted, watching each other through all the ice-cold hours. It was morning when they got out, cramped and frozen, at the little station, round which miles and miles of darkness, a black unfathomable ocean, seemed to lie – and which shone there with its little red sparkle of light among its wild waste of moors like the one touch of human life in a desert. They had a dreary hour to wait in the little wooden room by the stifling fire, divided between the smothering atmosphere within and the thrilling cold without, before a conveyance could be procured for them, in which they set out shivering over the seven darkling miles between them and Fordham. Vincent stood apart in elaborate indifference and carelessness, when the squire was recognised and done homage to; and Fordham's eye, even while lighted up by the astonished delight of the welcome given him by the driver of the vehicle who first found him out, turned instinctively to the Mordecai in the corner who took no heed. No conversation between them diversified the black road along which they drove. Mr Fordham took refuge in the driver, whom he asked all those questions about the people of the neighbourhood which are so interesting to the inhabitants of a district and so wearisome to strangers. Vincent, who sat in the dog-cart with his face turned the other way, suffered himself to be carried through the darkness by the powerful horse, which made his own seat a somewhat perilous one, with nothing so decided in his thoughts as a dumb sense of opposition and resistance. The general misery of his mind and body – the sense that all the firmament around him was black as this sky – the restless wretchedness that oppressed his heart – all concentrated into conscious rebellion and enmity. He seemed to himself at war not only with Mr Fordham who was helping him, but with God and life.

Morning was breaking when they reached the house. The previous day, as it dawned chilly over the world, had revealed his mother's ashy face to Vincent as they came up from Lonsdale with sickening thrills of hope that Susan might still be found unharmed. Here was another horror of a new day rising, the third since Susan disappeared into that darkness which was now lifting in shuddering mists from the bleak country round. Was she here in her shame, the lost creature? As he began to ask himself that question, what cruel spirit was it that drew aside a veil of years, and showed to the unhappy brother that prettiest dancing figure, all smiles and sunshine, sweet honour and hope? Poor lost child! what sweet eyes, lost in an unfathomable light of joy and confidence – what truthful looks, which feared no evil! Just as they came in sight of that hidden house, where perhaps the hidden, stolen creature lay in the darkness, the brightest picture flashed back upon Vincent's eyes with an indescribably subtle anguish of contrast; how he had come up to her once

– the frank, fair Saxon girl – in the midst of a group of gypsies – how he found she had done a service to one of them, and the whole tribe did homage – how he had asked, "Where you not afraid, Susan?" and how the girl had looked up at him with undoubting eyes, and answered, "Afraid, Arthur? – yes, of wild beasts if I saw them, not of men and women." Oh Heaven! – and here he was going to find her in shame and ruin, hidden away in this secret place! He sprang to the ground before the vehicle had stopped, jarring his frozen limbs. He could not bear to be second now and follow to the dread discovery which should be his alone. He rushed through the shrubbery without asking any question, and began to knock violently at the door. What did it matter to him though its master was there, looking on with folded arms and unsympathetic face? Natural love rushed back upon the young man's heart. He settled with himself, as he stood waiting, now he would wrap her in his coat, and hurry her away without letting any cold eye fall upon the lost creature. Oh, hard and cruel fate! oh, wonderful heart-breaking indifference of Heaven! The Innocents are murdered, and God looks on like a man, and does not interfere. Such were the broken thoughts of misery – half-thought, half-recollection – that ran through Vincent's mind as he knocked at the echoing door.

"Eugh! you may knock, and better knock, and I'se undertake none comes at the ca'," said the driver, not without a little complacence. "I tell the Squire, as there han't been man nor woman here for ages; but he don't believe me. She's deaf as a post, is the housekeeper; and her daughter, she's more to do nor hear when folks is wanting in – and this hour in the morning! But canny, canny, man! he'll have the door staved in if we all stand by and the Squire don't interfere."

Vincent paid no attention to the remonstrance – which, indeed, he only remembered afterwards, and did not hear at the moment. The house was closely shut in with trees,

which made the gloom of morning darker here than in the
open road, and increased the aspect of secrecy which had
impressed the young man's excited imagination. While he
went on knocking, Fordham alighted and went round to
another entrance, where he too began to knock, calling at
the same time to the unseen keepers of the place. After a
while some answering sounds became audible – first the
feeble yelping of an asthmatic dog, then a commotion up-
stairs, and at last a window was thrown up, and a female
head enveloped in a shawl looked out. "Eh, whae are ye?
vagabond villains – and this a gentleman's house!" cried a
cracked voice. "I'll let the Squire know – I'll rouse the
man-servants. Tramps! what are you wanting here?" The
driver of the dogcart took up the response well pleased.
He announced the arrival of the Squire, to the profound
agitation of the house, which showed itself in a variety of
scuffling sounds and the wildest exclamations of wonder.
Vincent leaned his throbbing head against the door, and
waited in a dull fever of impatience and excitement, as
these noises gradually came nearer. When the door itself
was reached and hasty hands began to unfasten its bolts,
Susan's brother pressed alone upon the threshold, forgetful and indifferent that the master of the house stood
behind, watching him with close and keen observation.
He forgot whose house it was, and all about his companion.
What were such circumstances to him, as he approached
the conclusion of his search, and thought every moment to
hear poor Susan's cry of shame and terror? He made one
hasty stride into the hall when the door was open, and
looked round him with burning eyes. The wonder with
which the women inside looked at him, their outcry of
disappointment and anger when they found him a stranger,
coming first as he did, and throwing the Squire entirely
into the shade, had no effect upon the young man, who
was by this time half frantic. He went up to the elder
woman and grasped her by the arm. "Where is she? show
me the way!" he said, hoarsely, unable to utter an un-

necessary word. He held the terrified woman fast, and thrust her before him, he could not tell where, into the unknown house, all dark and miserable in the wretchedness of the dawn. "Show me the way!" he cried, with his broken hoarse voice. A confused and inarticulate scene ensued, which Vincent remembered afterwards only like a dream; the woman's scream – the interference of Fordham, upon whom his fellow-traveller turned with sudden fury – the explanation to which he listened without understanding it, and which at first roused him to wild rage as a pretence and falsehood. But even Vincent at last, struggling into soberer consciousness as the day broadened ever chiller and more grey over the little group of strange faces round him, came to understand and make out that both Fordham and he had been deceived. Nobody had been there – letters addressed both to Fordham himself, and to Colonel Mildmay, had been for some days received; but these, it appeared, were only a snare laid to withdraw the pursuers from the right scent. Not to be convinced, in the sullen stupor of his excitement, Vincent followed Fordham into all the gloomy corners of the neglected house – seeing everything without knowing what he saw. But one thing was plain beyond the possibility of doubt, that Susan was not there.

"I am to blame for this fruitless journey," said Fordham with a touch of sympathy more than he had yet exhibited; "perhaps personal feeling had too much share in it; now I trust you will have some breakfast before you set out again. So far as my assistance can be of any use to you—"

"I thank you," said Vincent, coldly; "it is a business in which a stranger can have no interest. You have done all you cared to do," continued the young man, hastily gathering up the overcoat which he had thrown down on entering; "you have vindicated yourself – I will trouble you no further. If I encounter any one interested in Mr Fordham," he concluded, with difficulty and bitterness, but with a natural generosity which, even in his despair,

he could not belie, "I will do him justice." He made an
abrupt end, and turned away, not another word being
possible to him. Fordham, not without a sentiment of
sympathy, followed him to the door, urging refreshment,
rest, even his own society, upon his companion of the
night. Vincent's face, more and more haggard – his
exhausted excited air – the poignant wretchedness of his
youth, on which the older man looked, not without remi-
niscences, awoke the sympathy and compassion of the
looker-on, even in the midst of less kindly emotions. But
Fordham's sympathy was intolerable to poor Vincent. He
took his seat with a sullen weariness once more by the
talkative driver, who gave him an unheeded history of all
the Fordhams. As they drove along the bleak moorland
road, an early church-bell tingled into the silence, and
struck, with horrible iron echoes, upon the heart of the
minister of Salem. Sunday morning! Life all disordered,
incoherent, desperate – all its usages set at nought and
duties left behind. Nothing could have added the final
touch of conscious derangement and desperation like the
sound of that bell; all his existence and its surroundings
floated about him in feverish clouds, as it came to his mind
that this wild morning, hysterical with fatigue and excitement, was the Sunday – the day of his special labours – the
central point of all his former life. Chaos gloomed around
the poor minister, who, in his misery, was human enough
to remember Beecher's smile and Phoebe Tozer's invitation, and to realise how all the "Chapel folks" would
compare notes, and contrast their own pastor, to whom
they had become accustomed, with the new voice from
Homerton, which, half in pride and half in disgust,
Vincent acknowledged to be more in their way. He
fancied he could see them all collecting into their mean
pews, prepared to inaugurate the "coorse" for which
Tozer had struggled, and the offence upon their faces
when the minister's absence was known, and the sharp
stimulus which that offence would give to their appreciation

of the new preacher – all this, while he was driving over the bleak Northumberland wilds, with the cutting wind from the hills in his face, and the church-bell in his distracted ear, breaking the Sunday! Not a bright spot, so far as he could perceive, was anywhere around him, in earth, or sky, or sea.

Sunday night! – once more the church-bells, the church-going groups, the floating world, which he had many a time upbraided from the pulpit, seeking its pleasure. But it was in London now, where he stood in utter exhaustion but incapable of rest, now knowing where to turn. Then the thought occurred to him that something might be learned at the railway stations of a party which few people could see without remarking it. He waited till the bustle of arrival was over, and then began to question the porters. One after another shook his head, and had nothing to say. But the men were interested, and gathered in a little knot round him, trying what they could recollect, with the ready humanity of their class. "I'd speak to the detective police, sir, if I was you," suggested one; "it's them as finds out all that happens nowadays." Then a little gleam of light penetrated the darkness. One man began to recall a light-haired gentleman with a mustache, and two ladies, who "went off suddenly in a cab, with no luggage." "An uncommon swell he did look," said the porter, instinctively touching his cap to Vincent, on the strength of the connection; "and, my eyes! she was a beauty, that one in the blue veil. It was – let me see – Wednesday night; no – not Wednesday – that day as the train was an hour late – Friday afternoon to be sure. It was me as called the cab, and I won't deny as the gen'leman *was* a gen'leman. Went to the London Bridge station, sir; Dover line; no luggage; I took particular notice at the time, though it went out o' my head first minute as you asked me. – Cab, sir? Yes. Here you are – here's the last on the stand. – London Bridge station, Dover line."

Vincent took no time to inquire further. In the

impatience of his utter weariness and wretchedness, he seized on this slight clue, and went off at once to follow it out. London Bridge station! – what a world swarmed in those streets through which the anxious minister took his way, far too deeply absorbed in himself to think of the flood of souls that poured past him. The station was in wild bustle and commotion; a train just on the eve of starting, and late passengers dashing towards it with nervous speed. Vincent followed the tide instinctively, and stood aside to watch the long line of carriages set in motion. He was not thinking of what he saw; his whole mind was set upon the inquiry, which, as soon as that object of universal interest was gone, he could set on foot among the officials who were clanging the doors, and uttering all the final shrieks of departure. Now the tedious line glides into gradual motion. Good Heaven! what was that? the flash of a match, a sudden gleam upon vacant cushions, the profile of a face, high-featured, with the thin light locks and shadowy mustache he knew so well, standing out for a moment in aquiline distinctiveness against the moving space. Vincent rushed forward with a hoarse shout, which scared the crowd around him. He threw himself upon the moving train with a desperate attempt to seize and stop it but only to be himself seized by the frantic attendants, who caught him with a dozen hands. The travellers in the later carriages were startled by the commotion. Some of them rose and looked out with surprised looks; he saw them all as they glided past, though the passage was instantaneous. Saw them all! Yes; who was that, last of all, at the narrow window of a second-class carriage, who looked out with no surprise, but with a horrible composure in her white face, and recognised him with a look which chilled him to stone? He stood passive in the hands of the men, who had been struggling to hold him, after he encountered those eyes; he shuddered with a sudden horror, which made the crowd gather closer, believing him a maniac. Now it was gone into the black night, into the chill space, carrying a hundred innocent souls and light hearts, and among them deadly crime and vengeance – the doomed man and his executioner. His very heart shuddered in his breast as he made a faltering effort to explain himself, and get free from the crowd which thought him mad. That sight quenched the curses on his own lips, paled the fire in his heart. To see her dogging his steps, with her dreadful relentless promise in her eyes, overwhelmed Vincent, who a moment before had thrilled with all the rage of a man upon whom this villain had brought the direst shame and calamity. He could have dashed him under those wheels, plunged him into any mad destruction, in the first passionate whirl of his thoughts on seeing him again; but to see Her behind following after – pale with her horrible composure, a conscious Death tracking his very steps – drove Vincent back with a sudden paralysing touch. He stood chilled and horror-stricken in the crowd, which watched and wondered at him: he drew himself feebly out of their detaining circle, and went and sat down on the nearest seat he could find, like a man who had been stunned by some unexpected blow. He was not impatient when he heard how long he must wait before he could follow them. It was a relief to wait, to recover his breath, to realise his own position once more. That dreadful sight, diabolical and out of nature, had driven the very life-blood out of his heart.

As he sat, flung upon his bench in utter exhaustion and feebleness, stunned and stupified, leaning his aching head in his hands, and with many curious glances thrown at him by the bystanders, some of whom were not sure that he ought to be suffered to go at large, Vincent became sensible that some one was plucking at his sleeve, and sobbing his name. It was some time before he became aware that those weeping accents were addressed to him; some time longer before he began to think he had heard the voice before, and was so far moved as to look up. When he did raise his head it was with a violent start that he saw a little rustic figure, energetically, but with tears, appealing to him, whom his bewildered faculties slowly made out to be Mary, his mother's maid, whom Susan had taken with her when she left Lonsdale. As soon as he recognised her he sprang up, restored to himself with the first gleam of real hope which had yet visited him. "My sister is here!" he cried, almost with joy. Mary made no answer but by a despairing outbreak of tears.

"Oh no, Mr Arthur; no – oh no, no! never no more!" cried poor Mary, when she found her voice. "It's all been deceitfulness and lyin' and falsehood, and it ain't none o' her doing – oh no, no, Mr Arthur, no! – but now she's got nobody to stand by her, for he took and brought me up this very day; oh, don't lose no time! – he took and brought me up, pretending it was to show me the way, and he sent me right off, Mr Arthur, and she don't know no more nor a baby, and he'll take her off over the seas this very night – he will; for I had it of his own man. She's written letters to her Ma, Mr Arthur, but I don't think as they were ever took to the post; and he makes believe they're a-going to be married, and he'll have her off to France to-night. Oh, Mr Arthur, Mr Arthur, don't lose no time. They're at a 'otel. Look you here – here's the name as I wrote down on a bit o' paper to make sure; and oh, Mr Arthur, mind what I say, and don't lose no time!"

"But Susan – Susan – what of her?" cried her brother, unconsciously clutching at the girl's arm.

Mary burst into another flood of tears. She hid her face, and cried with storms of suppressed sobs. The young man rose up pale and stern from his seat, without asking another question. He took the crumpled paper out of her hand, put some money into it, and in few words directed her to go to his mother at Carlingford. What though the sight of her would break his mother's heart – what did it matter? Hearts were made to be broken, trodden on, killed – so be it! Pale and fierce, with eyes burning red in his throbbing head, he too went on, a second Murder,

after the first which had preceded him in the shape of the
Carlingford needlewoman. The criminal who escaped two
such avengers must bear a charmed life.

CHAPTER XXI.

Mrs Vincent rose from the uneasy bed, where she
had not slept, upon that dreadful Sunday morning, with
feelings which it would be vain to attempt any description
of. Snatches of momentary sleep more dreadful than
wakefulness had fallen upon her during the awful night –
moments of unconsciousness which plunged her into a
deeper horror still, and from which she started thinking
she heard Susan call. Had Susan called, had Susan come,
in any dreadful plight of misery, her mother thought she
could have borne it; but she could not, yet did, bear this,
with the mingled passion and patience of a woman; one
moment rising up against the intolerable, the next sitting
down dumb and steadfast before that terrible necessity
which could not be resisted. She got up in the dim wintry
morning with all that restless anguish in her heart, and
took out her best black silk dress, and a clean cap to
go under her bonnet. She offered a sacrifice and burnt-
offering as she dressed herself in her snow-white cuffs,
and composed her trim little figure into its Sunday neatness; for the minister's mother must go to chapel this
dreadful day. No whisper of the torture she was enduring
must breathe among the flock – nothing could excuse her
from attending Salem, seeing her son's people, and hearing
Mr Beecher preach, and holding up Arthur's standard at
this dangerous crisis of the battle. She felt she was pale
when she came into the sitting-room, but comforted herself

with thinking that nobody in Salem knew that by nature she had a little tender winter bloom upon her face, and was not usually so downcast and heavy-eyed. Instinctively she rearranged the breakfast-table as she waited for the young minister from Homerton, who was not an early riser. Mr Beecher thought it rather cheerful than otherwise when he came in somewhat late and hurried, and found her waiting by the white-covered table, with the fire bright and the tea made. He was in high spirits, as was natural. He thought Vincent was in very comfortable quarters, and had uncommonly pleasant rooms.

"Don't you think so? and one has just as great a chance of being uncomfortable as not in one's first charge," said the young preacher; "but we were all delighted to hear that Vincent had made an 'it. Liberal-minded people, I should say, if I may judge by Mr Tozer, who was uncommonly friendly last night. These sort of people are the strength of our connection – not great people, you know, but the flower of the middle classes. I am surprised you did not bring Miss Vincent with you for a little cheerful society at this time of the year."

"My daughter may perhaps come yet, before – before I leave," said Mrs Vincent, drawing herself up, with a little hauteur, as Mr Beecher thought, though in reality it was only a physical expression of that sob of agony to which she dared not give vent in audible sound.

"Oh, I thought it might be more cheerful for her in the winter," said the preacher, a little affronted that his interest in Vincent's pretty sister should be received so coldly. He was interrupted by the arrival of the post, for Carlingford was a profane country town, and had its letters on Sunday morning. The widow set herself desperately down in an arm-chair to read Arthur's letter. It made her heart beat loud with throbs so violent that a blindness came over her eyes, and her very life failed for an instant. It was very short, very assured and certain – he was going to Northumberland, where the fugitives had gone – he was going to bring Susan back. Mr Beecher over his egg watched her reading this, and saw that she grew ashy, deathly pale. It was not possible for him to keep silent, or to refrain from wondering what it was.

"Dear me, I am afraid you are ill – can I get you anything?" he said, rising from the table.

Mrs Vincent folded up her letter. "Thank you; my tea will refresh me," she said, coming back to her seat. "I did not sleep very much last night, and my head aches: when people come to my time of life," said the little woman, with a faint heroical smile, "they seldom sleep well the first few nights in a new place. I hope you rested comfortably, Mr Beecher. Mr Vincent, Arthur's dear papa, used to say that he never preached well if he did not sleep well; and I have heard other ministers say it was a very true rule."

"If that is all, I hope you will be pleased to-day," said the preacher, with a little complaisance. "I always sleep well; nothing puts me much out in that respect. Perhaps it is about time to start now? I like to have a few minutes in the vestry before going into the pulpit. You know the way, perhaps? or we can call at Mr Tozer's and get one of them to guide us."

"I think I know the way," said Mrs Vincent, faintly. It was a slight comfort, in the midst of her martyrdom, to leave the room and have a moment to herself. She sank down by her bedside in an inarticulate agony of prayer, which doubtless God deciphered, though it never came to words, and rose up again to put on her bonnet, her neat shawl, her best pair of gloves. The smile that might have come on the face of a martyr at the stake dawned upon the little woman's lips as she caught sight of her own pale face in the glass, when she was tying her bonnet-strings. She was not thrusting her hand into the scorching flames, she was only pulling out the bows of black ribbon, and giving the last touch to that perfection of gentle neatness in which Arthur's mother, for his sake, must present herself to his people. She took Mr Beecher's arm afterwards, and walked with him, through the wintry sunshine and streams of churchgoers, to Salem. Perhaps she was just a little sententious in her talk to the young preacher, who would have stared had anybody told him what active and feverish wretchedness was in her heart. She quoted Arthur's dear father more than usual; she felt a little irritated in spite of herself by the complaisance of the young man from 'Omerton. Notwithstanding the dreadful pressure of her trouble, she felt that his excitement in the prospect of preaching to Arthur's people was quite ill-timed. What did it matter to him whether the Salem flock liked him or not? were they not Arthur's people, pre-engaged to their own pastor? The gentle widow did what she could to bring Mr Beecher down as they walked through Grove Street. She remarked, gently, that where a minister was very popular, a stranger had but little chance of appreciation. "You must not be mortified if you see the congregation look disappointed when you come into the pulpit," said Mrs Vincent; "for my son, if he had not been called away so suddenly, was to commence a course of lectures to-day, and I believe a good deal of expectation was raised about them." The new preacher was perhaps a shade less buoyant when he resigned his friend's mother to Tozer at the door of the chapel, to be conducted to her pew. Salem was already about half filled; and the entering flock looked at Mrs Vincent, as she stood with the deacon in the porch, asking, with the courtesy of a royal personage, humble yet affable, after his wife and daughter. Tozer was a little overawed by the politeness of the minister's mother. He concluded that she was "quite the lady" in his private heart.

"If you tell me where the minister's seat is, I need not trouble you to go in," said Mrs Vincent.

"Mrs Tufton's uncommon punctual, and it's close upon her time," said Tozer; "being a single man, we've not set apart a seat for the minister – not till he's got some one as

can sit in it; it's the old minister's seat, as is the only one
we've set aside; for we've been a-letting of the pews
uncommon this past month, and it don't answer to waste
nothing in a chapel as is as expensive to keep up as Salem.
It's our pride to give our minister a good salary, as you
know, ma'am, and we've all got to pay up according; so
there ain't no pew set apart for Mr Vincent – not till he's
got a wife."

"Then I am to sit in Mr Tufton's pew?" said the
minister's mother, not without a little sharpness.

"There ain't no more of them never at Salem, but Mrs
Tufton," said Tozer. "Mr Tufton has had a shock, and the
only one of a family they've at home is a great invalid, and
never was within the chapel door in my time. Mr Tufton
he do come now and again. He would have been here to-
day, I make bold to say, but for the minister being called
away. I hope you've 'eard from Mr Vincent, ma'am, and as
he'll soon be back. It ain't a good thing for a congregation
when the pastor takes to going off sudden. Here she is a-
coming. Mrs Tufton, ma'am, this is Mrs Vincent, the
minister's mother; she's been waiting for you to go into
your pew."

"I hope I shall not be in your way," said Mrs Vincent,
with her dignified air. "I have always been accustomed to
see a seat for the minister; but as I am a stranger, I hope
for once I shall not be in your way."

"Don't say a word!" cried Mrs Tufton. "I am as glad
as possible to see Mr Vincent's mother. He is a precious
young man. It's not a right principle, you know, but it's
hard not to envy people that are so happy in their families;
nothing would make my Tom take to the ministry, though
his papa and I had set our hearts upon it; and he's in
Australia, poor dear fellow! and my poor girl is such an
invalid. I hope your daughter is pretty well? Come this
way. I hope I shall see a great deal of you. Mr Tufton
takes such an interest in his young brother; all that he
wants is a little good advice – that is what the minister

always tells me. All that Mr Vincent wants, he says, is a little good advice."

The latter part of this was communicated in a whisper, as the two ladies seated themselves in the minister's pew. After a momentary pause of private devotion, Mrs Tufton again took up the strain where she had left it off.

"I assure you, we take the greatest interest in him at the cottage. He doesn't come to see us so often as Mr Tufton would wish, but I daresay he has other things to do. The minister often says to me that he is a precious young man, is Mr Vincent, and that a little good advice and attention to those that know better is all he wants to make him a shining light; and I am sure he will want no good advice Mr Tufton can give him. So you may keep your mind easy – you may keep your mind quite easy. In any difficulty that could occur, I am sure the minister would act as if he were his own son."

"You are very kind; but I hope no difficulty will occur," said Mrs Vincent, with a little quiver in her lip.

"I hope not, indeed; but there are so many people to please in a flock," said the late minister's wife, with a sigh. "*We* always got on very well, for Mr Tufton is not one to take a deal of notice of any unpleasantness; but you know as well as I do that it takes a deal of attention to keep all matters straight. If you'll excuse me, it's a great pity Mr Vincent has gone away to-day. Nothing would have made my husband leave his post just as he was intimated to begin a course of lectures. It's *very* excusable in Mr Vincent, because he hasn't that experience that's necessary. I always say he's very excusable, being such a young man; and we have no doubt he'll get on very well if he does but take advice."

"My son was very unwilling to go; but it was quite necessary. His sister," said Mrs Vincent, clasping her hands tight under her shawl to balance the pang in her heart, "was with some friends – whom we heard something unpleasant about – and he went to bring her home. I expect them – to-morrow."

The poor mother shut her lips close when she had said the words, to keep in the cry or sob that seemed bursting from them. Yes, God help her, she expected them; perhaps to-morrow – perhaps that same dreadful night; but even in the height of her anguish there occurred to Mrs Vincent a forlorn prayer that they might not come back that Sunday. Rather another agonising night than that all the "Chapel folks" should be aware that their pastor was rushing wildly along distant railways on the day of rest. The fact that he was doing so added a pang to her own trouble. Total disarrangement, chaos, all the old habitudes of life gone to wreck, and only desperation and misery left, was the sensation produced by that interruption of all religious use and wont. It came upon her with an acute sting, to think that her poor young minister was travelling that Sunday; just as in Arthur's own experience at that same moment, the utter incoherence, chaos, and wretchedness into which his life had suddenly fallen, breathed upon him in the sound of the church-bells.

"Dear me, I am very sorry!" said Mrs Tufton; "some fever or something, I suppose – something that's catching? Dear, dear me, I am so sorry! but there are some people that never take infection; a little camphor is such a nice thing to carry about – it can't do any harm, you know. Mrs Tozer tells me he is a very nice young man, Mr Vincent's friend from 'Omerton. I don't like to say such a thing of a girl, but I do believe your son could have *that* Phoebe any day for asking, Mrs Vincent. I can't bear forward girls, for my part – that is her just going into the pew, with the pink bonnet; oh, you know her! – to be sure, Mrs Pigeon remarked you were sure to go *there;* though I should have hoped we would have seen you as soon as any one in Carlingford."

"Indeed, I have been much disappointed not to call. I – I hope I shall – to-morrow," said the widow, to whom to-morrow loomed dark like another world, and who could not help repeating over and over the dreaded name.

"That is Maria Pigeon all in white – to be only trades-people they *do* dress more than I approve of," said Mrs Tufton. "My Adelaide, I am sure, never went like that. Many people think Maria a deal nicer-looking than Phoebe Tozer, but her mother is *so* particular – more than particular – what I call troublesome, you know. You can't turn round without giving her offence. Dear me, how my tongue is going! the minister would say I was just at my old imprudent tricks – but you, that were a minister's wife, can understand. She *is* such a difficult woman to deal with. I am sure Mr Tufton is always telling them to wait, and that Mr Vincent is a young man yet, and experience is all he wants. I wish he had a good wife to keep him straight; but I don't know that *that* would be advisable either, because of Phoebe and the rest. Dear, dear, it is a difficult thing to know what to do! – but Mr Tufton always says, If he had a little more experience – Bless me, the young man is in the pulpit!" said Mrs Tufton, coming to a sudden standstill, growing very red, and picking up her hymn-book. Very seldom had the good woman such a chance to talk. She ran herself so out of breath that she could not join in that first hymn.

But Mrs Vincent, who had a sensation that the pew, and indeed the whole chapel, trembled with the trembling that was in her own frame, but who felt at the same time that everybody was looking at her, and that Arthur's credit was involved, stood up steadfastly, holding her book firm in both her hands, and with an effort almost too much for her, the heroism of a martyr, added her soft voice, touched with age, yet still melodious and true, to the song of praise. The words choked her as she uttered them, yet with a kind of desperate courage she kept on. Praise! – it happened to be a very effusive hymn that day, an utterance of unmitigated thanksgiving; fortunately she had not sufficient command of her mind or wits to see clearly what she was singing, or to enter into the wonderful bitter difference between the thanks she was uttering and

the position in which she stood. Could she give God thanks
for Susan's ruin, or rejoice in the light He had given, when
it revealed only misery? She was not called upon to
answer that hard question. She stood up mechanically
with her white face set in pale steadfastness, and was only
aware that she was singing, keeping the tune, and making
herself noways remarked among the crowd of strange
people, many of whom turned curious eyes towards her.
She stood with both her feet set firm on the floor, both her
hands holding fast to the book, and over the ache of
frightful suspense in her heart came the soft voice of
her singing, which for once in her life meant nothing
except a forlorn determination to keep up and hold herself
erect and vigilant, sentinel over Arthur's fortunes and his
people's thoughts.

Mr Beecher's sermon was undeniably clever; the Salem
folks pricked up their ears at the sound of it, recalling as it
did that period of delightful excitement when they were
hearing candidates, and felt themselves the dispensers of
patronage. That was over now, and they were wedded to
one; but the bond of union between themselves and their
pastor was far from being indissoluble, and they contemplated this new aspirant to their favour with feelings
stimulated and piquant, as a not inconsolable husband,
likely to become a widower, might contemplate the general
female public, out of which candidates for the problem-
atically vacant place might arise. Mrs Pigeon, who was the
leader of the opposition, and whose daughter Mr Vincent
had not distinguished, whose house he had not specially
frequented, and whom, most of all, he had passed in the
street without recognition, made a note of this man from
'Omerton. If the painful necessity of dismissing the present
pastor should occur – as such things did occur, deplorable
though they were – it might be worth while sending for Mr
Beecher. She made a note of him privately in her mind, as
she sat listening with ostentatious attention, nodding
her head now and then by way of assent to his statements.

Mrs Vincent remarked her as she watched the congregation
from the minister's pew, with her jealous mother's eyes.
The Tozers were not so devoted in their listening. Mrs
Tozer's brilliant cherry-coloured bonnet visibly drooped
once or twice with a blessed irregularity of motion; all
these signs Mrs Vincent perceived as she sat, in preternatural acute consciousness of everything round her, by
Mrs Tufton's side. She was even aware that the sermon
was clever; she remembered expressions in it long after,
which somehow got burned in, without any will of hers,
upon her breaking heart. The subdued anguish that was in
her collected fuel for its own silent consuming fire, even in
the congregation of Salem, where, very upright, very
watchful, afraid to relax her strained nerves even by
leaning back or forward, she lived through the long service
as if through a year of suffering.

The congregation dispersed in a buzz of talk and curiosity.
Everybody wanted to know where the minister had gone,
and what had taken him away. "I can't say as I think he's
using of us well," said somebody, whom Mrs Vincent could
hear as she made her way to the door. "Business of his
own! a minister ain't got no right to have business of his
own, leastways on Sundays. Preaching's his business. I
don't hold with that notion. He's in our employ, and we
pays him well—"

Here a whisper from some charitable bystander directed
the speaker's eyes to Mrs Vincent, who was close behind.

"Well! it ain't nothing to me who hears me," said this
rebellious member, not without a certain vulgar pleasure
in his power of insult. "We pays him well, as I say; I have
to stick to my business well or ill, and I don't see no reason
why the minister should be different. If he don't mind us
as pays him, why, another will."

"Oh, I've been waiting to catch your eye," said Mrs
Pigeon, darting forward at this crisis to Mrs Tufton;
"wasn't *that* a sweet sermon? that's refreshing, that is! I
haven't listened to anything as has roused me up like that

– no, not since dear Mr Tufton came first to Carlingford; as for what we've been hearing of late, I don't say it's not clever, but, oh, it's cold! and for them as like good gospel preaching and rousing up, I must confess as Mr Vincent—"

"Hush! Mrs Pigeon – Mrs Vincent," said Mrs Tufton, hurriedly; "you two ladies should have been introduced at the first. Mr Pigeon is one of our deacons and leading men, Mrs Vincent, and I don't doubt you've often and often heard your son talking of him. We are always discussing Mr Vincent, because he is our own pastor now, you know; and a precious young man he is – and all that he wants is a little experience, as Mr Tufton always says."

"Oh, I *am* sorry! – I beg your pardon, I'm sure," cried Mrs Pigeon; "but I am one as always speaks my mind, and don't go back of my word. Folks as sees a deal of the minister," continued the poulterer's wife, not without a glance at that cherry-coloured bonnet which had nodded during the sermon, and to which poor Mrs Vincent felt a certain gratitude, "may know different; but me as don't have much chance, except in chapel, I will say as I think he wants speaking to: most folks do – specially young folks, when they're making a start in the world. He's too high, he is, for us plain Salem folks; what we want is a man as preaches gospel sermons – real rousing-up discourses – and sits down pleasant to his tea, and makes hisself friendly. I never was one as thought a minister couldn't do wrong. I always said as they were just like other men, liking grand dinners and grand folks, and the vanities of this world; – not meaning no offence, Mrs Vincent, neither to you nor the minister – but I must say as I think, he's a deal too high."

"My son has had very good training," said the widow, not without dignity. "His dear father had many good friends who have taken an interest in him. He has always been accustomed to good society; and I must say, at the same time," added Mrs Vincent, "that I never knew Arthur to fail in courtesy to the poorer brethren. If he has

done so, I am sure it has been unintentionally. It is quite
against my principles and his dear father's to show any
respect to persons. If he has shown any neglect of Mrs
Pigeon's family," continued the mild diplomatist, "it must
have been because he thought them less, and not more in
need of him than the rest of the flock."

Mrs Pigeon listened with open mouth, but total discomfiture: whether this was a compliment or a reprimand
was totally beyond her power to make out. She cried,
"Oh, I'm sure!" in a tone which was half defensive and
half deprecating. Mrs Pigeon, however, intended nothing
less than to terminate the conversation at this interesting
point, and it was with utter dismay that she perceived Mrs
Vincent sweep past before she had recovered herself –
sweep past – though that black silk gown was of very
moderate dimensions, and the trim little figure was noways majestic. The minister's mother made a curtsy to the
astonished wife of the poulterer; she said "good morning"
with a gracious bow, and went upon her way before Mrs
Pigeon had recovered her breath. Perfect victory attended
the gentle widow in this little passage of arms. Her assailant
fell back, repeating in a subdued tone, "Well, I'm sure!"
Mrs Pigeon, like Tozer, granted that the minister's mother
was "quite the lady," henceforward, in her heart.

And Mrs Vincent passed on victorious; yes, victorious,
and conscious of her victory, though giddy with secret
anguish, and feeling as if every obstacle that hindered her
return was a conscious cruelty. They could not have
arrived this morning – it was impossible; yet she burned to
get back to see whether impossibility might not be accomplished for once, and Susan be there awaiting her. The
first to detain her was Mrs Tufton, who hurried, with
added respect, after her, triumphing secretly in Mrs
Pigeon's defeat.

"I am so glad you gave her her answer," said Mrs Tufton;
"bless me! how pleased Adelaide will be when I tell her! I
always said it would be well for a minister's wife to have a

spirit. Won't you come and take a bit of dinner with us, as Mr Vincent is not at home? Oh, I daresay somebody will ask Mr Beecher. It does not do to pay too much attention to the young men that come to preach – though I think he *was* clever. You won't come? – a headache? – poor dear! You're worrying about your daughter, I am sure; but I wouldn't, if I were you. Young girls in health don't take infection. She'll come back all right, you'll see. Well – good-bye. Don't come in the evening if you have a headache. I shouldn't, if I were you. Good-bye – and to-morrow, if all is well, we'll look for you. Siloam Cottage – just a little way past Salem – you can't miss the way."

"Yes, thank you – to-morrow," said Mrs Vincent. If only anybody could have known what dreadful work it was keeping up that smile, holding upright as she did! Then she went on a little way in peace, half crazed with the misery that consumed her, yet unnaturally vigilant and on the alert, always holding up Arthur's standard at that critical hour when he had no representative but herself in his field of battle. But the poor mother was not long allowed this interval of peace. After a few minutes, the Tozers, who were going the same way, came up to her, and surrounded her like a bodyguard.

"I liked that sermon, ma'am," said Tozer; "there was a deal that was practical in that sermon. If ever we should be in the way of hearing candidates again – and short-sighted creatures like us never knows what's a-going to happen – I'd put down that young man's name for an 'earing. There ain't a word to be said again' the minister's sermons in the matter of talent. They're full of mind, ma'am – they're philosophical, that's what they are; and the pews we've let in Salem since he come, proves it, let folks say what they will. But if there *is* a want, it's in the application. He don't press it home upon their consciences, not as some on us expected; and Mr Tufton being all in that line, as you may say, makes it show the more. If I was going to make a change again – not as I mean nothing of the kind, or as the Salem folks has ever took it into their heads – I'd like to have a little o'both ways, that's what I'd like."

"When you get a minister of independent mind, Mr Tozer, if he gives you the best he has, he ought to be allowed to choose his own way," said Mrs Vincent. "My dear husband always said so, and he had great experience. Mr Vincent's son, I know, will never want friends."

"I am sure as long as the minister keeps to his duty, he'll always find friends in Tozer and me," said the deacon's wife, striking in; "and though there may be folks in a finer way, there ain't no such good friends a pastor can have as in his own flock. As for hearing candidates and that, Tozer ought to know as none on us would hear of such a thing. I don't see no reason why Mr Vincent shouldn't settle down in Carlingford and make himself comfortable. We're all his friends as long as he's at his post."

"Oh, Ma, I am sure he *is* at his post," cried Phoebe; "he has gone away because he could not help it. I am quite sure," continued the modest maiden, casting down her eyes, "that he would *never* have left but for a good reason! Oh, I am confident he is fond of Carlingford *now*. He would not go away if he had not some duty – I am certain he would not!"

"If Phoebe is better informed than the rest of us, it ain't nobody's business as I can see," said the father, with a short laugh. "I always like the young folks to manage them matters among themselves; but I take my own view, miss, for all that."

"O, Pa, how can you talk so," cried Phoebe, in virgin confusion, "to make Mrs Vincent think—"

"Indeed, nothing will make me think otherwise than I know," said Mrs Vincent, with a voice which extinguished Phoebe. "I understand my son. He does not bestow his confidence very easily; and I am sure he is quite able to manage *all* the matters he may have in hand," added the widow, not without significance. Not all her anxiety for

Arthur, not all her personal wretchedness, could unwoman the minister's mother so much as to make her forgive or overlook Phoebe's presumption. She could not have let this pretendant to her son's affections off without trans-fixing her with a passing arrow. Human endurance has its limits. Mrs Vincent could bear anything for Arthur except this pretence of a special interest in him.

"Oh, I am sure I never meant—!" faltered Phoebe; but she could get no further, and even her mother did not come to the rescue.

"Them things had much best not be talked of," said Mrs Tozer, sharply. "Mr Beecher is coming in to have a bit of dinner. You mightn't have things comfortable where you are, the minister being away, and you used to your own house. Won't you come in with us and eat a bit of dinner? I never can swallow a morsel when I'm by myself. It's lonesome for you in them rooms, and us so near. There ain't no ceremony nor nonsense, but we'll be pleased if you'll come."

"Thank you very much," said Mrs Vincent, who could not forget that the cherry-coloured bonnet had nodded during Mr Beecher's sermon, "but I slept badly last night. At my time of life a new bed often makes one sleepless, and I have a bad headache. I think I will go and lie down. Many thanks. It is very kind of you to ask me. I hope I shall see you," said the widow, with a slight shiver, repeating her formula, "to-morrow."

"You can't take us amiss," said Mrs Tozer; "there's always enough for an extra one, if it isn't grand or any ceremony; or if you'll come to tea and go to church with us at night? Phoebe can run over and see how you find yourself. Good mornin'. I'm sorry you'll not come in."

"Oh, I wish you would let me go with you and nurse you," said Phoebe, not without a glance in the other direction at the approaching form of the young man from 'Omerton, "I *am* so frightened you don't like me! – but I'll come over before tea and sit with you if your headache is not better. If I could only make you fancy I was Miss Vincent!" said Phoebe, with pink pleading looks.

Mrs Vincent turned away more smartly under the effect of that stimulant. She crossed George Street, towards her son's rooms, a solitary little figure, in the flood of winter sunshine – not dismal to look at, save for its black dress, trim, alert, upright still. And the heart within, which ached with positive throbs of pain, had roused up under that last provocation, and was stinging with indignation and anger, pure womanly, and not to be deadened by any anguish. Phoebe's impertinence, as she called it to herself, took her out of her own far heavier trouble. To think of that pink creature having designs upon *her* boy, and taking upon herself little airs of conquest! To encounter Phoebe's wiles overwhelmed Arthur with shame and annoyance; but they exasperated his mother. She went home with a steadier ring in her little light footstep. But the fumes of that temporary excitement had faded when the door opened upon her – the blank door, with the little maid open-mouthed behind, who did not look her in the face, and who had nothing to communicate; the sitting-room up-stairs lay blank in utter solitude – all the books put away according to Sunday custom, and the cover of Arthur's letter lying on the table startling his mother into wild hopes that some other communication had come for her. She sank down upon a chair, and covered her pale face with her hands – torture intolerable, unendurable; but oh, how certainly to be endured and put up with! This poor mother, who had met with many a heavy sorrow in her day, though never any so hideous as this, was no excitable, passionate creature, but a wholesome, daylight woman, in whom no strain of superlative emotions had choked up the natural channels of relief. She wept a few bitter, heavy tears under cover of her clasped hands – tears which took away the dreadful pressure upon her brain, and made it easier to bear for the moment. Then she went away in her patience, and took off her bonnet, and prepared herself for the calm of the dreadful day of which so small a portion had yet passed. She pretended to dine, that no outlet might be left to gossip on that score. She took a good book and lay down upon the sofa in the awful silence – the moments creeping, stealing over her in a tedious procession which she could almost see – the silence throbbing all around as if with the beats of her own heart; how was it that the walls of the house stood steady with those throbs palpitating within their dull enclosure? But there was this comfort at least, that nobody fathomed Mrs Vincent in that speechless martyrdom of hers – nobody guessed the horror in her heart – nobody imagined that there was anything of tragic meaning under that composed aspect. She went to church again in the evening to escape Phoebe's "nursing," and sat there choking with the anticipation that meantime her son was bringing Susan home. She walked home with Beecher, devoured by feverish hopes and fears, found still no one there, with an unutterable pang, yet relief, and sat with the young man from 'Omerton for a horrible hour or two, till the strain had all but killed her. But nobody came; nobody came all through the hideous night. Holding with half-frantic hands to the thread of life, which could ill bear this total want of all its usual sustenance, but which must not be sacrificed for her children's sake – keeping alive, she could not tell how, without food, without rest, without even prayer – nothing but a fever of dumb entreaty coming to her mind when she sought some forlorn comfort from the mere fact of going on her knees – Mrs Vincent lived through the night and the morning. Another horrible, sunshiny, cheerful day; but no sound on earth or heaven to say they were coming – no arrival, no letter – nothing but hopeless, sickening, intolerable suspense – suspense all the more intolerable because it had to be borne.

CHAPTER XXII.

To-morrow! to-morrow was Monday morning, a new day,
a new work-week – cheerful, healthful, and exhilarating –
bright with that frosty sunshine, which carried comparative
comfort to many a poor house in Carlingford. The widow's
face was sharper, paler, of a wonderful ashy colour. Nature
could not go on under such a struggle without showing signs
of it. Beecher, who was not to go until a late train, took
leave of her as soon as he could, not without a little fright,
and betook himself to Tozer's, where he said she overawed
him with her grand manners, and where he was led to admit
that Vincent had always been a little "high." If she could
have abandoned herself to her dreadful vigil, perhaps Mrs
Vincent might have found it easier, perhaps harder – she
herself thought the former; but she dared not give up to it.
She had to set her face like a flint – she was Arthur's
representative, and had still to show a steadfast front of
battle for him, and if not discomfit, still confront his
enemies. She had to call at Siloam Cottage, at Mrs Tozer's,
to do what else might be necessary for the propitiation of
the flock. She never dreamed of saying to herself that she
could not do it; there was no question of that; the flag had to
be kept flying for Arthur. No friend of his must be
jeopardised, no whisper allowed to rise which his mother
could prevent: she had been a minister's wife for thirty
years; well had she learned in that time, like Mrs Tufton,
that a deal of attention was needed to keep all things straight.

Accordingly, in the height of her excitement and anxiety,
believing that any moment the poor fugitive might be
brought home, the widow, in her unflinching martyrdom,

once more put on her bonnet, and drew out her black ribbon into bows of matchless neatness. Though she wrung her poor hands in speechless anguish as she went out of the room, it was with composed, though colourless lips, that she spoke to the little maid in the hall. "Mr Vincent may come home any time to-day," said the widow; "you must have some lunch ready, and tea; perhaps his sister may be with him – or – or she may come alone. Any one who comes is to be taken up-stairs. I will not be long gone; and I am going to Mrs Tufton's, if anybody should want me—"

At this moment a knock came to the door – a hurried single knock, always alarming, and sounding like an evil omen. Mrs Vincent's voice failed her at that sound – most likely her face went into convulsive twitches, for the maid stood staring at her, too much startled to open the door, until a wild gesture from the speechless woman, who was herself unable to move, her breath almost forsaking her, and coming in sobs, recalled the girl to her senses. The door was opened, and Mrs Vincent stood with burning eyes gazing out. Ah, not Susan! never Susan! – a little, stout, rustic figure, all weary and dishevelled, looking ashamed, frightened, almost disreputable in utter forlornness and unhappiness. Mrs Vincent gave a great sob to get breath, and dropped upon the chair, and held out her hand to Mary. She had forgotten Mary – forgotten her momentary comfort in the fact that Susan's flight was not alone. Now was it life or death the girl was bringing? She drew the frightened creature near, close, and shrieked, as she thought, her question in her ear. "What? what?" said Mrs Vincent in her own mind; but no sound came to Mary's ears.

"O missis dear, missis dear!" sobbed the girl. "I've been and told Mr Arthur exact where she is – he's gone to fetch her home. O missis, don't take on! they'll soon be here. Miss Susan's living, she ain't dead. O missis, missis, she ain't dead – it might be worse nor it is."

At these words Mrs Vincent roused herself up once more. "My daughter has been ill," she said in gasps, turning a dreadful look upon the servant of the house. Then she rose, took hold of Mary's arm, and went up-stairs with her, holding her fast. She shut the door with her own hands when they got back to the lonely parlour full of daylight and silence. "Miss Susan has been ill?" she said once more with parched lips, looking again, with that full blank gaze which seemed to deny and defy any other answer, in Mary's frightened face.

"O missis, don't take on!" sobbed the terrified girl.

"No, oh no, no, that is impossible. I can't take on, Mary, if I would – oh no, not now," said the poor widow, with what seemed a momentary wandering of her strained senses. "Tell me all – I am ready to hear it all."

And then Mary began the pitiful story, the same they had heard in Lonsdale – the sudden arrival of the girl and her governess, and innocent Susan's puzzled interest in them; Mr Fordham's appearance afterwards, his sudden snatch at the stranger, his ready use of Arthur's letter, which Susan was disturbed about, to persuade her that she must instantly go to her mother and set all right; the journey bringing them late at night to an unknown place, which, with the boom of the unexpected sea in their ears, the defenceless deceived creatures found out not to be Car-lingford. Mary knew nothing of the scene which had been enacted up-stairs, when the villanous scheme was made known to the unhappy victim. She could tell nothing but by guesses of what had passed and followed, and Mary, of course, by a natural certainty, guessed the worst. But next day Susan had written to her mother, either because she was still deceived or still innocent; and the next day again Mary was sent away under a pretence of being sent to church, and the false Fordham himself had conducted her to town and left her there. Such was Mary's tale. Last night she had met Mr Arthur and given him the address. Now, no doubt, they were on their way, – if only missis would not take on! "No," said the widow once more, with speechless lips. Take on! oh no, never more. Surely all these light afflictions that could bring tears were over now – nothing but horror and agony remained. The poor mother sat for a little in a dreadful silence, aching all over her anguished frame. Nothing was to be said or done; the pause of utter misery, in which thought itself had no place, but one horrible sensation of suffering was all that remained of life, passed over her; then a faint agonised smile fluttered upon her white lips. She drew on her glove again slowly and with pain. "I must go out, Mary," said Arthur's mother. "I must do my duty if the world were all breaking up, as I – I think it is; and you must stay here and tell my poor darling her mother will come back to her directly. And don't talk to the other servant, Mary. You shall be like my own child if you will stand by us now."

"O missis dear, not a word – not if it was to save my life!" said poor Mary, through her tears.

And in her bravery and desperation the widow went out to her other forlorn hope. She went away out of the doors which enclosed at least the knowledge of this event, through the everyday streets, where, if there were other tragedies, nobody knew of them any more than of hers. She had her veil over her face, on which that shadow had settled, and no one could have suspected her of carrying a broken heart through those sunshiny ways. She could not think or anticipate or even fear anything further. Susan might die under that load of shame and anguish, but her mother apprehended, was sensible of, nothing more. The worst had come, except for Arthur, who might be helped out of his troubles. So, stunned and hopeless, she set out to visit Arthur's people, with a courage more desperate than that of battle. That was the duty which must be done if the world went to pieces – to talk to Adelaide Tufton and hear her sharp criticism and bitter gossip – to listen to the old minister dawdling forth his slow sentiments – to visit the Tozers and soothe their feelings, and hear what they had to say. An *auto-da-fé* in the old Spanish fashion would have been easier, to be sure; but this was how the minister's mother, in the depths of unknown anguish and calamity, was expected to exert herself, the only way she could serve her son.

The parlour in Siloam Cottage was as green and obscure, as warm and close, as of old. The big geranium had grown, and covered the little window still more completely, and the fire burned with virulence, conscious of the frost. The minister's invalid daughter, with the colourless face and sharp eyes, was still knitting, leaning back upon her pillows. Poor Mrs Vincent, when she sat down, as near the door as possible, feeling as if she could not get breath, became immediately aware that to confront those eyes was a more dangerous process than any which she had yet been subjected to in Carlingford. They penetrated through her, keen with the restless life and curiosity which made up to that disabled woman for the privations of her existence. In the dim green parlour the minister's mother saw nothing but Adelaide Tufton's eyes. If they had been beautiful eyes, the effect would have been less surprising; but they were not beautiful; they were pale blue, and had something of the shrill shining of a rainy sky in the glistening white, which counted for far more than the faint watery colour. Mrs Vincent gave way before them as she had never yet done. She cast down her own eyes, and drew back her chair, and even faltered in her speech, when she was obliged to face their observation. The danger was all the greater for being unexpected. As for Mrs Tufton, that good woman was in a flutter of interest and sympathy. She wanted to know whether Susan had gone through all the orthodox number of fevers and youthful ailments, and was in her element talking of the merits of camphor as a preventive, and of all the means that might be used to avoid infection.

"When my children were young, and their papa always being noted for so active a man among his people, I don't know what I should have done if I had been easily frightened," said Mrs Tufton. "Don't worry – keep her quiet, and give her—"

"Mrs Vincent never said she was afraid of infection," said Adelaide. "Is it typhus fever? My mother jumps at everything, and never stops to inquire. I daresay it's something quite different. Love affairs? Oh no; of course we don't want you to tell us. I don't think Phoebe Tozer will die of her failure. This young man from Homerton will console her. Has your son recovered his little affair with the young Dowager, Mrs Vincent? He dined there, you know. I daresay his head was turned; but there is one safeguard with those fine ladies. If a man has his wits about him, he can always know that they mean nothing all the time."

"Indeed, I don't know what you mean. My son knows Lady Western, I believe; I remember one time he dined there. My Arthur," said the mother, with a faint smile, "is not one to have his head turned. He has been used to be thought a great deal of at home."

"Ah, he's a precious young man!" said Mr Tufton, seesawing the air with his large grey hand. "I am much interested in my dear young brother. He thinks too much, perhaps – too much – of pleasing the carnal mind; and my people, that have been used to practical preaching so long, find the difference. But when he has deeper experiences—"

"Stuff!" said the invalid, turning her head half aside; "you know the chapel has filled since he came. Even when they are asses like your Salem people, you know they like a man with brains. I don't see that it matters much what Mr Vincent goes wrong in; he was sure to go wrong somehow. I gave him six months, but he has got through the six months, and they have not killed him off yet. What does he mean, thrusting himself into other people's messes? As far as I can make out, it's quite a little tragedy. There was that Mrs Hilyard, you know – the woman in Back Grove Street. Ah, you know her!" said Adelaide, keenly, seeing the little shiver with which the visitor received the name.

"I have heard my son speak of her," said the widow, faintly.

"She was some connection of the Bedford family," said Adelaide, going on, with her curious eyes fixed on Mrs Vincent's face, who quailed before her, "and she married a half-brother of Lady Western's – a desperate rascal he was. They had one baby, and then she left him – one baby, a girl, that has grown up an idiot; and here this lady lives – a poor needlewoman – to keep the girl safe, somehow, out of her father's hand. Why he should want to have her I can't exactly tell. I suspect, because she's pretty, to make a decoy of her, and sell her somehow, either to be married, or worse—"

"Adelaide!" cried Mrs Tufton; "oh, my dear, do mind what you're saying; Mrs Vincent does not know you. What can she think if you talk like that?"

"Mrs Vincent sees well enough I am not a girl to be frightened for words," said the sick woman. "Now, what I want to know is, what has your son to do with it? He's gone off after them, now, for some reason or other; of course I don't expect you to tell me. Perhaps Lady Western has sent him? – never mind, I will find out; but I know it has something to do with Mrs Hilyard, for they both went off from Carlingford the same day. I have no share in life for myself," said Adelaide, with another keen look at the stranger; "and so, instead of comforting myself that it's all for the best, as papa says, I interfere with my fellow-creatures. Oh, pray, don't be sorry for me. I get on as well as most people. Nobody in this place ever succeeds in concealing anything from me."

"Indeed it is a pity when people have anything to conceal," said poor Mrs Vincent, thinking, with a sensation of deadly sickness at her heart, of the awful secret which was in Mary's keeping, and faltering, in spite of all her self-command. She rose up hurriedly, when she met once more the glance of those sharp eyes: she could not bear that investigation; all her dreadful suspense and excite-

ment seemed to ooze out unawares, and betray themselves;
her only safety seemed in flight.

"This is a very short visit," said Mr Tufton. "My dear
anxious sister, we can only pray you may be comforted.
All things work together for good; you don't need to be
told that. It's sure to be for the best, whatever happens:
take that consolation to your heart – it's sure to be for the
best."

"If her daughter dies and her son is dismissed, I wonder
will that be for the best?" said Adelaide Tufton, as soon as
the widow had left the room. Mrs Vincent's ears, made
acute by suffering, caught enough of this valedictory
address to realise, if that were possible, an additional
pang. Kind Mrs Tufton did not hear it, not being in any
such state of feverish susceptibility. She, on the contrary,
kissed the mother, whom she pitied with all her heart, and
entreated her not to worry. "A young healthy girl does not
fall ill for nothing. You'll see things will turn out all right,"
said the kind soul; and Mrs Vincent went upon her forlorn
way.

At Mrs Tozer's the minister's mother found a little
committee assembled. Mrs Brown was there from the
Devonshire Dairy, and Mrs Pigeon, whose gratification in
being able to hail Mrs Vincent as an acquaintance, to
the confusion of the dairywoman and amazement of Mrs
Tozer, almost restored the minister to the lady's favour.
They were in the drawing-room, where, in honour of the
expected visitors, a fire had been lighted; and as Mrs
Vincent ascended the dark staircase, she obtained a passing
glimpse of Mr Beecher seated at the table in the parlour
studying 'The Railway Guide,' which Phoebe expounded
to him, until they were both sent for up-stairs. Altogether
the conjunction did not look promising for Arthur's interests.
She went in thrilling with a touch of exasperation and
defiance. Now was the time to make a final stand for
Arthur. This covert rebellion could be deprecated no
longer.

"I expect my son home to-day," said the brave mother, gulping down all the pangs of her expectation. "I think, now that I see for myself how much he is thought of in Carlingford, I ought to make an apology to the Salem people. It was I that induced him to go away, not thinking that one Sunday would be such a great matter; but indeed it was very gratifying to me to see how disappointed everybody was. I hope Mr Beecher will pardon me, for I am sure he preached us a very nice sermon, and we were all grateful for it; but, naturally on my dear boy's account, to see how disappointed everybody was, was a great gratification to me."

"Oh! I did not mind," said Mr Beecher, with a little laugh of embarrassment; but the young man was much taken aback, and stared with astonished looks before he answered, at this totally unexpected address. Having thus floored one of her adversaries, and seeing the female foe more voluble and ready, quite prepared to answer her, Mrs Vincent blandly proceeded.

"And this, you know, Mrs Tozer, was all the more gratifying to me, because I was not quite sure that Arthur had done wisely in choosing Carlingford. His dear father had so many friends in our denomination, and people are so kind as to speak of my boy as such a rising young man. Before I knew Carlingford," said the widow, looking round her with an air of gentle superiority, "I used to regret my son had not accepted the invitation from Liverpool. Many people said to me that his talents would have had so much more room there; but I am reconciled now," she added, turning her mild eyes upon Mrs Pigeon, who showed symptoms of resistance. "I may say I am quite satisfied now. He would have been better off, and had more opportunity of making himself a position in Liverpool, but what is that in comparison with the attachment of a flock?"

"Well, indeed, that's just the thing, ma'am," said Mrs Brown, who imagined herself addressed; "we *are* fond of him. I always said he was an uncommon nice young man; and if he was but to settle down—"

"That will come in time," said the minister's mother, graciously; "and I am glad, for my part, that he has been away, for it shows me how his dear people feel towards him; and though he would have been, of course, better off in Liverpool, I would never consider that in comparison. They still want to have him, you know, and keep writing me letters, and him too, I don't doubt; but after what I have seen, I could *never* advise him to break the link that has been formed here. The connection between pastor and people is a sacred tie; it should *never* be broken," said Mrs Vincent, with mild grandeur, "for anything so poor as a money object; but my dear boy is far above any such consideration as that."

"Ah!" said Mrs Pigeon, drawing a long breath of involuntary awe and admiration; "and I don't doubt as the pastor would have been a deal better off in Liverpool," she added, after a pause, quite overpowered by that master-stroke.

"It's a deal bigger a place," suggested Mrs Tozer; "and grander folks, I don't have a doubt," she too added, after an interval. This new idea took away their breath.

"But, ah! what is that to affection," said Arthur's artful mother, "when a minister has the love of his flock! My dear Mrs Pigeon, though a mother is naturally anxious for her son, nothing on earth would induce me to advise him to break such a tie as that!"

"And indeed, ma'am, it's as a Christian mother should act," gasped the poulterer's subdued wife. Mrs Brown made a little movement of admiring assent, much impressed with the fine sentiments of the minister's mother. Phoebe put her handkerchief to her eyes, and Mr Beecher found it was time for his train. "Tell Vincent I am very glad to have been of use to him. We were all delighted in 'Omerton to hear of him making such an 'it," said Mr Beecher, friendly but discomfited. He made his leave-taking all

round, before Mrs Vincent, at the height of victory, rose
and went her way. Then she, too, shook hands, and
blandly parted with the astonished women. They remained
behind, and laid their heads together, much subdued,
over this totally new light. She departed, gently victorious.
This little demonstration had done her good. When she got
out into the street, however, she fell down again into
those depths of despair out of which she had risen so
bravely for Arthur's sake. She began to plan how she
and Susan could go away – not to Lonsdale – never again
to Lonsdale – but to some unknown place, and hide their
shame-stricken heads. She was so weary and sick in her
heart, it was almost a comfort to think of creeping into
some corner, taking her poor darling into her arms, healing
those dreadful wounds of hers, hiding her from the
sight of men. This was what they must do as soon as her
dearest child came back – go to Scotland, perhaps, or into
the primitive south country, where nobody knew them,
or— but softly, who was this?

A new claim upon the overworked anxious soul. At the
door of her son's house stood a carriage – an open carriage
– luxurious and handsome, with two fine horses impatiently
pawing the air, and a very fine footman at the door,
talking to the little maid. Within the carriage, the same
beautiful young woman whom Mrs Vincent remembered
to have seen waving a lovely hand to Arthur. No doubt it
was Lady Western. The beauty did not bewilder Mrs
Vincent as she had bewildered Mrs Vincent's son; but,
with a thrill of mingled pride, admiration, and disapproval,
she hastened forward at sight of her. Could she be asking
for Arthur? – and could Arthur have ventured to love that
lovely creature in her radiance of wealth and rank? With a
mother's involuntary self-delusion Mrs Vincent looked at
the beautiful vision as at Arthur's possible bride, and was
proud and displeased at the same moment; proud, that
anything so lovely and splendid was to fall to her son's lot
– disapproving, that Arthur's chosen should offer a mark

of favour even to Arthur, so much more decided than
accorded with the widow's old-fashioned notion of what
became a woman. Mrs Vincent did not think of the other
figure by Lady Western's side – a man of great height,
very slight, and rapid in his movements, with a long
brown beard and thoughtful eyes – eyes which lightened
up and became as keen as they were dreamy, whenever
occasion arose. Why should the widow look at him?
She had nothing to do with him. This once in their life
they were to come into momentary contact – never more.

"Mr Vincent ain't at home – but oh, look dear! –
here's his mother as can tell you better nor me," cried the
half-frightened maid at the door.

"His mother?" said the beautiful creature in the carriage;
she had alighted in a moment, and was by Mrs Vincent's
side – "Oh, I am so glad to see Mr Vincent's mother! I am
Lady Western – he has told you of me?" she said, taking
the widow's hand; "take us in, please, and let us talk to
you – we will not tease you – we have something important
to say."

"Important to us – not to Mrs Vincent," said the gentleman who followed her, a remarkable figure, in his loose
light-coloured morning dress; and his eyes fell with
a remorseful pity upon the widow, standing drawn-back
and self-restrained, upon the ground of her conscious
misery, not knowing whether to hope that they brought
her news, or to steel herself into a commonplace aspect
of civility. This man had a heart; he looked from the
brilliant creature before him, all flushed and radiant
with her own happiness, to the little woman by her side,
in her pitiful widow's dress, in her visible paleness
and desperation of self-control. It was he who had brought
Lady Western here to put his own innocence beyond
doubt, but the cruelty of that selfish impulse struck
him now as he saw them stand together. "Important to us
– not to Mrs Vincent," he said again, taking off his hat
to her with devout respect.

"Ah, yes! to us," said Lady Western, looking up to him with a momentary gleam of love and happiness. Then the pretty tender-hearted creature changed her look, and composed her countenance into sympathy. "I am so sorry for you, dear Mrs Vincent!" she said, with the saddest voice. At this the widow on her part started, and was recalled to herself.

"I am a stranger in Carlingford," said the mild little woman, drawing up her tiny figure. "I do not know what has procured me this pleasure – but all my son's friends are welcome to me. I will show you the way up-stairs," she continued, going up before them with the air of dignity which, after the hard battles and encounters and bitter wounds of this day, became the heroic little figure. She sent Mary, who started up in dismay at her entrance, into another room, and gave Lady Western a chair, but herself continued standing, always the conservator of Arthur's honour. If Arthur loved her, who was this man? why did such glances pass between them? Mrs Vincent stood erect before Lady Western, and did not yield even to the winning looks for which poor Arthur would have given his life.

"Oh, dear Mrs Vincent, I am so sorry for you!" said Lady Western again; "I know it all, and it makes my heart bleed to think of it. I will be your friend and your daughter's friend as long as I live, if you will let me. Oh, don't shut your heart against me! Mr Vincent trusts me, and so must you; and I am heartbroken to think all that you must have gone through—"

"Stop!" said Mrs Vincent, with a gasp. "I – I cannot tell – what you mean," she articulated, with difficulty, holding by the table to support herself, but looking with unflinching eyes in her new persecutor's face.

"Oh, don't shut your heart against me!" cried the young Dowager, with genuine tears in her lovely eyes. "This gentleman was with Mr Vincent yesterday – he came up here this morning. He is – Mr Fordham." She broke off

abruptly with a terrified cry. But Mrs Vincent had not
died or fainted standing rigid there before her, as the soft
creature thought. Her eyes had only taken that blank
lustreless gaze, because the force of emotion beneath
was too much for them, and inexpressible. Even in that
extremity, it was in the widow's heart, wrung to desperation,
to keep her standing-ground of assumed ignorance, and
not to know what this sudden offer of sympathy could
mean.

"I do not know – the gentleman," she said, slowly,
trying to make the shadow of a curtsy to him. "I am sorry
to seem uncivil; but I am tired and anxious. What – what
did you want of me?" she asked, in a little outburst of
uncontrollable petulance, which comforted Lady Western.
It was a very natural question. Surely, in this forlorn
room, where she had passed so many wretched hours, her
privacy might have been sacred; and she was jealous and
angry at the sight of Fordham for Arthur's sake. It was
another touch in the universal misery. She looked at Lady
Western's beauty with an angry heart. For these two, who
ventured to come to her in their happiness, affronting her
anguish, was Arthur's heart to be broken too?

"We wanted – our own ends," said Fordham, coming
forward. "I was so cruel as to think of myself, and that you
would prove it was another who had assumed my name.
Forgive me – it was I who brought Lady Western here;
and if either of us can serve you, or your daughter – or
your son—" added Fordham, turning red, and looking
round at his beautiful companion.

Mrs Vincent could bear it no longer. She made a hasty
gesture of impatience, and pointed to the door. "I am not
well enough, nor happy enough to be civil," cried Arthur's
mother; "we want nothing – nothing." Her voice failed her
in this unlooked-for exasperation. A few bitter tears came
welling up hot to her eyes. It was very different from the
stupor of agony – it was a blaze of short-lived passion,
which almost relieved, by its sense of resentment and

indignation, a heart worn out with other emotions.
Fordham himself, filled with compunction, led Lady
Western to the door; but it was not in the kind, foolish
heart of the young beauty to leave this poor woman in
peace. She came back and seized Mrs Vincent's trembling
hands in her own; she begged to be allowed to stay to
comfort her; she would have kissed the widow, who drew
back, and, half fainting with fatigue and excitement, still
kept her erect position by the table. Finally, she went
away in tears, no other means of showing her sympathy
being practicable. Mrs Vincent dropped down on her
knees beside the table as soon as she was alone, and
leaned her aching, throbbing head upon it. Oh, dreadful
lingering day, which was not yet half gone! Unconsciously
groans of suffering, low but repeated, came out of her
heart. The sound brought Mary, with whom no concealment was possible, and who gave what attendance and
what sympathy she might to her mistress's grievous trouble.
Perhaps the work of this dreadful day was less hard than
the vigil to which the mother had now to nerve her heart.

CHAPTER XXIII.

WAS it possible that she had slept? A moment ago and it
was daylight – a red sunset afternoon: now the pale half-
light, struggling with the black darkness, filled the apartment. She was lying on the sofa where Mary had laid her,
and by her side, upon a chair within her reach, was some
tea untasted, which Mary must have brought after she had
fallen into that momentary slumber. The fire burned
brightly, with occasional little outbreaks of flame. Such a
silence seemed in the house – silence that crept and
shuddered – and to think she should have slept!

The night had found covert in all the corners, so dark
they were; but one pale line of light came from the
window, and the room had a little ruddy centre in the fire.
Mrs Vincent, in the poignant anguish of her awakening,
grew superstitious; some other breath – some other
presence – seemed in the room besides her own. She
called "Mary," but there was no answer. In her excited
condition anything was possible – the bounds of the living
world and the possible seemed gone for ever. She might
see anything – hear anything – in the calm of her desperation. She got up, and hastily lighted the candle which
stood on the table. As she looked over the little light a
great cry escaped her. What was it? rising darkly, rising
slowly, out of the shadows in which it had been crouching,
a huddled indistinct figure. Oh God! not Susan! not her
child! As it rose slowly facing her, the widow cried aloud
once more, and put her hand over her eyes to shut out the
dreadful vision. Ghastly white, with fixed dilated eyes –
with a figure dilated and grandiose – like a statue stricken
into marble, raised to grandeur – could it be Susan who
stood there, without a word, without a movement, only
with a blank gaze at the horrified woman, who dared
not meet those dreadful eyes? When life rallied in Mrs
Vincent's horror-stricken heart, she went to the ghastly
creature, and put warm arms round it, and called it Susan!
Susan! had it any consciousness at all, this dreadful ghost?
had it come from another world? The mother kissed it with
lips that woke no answer – held it motionless in her
trembling arms. She cried again aloud – a great outcry –
no longer fearing anything. What were appearances now?
If it was Susan, it was Susan dead whom she held, all
unyielding and terrible, in her warm human arms.

Mary heard and came with exclamations of terror and
sympathy. They got her between them to the fire, and
chafed her chill hands and feet. Nobody knew how she
had got in, where she had come from; no one was with her
– no one had admitted her. She sat a marble woman in the

chair where they had placed her, unresistant, only gazing, gazing – turning her awful eyes after her mother. At last she drew some long gasping breaths, and, with a shudder which shook her entire frame, seemed to come to herself. "I am Susan Vincent," said the awful ghost. No tears, nor cries, nor wild pressure of her mother's arms, nor entreaties poured into her cold ear, could extract any other words. Mrs Vincent lost her self-possession: she rushed out of the room for remedies – rung the bell – called for Arthur in a voice of despair – could nobody help her, even in this horrible crisis? When she had roused the house she recollected herself, and shut the door upon the wondering strangers, and returned once more to her hopeless task. "Oh, Mary! what are we to do? Oh, Susan, my child, my darling! speak to your poor mother," cried the widow; but the marble figure in the chair, which was Susan, made no reply. It began to shiver with dreadful trembling fits – to be convulsed with long gasping sobs. "I am – Susan – Susan Vincent," it said at intervals, with a pitiful iteration. The sight of her daughter in this frightful condition, coming after all her fatigue and strain of excitement, unnerved Mrs Vincent completely. She had locked the door in her sudden dismay. She was kneeling, clasping Susan's knees – wasting vain adjurations upon her – driven beyond hope, beyond sense, beyond capacity. Little rustic Mary had all the weight of the emergency thrown upon her shoulders. It was she who called to the curious landlady outside to send for the doctor, and who managed to get Susan put into her mother's bed. When they had succeeded in laying her down there, a long interval, that seemed like years, passed before Dr Rider came. The bed was opposite the window, through which the pale rays of the twilight were still trembling. The candle on the other side showed Mrs Vincent walking about the room wringing her hands, now and then coming to the bedside to look at the unconscious form there, rent by those gasping sobs, uttering those dreadful words.

Mary stood crying at the foot of the bed. As for the widow, her eyes were tearless – her heart in an intolerable fever of suffering. She could not bear it. She said aloud she could not bear it – she could not bear it! Then she returned again to call vainly upon her child, her child! Her strength had given way – she had spent all her reserves, and had nothing to resist this unexpected climax of misery.

It was quite dark when Dr Rider came. Mary held the candle for him as he felt Susan's pulse, and examined her wide-open eyes. The doctor knew nothing about her any more than if he had not been a doctor. He said it must have been some dreadful mental shock, with inquiring looks at Mrs Vincent, who began to recover herself. He put back the heavy locks of golden brown hair, which had been loosened down from Susan's head, and said he was afraid there was pressure on the brain. What could he say? – he knew nothing more about it. He left some simple directions, said he would send some medicine, and took Mrs Vincent into the corner to ask what it was. "Some severe mental shock?" asked Dr Rider; but, before she could reply, a cab drove rapidly up to the door, and sounds of a sudden arrival were audible in the house. "Oh, doctor, thank God, my son is come – now I can bear it," said the widow. Dr Rider, who was of a compassionate nature, waited with pitying eyes till the minister should come up, and went to take another look at the patient, relieved to think he could speak to her brother, instead of racking her mother's heart. Mrs Vincent grew calm in the sudden consolation of thinking Arthur at hand. She sat down by the bedside, with her eyes fixed on the door, yearning for her son, the only living creature from whom she could have entire sympathy. Was it necessary that they should speak so loudly as they came up-stairs? – could he be bringing a stranger with him to Susan's sick-room? Her heart began to beat louder with mingled expectation and displeasure. It was not like Arthur – and there was no sound of his voice in the noise that swept up the

stair. She rose up instinctively as the footsteps approached
– heavy steps, not like her son's. Then the door was
thrown open. It was not Arthur who stood upon the dim
threshold. It was a stranger in a rough travelling-coat,
excited, resolute, full of his own errand. He made a stride
into the room to the bedside, thrusting Mrs Vincent aside,
not wittingly, but because she was in his way. Mary stood
at the other side with the doctor, holding up the one pale
candle, which threw a flickering light upon the marble
white figure on the bed, and the utter consternation
and surprise in Dr Rider's face. Mrs Vincent, too much
alarmed and astonished to offer any resistance, followed
the man who had thus entered into her sanctuary of
anguish. He knew what he was doing, though nobody else
did. He went straight forward to the bed. But the sight
of the unconscious figure there appalled the confident
stranger. "It is she, sure enough," he said; "are you a
doctor, sir? is the lady taken ill? I've come after her every
step of the way. She's in my custody now. I'll not give any
trouble that I can help, but I must stay here."

Mrs Vincent, who scarcely could endure to hear,
and did not understand, rushed forward while he was
speaking, and seized him by the arm – "Leave the room!"
she cried with sudden passion – "He has made some
impudent mistake, doctor. God help me! – will you let my
child be insulted? Leave the room, sir – leave the room, I
say! This is my daughter, Miss Vincent, lying here. Mary,
ring the bell – he must be turned out of the room. Doctor,
doctor! you are a man; you will never let my child be
insulted because her brother is away."

"What does it mean?" cried Dr Rider – "go outside and
I will come and speak to you. Miss Vincent is in a most
dangerous state – perhaps dying. If you know her"

"Know her, doctor! you are speaking of my child," cried
Mrs Vincent, who faced the intruder with blazing eyes.
The man held his ground, not impertinently, but with
steadiness.

"I know her fast enough," he said; "I've tracked her every step of the way; not to hurt the lady's feelings, I can't help what I'm doing, sir. It's murder;—I can't let her out of my sight."

Mrs Vincent clasped her hands together with a grasp of desperation. "What is murder?" she said, in a voice that echoed through the room. The doctor, with an exclamation of horror, repeated the same question. Murder! it seemed to ring through the shuddering house.

"It's hard upon a lady, not to say her mother," said the man, compassionately; "but I have to do my duty. A gentleman's been shot where she's come from. She's the first as suspicion falls on. It often turns out as the one that's first suspected isn't the criminal. Don't fret, ma'am," he added, with a glance of pity, "perhaps it's only as a witness she'll be wanted – but I must stay here. I daren't let her out my sight."

There was a dreadful pause. Mrs Vincent looked up at the two men before her with a heartrending appeal in her eyes. Would anybody tell her what it meant? – would nobody interfere for Susan? She moaned aloud, inarticulate in her voiceless misery. "And Arthur is not here!" was the outcry which at last burst from her heart. She was beyond feeling what this was – her senses were confused with extremity of suffering. She only felt that another blow had been dealt at her, and that Arthur was not here to help to bear it. Then the stranger, who had put himself so horribly in possession in Susan's sick-room, once more began to speak. The widow could not tell what he said – the voice rang in her ears like a noise of unmeaning sound, but it stirred her to a flush of female passion, as violent as it was shortlived. She sprang forward and took hold of his arm with her white little trembling hand: "Not here – not here!" cried the mother in her passion. With her feeble force excited into something irresistible, she put the astonished stranger out of the room before he knew what she was doing. If an infant had done it the man could not have been more utterly astonished. Outside, the people of the house were standing in an excited group. She thrust the dreadful messenger of justice out with those hands that shook with tremors of anguish and weakness. She shut the door upon him with all her feeble strength, locked it, put a chair against it; then she stumbled and fell as she stretched out for another – fell down upon her knees, poor soul! and remained so, forgetting, as it seemed, how she came there, and gradually, by instinct, putting together the hands which trembled like leaves in the wind – "Lord, Lord!" cried the mother, hovering on the wild verge between passion and insensibility. She called Him by name only as utter anguish alone knows how; she had nothing to tell Him; she could only call upon Him by His name.

Dr Rider took the half-insensible form up in his arms and carried her to the bedside, where Susan still lay motionless with her eyes wide open, in an awful abstraction and unconsciousness. He put Mrs Vincent tenderly into the chair, and held the hands that shook with that palsied irrestrainable tremor. "No one can bring her to life but you," said the doctor, turning the face of the miserable mother towards her child. She has kept her senses till she reached you; when she was here she no longer wanted them; she has left her life in your hands." He held those hands fast as he spoke; pressed them gently, but firmly; repeated his words over again. "In your hands," said the doctor once more, struck to his heart with horror and pity. Susan's bare beautiful arm lay on the coverlid, white, round, and full, like marble. The doctor, who had never seen the fair Saxon girl who was Mrs Vincent's daughter a week ago, thought in his heart that this full developed form and face, rapt to grandeur by the extremity of woe, gave no contradiction to the accusation he had just heard with so much horror. That week had obliterated Susan's soft girlish innocence and the simplicity of her eighteen years. She was a grand form as she lay there upon that bed – might have loved to desperation – fallen – killed. Unconsciously he uttered aloud the thought in his heart – "Perhaps it would be better she should die!"

Then the mother rose. Once more her painful senses came back to the woman who was still the minister's mother, and, even in this hideous dream of misery, had not forgotten the habits of her life. "When my son comes he will settle it all," said Mrs Vincent. "I expect him – any time – he may come any minute. Some one has made – a mistake. I don't know what that man said; but he has made – a mistake, doctor. My son, Mr Vincent, will see to all that. It has nothing to do with us. Tell me what we are to do for my child. Cut off her hair? Oh, yes, yes, anything? I don't mind it, though it is a sacrifice. She has had – a – a great fright doctor. She could not tell me particulars. When her brother comes home, we will hear all—" said the widow, looking with a jealous gaze in his eyes to see if he believed her. The scene altogether overcame Dr Rider. He turned away and went to the other side of the room, and took a glass of water from the table before he could answer her or meet that appeal. Then he soothed her as he best could with directions about Susan. He went away immediately to come back in an hour, if perhaps there might be any change – so he said; but, in reality, he wanted to escape, to hear this dreadful story, to think what was best. Friendless, with nobody near to protect them, and the officer of justice waiting at the door, what were these women to do? perhaps death waited closer than the visible messenger of fate. Would it be well to stay that more merciful executioner on his way?

The doctor found the officer outside the door, waiting, not without pity, at his post. He heard what was this man's version of the strange tragedy – strange, and yet not unfamiliar to human ears. The young woman had been betrayed and ruined. In wild vengeance and misery she had seized one of her seducer's pistols and shot him through the head – such was the story. And now she had

fled from the scene of the murder, tracked step by step by
the avenger. The whole house was in a tumult, as may
be supposed. The indignant landlady, who was a member
of Salem, could scarcely be prevented going into the
jealously-closed room and turning out the unhappy
criminal. Another lodger, a nervous woman, had already
collected her goods to fly from the place. Outside, some
mysterious instinct had collected a few people about the
door of the hitherto irreproachable house, which imagination magnified into a crowd. Already Tozer had set out
from his shop, red with anger, to inquire into this incipient
excitement, which nobody could explain. And still Arthur
had not appeared to stand by the miserable woman in this
horrible climax of fate.

When the doctor went back to the room where Susan
was, he found Mrs Vincent in a state of agitated activity.
Mary and she were flitting about the room, moving lights
before Susan's eyes, making what noises they could with
the furniture, keeping a fantastic commotion about the
bed. "She stirred, doctor, and we were trying to rouse
her," said the widow, who had put everything but Susan's
bodily extremity from her eyes at the moment. The
doctor, who was desperate, and whose heart was moved,
resorted to desperate measures. He gathered them about
the bed, set Mrs Vincent to support the insensible form,
and raising that white marble arm which had developed
into such glorious proportion, touched the swollen blue
vein with his lancet. The touch acted like magic. In
another moment she had struggled up out of her mother's
grasp, and thrown out the arm, from which the blood
flowed, up above her head: the crimson stream caught her
wild eye as she raised her arm in the air. A convulsive
shudder shook her frame. She threw herself over on her
face with a cry of horror, far more than a match, in her
strength of youth and passion, for the agitated arms that
held her. "Mother, mother, mother! it is his blood! it is his
life!" cried that despairing voice. The confused bed, the

convulsed frame, the flowing blood, all pitifully lighted up
by Mary's candle, made up of themselves a scene like a
murder; and Dr Rider vainly tried to forget the dreadful
words which forced upon his mind their untimely testimony.
He shuddered at the touch of that white woman's hand as
he bound up the wounded arm. He withdrew his eyes
from the pallid grandeur of the stricken face. In spite of
himself, horror mingled with his pity. A heavier stain was
upon her than those crimson traces on her pearly skin.
Other words followed in an incoherent stream. Fever of
the heart and brain, burning up into consuming frenzy,
had seized upon this lost creature, who was no longer a girl
or innocent. Ere long they had to send for nurses, to
restrain her delirium. She, raving with a wild madness
which betrayed in every wandering exclamation the horror
upon her soul, lay desperate in the room which had
enclosed for so many lingering hours her mother's anguish
of suspense and fear. In an adjoining room, the man who
had followed her to this refuge still waited, watchful yet
pitiful, intent that his prisoner should not escape him.
While outside a few gazers lingered, looking up at the
lights in the windows, with a strange perception that
something unusual had happened, though nobody knew
what it was. Such was the scene upon which Arthur
Vincent, not unwarned, yet incredulous, came suddenly
with eyes of horror and wild indignation as he reached his
own door.

CHAPTER XXIV.

WHEN Vincent was set down, in the darkness and silence
of the Sunday night, in the Dover railway station, it was

some minutes before he could collect himself, and understand where he was. He had fallen into a feverish sleep during the journey, little as he could have supposed himself capable of sleeping at such a moment; but he was young, and unused to the ceaseless fatigue and excitement and total want of rest which had obliterated for him the natural distinction between night and day. While his fellow-passengers trooped away, with all the bustle and excitement of travellers, to the pier and the night-boat which waited to carry them across the Channel, he, whom various porters and attendants stimulated with adjurations to make haste, and warnings that he would be late, stumbled out into the dark, collecting his faculties, and trying to think what he must do first. He was giddy and feverish with that insufficient snatch of sleep which had lost him the time in which he might have been laying his plans. But when he got outside the station into the unknown place, into the gloom of night, and heard the "moanings of the homeless sea" sounding sullen against the unseen shore, recollection and energy came back to him. That very sound, booming through the darkness, inspired Susan's brother. He thought of her forlorn, desolate, succourless, a weary wanderer seeking rest and finding none, shrouded up in darkness and danger, lost in the mysterious gloom – such was the sentiment of the night. The minister went on rapidly to the town, with its restless lights, through which everybody seemed to be passing towards the unseen sea. Should he follow with the stream, or should he stop at the hotel of which Mary had told him? He quickened his steps as he reached the open door of the inn, and plunged in to make rapid inquiries. Nobody knew either Colonel Mildmay or Mr Fordham, but the party which he described had been there, and had left only an hour before – not for the boat, the attendants thought; but the boat was ringing its bells through the night; and if by chance they had gone there, no time was to be lost. He rushed from the inn as fast as his wearied limbs could

carry him to the pier, where the lookers-on stood aside out
of his way, recognising his excitement. He went through
among all the passengers with the rough captain and his
lantern, having briefly explained to that functionary
what he wanted. But they were not there. When he had
satisfied himself, he left the boat, and stood with suspicious
reluctance, unwilling to lose sight of it, on the pier, and
watched the coloured lamp on the mast of the steamer
gradually gliding through the darkness out of the sheltering
harbour, till it began to plunge and heave on the unseen
sea. Then he took his troubled way back to the inn. It was
very late, and all the population seemed to disappear out
of the streets, with the little attendant crowd which had
been waiting upon the last event of the day, the departure
of this night-boat. The inn itself looked half asleep, and
was half closed when he returned. No further arrivals, no
incidents in the shape of trains or boats, were to be looked
for till the morning. It was the first time that Arthur had
encountered this compulsory pause of night. He struggled
against it for some time, questioning the waiters, and
gleaning some particulars which did but increase his
anxiety; but the waiters themselves were sleepy, and all
the world around had closed itself up in utter quietness
and rest.

Vincent went out again, but he could get admittance
nowhere, save at the office of the police, where he went in
desperation to ask the services of some one skilful in such
inquiries. He found this not without difficulty, but nothing
was to be done that night. he had to go back to the hotel,
to consent to the necessary rest for which, notwithstanding
the fever of his mind, his worn-out frame craved. Weariness, indeed, had gradually overpowered and absorbed
him; stronger than anxiety, more urgent even than his
love for his sister, was this present and overpowering
exhaustion which began to occupy all his thoughts.
Though he struggled with it, he could not but feel in his
heart, with a certain guilt, how this overwhelming desire

to throw himself down somewhere and rest possessed him to the exclusion of more worthy impulses. After he had ordered some refreshment, of which, indeed, he stood as much in need, the young man threw himself upon a sofa, and there fell into a deep sleep of utter weariness. He could do no more. He slept as youth must sleep, were it on the edge of a precipice, were it at the deathbed of its dearest friend. The very waiter who brought in the food he had ordered, took pity upon the worn-out slumberer. The man heaped up the fire, and covered Vincent with his railway wrapper before he withdrew; and it was not till morning that the young minister awoke out of that profound slumber – awoke chilled and aching and confused, in the dark, with the untouched meal still on the table, the candle flaming in its socket, and he himself totally unaware how long he had been asleep. In the interval that elapsed before the first sounds of awakening life in the house, he had time to collect himself, and when he went down-stairs to the coffee-room, still in the dark of the winter morning, had regained more command of himself and his powers than at any previous moment since this misery came upon him.

But it was still so early that the fire was scarcely alight, and he had to wait for the cup of coffee he ordered. Vincent went to the window, as was natural – a large window looking into the dark street, faintly lighted with lamps, which somehow burned less bright in the chill of the morning than they did at night. Looking out vaguely, yet with the vigilance of anxiety, without being able to discriminate anything except here and there a dark figure passing in the darkness, the young man waited with his face close to the uncurtained panes. There was nothing in that blank undecipherable street to interest him, and yet he gazed out mechanically in the anxious preoccupation of his mind. When the attendant came into the room with his coffee, his attention was temporarily distracted. He got up to go to the table where breakfast was being arranged for him; but, as he rose, his eye was caught by the gleam of a passing face, ghastly white in the darkness, looking in. Before he could draw breath, the apparition was gone. Without saying a word to the astonished waiter, who began to think him mad, Vincent dashed out after this vanished vision. Two female figures were visible a little farther on in the gloomy street. He pursued them with breathless, noiseless speed, and grasped at the arm of a terrified woman who, gasping with sudden fright, turned upon him a face he had never seen before. Nobody else was to be seen in any direction. The minister made an inarticulate apology, and turned back to search for some opening or passage through which that face could have disappeared. It was no fancy of his that painted that pale countenance upon the darkness – the same face that he had seen in the railway carriage following Colonel Mildmay – the same, but with a new look of horror and desperation in its eyes. The young man investigated, as he thought, every doorway, every corner which could have given shelter to such a fugitive. He returned, excited and agitated, to the inn, to ask if there was any passage through the line of houses which he might have over-looked, but could hear of none. It was on his lips to ask if they had heard of any crime or accident during the night – any – murder; but prudence restrained the incautious utterance. He went out with the wildest agitation in his mind; something had happened. Mrs Hilyard's face, gleaming in unconscious at the window, betrayed to him much more clearly than any confession, that some new and awful event had been added to that woman's strange experiences of life; and in the darkness he had been aware of some shadowy figure beside her, accompanying her ghostly way. Perhaps her child – perhaps – could it be Susan? The young man went out, not knowing where he went, into the darkness of the winter morning; he hastened to the pier, to the railway, startling the half-awakened people about, but nowhere could either see or hear of her.

Could it be a delusion? but the wildest imagination in the world could not have inspired with such a new horror of expression the eyes that gleamed out of that ghastly pale face.

The grey daylight had just got final mastery of the dark, when Vincent met the man whom he had employed the night before to help him in his inquiries. This agent, more skilful than the minister, had found out the cab-driver who conveyed the party from the hotel on the previous evening. Colonel Mildmay seemed to have made the precipitate retreat of a man suddenly startled and frightened out of his plans. The cabman gave a detailed account of the strange conduct of his fare. "We was a-going to the pier to the Ostend steamer, sir," said the driver, "when I was pulled up sharp, and got my directions to turn about sudden and go to the railway. There was a lady as I see keeping her eyes on us, a-standing by the pier-gates with her bag in her hand; but it was dark, and she couldn't have seen who was in the cab. The same occurred, sir, as we came up to the railway. I don't say as I see the lady there – but sure enough I was pulled up second time, and ordered out along the Folkestone road, a matter o'three mile or so. Then I was turned back again; and the end of all was that I took them to the Swan in Walmer Street, as is a place where there's well-aired beds and chops, and that style o'thing. That ain't the style of thing as is done in the Lord Warden. To take a fare, and partic'lar along with ladies, from the one of them places to the other, looks queer – that's what it does; it looks very queer, sir. It made me take a deal of notice. Gen'leman tall, light-haired, hook nose, awful swell to look at. Ladies, one on 'em pretty tall, one little; pretty creatures, but dreadful skeared, as far as I could see. The little one had a blue veil. That's them, sir; thought as I was right."

"And you can take me to the place?" said Vincent.

"Jump into my cab, and I'll have you there, sir, in five minutes," said the man.

The minister sprang into the cab alone. He no longer wanted the aid of a stranger; the darkling streets seemed to glide past him, and not he past them, as he dashed on at last to find his sister, this time there could be no mistake. After they had threaded several obscure streets, the driver came to a sudden pause, got off his box, and touched his hat with an alarmed look. "I can't drive up to the very 'ouse, sir – there's a crowd around the door; they do say as something has happened. I hope it ain't to any of your friends?" said the cabman. Vincent flung the door open as he was speaking, and rushed out. A horrified and excited crowd was besieging the door of the shabby public-house to which he had been brought. Seeing his hasty arrival, and the passionate anxiety in his eyes, the crowd gave way before him, recognising his right of entry; the very policeman at the door yielded to him in the force of his passion. "What is it?" he cried, aware of putting away some women and babies from the door, with mechanical kindness, but unconscious that he had stumbled up the steps like a man in a dream, and was demanding an answer to his question with an almost wild vehemence. The question was answered by a dozen eager voices. It was murder – murder! He could make out nothing but the word in the confusion of many speakers and of his own mind. Nobody opposed his entrance or asked what business he had there. He sprang up the stairs in two or three steps, pressed forward to a half-open door, within which he saw some people assembled, and, unawares thrusting aside a man who stopped him, went into the chamber of death. Several people were around the bed – one, a surgeon, occupied with a prostrate figure there. Vincent, over the heads of the spectators, gazed with burning eyes at this horrible spectacle. Susan herself, whom he did not expect to find there, nor could associate in any way with such a scene, faded out of his mind as he gazed with haggard face and horror-stricken soul at the shattered head, bound up in bloody bandages, scarce recognisable except by sharp eyes of love or hate, which rested on that mean pillow. He asked no questions for the moment. To him alone the business needed no explanation. He was not even surprised – he stood gazing in a momentary trance of horror at the lamentable sight. It was a wretched room, shabby and meagre, such a place as only terror could have driven Mildmay to. Villain as he was, his punishment had begun before that pistol-shot brought it to a climax – even in his success he had been conscious that she would keep her word.

The policeman at the door touched Vincent on the sleeve, just as he turned from the dreadful spectacle before him. "Nobody is allowed in here but for a good reason," said this man, gazing suspiciously at the stranger; "unless you knows something about it, or have come to identify the poor gentleman, or are of some use somehow, I can't let you stay here."

"I do not wish to stay here," said Vincent, turning away with a shudder. "I want to see the ladies who were with him. Yes, I know who he is – but I am not a friend of his; I have nothing to do with the matter. Where are the ladies who were with him? Miss Vincent," said the minister, with a pang, "and – and Miss Mildmay. I have come to take them away."

"The ladies as were with him? Oh, it's them as you're a-wanting; perhaps you'll stop a minute and talk to the inspector," said the policeman. "The ladies as were with him? Maybe you can tell the inspector something as will help justice? You didn't know the reason as brought out two young women a-travelling with a gen'leman, did you? They'll want all the friends they can collect afore all's done. You come this way with me."

It was a relief to get out of sight of that which horrified yet fascinated his eyes. Vincent followed the man into another room without observing the evident suspicion with which he was regarded. "Where are they?" he asked again. "I have a cab below. This is not a place for women. I have come to take them away. Where are the people of the house? What do you mean by keeping your hand on me? I want Miss Vincent. Do you hear me? I have nothing to do with Colonel Mildmay. He has plenty of friends to avenge him. I want my sister. Where is she? Call the people of the house."

Vincent threw off the policeman's hand from his arm, and, looking for a bell, rang violently. He was too much horror-stricken, and too secure of finding Susan, weeping and helpless in some corner, to show any of the passionate eagerness with which he had started on his search. Little doubt she was there, poor lost soul. He shrank from meeting her, now that the meeting was so near; and his thoughts went after that other desperate wretched woman, flying – who could tell where? – in despair and darkness. The house was in utter disorder, as was natural; none of its humble occupants being capable, at the present exciting moment, of attending to their usual duties. Vincent rang the bell again, till it pealed and echoed through the place. Then he bethought himself, with a natural shudder, of the death-chamber close by. He turned to the man by his side, with an instinctive involuntary curiosity. "Is any one suspected?" said the minister, feeling his face grow pale with a dreadful consciousness of the secret which he shared. But before he could hear the answer, his second summons had brought up the terrified mistress of the house, attended half-way up the stair by a throng of curious women. He went hurriedly to meet her at the door.

"Where are the ladies?" said the minister. "I have just heard that my sister was brought here last night. Tell her I am here. Take me to her. Don't be alarmed. You know what I mean? The two ladies – young ladies who came here with Colonel Mildmay last night – where are they? Good heavens! do you not understand what I mean?"

"The young ladies, sir?" faltered the landlady, gasping, and looking at the man who still kept by Vincent's side. "Oh, Lord bless us! The young ladies—"

"Make haste and let them know I am here," said Vincent, gradually growing more and more anxious. "I will undertake to produce them if they are wanted as witnesses. Where are they? – where is my sister? I tell you she is my sister. I have come for her. Tell Miss Vincent. Surely I am speaking plain English," said the young man, with a flush of sudden dread. "The elder one, Miss Vincent – you understand me? Let her know that I am here."

"His sister! Oh, Lord bless us; and he don't know no more than the unborn," cried the woman of the house. "Oh, Lord! p'liceman, can't you tell the poor gentleman? His sister! oh, that's worse than ever, that is. Some poor young thing as has been beguiled and led astray. Lord bless us! don't look at me o' that way. I ain't to blame. Oh, gracious me, that I should have to tell the gentleman, and you standing there! Oh, sir, it's her as has done it. She's gone away from here afore break of day. I don't blame her; oh, I don't blame her; don't look o' that dreadful way at me. He's drove her to it with bad usage. She'll have to suffer for it; but I don't blame her. I don't blame her if it was my last word in life."

Vincent felt his tongue cleave to his mouth. He was stunned; he did not know what he said – what he was hearing. "Blame her? whom? for what?" he said, with a mechanical effort. He seemed to himself to be suddenly engulfed in some horrible cloud, but he did not know what it meant.

"Oh, Lord! don't look o' that dreadful way at me; she's gone off from here as soon as she done it," cried the woman. "She had that much sense left, poor soul. He's drove her mad; he's drove her to it. My man says it can't be brought in no worse than manslaughter—"

"You don't understand me," Vincent broke in; "you are

talking of the criminal. Who are you talking of? – but it does not matter. I want Miss Vincent. Do you hear me? – the young lady whom he brought here last night. Where is my sister? Gone away before daybreak! You mean the criminal, but I want my sister – Susan! take me to where she is. She had nothing to do with it. I will give you anything – pay you anything, only take me to where she is."

He moved towards the door as he spoke, half believing that, if he could but hold out and refuse to credit this horror, Susan might still be found. "Lord bless us! the poor young gentleman's gone out of his senses," cried the landlady. "Let him go through all the house, if that's what he wants. There ain't nothing to conceal in my house. I'll take you to the room as they were in – she and the other one. This way, sir. They hadn't nothing with them but two little bags, so there wasn't much to leave; but such as it is, being her night-things, is there. She wasn't thinking of bags, nor any of her little comforts, when she went away. Here, sir; walk in here."

The woman took him to a room up-stairs, where Vincent followed her mechanically. The room had evidently been occupied a very short time before. Upon a chair, open, with the contents only half thrust in, was a travelling-bag, which the minister recognised at once – a piece of family property dreadful to see in such a place. Susan had been putting her things away with the orderly instinct of her mother's daughter when this sudden shock of terror came upon her. "Do you mean to tell me that it is she who has gone away," said Vincent, with a look of incredulous wonder and appeal – "she – Susan Vincent, my sister? Take time to think. It was not *she* – somebody else. Tell me where she is—"

"Oh, sir, don't say anything as may come against her," cried the landlady. "It's nobody but her, poor soul, poor soul. If it was possible to think as it could be another, I would – but there was nobody else to do it. As soon as we

heard the shot and the groan the master got up. He met
her on the stair, sir, if you'll believe me, like a woman as
was walking in her sleep. He was that struck he daren't
say a word to her. He let her pass by him and go out at the
door – and when he went into the gentleman's room and
found him there a-dying, she was gone clean off, and
couldn't be heard of. Folks say as my husband should
have stopped her, but it wasn't none of his business. Oh,
sir, don't say nothing as'll put them on her track! There's
one man gone off after her already – oh, it's dreadful! – if
you'll be advised by me, you'll slip out the back way, and
don't come across that policeman again. If she did kill
him," cried the weeping landlady, "it was to save herself,
poor dear. I'll let you out the back way, if you'll be guided
by me."

The horror of this accusation had come home to
Vincent's mind at last. He saw, as if by a sudden flash of
dreadful enlightenment, not guilt indeed, or its awful
punishment, but open shame – the disgrace of publicity –
the horrible suspicions which were of themselves more
than enough to kill the unhappy girl. He made a great
effort to speak, but could not for the moment. He thrust in
the white soft garments which were hanging out of it, into
that familiar bag, which somehow gave him a pang more
acute than all the terrible news he was hearing. He had
travelled with it himself on innocent boyish journeys, had
seen it in his mother's innocent hands – and now to find it
in this shuddering atmosphere of crime and mystery! He
too shuddered as he roused himself to speak. "Hush –
hush," said Vincent, "you mistake, my sister has nothing
to do with it; I – I can prove that – easily," said the
minister, getting the words out with difficulty. "Tell me
how it all happened – when they came here, what passed;
for instance—" He paused, and his eye caught another
evidence of the reality of his horrible position. It was the
blue veil which he had followed and described, and looked
for through all these weary hours. He took it up in his

hand, crushing it together with an almost ungovernable
impulse of rage, from where it had been thrown down on
the shabby carpet. "For instance," said Susan's brother,
restraining himself, "where is the girl who wore this? You
said Miss Vincent went away alone – where was the other?
was she left behind – is she here?"

The policeman had followed them up into the room in
natural curiosity and suspicion. The landlady's husband
had sworn that Susan left the house by herself. Then,
where was the girl? The fugitive had been tracked to the
railway, the policeman said; but she was alone. Nobody
had thought before of her helpless companion. The inspector arrived while they were going over the house
trying if it were possible to find any traces of this forlorn
creature. Vincent was much too profoundly concerned
himself to keep silence about the mysterious movements
of the woman whom he had seen on his way to Dover –
whom he had seen that very morning in the darkness –
whom he knew to be the bitterest enemy of the murdered
man. It was only when he described her – when he tried to
collect all the information he had ever had about her for
the guidance of justice – that he saw how little he knew of
her in reality. His very description was tinged with a touch
of fancy; and in this frightful emergency he perceived, for
the first time, how much his imagination had supplied of
the interest he felt in this woman. When he had done all
it was possible to do to set the pursuer on her track,
and gathered all he could of the supposed proofs against
Susan, he left the place where he could do nothing further.
He had to describe himself fully – to prove his identity by
a reference to the Dissenting minister of the place, and
explain whence he had come and whither he was going –
before the officers in charge of the house, although conscious that they had no grounds for detaining him, would
let him go. But he was permitted to leave at last. While he
waited for the next train to Carlingford, he questioned the
cabman, who could give but a very faint and indistinct

description of the lady whom he had seen at the pier-gates, whose appearance had stopped Colonel Mildmay in the prosecution of his journey. She was standing under a lamp, the man said: the gentleman might see her, but he didn't think as she could see him; but dim as the vision was, this was another little link in the chain of evidence. If it did but vindicate Susan – save her, not from the penalty, but from the very shadow and suspicion of such a horror! It was this which filled the minister's mind with every sort of frightful apprehension. To have Susan's name exposed to such a horrible publicity – to have such a scene, such a crime anyhow connected with his sister – the idea shook Vincent's mind utterly, and almost disabled him from thought at all. And where was she, poor horror-stricken fugitive? He scarcely dared hope that she had gone to her mother. Sudden death, madness, any misery, seemed possible to have overtaken the unhappy girl thus suddenly reft out of the peacefulness of her youth into circumstances so horrible. When he entered Carlingford, late at night, it was with insupportable pangs of suspense and alarm that he looked into the faces he met on the lighted streets. Were they looking at him already with a consciousness that some frightful shadow enveloped him? Tozer's shop was already shut – earlier than usual, surely – and two or three people stood talking at the open door, clearly visible against the gaslight, which still burned bright within. Farther up opposite his own house, two or three passengers had stopped to look up at the lighted windows. When Vincent thrust aside a lad who happened to be in his way, asking, with uncontrollable irritation, what he wanted there, the door opened suddenly at the sound of his voice. All was excited and confused within – common life, with its quiet summonses and answers, was over there. Wild confusion, agitation, reproach, sur-rounded the unfortunate minister. His landlady came forward to meet him, to bewail her own misfortune, and upbraid him with the wrong he had done her. "I took in

the pastor for a lodger, because he was sure to be steady
and respectable, and this is what he has brought to me!"
cried the hysterical woman. "What is the meaning of all
this?" cried Vincent, looking round him with restrained
fury; but he did not wait for an answer. He went up to his
rooms to know the worst. As he rushed breathless up-
stairs, loud outcries of delirium reached him. In his horror
and anguish he could not recognise the voice – was it his
mother who had given way under the terrible burden? He
dashed open the door of the sitting-room in which he had
spent so many quiet hours – neither mother nor sister were
there; instead of them a rough-featured man, in a blue
travelling-coat, and Tozer, flushed and argumentative,
standing by the table. Vincent had not time to ask what
the controversy was that was going on between the two.
The butterman grasped his hand with an almost violent
pressure, and took the stranger's arm. "Beg your pardon
for being in your room, Mr Vincent, but me and this
gentleman has a little business. I'll be back presently and
explain," said the good deacon, with a compassionate look
at the young man, whose weary eyes sought with instinctive suspicion that unknown face. "I'm your friend, Mr
Vincent – I always was; I'm not one as will desert a friend
in trouble," said Tozer, with another shake of his hand,
lowering his voice. Then he disappeared with his strange
companion. The minister was alone with those cries,
with this agitation. He threw himself down in momentary
despair. The worst, it appeared, had happened – the
horror had travelled before him. He gave up everything in
the anguish of that moment. There seemed to be no use
for any further struggle. To this sensitive, spotless,
inexperienced household, suspicion was worse than death.

CHAPTER XXV.

WHEN Vincent came to himself, and began to see clearly
the true horrors of his position, his mind, driven to its last
stronghold, rallied convulsively to meet the worst. It was
Susan who was raving close by; but her brother, in the
sickening despair of his heart, had not the courage to go into
that agitated sick-room. He sat waiting for Tozer's return
with a sense of helplessness, a sense of irritation, against
which he had not strength to contend. In that bitter
moment he gave up everything, and felt himself no longer
capable of striving against his fate. He felt in his heart that
all Carlingford must already be discussing the calamity that
had come upon him, and that his innocent honourable
name was already sullied by the breath of the crowd; and,
with a strange mixture of intolerance and eagerness, he
waited the return of the man who had first, as it appeared,
thrust himself into the secret – a man whom the minister
must not affront, must not defy, on peril of all he had in the
world. These few silent moments were more terrible to
Vincent than any that had gone before them. Was it any
good holding out, attempting to keep a brave face to the
world, struggling against this crushing blow? – or would it
not be easiest to give in, to drop the useless arms, to fly from
the inevitable downfall? Some corner of the earth there
surely remained where he could hide his head and find a
shelter for the two poor women who were greater sufferers
than he. It was with such feelings that he awaited the return
of Tozer – feelings aggravated by the consciousness that
somehow the butterman was engaged in his service at this
very moment, and by a shadowy and unexpressed suspicion

in his mind as to the character of the stranger whom Tozer
had taken away. The excellent deacon returned at last with
looks of conscious importance. He was very sorry and
anxious, but he could not help looking confidential, and
standing a little higher upon the ground of this mystery,
which nobody shared but himself. Once more he shook
hands with Vincent, sympathetically, and with a grasp full
of meaning.

"The thing for us to do is to keep it quiet – to keep it
quiet, sir," said Tozer, lowering his voice as he spoke.
"Nothing must be said about it – no more nor can be helped,
Mr Vincent. As far as it has gone, there's nobody as has
heard but me. If it could be kept private from the Salem
folks," continued the butterman, taking a seat at the table,
and looking cautiously round him, as if to make sure that no
one was within hearing, "it would be for the best. Them
women do make such a talk about everything. Not to tell a
falsehood, sir, as I wouldn't, not to save my own, if so be as
my own could be in such a position – we'll say as your
sister's took bad, sir, that's what we'll say. And no lie
neither – hear to her, poor soul! – But, Mr Vincent," said
Tozer, drawing closer, and confiding his doubt in a whisper,
"what she says is best not to be listened to, if you'll take my
advice. It ain't to be built upon what a poor creature says in
a fever, but them sort of words and screechings don't come
out of nothing but a troubled mind. She was aggravated
awful – so the man tells me."

"Who was the man?" asked Vincent, hurriedly.

"The man? oh! – which man was you meaning, sir?"
asked Tozer, with a little fright, recurring to his more
generous intention of keeping this intruder altogether from
the knowledge of the minister; "nobody in particular, Mr
Vincent – nobody as is worth mentioning. One as was sent
to inquire – that's all. I've cleared him away out of the
road," said the butterman, not without some natural complacency: "there ain't no matter about him. Don't ask me
no more, Mr Vincent, for it's losing time as is precious.

If there's anything as can be done, it's best to do it directly. I'd speak to John Brown as is the cleverest attorney in Carlingford, sir, if I was you. She's young, and, as I was saying, she was aggravated awful. She might be got off."

"Hush!" said Vincent, who had to put a desperate curb upon himself, lest the restrained rage with which he heard this implication of guilt should burst out; "you think there is something in this horrible business – that my sister has something to do with it. It is all a frightful delusion – an infernal—"

"Mr Vincent, sir, you mustn't swear. I'm as sorry for you as a man can be; but you're a minister, and you mustn't give way," said Tozer. "If there ain't nothing in it, so much the better; but I'm told as the evidence is clean again' her. Well, I won't say no more; it's no pleasure to me to think of a young creature, and a minister's daughter, with a mother like what she's got, going any ways astray – far the contrary, Mr Vincent: your own father, if he was living, couldn't be more sorry than me. But my advice is, keep quiet, and don't let anything get out no more nor can be helped. I don't mean to say as it can be altogether kep' quiet – that ain't in the nature of things; nor I don't mean to make you suppose as all is likely to go smooth, and no fault found. There's pretty sure to be some unpleasantness, one way or another; and the only thing as I can see is just to put up with it, and stand your ground, and do your duty all the same. And I for one will stand by you, sir," said Tozer, rising to his feet with a little glow of conscious generosity and valour, and shaking the hand of the poor young minister with cordial kindness – "I'll stand by you, sir, for one, whatever happens; and we'll tide it out, Mr Vincent, that's what we'll do sir, if you can but hold on."

"Thank you," said poor Vincent, moved to the heart – "thank you. I dare not think how it is all to end, but thank you all the same; I shall not forget what you say."

"And tell your mother," continued Tozer, swelling to a little triumph in his own magnanimity – "tell your mother as I said so; tell her as I'll stand by you through thick and thin; and we'll pull through, we'll pull through!" said the butterman, slowly disappearing, with a face radiant with conscious bounty and patronage, through the open door.

Vincent had followed him with an instinct of civility and gratitude. Just as Tozer withdrew, a fresh burst of outcry came from the sick-room, ringing through the excited house. The deacon turned round half-way down the stair, held up his hands, listened, and made a movement of wondering pity towards the closed door which hid Susan, but did not keep in her cries. The wretched minister drew back from that compassionate gesture as if some one had struck him a blow. He went back and threw himself down on the sofa, and covered his face with his hands. The pity and the patronage were the last drop of humiliation in his bitter cup. Hot tears came to his eyes; it seemed to him more than flesh and blood could bear.

Some time elapsed, however, before Vincent had the courage to meet his mother. When those dreadful outcries sank into exhaustion, and all for the moment was quiet in the sick-room, he sent to tell her he had arrived, and went to the dreadful door which she kept closed so jealously. He was afraid to meet her eye when she came to him, and noiselessly drew him within. Judging by himself, he had not ventured to think what his mother's horror and despair would be. But Mrs Vincent put her arms round her son with an exclamation of thanksgiving. "Oh, Arthur! thank God, you are come. Now I shall be able to bear it," cried his mother. She cried a little upon his breast, and then wiped her eyes and looked up at him with quivering lips. "Oh, Arthur, what my poor darling must have come through!" said Mrs Vincent, with a wistful appeal to him in her tender eyes. She said nothing of the darker horror. It lay upon her soul a frightful, inarticulate shadow; but in the mean time she could only think of Susan and her fever – that fever which afforded a kind of comfort to the mother – a proof that her child had not lost her innocence lightly, but that the

shock had been to Susan a horrible convulsion, shaking earth
and heaven. the mother and son went together to the bedside to look at the unhappy cause of all their sorrows – she
clinging with her tender hand to his arm, wistful now, and
afraid in the depths of her heart lest Arthur, who was only a
man, might be hard upon Susan in her terrible abasement.
It was more than a year since Vincent had seen his sister.
Was it Susan? The grandeur of the stricken form, the features
sublimed and elevated, the majestic proportions into which
this awful crisis of fate had developed the fair-haired girl of
Lonsdale, struck her brother with unspeakable awe and pity.
Pity and awe; but yet another feeling mingled in the wonder
with which he gazed upon her. A thrill of terror came over
him. That frightful, tropical blaze of passion, anguish, and
woe which had produced this sudden development, had it
developed no unknown qualities in Susan's heart? As she
lay there in the majesty of unconsciousness, she resembled
more a woman who could avenge herself, than a soft girl,
the sudden victim of a bad man. Vincent turned away from
the bed with an involuntary shudder. He would not, could
not, look at her again: he left his mother to her unceasing
vigil, and himself went to his own room, to try if rest were
possible. Rest was not easy in such a terrible complication
of affairs; but weariness is omnipotent with youth. He did
sleep by snatches, in utter fatigue and exhaustion – slept
long enough to secure for himself the unspeakable torture
of waking to the renewed horror of a new day.

CHAPTER XXVI.

Next morning the minister rose to the changed life and
world which now surrounded his way, if not with much less

excitement, at least with a more familiar knowledge of all the troubles which encompassed him. As he sat over the pretended breakfast, for which he had no appetite, and not even heart enough to make a show of eating, hearing close by the voice of his sister's delirium, sometimes in faint murmurs, sometimes rising into wild outcries of passion, and pondered all the circumstances of this frightful calamity, it is not wonderful that his heart fainted within him. He had found out quickly enough that it was an officer of justice whom Tozer had succeeded, by what means he could not tell, in removing from the house. His landlady knew all the facts sufficiently well to be by times reproachful and by times sympathetic. The other lodgers in the house, some of whom had already left for fear of pollution, were equally aware of all the circumstances of the case; and it was impossible to hope that a tale so exciting, known to so many, could be long of spreading. The minister seemed to himself to look ruin in the face, as he sat in profound dejection, leaning his head in his hands. He had committed his sister's interests into the hands of the best attorney he could hear of in Dover, that watch and search might be made on the spot for any further information; and now the only thing possible to be done was to secure some still more skilful agent in London to superintend the case, and set all the machinery of detection in motion to discover Mrs Hilyard. Vincent had nothing in the world but the income which he drew from the liberality of Salem; an income which could ill stand the drain of these oft-repeated journeys, not to speak of the expenses of Susan's defence. All the minister had would not be enough to retain a fit defender for her, if she had to undergo the frightful ordeal of a trial. The very thought of it drove her unhappy brother desperate. Would it not be better if she died and escaped that crowning misery, which must kill her anyhow, if she survived to bear it? But these ponderings were as unprofitable as they were painful. When he had seen his mother, who whispered to him accounts of Susan's illness, which his mind was too much preoccupied to under-

stand, he went away immediately to the railway, and
hastened to town. While he stood waiting in the lawyer's
office, he took up listlessly, without knowing what he was
doing, the newspaper of the day. There he found the whole
terrible tale made into a romance of real life, in which his
sister's name, indeed, was withheld, but no other particular
spared. As he stood wiping the heavy dew from his forehead,
half frantic with rage and despair, the quick eye of his
misery caught a couple of clerks in another corner of the
office, talking over another newspaper, full of lively interest
and excitement. It was Susan's story that interested them;
the compiler had heightened with romantic details those
hideous bare facts which had changed all his life, and made
the entire world a chaos to Vincent; and all over the country
by this time, newspaper readers were waking up into excitement about this new tale of love, revenge, and crime. The
poor minister put down the paper as if it had stung him, and
drew back, tingling in every nerve, from the table, where
he could almost hear the discussion which was going on
about Miss—; where she could have escaped to, and whether
she would be found. It restored him to his senses and self-
command when he found himself face to face with the cool
lawyer, who waited for his tragic story as a matter of
business, and who had nothing to do with the heartbreaks
or the disgrace which it involved. He was detained there for
some time, giving as full an account as he could of all the
circumstances, and describing as well as he could his reason
for suspecting Mrs Hilyard, and her mysterious appearance
at the scene of the murder. Vincent perceived, with a
sensation of comfort at his heart, that his story interested
the acute attorney, accustomed to the tricks and expedients
of crime, who perceived at once the circumstances of suspicion, and understood at once how to go about it, and ferret
the secret out. The minister himself grew steadier as he
entered into his narrative. No shivers of wonder or pain
convulsed the calm lawyer as he listened. Under his touch,
Susan's dreadful position became one not unprecedented,

to be dealt with like any other condition of actual life; and
when Vincent, after furnishing all the information he could,
and satisfying himself that no time was to be lost in the
prosecution of the search for the real criminal, left the office
to return to Carlingford, it was with a mind somewhat calmed
out of its first horror. He went back again by the train,
deeply depressed and anxious, but not so susceptible to every
glance and word as he had been an hour or two before. He
tried, indeed, to take a certain gloomy satisfaction from the
idea that now everything was known. Fear of discovery
could no longer appal the stricken household; and to meet
the horror in the face was less dreadful than to feel themselves
skulking under a secret shadow which might at any moment
be found out. He set his face sternly, and looked everybody
full in the eyes who looked at him, as he once more alighted
at the familiar station. He accepted the fact that people
were talking of him, pitying him, contemplating him with
wonder and fright, as somehow involved in an atmosphere
of tragedy and crime. With this feeling he went slowly
along George Street on his homeward way, with no susceptibility left in him, so far as he was aware, except as concerned
this sudden calamity which had swallowed up his life.

When suddenly the sound of a carriage stopping came
dully upon his ears; he would not have noted or heard it but
for the sound that followed of some one calling his own
name, and the soft rush of footsteps on the pavement; even
then he did not turn round to see who called him. It was
accordingly with a thrill of strange emotion – a strange,
sudden, guilty suffusion of delight over all his tingling
frame and aching heart, even in the midst of his suffering,
that he felt the light touch of Lady Western's hand first laid
on his arm, then softly stealing within it in the sudden
sympathy which possessed her as she looked up into his
colourless face. It was pity and natural kindness which
prompted the young Dowager to this unwonted familiar
touch. She was sorry for him to the bottom of her heart – she
would fain have made him amends somehow for the

terrible evil which had come upon him. With the natural impulse of a woman to caress or soothe, or cheat a man anyhow out of that look of suffering which it is intolerable to her to see on his face, Lady Western acted instinctively, without thinking what she did. She slid her beautiful hand into his arm, clung to him, looked up with her lovely appealing face and eyes full of tears to the pale face of the minister, which that touch moved beyond all expression. If he did not stop and take her into his arms, and lean his great anguish upon her in a sweetness of relief unspeakable and measureless, it was only because ordinary rule and custom are stronger than even passion. He was as much deceived as if he had done it, the poor young deluded soul. Out of the thunder and storm, all at once, without prelude or warning, he thought it was the light of love that broke upon him all radiant and glorious. With that he could brave all, overcome all; for that he could be content to fathom any depths of wretchedness. So he thought, as he looked down from those sudden heights of unhoped-for tremulous blessedness into that lovely face, and saw it trembling with divine compassion and tenderness. So he thought the ice breaking, the depths stirring in his own soul. Hope, deliverance, happiness, a delight more exquisite still, that consolation of love which makes anguish itself sweet, breathed over the poor young Nonconformist as that hand slid within his arm. His very brain grew dizzy with the sweetness of relief, the sudden ease that possessed his soul.

"Oh, Mr Vincent, my heart is breaking; what shall we do – what shall we do?" cried Lady Western. "If it is true, I shall never dare speak to you again, and I feel for you to the bottom of my heart. Oh, Mr Vincent, you don't think she did it? I am sure she did not do it – *your* sister! It was bad enough before," cried the lovely creature, crying without restraint, but still holding his arm and gazing up into his face, "but now my heart is broken. Oh, will you tell me what I must do? I will not go to *him*, for he has been a bad man; and I dare not go to your dear mother as I should like to go; and I feel for you, oh, to the very bottom of my heart!"

"Then I can bear it," said Vincent. Though he did not speak another word, the sound of his voice, the expression of his face, betrayed him. He put his hand involuntarily upon the little hand that rested on his arm. It was all so sudden that his self-command forsook him. A smile trembled upon his face as he looked down at her with all his heart in his eyes. "Then I can bear it," said the poor young minister, overwhelmed and penetrated by that exquisite consolation. Lady Western gave a little start of alarm as she read the unmistakable meaning in his face. She withdrew her hand hastily with a flush of radiant colour and downcast look of fright and shame. What had she done? Her confusion, her agitation, her sudden withdrawal, did but increase the spell. To Vincent's charmed soul it seemed that *she* had betrayed herself, and that womanly reserve alone drew her back. He attended her to her carriage with a tender devotion which could not express itself in words. When he had put her in, he lingered, gazing at the face, now so troubled and downcast, with a delicious feeling that he had a right to gaze at her. "You have made me strong to bear all things," he said, in the low tone of passion and secret joy. In the depth of his delusion he saw no other meaning than sudden timidity and womanly reticence in her confused and alarmed looks. When the carriage drove off he stood looking after it with eyes full of dreamy light. Darkness surrounded him on every side, darkness more hideous than a nightmare. The poor young soul believed for that delicious moment that superlative and ineffable, like his misery, was to be his joy.

Harder thoughts regained the mastery when he got within his own house again. It was no longer the orderly, calm, well-regulated house which had taken in the minister of Salem by way of adding yet a finer touch to its own profound respectability. Susan's unhappy presence pervaded the place. Boxes of other lodgers going away

encumbered the hall, where the landlady hovered weeping
and admitted the pastor sullenly with an audible sob.

Though he had imagined himself invested in armour of
light against all these petty assaults, Vincent was not strong
enough, even in the fictitious strength given him by Lady
Western's kindness, to bear the reality of his position. The
very face of his landlady brought before him the whole
array of faces at Salem, which he must shortly encounter,
all directed towards him in judicial severity – an awful
tribunal. When he reached the shelter of his room up-stairs,
the 'Carlingford Gazette' lay upon his table, folded out so
as to show that mysterious story of Miss—, which some
one in the house had certainly identified. The poor minister
took it in his hands with an impulse to tear it in pieces – to
trample it under foot – to give some outlet, now he was by
himself, to the rage and indignation with which he saw his
own calamity turned into a romance for the amusement of
the public. He checked himself with a bitter smile at his
own folly; unconsciously he bethought himself of Tozer's
back-parlour, of Mr Tufton's sitting-room, of all the places
about where he had seen his people gleaning information
and amusement from the 'Carlingford Gazette.' How the
little paper, generally so harmless, would amuse and
excite its readers to-day! What surmises there would be,
and how soon the fatal knowledge would ooze out and be
talked over on all sides! It was no matter of feeling to him
– it was ruin in every way to the poor young minister,
whose credit and living depended solely upon the caprice
of his "flock." The sight of the newspaper had so stunned
him, that it was some time before he perceived a letter
lying under it on the table. When he saw that the post-
mark was Dover, he snatched up this letter eagerly
and tore it open. It was from the lawyer whom he had
consulted there. For the first moment he did not comprehend the information it conveyed. Good news! – what
news could be good under his dreadful circumstances?
The young man's mind was stupified, and could not take it

in. It was the copy of a doctor's certificate – the opinion of
a famous surgeon who had been summoned from London
– to the effect that Colonel Mildmay's wound was not
necessarily fatal, and that if fever did not come on he
might recover. The minister read it over again and again
before he could comprehend it; and when he did comprehend it, the fact seemed rather an aggravation than a
comfort to his misery. He was not dead – this destroyer.
Perhaps at this moment, when his unhappy victim lay
struggling between life and death, he, with the horrible
good fortune of wickedness, was coming back from the
edge of the grave. At the first shock it did not seem good
news to Vincent. Not dead! – "the cursed villain," he said
through his clenched teeth. The earth was not rid of that
pitiless wretch. It looked like another grand injustice in
the world, where all the landmarks were overturned, and
only evil seemed to prosper. He did not connect it anyhow
with possible relief or deliverance to Susan; on the contrary,
it raised in his own mind all the resentment and rage
which had been quenched by Mildmay's supposed death.
He could scarcely compose himself after that unexpected
information. If all went well, it would naturally change the
character of the case – perhaps, under the circumstances,
there might be no prosecution, said the lawyer's letter.
Vincent was young – excited out of all self-command or
prudential considerations. In his soul he resented even
this hope, which might still save his sister, and grudged
what he felt to be the diabolical good-luck of her destroyer.
Not dead! – not going to die! – not punished anyhow.
About, after all the misery he had occasioned, to recover,
and go on prosperously again, and spread wretchedness
and ruin upon others. "He shall render me an account!"
cried the minister fiercely to himself. "He shall answer for
it to me!" He felt it intolerable, that this guilty soul should
escape punishment.

Thoughts more reasonable, however, came to him
after a time. He began to see the importance of the

intelligence to Susan – and even to himself. At least she could not be accused of shedding blood – at least she might be hidden somewhere in her shame, poor lost soul, and kept from the cruel eyes of the world. When he began to feel the influence of this gleam of comfort, he ventured to go to the sick-room to tell his mother, whom he had not yet seen; but Mrs Vincent was deaf and insensible to everything but her child, whose need and danger were too urgent to permit more distant spectres, however terrible, to be visible in her sick-chamber. Mary, already worn out with fatigue, had gone to bed with a headache, with the liveliest conviction in her mind that she had taken the fever too. The widow, who had lived for the past week as though she had no physical frame at all, sat sleepless, with hot eyes and pallid face, by her daughter's bed. She could still smile – smiles more heart-breaking than any outcry of anguish – and leaned her poor head upon her son, as he came near to her, with a tender pressure of her arms and strain of absolute dependence which went to his heart. She could not speak, or say, as she had said so often, that her boy must take care of his sister – that Susan had no one else to stand by her. Leaning upon him in an unspeakable appeal of love and weakness, smiling on him with her wistful quivering lips, was all the poor mother could do now.

All; for in that room no one could speak. One voice filled its silence. The restless movement of the head on that pillow turning from side to side in search of the rest which was nowhere to be found, stilled every other motion. Not even fever could flush the marble whiteness of her face. Awfully alone, in her mother's anxious presence, with her brother by her bedside, Susan went on unconscious through the wild distracted world of her own thoughts – through what had been her own thoughts before horror and anguish cast them all astray. Vincent stood aside in breathless attention like the rest, before he had been many minutes in the room. We say to each other how

strange it is that no heart can ever fully communicate itself
to another; but when that revelation does take place,
awful is the spectacle. All unawares, in her dread distraction, Susan opened up her heart.

"What does it matter what they will say?" said Susan; "I
will never see them again. Unless – yes, put down her veil;
she is pretty, very pretty; but what has Herbert to do with
her? He said it was me he wanted; and why did he bring
me away if he did not love me? Love me! and deceived
me, and told me lies. Oh God, oh God! is it not Carlingford?
Where is it? I am taking God's name in vain. I was not
thinking of Him; I was thinking—. His name is Fordham,
Herbert Fordham, – do you hear? What do you mean by
Mildmay? I know no Mildmay. Stop and let me think.
Herbert – Herbert! Oh, where are you – where are you?
Do you think it never could be him, but only a lie? Well! if
he did not love me, I could bear it; but why, why did he
cheat me, and bring me away? The door is locked; they
will not let me get out. Herbert! was there never, never
any Herbert in the world? Oh, come back, even if you are
only a dream! Locked! If they would only kill me! What do
they mean to do with me? Oh, God, oh God! but I must
marry him if he says so. I must, *must* marry him, though
he has told me lies. I must, whatever he does. Even if I
could get through the window and escape; for they will call
me wicked. Oh, mamma, mamma! and Arthur a minister,
and to bring disgrace on *him!* But I am not disgraced. Oh
no, no; never, never! – I will die first – I will kill him first.
Open the door; oh, open the door! Let me go!"

She struggled up in one of her wilder paroxysms. She
had thrown herself half out of bed, rising up wildly, and
tossing her arms into the air, before her startled brother
could rush forward to control her. But as the voice of the
unhappy girl rose into frenzy, some unseen attendants
stole in and took her out of his unskilful hands. The sight
was too painful for unaccustomed eyes – for eyes of love,
which could scarcely bear, even for her own sake, to

see such means of restraint employed upon Susan. Mrs Vincent stood by, uttering unconscious cries, imploring the two strong women who held her daughter, oh, not to hurt her, not to grasp her so tightly; while Susan herself beat the air in vain, and entreated, with passionate out-cries, to be set free — to be let go. When she was again subdued, and sank into the quiet of exhaustion, Vincent withdrew from this saddest scene of all, utterly depressed and broken-spirited. The wretch lived who had wrought this dread wreck and ruin. What did it matter? Within that room it gave no relief, eased no heart, to say that he was not dead. Forms more terrific still than those of law and public vengeance — madness and death — stood on either side of Susan's bed; till they had fought out the desperate quarrel, what matter to those most immediately concerned whether a greater or a lesser penalty lowered over her head? The minister went back to his own retirement with an aching heart, utterly dejected and depressed. He threw himself into a chair to think it all over, as he said to himself; but as he sat there, hopeless and solitary, his mind strayed from Susan. Could any one blame him? Who does not know what it is to have one secret spot of personal consolation to fly to in the midst of trouble? Vincent betook himself there in the utter darkness of everything around. Once more he seemed to feel that sudden touch which took away half his burden. No words could have spoken to his heart like that fairy hand upon his arm. He brooded over it, not thinking, only living over again the moment which had made so great a difference in the world. He forgot Fordham; he forgot everything; he took neither reason nor likelihood with him in his self-delusion. A sudden rosy mist suffused once more the cruel earth upon which he was standing; whatever came, he had something of his own to fall back upon, an ineffable secret sweetness, which stanched every wound before it was made. The young minister, out of the very depths of calamity, escaped into this garden of delights; he put aside the intolerable misery of the house; he thrust away from him all the lesser troubles which bristled thick in front of him in the very name of Salem. He fled to that one spot of joy which he thought remained to him in the middle of the waste, doubly sweet and precious. It gave him strength to hold out through his trouble, without being overwhelmed. He escaped to that delicious resting-place almost against his will, not able to resist the charm of the indescribable solace he found there. He alone, of all concerned, had that footbreadth of personal happiness to take refuge in amid the bitter storm. He did not know it was all delusion, self-deception, a woeful miserable blunder. He hugged it to his heart in secret, and took a comfort not to be spoken from the thought. Vanity of vanities; but nothing else in the world could have stolen with such fairy balms of consolation and strength to the heart of the poor minister. It was not long till he was called to face his fate again, and all the heavy front of battle set in array against him; but it was with a feeling of sweet guilt that he started up in the winter twilight, and left his room to see Tozer, who waited for him below. That room henceforward was inhabited by the fairy vision. When he went back to it, Love, the consolatrix, met him again, stealing that visionary hand within his arm. Blank darkness dwelt all around; here, falsest, fairest mirage of imagination, palpitated one delicious gleam of light.

CHAPTER XXVII.

SOMEHOW the heavy week stole round without any other fluctuations but those terrible ones of Susan's fever. Dreadful consolation and terrible doubt breathed forth in those heart-rending revelations which her poor unconscious soul was continually pouring forth. The unhappy girl showed her heart all naked and undisguised to the watchers round her – a heart bewildered, alarmed, desperate, but not overwhelmed with guilty passion. Through the dreadful haze which enveloped her mind, flashes of indignation, bursts of hope, shone tragical and fierce; but she was not a disgraced creature who lay there, arguing pitifully with herself what she must do; not disgraced – but in an agony of self-preservation could she have snatched up the ready pistol – could it be true? When Vincent went into that room, it was always to withdraw with a shuddering dread. Had she escaped one horror to fall into another yet more horrible? That evidence of which, with Mrs Hilyard's face before his eyes, he had been half contemptuous at first, returned upon him with ever-growing probability. Driven to bay, driven mad, reason and self-control scared by the horrible emergency, had the desperate creature resorted to the first wild expedient within her reach to save herself at last? With this hideous likelihood growing in his mind, Vincent had to face the Sunday, which came upon him like a new calamity. He would fain have withdrawn, and, regardless of anything else which might happen, have sent once more for Beecher. To confront the people of Salem, to look down upon those familiar rows of faces, all of them bearing a consciousness of the story in the newspapers, acquainted with all that his landlady could tell, and guessing but too distinctly the terrible misfortune which had befallen his family, seemed more than flesh and blood could bear. He was sitting alone, pondering all this, with a letter which he had commenced to write to Beecher before him, when Tozer, who was now his constant visitor, came in. There could be no doubt of the butterman's honest and genuine sympathy, but, unfortunately, there was just as little doubt that Tozer took a pleasure in managing the minister's affairs at this crisis, and piloting him through the troubled waters. Tozer did all but neglect his business

to meet the emergency; he carried matters with rather a
high hand in the meetings of the managing committee; he
took absolute control, or wished to do so, of Vincent's
proceedings. "We'll tide it over, we'll tide it over," he said,
rubbing his hands. To go in, in this state of mind, secure in
his own resources and in the skill with which he could guide
the wavering and half-informed mind of Salem, fluctuating
as it did between horror and sympathy, doubtful whether to
take up the minister's cause with zeal, or to cast him off and
disown him, and to find the minister himself giving in,
deserting his post at the most critical moment, and making
useless all that his patron was doing for him, was too much
for the deacon's patience. He sat down in indignant surprise
opposite Vincent, and struck his stick against the floor
involuntarily, by way of emphasis to his words.

   "Mr Vincent, sir, this ain't the thing to do – I tell you it
ain't the thing to do. Salem has a right to expect different,"
cried Tozer, in the warmth of his disappointment; "a
congregation as has never said a word, and office-bearers
as have stuck by you and stood up for you whatever folks
liked to say! I'm a man as will never desert my pastor in
trouble; but I'd like to know what you call this, Mr Vincent,
but a deserting of *me?* What's the good of fighting for
the minister, if he gives in and sends for another man, and
won't face nothing for himself? It's next Sunday as is all
the battle. Get that over, and things will come straight.
When they see you in the pulpit in your old way, and all
things as they was, bless you, they'll get used to it, and
won't mind the papers no more nor – nor I do. I tell you
sir, it's next Sunday as is the battle. I don't undertake to
answer for the consequences, not if you gives in, and has
Mr Beecher down for next Sunday. It ain't the thing to do,
Mr Vincent; Salem folks won't put up with that. Your
good mother, poor thing, wouldn't say no different. If you
mean to stay and keep things straight in Carlingford,
you'll go into that pulpit, and look as if nothing had
happened. It's next Sunday as is the battle."

"Look as if nothing had happened! – and why should I
wish to stay in Carlingford, or – or anywhere?" cried
Vincent, in a momentary outbreak of dejection. But he
threw down his pen, and closed his blotting-book over the
half-written letter. He was too wretched to have much
resolution one way or another. To argue the matter was
worse than to suffer any consequences, however hard they
might be.

"I don't deny it's natural as you should feel strange,"
admitted Tozer. "I do myself, as am only your friend, Mr
Vincent, when folks are a-talking in the shop, and going
over one thing and another – asking if it's true as she
belongs to you, and how a minister's daughter ever come
to know the likes of him—"

"For heaven's sake, no more, no more! – you will drive
me mad!" cried Vincent, springing to his feet. Tozer, thus
suddenly interrupted, stared a little, and then changed the
subject, though without quite finding out how it was that
he had startled his sensitive companion into such sudden
impatience. "When I was only telling him the common
talk!" as he said to his wife in the privacy of their own
parlour. In the mean time he had other subjects equally
interesting.

"If you'll take my advice, you'll begin your coorse all
the same," said Tozer; "it would have a good effect, that
would. When folks are in a state of excitement, and a-
looking for something, to come down upon them as before,
and accordin' to intimation, would have a wonderful effect,
Mr Vincent. You take my word, sir, it would be very
telling – would that. Don't lose no time, but begin your
coorse as was intimated. It's a providence, is the intimation.
I wouldn't say nothing about what's happened – not plain
out; but if you could bring in a kind of an inference like,
nothing as had anything to do with the story in the papers,
but just as might be understood—"

The butterman sat quite calmly and at his ease, but
really anxious and interested, making his sober suggestions.

The unfortunate minister, unable otherwise to subdue his
impatience and wretchedness, fell to walking up and down
the room, as was natural. When he could bear it no longer,
he came back to the table at which Tozer sat in all the
pomp of advice and management. He took his unfinished
letter and tore it in little pieces, then stopped the calm
flow of the deacon's counsel by a sudden outburst.

"I will preach," cried the young man, scattering the bits
of paper out of his hand unawares. "Is not that enough?
don't tell me what I am to do – the evil is sufficient without
that. I tell you I will preach. I would rather cut off my
right hand, if that would do as well. I am speaking like a
child or a fool: who cares for my right hand, I wonder, or
my life, or my senses? No more of this. I will preach –
don't speak of it again. It will not matter a hundred years
hence," muttered the minister, with that sudden adoption
of the philosophy of recklessness which misery sometimes
plays with. He threw himself into his chair again, and
covered his face with his hands. He was thinking of Salem,
and all those rows of gazing eyes. He could see them all in
their pews; imagination, with a cruel freak like a mocking
spirit, depicting all the finery of Mrs Pigeon and Mrs
Brown upon that vivid canvass. The minister groaned at
the thought of them; but to put it down on paper, and
record the pang of exasperation and intolerable wretchedness which was thus connected with the fine winter bonnets
of the poulterer's wife and the dairywoman would make a
picture rather grotesque than terrible to unconcerned
eyes. It was dreadful earnest to poor Vincent, thinking
how he should stand before them on that inexorable
Sunday, and preach "as if nothing had happened;" reading
all the while, in case his own mind would let him forget
them, the vulgarest horrors of all that had happened in all
that crowd of eyes.

"And you'll find a great consolation, take my word,
sir, in the thought that you're a-doing your duty," said
Tozer, shaking his head solemnly, as he rose to go away:

"that's a wonderful consolation, Mr Vincent, to all of us; and especially to a minister that knows he's a-serving his Master and saving souls."

Saving souls! Heaven help him! the words rang in his ears like mocking echoes long after the butterman had settled into his arm-chair, and confided to his wife and Phoebe that the pastor was a-coming to himself and taking to his duties, and that we'll tide it over yet. "Saving souls!" the words came back and back to Vincent's bewildered mind. They formed a measure and cadence in their constant repetition, haunting him like some spiritual suggestion, as he looked over, with senses confused and dizzy, his little stock of sermons, to make preparation for the duty which he could not escape. At last he tossed them all away in a heap, seized his pen, and poured forth his heart. Saving souls! what did it mean? He was not writing a sermon. Out of the depths of his troubled heart poured all the chaos of thought and wonder, which leapt into fiery life under the quickening touch of personal misery and unrest. He forgot the bounds of orthodox speculation – all bounds save those of the drear mortal curtain of death, on the other side of which that great question is solved. He set forth the dark secrets of life with exaggerated touches of his own passion and anguish. He painted out of his own aching fancy a soul innocent, yet stained with the heaviest of mortal crimes: he turned his wild light aside and poured it upon another, foul to the core, yet unassailable by man. Saving souls! – which was the criminal? which was the innocent? A wild confusion of sin and sorrow, of dreadful human complications, misconceptions, of all incomprehensible, intolerable thoughts, surged round and round him as he wrote. Were the words folly that haunted him with such echoes? Could he, and such as he, unwitting of half the mysteries of life, do anything to that prodigious work? Could words help it – vain syllables of exhortation or appeal? God knows. The end of it all was a confused recognition of the One half-known, half-identified, who, if any hope were to be had, held that hope in His hands. The preacher, who had but dim acquaintance with His name, paused in the half idiocy of his awakened genius, to wonder, like a child, if perhaps his simple mother knew a little more of that far-off wondrous figure – recognised it wildly by the confused lights as the only hope in earth or heaven – and so rose up, trembling with excitement and exhaustion, to find that he had spent the entire night in this sudden inspiration, and that the wintry dawn, cold and piercing to the heart, was stealing over the opposite roofs, and another day had begun.

This was the sermon which startled half the population of Carlingford on that wonderful Sunday. Salem had never been so full before. Every individual of the Chapel folks was there who could by any means come out, and many other curious inhabitants, full of natural wonder, to see how a man looked, and what he would preach about, concerning whom, and whose family, such mysterious rumours were afloat. The wondering congregation thrilled like one soul under that touch of passion. Faces grew pale, long sobs of emotion burst here and there from the half-terrified excited audience, who seemed to see around them, instead of the everyday familiar world, a throng of those souls whom the preacher disrobed of everything but passion and consciousness and immortality. Just before the conclusion, when he came to a sudden pause all at once, and made a movement forward as if to lay hold of something he saw, the effect was almost greater than the deacons could approve of in chapel. One woman screamed aloud, another fainted, some people started to their feet – all waited with suspended breath for the next words, electrified by the real *life* which palpitated there before them, where life so seldom appears, in the decorous pulpit. When he went on again the people were almost too much excited to perceive the plain meaning of his words, if any plain meaning had ever been in that passionate outcry of a wounded and bewildered soul. When the

services were over, many of them watched the precipitate
rush which the young preacher made through the crowd
into his vestry. He could not wait the dispersion of the
flock, as was the usual custom. It was with a buzz of
excitement that the congregation did disperse slowly, in
groups, asking each other had such a sermon ever been
preached before in Carlingford. Some shook their heads,
audibly expressing their alarm lest Mr Vincent should go
too far, and unsettle his mind; some pitied and commented
on his looks – women these. He sent them all away in a
flutter of excitement, which obliterated all other objects of
talk for the moment, even the story in the papers, and left
himself in a gloomy splendour of eloquence and uncertainty,
the only object of possible comment until the fumes of his
wild oration should have died away.

"I said we'd tide it over," said Tozer, in a triumphant
whisper, to his wife. "That's what he can do when he's
well kep' up to it, and put on his mettle. The man as says
he ever heard anything as was finer, or had more mind in
it," added the worthy butterman to his fellow-deacons,
"has had more opportunities nor me; and though I say it,
I've heard the best preachers in our connection. That's
philosophical, that is – there ain't a man in the Church as
I ever heard of as could match that, and not a many as
comes out o' 'Omerton. We're not a-going to quarrel with
a pastor as can preach a sermon like that, not because he's
had a misfortune in his family. Come into the vestry,
Pigeon, and say a kind word – as you're sorry, and we'll
stand by him. He wants to be kep' up, that's what he
wants. Mind like that always does. It ain't equal to doing
for itself, like most. Come along with me, and say what's
kind, and cheer him up, as has exerted hisself and done
his best."

"It *was* rousing up," said Pigeon, with a little reluctance;
"even the missis didn't go again' that; but where he's weak
is in the application. I don't mind just shaking hands—"

"If we was all to go, he might take it kind," suggested

Brown, the dairyman, who had little to say, and not much confidence in his own opinion; and pride and kindness combined won the day. The deacons who were in attendance went in, in a body, to shake hands with the pastor, and express their sympathy, and congratulate him on his sermon, the latter particular being an established point of deacon's duty in every well-regulated and harmonious community. They went in rather pleased with themselves, and full of the gratification they were about to confer. But the open door of the vestry revealed an empty room, with the preacher's black gown lying tossed upon the floor, as if it had been thrown down recklessly in his sudden exit. The little procession came to a halt, and stared in each other's faces. Their futile good intentions flashed into exasperation. They had come to bestow their favour upon him, to make him happy, and behold he had fled in contemptuous haste, without waiting for their approval; even Tozer felt the shock of the failure. So far as the oligarchs of Salem were concerned, the sermon might never have been preached, and the pastor sank deeper than ever into the bad opinion of Mr Pigeon and Mr Brown.

In the mean time Vincent had rushed from his pulpit, thrown on his coat, and rushed out again into the cold midday, tingling in every limb with the desperate effort of self-restraint, which alone had enabled him to preserve the gravity of the pulpit and conclude the services with due steadiness and propriety. When he made that sudden pause, it was not for nought. Effective though it was, it was no trick of oratory which caught the breath at his lips, and transfixed him for the moment. There, among the crowded pews of Salem, deep in the further end of the chapel, half lost in the throng of listeners, suddenly, all at once, had flashed upon him a face – a face, unchanged from its old expression, intent as if no deluge had descended, no earthquake fallen; listening, as of old, with gleaming keen eyes and close-shut emphatic mouth. The whole building reeled in Vincent's eyes as he caught sight of that thin head, dark and silent, gleaming out in all its expressive refinement and intelligence from the common faces round. How he kept still and went on was to himself a kind of miracle. Had she moved or left the place, he could not have restrained himself. But she did not move. He watched her even while he prayed, with a profanity of which he was conscious to the heart. He watched her with her frightful composure finding the hymn, standing up with the rest to sing. When she disappeared, he rushed from the pulpit – rushed out – pursued her. She was not to be seen anywhere when he got outside; and the first stream of the throng of dispersing worshippers – which fortunately, however, included none of the leading people of Salem – beheld with amazed eyes the minister who darted through them, and took his hurried way to Back Grove Street. Could she have gone there? He debated the question vainly with himself as he hastened on the familiar road. The door was open as of old, the children playing upon the crowded pavement. He flew up the staircase, which creaked under his hasty foot, and knocked again at the well-known door, instinctively pausing before it, though he had meant to burst in and satisfy himself. Such a violence was unnecessary – as if the world had stood still, Mrs Hilyard opened the door and stood before him, with her little kerchief on her head, her fingers still marked with blue. "Mr Vincent," said this incomprehensible woman, admitting him without a moment's hesitation, pointing him to a chair as of old, and regarding him with the old steady look of half-amused observation, "you have never come to see me on a Sunday before. It is the best day for conversation for people who have work to do. Sit down, take breath; I have leisure, and there is time for everything we can have to say."

CHAPTER XXVIII.

Vᴏɴᴄᴇɴᴛ put out his hand to seize upon the strange woman
who confronted him with a calmness much more confounding
than any agitation. But her quick eye divined his purpose.
She made the slightest movement aside, extended her own,
and had shaken hands with him in his utter surprise before
he knew what he was doing. The touch bewildered his
faculties, but did not move him from the impulse, which
was too real to yield to anything. He took the door from her
hand, closed it, placed himself against it. "You are my
prisoner," said Vincent. He could not say any more, but
gazed at her with blank eyes of determination. He was no
longer accessible to reason, pity, any sentiment but one.
He had secured her. He forgot even to be amazed at her
composure. She was his prisoner – that one fact was all he
cared to know.

"I have been your prisoner the entire morning," said Mrs
Hilyard, with an attempt at her old manner, which scarcely
could have deceived the minister had he preserved his wits
sufficiently to notice it, but at the same time betraying a
little surprise, recognising instinctively that here she had
come face to face with those blind forces of nature upon
which no arguments can tell. "You were in much less doubt
about your power of saving souls the last time I heard you,
Mr Vincent. Sit down, please. It is not long since we met,
but many things have happened. It is kind of you give me
so early an opportunity of talking them over. I am sorry to
see you look excited – but after such exertions, it is natural,
I suppose—"

"You are my prisoner," repeated Vincent, without

taking any notice of what she said. He was no match for her in any passage of arms. Her words fell upon his ears without any meaning. Only a dull determination possessed him. He locked the door, while she, somewhat startled in her turn, stood looking on; then he went to the window, threw it open, and called to some one below – any one – he did not care who. "Fetch a policeman – quick – lose no time!" cried Vincent. Then he closed the window, turned round, and confronted her again. At last a little agitation was visible in this invulnerable woman. For an instant her head moved with a spasmodic thrill, and her countenance changed. She gave a rapid glance round as if to see whether any outlet was left. Vincent's eye followed hers.

"You cannot escape – you shall not escape," he said, slowly; "don't think it – nothing you can do or say will help you now."

"Ah!" said Mrs Hilyard, with a startled, panting breath. "You have come to the inexorable," she said, after a moment; "most men do, one time or another. You decline meeting us on our ground, and take to your own. Very well," she continued, seating herself by the table where she had already laid down one of the Salem hymn-books; "till this arrival happens, we may have a little conversation, Mr Vincent. I was about to tell you something which ought to be good news. Though you don't appreciate my regard for you, I will tell it you all the same. What noise is that? Oh, the boys, I suppose, rushing off for your policeman. I hope you know what you are going to say to that functionary when he comes. In the mean time, wait a little – you must hear my news."

The only answer Vincent made was to look out again from the window, under which a little group of gazers had already collected. His companion heard the sounds below with a thrill of alarm more real than she had ever felt before. She sat rigidly, with her hand upon the hymn-book, preserving her composure by a wonderful effort, intensely alive and awake to everything, and calculating her chances with a certain desperation. This one thing alone of all that had happened, the Back Grove Street needlewoman, confident in her own powers and influence, had not foreseen.

"Listen!" she cried, with an excitement and haste which she could not quite conceal. "That man is not dead, you know. Come here – shut the window! Young man, do you hear what I say to you? Am I likely to indulge in vain talk now? Come here – here! and understand what I have to say."

"It does not matter," said Vincent, closing the window. "What you say can make no difference. There is but one thing possible now."

"Yes, you are a man!" cried the desperate woman, clasping her hands tight, and struggling with herself to keep down all appearance of her anxiety. "You are deaf – blind! You have turned your back upon reason. That is what it always comes to. Hush! come here – closer; they make so much noise in the street. I believe," she said, with a dreadful smile, "you are afraid of me. You think I will stab you, or something. Don't entertain such vulgar imaginations, Mr Vincent. I have told you before, you have fine manners, though you are only a Dissenting minister. I have something to tell you – something you will be glad to know—"

Here she made another pause for breath – merely for breath – not for any answer, for there was no answer in her companion's face. He was listening for the footsteps in the street – the steps of his returning messengers. And so was she, as she drew in that long breath, expanding her forlorn bosom with air, which the quick throbs of her heart so soon exhausted. She looked in his eyes with an eager fire in her own, steadily, without once shifting her gaze. The two had changed places. It was he, in his inexorableness, close shut up against any appeal or argument, that was the superior now.

"When you hear what I have to say, you will not be so calm," she went on, with another involuntary heave of her breast. "Listen! your sister is safe. Yes, you may start, but what I say is true. Don't go to the window yet. Stop, hear me! I tell you your sister is safe. Yes, it may be the people you have sent for. Never mind, this is more important. You have locked the door, and nobody can come in. I tell you again and again, your sister is safe. That man is not dead – You know he is not dead. And yesterday – hush! never mind! – yesterday," she said, rising up as Vincent moved, and detaining him with her hand upon his arm, which she clutched with desperate fingers, "he made a declaration that it was not she; a declaration before the magistrates," continued Mrs Hilyard, gasping as her strength failed her, and following him, holding his arm as he moved to the window, "that it was not she – not she! do you understand me – not she! He swore to it. He said it was another, and not that girl. Do you hear me?" she cried, raising her voice, and shaking his arm wildly in the despair of the moment, but repeating her words with the clearness of desperation – "He said on his oath it was not she."

She had followed him to the window, not pleading for herself by a single word, but with her desperate hand upon his arm, her face pinched and pale to the lips, and a horrible anxiety gleaming in the eyes which she never removed from his face. The two stood together there for a moment in that silent encounter; he looking down at the group of people below, she watching his face with her eyes, clutching his arm with her hand, appealing to him with a speechless suspense and terror, which no words can describe. Her fate hung upon the merest thread, and she knew it. She had no more power to move him in her own person than any one of the ragged children who stood gazing up at the window. There he stood, silent, blank, immovable; and she, suffering no expression of her dreadful suspense to escape her, stood clutching his arm, seeing, as she had never seen before, a pale vision of prisons, scaffolds, judgments, obscuring earth and heaven. She was brave, and had dared them all wittingly in the crisis of her fate, but the reality caught the labouring breath from her lips, and turned her heart sick. This morning she had woke with a great burden taken off her mind, and, daring as she was, had faced the only man who had any clue to her secret, confident in his generous nature and her own power over him. But this confidence had failed her utterly, and in the very ease and relief of her mind – a relief more blessed and grateful than she could have acknowledged to any mortal – lo! here arose before her close and real the spectre which she had defied. It approached step by step, while she gazed with wild eyes and panting breath upon the inexorable man who had it in his power to deliver her over to law and justice. She dared not say a word of entreaty to him; she could only watch his eyes, those eyes which never lighted upon her, with speechless dread and anxiety. Many evils she had borne in her life – many she had confronted and overcome – obstinate will and unscrupulous resolution had carried her one way or other through all former dangers. Here for the first time she stood helpless, watching with an indescribable agony the face of the young man at whom she had so often smiled. Some sudden unforeseen touch might still set her free. Her breath came quick in short gasps – her breast heaved – her fate was absolutely beyond her own control, in Vincent's hands.

Just then there came into the narrow street a sound of carriage-wheels. Instinctively Vincent started. The blank of his determination was broken by this distant noise. Somehow it came naturally into the silence of this room and woke up the echoes of the past in his mind; the past – that past in which Lady Western's carriage was the celestial chariot, and she the divinest lady of life. Like a gleam of light there suddenly dawned around him a remembrance of the times he had seen her here – the times he had seen her anywhere; the last time – the sweet hand she had laid upon his arm. Vincent's heart awoke under that touch. With a start he looked down upon the hand which was at this moment on his arm, – not the hand of love, – fingers with the blood pressed down to the very tips, holding with desperation that arm which had the power of life and death. A hurried exclamation came from his lips; he looked at the woman by him, and read vaguely in her face all the passion and agony there. Vaguely it occurred to him that to save or to sacrifice her was in his hands, and that he had but a moment now to decide. The carriage-wheels came nearer, nearer, ringing delicious promises in his ears – nearer too came the servants of that justice he had invoked; and what plea was it, what strange propitiation, which his companion had put forth to him to stay his avenging hand? Only a moment now; he shook her hand off his arm, and in his turn took hold of hers; he held her fast while she faced him in an agony of restrained suspense and terror. How her worn bosom panted with that quick-coming breath! Her life was in his hands.

"What was that you said?" asked Vincent, with the haste and brevity of passion, suddenly perceiving how much had to be done in this moment of fate.

The long-restrained words burst from his companion's lips almost before he had done speaking. "I said your sister was safe!" she cried; "I said he had declared her innocent on his oath. It was not she – he has sworn it, all a man could do. To sacrifice another," she went on breathlessly, with a strong momentary shudder, pausing to listen, "will do nothing for her – nothing! You hear what I say. It was not she; he has sworn upon his solemn oath. Do as you will. She is safe – safe! – as safe as – as – God help me – as safe as my child; – and it was for her sake—"

She stopped – words would serve her no further – and just then there came a summons to the locked door. Vincent dropped her arm, and she recoiled from him with an involuntary movement; unawares she clasped her thin hands and gave one wild look into his face. Not even now could she tell what he was going to do, this dreadful arbiter of fate. The key, as he turned it in the door, rang in her ears like thunder; and his hand trembled as he set

open the entrance of the needlewoman's mean apartment.
On the threshold stood no vulgar messenger of fate, but a
bright vision, sad, yet sweeter than anything else in earth
or almost in heaven to Vincent. He fell back without
saying anything before the startled look of that beautiful
face. He let in, not law and justice, but love and pity, to
this miserable room.

"Oh, Rachel! where have you been? have you seen
him? have you heard of him? where have you been?"
cried the visitor, going up to the pallid woman, whose eyes
were still fixed on Vincent. Mrs Hilyard could not speak.
She dropped upon her knees by the table, shivering and
crouching like a stricken creature. She leaned her head
upon the hymn-book which lay there so strangely at
variance with everything else around it. Pale with fright
and horror, Lady Western appealed to Vincent. "She is ill,
she is fainting – oh, Mr Vincent, what have you been
saying to her? She was not to blame," cried the new-comer
in her ignorance. Vincent attempted no reply, offered
no help. In his heart he could have snatched away
those beautiful hands which embraced and comforted his
"prisoner," thus rescued out of his grasp. It was hard to
see her touch that guilty conscious woman whom his own
heart refused to pity. He stood by looking on, watching
her still; the instinct of vengeance had been awakened
within him. He was reluctant to let her go.

"You have been saying something to her," said Lady
Western, with tears in her eyes; "and how could *she* be to
blame? Rachel! Oh, I wonder, I wonder if she loved him
after all?" cried the beautiful creature in the bewilderment of her innocence and ignorance. She stood bending
over the kneeling figure, troubled, perplexed almost more
than her strange sister-in-law had ever yet perplexed her.
She could not account for this extraordinary access of
agitation. It was nohow explainable, except upon that
supposition which opened at once the warmest sympathies
of the gentle young woman's heart.

"Rachel, dear!" she cried, kissing softly the thin hands worn with toil that covered Mrs Hilyard's face – "he is still living, there is hope; perhaps he will get better; and he is showing a better mind too," she added, after a little tremulous pause. "I came to see if you had come home, to tell you; he has sworn that it was not – oh, Mr Vincent, I sent you word immediately when I got the message – he says it was not your sister; she had nothing to do with it, he says. Now, I can look you in the face again. The first thing he was able to do when he came to himself was to clear her; and now she will get better – and your dear mother?" said Lady Western, looking wistfully into the young man's face. In that moment, while her attention was directed otherwise, Mrs Hilyard rose up and took her seat again; took her seat because she was not able to stand, and scarcely able, by all the power of her will, to compose the nerves which, for the first time in her life, had utterly got the better of her. She wiped off the heavy moisture from her face with a furtive hand before the young Dowager turned her eyes again that way. She grasped fast hold of the only thing on the table, the Salem hymn-book, and with a vast effort regained some degree of self-command. For that precious moment she was free from observation, for nothing in the world could have prevented Vincent from returning with his own fascinated eyes the look which Lady Western turned upon him. While the two looked at each other, she was safe; she collected her scattered forces in that invaluable instant. She was herself again when Lady Western looked round, somewhat nervous and embarrassed, from the gaze of passion with which her look of deprecation and sympathy had been met. If a slight shiver now and then thrilled over Mrs Hilyard's figure, it was as like to be cold as emotion. Otherwise, she sat with her arm resting on the table and her hand clenched upon the hymn-book, her thin lips clinging spasmodically to each other, and her face pallid, but to an uncritical observer scarcely changed from the grey and vigilant composure of her usual appearance. So many storms had passed over that countenance, that the momentary agony of horror and fright from which she had scarcely yet emerged did not tell as it would have done on a face less worn. Her voice was sharp and strained when she spoke, and she watched Vincent's eye with a keenness of which he was vividly conscious; but Lady Western, who did not go deep into looks and meanings, found nothing very unusual in what she said.

"I think Mr Vincent was doubtful of my information," she said. "I heard it last night from Langridge, the groom, who once belonged to my family, you know, Alice; and – and lets me know if anything more than usual happens," she said, abruptly stopping to draw breath. "I travelled all night to get here to-day. Mr Vincent was doubtful of me. Now this matter is cleared up, I daresay he will understand me when I say that I never could have allowed things to go further. I am only a needlewoman, and live in Back Grove Street," continued Mrs Hilyard, recovering gradually as she spoke; "but I have certain things still in my power. Mr Vincent will understand what I mean," she went on, fixing her eyes upon him, and unable to repress an occasional gasp which interrupted her words, "when I say that I should not have suffered it to go further. I should not have shrunk from any sacrifice. My dear, I have been a little shaken and agitated, as you perceive. Mr Vincent wants to keep his eye upon me. Take me with you, Alice," said the bold woman, once more looking Vincent full in the face; "take charge of me, keep me prisoner, until all this is cleared up. I am about tired of living a disguised princess. Send up your people for my possessions here and take me with you. You will find me safe, Mr Vincent, when you happen to want me, with Lady Western in Grange Lane."

"Oh, Rachel, I am so glad!" cried Lady Western; "I cannot for my life imagine what you mean by keeping you my prisoner, and all that; but Mr Vincent may be very sure you will be safe, with me; – since he has so much interest in your movements," continued the young Dowager, turning her perplexed eyes from one to the other. She had not the remotest idea what it all meant. She was perhaps a little surprised to perceive that, after all, Vincent's interest was less with herself than with this strange woman, whose calmness and agitation were equally confusing and unintelligible. "We shall, of course, always be happy to see Mr Vincent in Grange Lane," she concluded, with a somewhat stately courtesy. He did not look at her; he was looking at the other, whose eyes were fixed upon his face. Between these eyes Lady Western, much amazed, could perceive a secret communication passing. What could it mean? The consciousness of this mystery between them which she did not know, annoyed her, notwithstanding her sweet temper. She withdrew her hand instinctively from Mrs Hilyard's, which she had taken in momentary enthusiasm, and watched their looks of intelligence with half-offended eyes.

"Yes," said the needlewoman, speaking with her eyes fixed upon Vincent, though she did not address him, and making a desperate effort after her usual manner; "I do not think Back Grove Street will do any longer. One may as well take advantage of the accident which has brought our family affairs before the world to come alive again. It is a thing one must do sooner or later. So, if your carriage is close, Alice, I will go home with you. I shall miss Salem," said the audacious woman, "though you are so much less sure about doing good than you used to be, Mr Vincent. If my soul happens to be saved, however," she continued, with a strange softening of her fixed and gleaming eyes – "if that is of much importance, or has any merit in it – you will have had some share in the achievement. You will?" She said the words with a keen sharpness of interrogation, much unlike their more obvious meaning. "You will," she repeated again, more softly – "you will!" Her thin hands came together for a moment in a clasp of mute supplication; her eyes, always hitherto looking down upon him from heights of dark knowledge and experience, looked up in his face with an anguish of entreaty which startled Vincent. Just at that moment the sounds in the street grew louder, and a voice of authority was audible ordering some one to clear the way. Mrs Hilyard did not speak, but she put out her hand and touched Lady Western's shawl, lifting its long fringes, and twisting them round those fingers on which the marks of her long labour were still visible. She withdrew as she did this her eyes from his face. Her fate was absolutely in his hands.

"Ladies," said Vincent, hoarsely, after vainly trying to clear his agitated voice, "it is better you should leave this place at once. I will see you to your carriage. If I do wrong, the consequences will fall hardest on me. Don't say anything; either way, talking will do little good. You are her shield and defence," he said, looking at Lady Western, with an excitement which he could not quite keep under. "When she touches you she becomes sacred. You will keep her safe – safe? you will not let her go?"

"Yes; I will keep her safe," said the beauty, opening her lovely astonished eyes. "Is she in danger? Oh, Mr Vincent, your trouble has been too much for you! remember your sister is safe now."

"Is she?" said the minister; he was bitter in his heart, even though that hand was once more laid on his arm. "Safe! – with a broken heart and a ruined life; but what does that matter? It is all we are good for; though we may go mad and die."

"Oh, not you! not you!" said Lady Western, gazing at him with the tenderest pity in her sweet eyes. "You must not say so; I should be so unhappy." Her beautiful hand pressed his arm with the lightest momentary pressure. She could not help herself; to see suffering and not to do what was in her to soothe it, was not possible to her soft heart. Whatever harm that temporary opiate might do, nothing in the world could have prevented her gentle kindness from administering it. She went down the humble stairs leaning on his arm, with Mrs Hilyard following close. The young man put aside the little crowd he himself had collected, and put them in the carriage. He saw them drive away with a kind of despairing exaltation and excitement, and turned to the difficulties which remained to him – to explain himself and send the tardy ministers of justice away. He explained as he best could that he had been mistaken, and once more emptied his scanty purse, where there was now little enough left. When he had got rid of the disappointed group about the door, he went home slowly in the reaction of his violence and haste. Susan was safe; was she safe? delivered from this dreadful accusation – allowed to drop back at least with her broken heart into the deep silences of privacy and uninvadable domestic life. Well, it was a mercy, a great mercy, though he could not realise it. He went home slowly, tingling with the strain of these strange hours; was it Sunday still? was it only an hour ago that Salem had thrilled to the discourse in which his passion and despair had found vent? Vincent neither comprehended himself nor the hours, full of strange fate, which were gliding over him. He went home exhausted, as if with a great conflict; conscious of some relief in his heart, but half unwilling to confess to it, or to realise the means by which it had dawned upon him.

CHAPTER XXIX.

When Vincent entered the house, the sensation of quiet in it struck him with a vague consolation which he could scarcely explain. Perhaps only because it was Sunday; but there was no reproachful landlady, no distracting sound from above – all quiet, Sunday leisure, Sunday decorum, as of old. When he went up hurriedly to his sitting-room, he found two letters lying on his table – one a telegraphic despatch from Dover, the other a dainty little note, which he opened as a man opens the first written communication he receives from the woman of all women. He knew what was in it; but he read it as eagerly as if he expected to find something new in the mild little epistle, with its gentle attempt at congratulation. The news was true. Either remorse had seized upon Mildmay in the prospect of death, or the lingering traditions of honour in his heart had asserted themselves on Susan's behalf. He had declared her entirely innocent; he had even gone farther, he had sworn that it was only as the companion of his daughter that Susan had accompanied them, and as such that he had treated her. The deposition taken by the magistrates was sent to Vincent in an abridged form, but what it conveyed was clear beyond dispute. So far as the words of this apparently dying man could be received, Susan was spotless – without blood on her hand, or speck upon her good fame. The lesser and the greater guilt were both cleared from that young head which had not been strong enough to wait for this vindication. Though he said, Thank God, from the bottom of his heart, an unspeakable bitterness filled Vincent's soul as he read. Here was a deliverance, full, lavish, unlooked for; but who could tell that the poor girl, crazed with misery, would ever be any the better for it? who could tell whether this vindication might be of any further use than to lighten the cloud upon Susan's grave?

With this thought in his mind he went to the sick-room, where everything seemed quiet, not quite sure that his mother, absorbed as she was in Susan's present danger, could be able to realise the wonderful deliverance which had come to them. But matters were changed there as elsewhere. Between the door and the bed on which Susan lay, a large folding-screen had been set up, and in the darkened space between this and the door sat Mrs Vincent, with Dr Rider and his wife on each side, evidently persuading and arguing with her on some point which she was reluctant to yield to them. They were talking in whispers under their breath, and a certain air of stillness, of calm and repose, which Vincent could scarcely comprehend, was in the hushed room.

"I assure you, on my word," said Dr Rider, lifting his eyes as Vincent opened the door, and beckoning him softly to come in, "that this change is more than I dared hope for. The chances are she will wake up out of danger. Nothing can be done for her but to keep her perfectly quiet; and my wife will watch, if you will rest; – for our patient's sake!" said the anxious doctor, still motioning Vincent forward, and appealing to him with his eyes.

"Mr Vincent has something to tell you," said the quick little woman, impetuous even in her whisper, who was Dr Rider's wife. "He must not come and talk here. He might wake her. Take him away. Edward, take them both away. Mrs Vincent, you must go and hear what he has to say."

"Oh, Arthur! my dear boy," cried his mother, looking up to him with moist eyes. "It is I who have something to tell. My child is perhaps to get well, Arthur. Oh! my own boy, after all, she is going to get better. We shall have Susan again. Hush! doctor, please let me go back again; something stirred – I think something stirred; and perhaps she might want something, and the nurse would not observe. Tired? – no, no; I am not tired. I have always watched them when they were ill, all their lives. They never had any nurse in sickness but their mother. Arthur, you know I am not tired. Oh! doctor, perhaps you would order something while he is here, for my son; he has been agitated and anxious, and he is not so strong – not nearly so strong as I am; but, my dear," said the widow, looking up in her son's face with a wistful eagerness, "when Susan gets better, all will be – well."

She said the last words with a trembling, prolonged sigh. Poor mother, in that very moment she had recalled almost for the first time how far from well everything would be. Her face darkened over piteously as she spoke. She rose up, stung into new energy by this dreadful thought, which had been hitherto mercifully obscured by Susan's danger. "Let me go back – don't say anything. Nobody can watch my child but me," said the heart-broken woman; and once more she looked in her son's face. She wanted to read there what had happened – to ascertain from him, without any one else being the wiser, all the dreadful particulars which now, in the first relief of Susan's recovery, had burst into sudden shape upon her sight. "Doctor, we will not detain you; her brother and I will watch my child," said Mrs Vincent. The light forsook her eyes as she rose in that new and darker depth of anxiety; her little figure tottered trying to stand as she held out her hand to her son. "You and me – only you and me, Arthur – we must never leave her; though everybody is so kind—" said the minister's mother, turning with her smile of martyrdom, though her eyes were blind and she could not see them, to Dr Rider and his wife.

Vincent took his mother's hands and put her tenderly back in her chair. "I have good news, too," he said; "all will be well, mother dear. This man who has wrought us so much trouble is not dead. I told you, but you did not understand it; and he declares that Susan—"

"Arthur!" cried Mrs Vincent, with a sharp outcry of alarm and remonstrance. "Oh, God forgive me! I will wake my child. Arthur! The doctor is is very good," added the widow, looking round upon them always with the instinct of conciliating Arthur's friends; "and so is Mrs Rider; but every family has its private affairs," she concluded, with a wistful deprecating smile, all the time making signs to Arthur to stop him in his indiscreet reve-lations. "My dear, you will tell me presently when we are alone."

"Ah, mother," said Vincent, with a suppressed groan, "there is nothing private now in our family affairs. Hush! listen – Susan is cleared; he swears she had nothing to do with it; he swears that she was his daughter's companion only. Mother! Good heavens! doctor, what has happened? She looks as if she were dying. Mother! What have I done? I have killed her with my good news."

"Hush, hush – she has fainted – all will come right; let us get her away," cried Dr Rider under his breath. Between them the two young men carried her out of the room, which Mrs Rider closed after them with a certain triumph. The widow was not in so deep a faint but the fresher air outside and the motion revived her. It was more a sudden failing of her faculties in the height of emotion than actual insensibility. She made a feeble effort to resist and return into Susan's room. "You will wake her," said Dr Rider in her ear; and the poor mother sank back in their arms, fixing her wistful misty eyes, in which everything swam, upon her son. Her lips moved as she looked at him, though he could not hear her say a word; but the expression in her face, half awakened only from the incomprehension of her swoon, was not to be mistaken or resisted. Vincent bent down over her, and repeated what he had said as he carried her to another room. "Susan is safe – Susan is innocent. It is all over; mother, you understand me?" he said, repeating it again and again. Mrs Vincent leaned back upon his shoulder with a yielding of all her fatigued frame and worn-out mind. She understood him, not with her understanding as yet, but with her heart, which melted into unspeakable relief and comfort without knowing why. She closed her eyes in that wonderful consciousness of some great mercy that had happened to her; the first time she had closed them voluntarily for many nights and days. When they laid her down on the bed which had been hurriedly prepared for her, her eyes were still closed, and tears stealing softly out under the lids. She could not break out into expressions of thankfulness – the joy went to her heart.

Dr Rider thought it judicious to leave her so, and retired from the bedside with Vincent, not without some anxious curiosity in his own mind to hear all "the rights" of the matter. Perhaps the hum of their voices, quietly though they spoke, aroused her from her trance of silent gratitude. When she called Arthur faintly, and when they both hurried to her, Mrs Vincent was sitting up in her bed wiping off the tears from her cheeks. "Arthur, dear," said the widow, "I am quite sure Dr Rider will understand that what he has heard is in the strictest confidence; for to be sure," she continued, with a faint smile breaking over her wan face, "nobody could have any doubt about my Susan. It only had to be set right – and I knew when my son came home he would set it right," said Mrs Vincent, looking full in Dr Rider's face. "It has all happened because I had not my wits about me as I ought to have had, and was not used to act for myself; but when my son came back – Arthur, my own boy, it was all my fault, but I knew you would set it right – and as for my Susan, nobody could have any doubt; and you will both forgive your poor mother. I don't mind saying this before the doctor," she repeated once more, looking in his face; "because he has seen us in all our trouble, and I am sure we may trust Dr Rider; but, my dear, you know our private affairs are not to be talked of before strangers – especially," said the widow, with a long trembling sigh of relief and comfort, "when God has been so good to us, and all is to be well."

The two young men looked at each other in silence with a certain awe. All the dreadful interval which had passed between this Sunday afternoon and the day of Susan's return, had been a blank to Mrs Vincent so far as the outer world was concerned. Her daughter's illness and danger had rapt her altogether out of ordinary life. She took up her burden only where it had dropped off from her in the consuming anxiety for Susan's life and reason, in which all other fears had been lost. Just at the point where she had forgotten it, where she had still faced the world with the despairing assumption that all would be right when Arthur returned, she bethought herself now of that frightful shadow which had never been revealed in its full horror to her eyes. Now that Arthur's assurance relieved her heart of that, the widow took up her old position instinctively. She knew nothing of the comments in the newspapers, the vulgar publicity to which poor Susan's story had come. She wanted to impress upon Dr Rider's mind, by way of making up for her son's imprudence, that he was specially trusted, and that she did not mind speaking before him because he had seen all their trouble. Such was the poor mother's idea as she sat upon the bed where they had carried her, wiping the tears of joy from her wan and worn face. She forgot all the weary days that had come and gone. She took up the story just at the point where she, after all her martyrdom and strenuous upholding of Arthur's cause, had suddenly sunk into Susan's sick-room and left it. Now she reappeared with Arthur's banner once more in her hands – always strong in that assumption that nobody could doubt as to Susan, and that Arthur had but to come home to set all right. Dr Rider held up his warning finger when he saw Vincent about to speak. This delusion was salvation to the widow.

"But I must go back to Susan, doctor," said Mrs Vincent. "If she should wake and find a stranger there! – though Mrs Rider is so kind. But I am much stronger than I look – watching never does me any harm; and now that my mind is easy – People don't require much sleep at my time of life. And, Arthur, when my dear child sees me, she will know that all is well – all is well," repeated the widow, with trembling lips. "I must go to Susan, doctor; think if she should wake!"

"But she must not wake," said Dr Rider; "and if you stay quietly here she will not wake, for my wife will keep everything still. You will have a great deal to do for her when she *is* awake and conscious. Now you must rest."

"I shall have a great deal to do for her? Dr Rider

means she will want nursing, Arthur," said Mrs Vincent, "after such an illness; but she might miss me even in her sleep, or she might—"

"Mother, you must rest, for Susan's sake; if you make yourself ill, who will be able to take care of her?" said Vincent, who felt her hand tremble in his, and saw with how much difficulty she sustained the nervous shivering of her frame. She looked up into his face with those anxious eyes which strove to read his without being able to comprehend all the meanings there. Then the widow turned with a feminine artifice to Dr Rider.

"Doctor, if you will bring me word that my child is still asleep – if you will tell me exactly what you think, and that she is going on well," said Mrs Vincent; "you are always so kind. Oh, Arthur, my dear boy," cried the widow, taking his hand and caressing it between her own, "now that he is gone, tell me. Is it quite true? – is all well again? but you must never bring in Susan's name. Nobody must have it in their power to say a word about your sister, Arthur dear. And, oh, I hope you have been prudent and not said anything among your people. Hush! he will be coming back; it is quite true, Arthur? Tell me that my dear child has come safe out of it all, and nothing has happened. Tell me! Oh, speak to me, Arthur dear!"

"It is quite true," said Vincent, meeting his mother's eyes with a strange blending of pity and thankfulness. He did not say enough to satisfy her. She drew him closer, looking wistfully into his face. The winter afternoon was darkening, the room was cold, the atmosphere dreary. The widow held her son close, and fixed upon him her anxious inquiring eyes. "It is quite true, Arthur! There is nothing behind that you are hiding from me?" she said, with her lips almost touching his cheek, and her wistful eyes searching his meaning. "Oh, my dear boy, don't hide anything from me. I am able to bear it, Arthur. Whatever it is, I ought to know."

"What I have told you is the simple truth, mother," said

Vincent, not without a pang. "He has made a declaration before the magistrates—"

Mrs Vincent started so much that the bed on which she sat shook. "Before the magistrates!" she said, with a faint cry. Then after a pause – "But, thank God, it is not here, Arthur, nor at Lonsdale, nor anywhere where we are known. And he said that – that – he had never harmed my child? Oh, Arthur, Arthur – your sister! – that she should ever be spoken of so! And he was not killed? I do not understand it, my dear. I cannot see all the rights of it; but it is a great comfort to have you to myself for a moment, and to feel as if perhaps things might come right again. Hush! I think the doctor must be coming. Speak very low. My dear boy, you don't mean it, but you are imprudent; and, oh, Arthur, with a troublesome flock like yours you must not commit yourself! You must not let your sister's name be talked of among the people. Hush, hush, I hear the doctor at the door."

And the widow put her son away from her, and leant her head upon her hands instead of on his shoulder. She would not even let the doctor suppose that she had seized that moment to inquire further, or that she was anything but sure and confident that all was going well.

"She is in the most beautiful sleep," said the enthusiastic doctor, "and Nettie is by her. Now, Mrs Vincent, here is something you must take; and when you wake up again I will take you to your daughter, and I have very little doubt you will find her on the fair way for recovery – recovery in every sense," added Dr Rider, incautiously; "twice saved – and I hope you will have no more of such uneasiness as you have suffered on her behalf."

"Indeed, I have had very little uneasiness with my children," said Mrs Vincent, drawing up her little figure on the bed. "Susan never had a severe illness before. When she came here first she was suffering from a – a bad fright, doctor. I told you so at the time; and I was so weak and so alarmed, Arthur dear, that I fear Dr Rider has

misunderstood me. When one is not much used to illness,"
said the mother, with her pathetic jesuitry, "one thinks
there never was anything so bad as one's own case, and I
was foolish and upset. Yes, I will take it, doctor. Now that
I am easy in my mind, I will take anything you please;
and you will let me know if she wakes, or if she stirs.
Whatever happens, you will let me know that moment?
Arthur, you will see that they let me know."

The doctor promised, anxiously putting the draught into
her hands: he would have promised any impossible thing
at the moment, so eager was he to get her persuaded to
rest.

"I have not talked so much for – I wonder how long it
is?" said the widow, with a faint smile. "Oh, Arthur dear, I
feel as if somehow a millstone had been on my heart, and
God had taken it off. Doctor, it is – it is – all your doing,
under Providence," said the little woman, looking full
in his face. Perhaps she believed it – at least she meant
him to believe so. She swallowed the draught he gave her
with that smile upon her face, and laid down her throbbing
head in the quietness and darkness. "Go with the doctor,
Arthur dear," she said, denying the yearning in her heart
to question her son further, lest Dr Rider might perhaps
suppose all was not so well as she said; "and, oh, be sure to
tell me the very moment that Susan wakes?" She watched
them gliding noiselessly out of the room, two dark figures,
in the darkness. She lay down alone, throbbing all over
with thrills of pain, which were half pleasure. She began to
be conscious again of her own body and life; and the
wistful curiosity that possessed her was not strong enough
to neutralise the positive unmistakable joy. Susan was
recovering. Susan was innocent. What trouble could there
be heavy enough to take away the comfort out of words
like these!

"Now she will sleep. Mr Vincent, I congratulate you on
having such pure blood in your veins; not robust, you
know, but far better – such sweet, perfect health as one

rarely meets with nowadays," said the doctor under his breath, with professional enthusiasm; "all the better for your sister that she came of such a stock. My wife, now, is another example – not robust, as I say – natures delicately organised, but in such exquisite adjustment, and with such elasticity! Mrs Vincent will go to sleep like a baby, and wake able for – anything that God may please to send her," said Dr Rider with reverence. "They will both sleep till to-morrow if all goes well. Hush! – Well, I may be absurd, for neither of them could hear us here; but still it is best to err on the safe side."

"But Susan – you are not deceiving us – Susan is—" said Vincent, with sudden alarm.

"She is asleep," said Dr Rider; "and, if I can, I will remain till she wakes; it is life or death."

They parted thus – the doctor to the little room below-stairs, where Vincent's dinner awaited him, and the young minister himself to his own room, where he went into the darkness with a kind of bewildered uncertainty and in-comprehension of the events about him. To think that this day, with all its strange encounters and unexpected inci-dents, was Sunday, as he suddenly remembered it to be – that this morning he had preached, and this evening had to preach again, completed in Vincent's mind the utter chaos and disturbance of ordinary life. It struck him dumb to remember that by-and-by he must again ascend the pulpit, and go through all his duties. Was he an imposter, doing all this mechanically? He debated the question dully in his mind, as he sat too much bewildered to do anything else in the dark in his bed-chamber, pondering with a certain confused gravity and consolation over all that had happened. But faculties which are confused by sudden comfort and relief, are very different from faculties obscured and confounded by suffering. He sat vaguely in the dark, wondering over his strange position. This morning, even in the height of his despair, he had at least some idea what he was going to do in that pulpit of Salem. It was a sacrifice – a martyrdom to accomplish – a wild outcry and complaint to pour forth to the world. This evening he sat wasting the precious moments in the soft darkness, without knowing a word of what he was to say – without being able to realise the fact, that by-and-by he should have to go out through the sharp air echoing with church-bells – to see once more all those watchful faces turned upon him, and to communicate such instruction as was in him to his flock. A sense of exhaustion and satisfaction was in Vincent's heart. He sat listless in a vague comfort and weariness, his head throbbing with the fumes of his past excitement, yet not aching. It was only now that he realised the rolling off from his head of this dark cloud of horror and shame. Susan was recovering – Susan was innocent. He became aware of the facts much in the same way as his mother became aware of them ere she dropped to sleep in the blessed darkness of the adjoining room. Confused as he was, with his brain still full of the pulsations of the past, he was so far conscious of what had happened. He sat in his reverie, regardless of the time, and every-thing else that he ought to have attended to. The little maid came and knocked at his door to say his dinner had been waiting for an hour, and he answered, "Yes; he was coming," but sat still in the darkness. Then the landlady herself, compunctious, beginning to feel the thrills of returning comfort which had entered her house, came tapping softly to say it was near six, and wouldn't Mr Vincent take something before it was time for chapel? Mr Vincent said "Yes" again, but did not move; and it was only when he heard the church-bells tingling into the night air that he got up at last, and, stealing first to the door of Susan's room, where he could hear soft regular breathing in the darkness, he went away in an indescribably exalted condition of mind to Salem and his duty. There is a kind of weakness incident to excitement of mind and neglect of body, which is akin to the ecstatic state in which men dream dreams and see visions. Vincent was in that condition to-night. He was not careful what anybody would say or think; he no longer pictured to himself the upturned faces in Salem, all conscious of the tragedy which was connected with his name. The sense of deliverance in his heart emancipated him, and gave a contrary impulse to his thoughts. In the weakness of an excited and exhausted frame, a certain gleam of the ineffable and miraculous came over the young man. He was again in the world where God stoops down to change with one touch of His finger the whole current of man's life – the world of childhood, of genius, of faith; that other world, dark sphere of necessity and fate, where nothing could stay the development into dread immortality of the obstinate human intelligence, and where dreary echoes of speculation still questioned whether any changes were possible in heart and spirit, or if saving souls were a mere figure of speech, floated away far off over his head, a dark fiction of despair. In this state of mind he went back to the pulpit where, in the morning, he had thrilled his audience with all those wild complications of thought which end in nothing. Salem was again crowded – not a corner of the chapel remained unfilled; and again, many of the more zealous members were driven out of their seats by the influx of the crowd. Vincent, who had no sermon to preach, and nothing except the fulness that was in his heart to say, took up again his subject of the morning. He told his audience with the unpremeditated skill of a natural orator, that while Reason considered all the desperate chances, and concluded that wonderful work impossible, God, with the lifting of His countenance, with the touch of his power, made the darkness light before Him, and changed the very earth and heavens around the wondering soul. Lifted out of the region of reasonableness himself, he explained to his astonished audience how Reason halts in her conclusions, how miracle and wonder are of all occurrences the most natural, and how, between God and man, there are no boundaries of possibility. It was a strange sermon, without any text or divisions, irregular in its form, sometimes broken in its utterance; but the man who spoke was in a "rapture" – a state of fasting and ecstacy. He saw indistinctly that there were glistening eyes in the crowd, and felt what was somewhat an unusual consciousness – that his heart had made communications to other hearts in his audience almost without his knowing it; but he did not observe that nobody came to the vestry to congratulate him, that Tozer looked disturbed, and that the deacons averted their benign countenances. When he had done his work, he went home without waiting to talk to anybody – without, indeed, thinking any more of Salem – through the crowd, in the darkness, passing group after group in earnest discussion of the minister. He went back still in that exalted condition of mind, unaware that he passed Mrs Tozer and Phoebe, who were much disposed to join him – and was in his own house sooner than most of his congregation. All within was quiet, lost in the most grateful and profound stillness. Sleep seemed to brood over the delivered house. Vincent spoke to the doctor, who still waited, and whose hopes were rising higher and higher, and then ate something, and said his prayers, and went to rest like a child. The family, so worn out with labour, and trial, and sorrow, slept profoundly under the quiet stars. Those hard heavens, from which an indifferent God saw the Innocents murdered and made no sign, had melted into the sweet natural firmament, above which the great Father watches unwearied. The sudden change was more than mere deliverance to the young Nonconformist. He slept and took rest in the sweet surprise and thankfulness of his soul. His life and heart, still young and incapable of despair, had got back out of hard anguishes and miseries which no one could soften, to the sweet miraculous world in which circumstances are always changing, and God interferes for ever.

CHAPTER XXX.

WHEN Vincent awoke next morning, his mother was standing by his bedside. Her eyes were dewy and moist, a faint tingle of colour was on her sweet old cheek, and her steps tottered a little as she came up to his bed, and stooped to kiss him. "Oh, Arthur, my dear boy, she knows me!" said Mrs Vincent, putting up her hand to her eyes. "I must not be away from her a moment, but I could not resist coming to tell you. She knows me, dear. Make haste and dress, and come and see your sister, Arthur; and I will give orders about your breakfast as I go back. My dear, I know you have been anxious," said the widow, putting back his hair fondly with the soft little hand which still trembled; "though men have not the way of showing it, I know you have been very anxious. You looked quite pale and thin as you slept. But I must speak to the landlady now and see about your food. Come to Susan's room as soon as you are dressed, and I will order your breakfast, my dear boy," said his mother, going softly out again, with her tender little figure all beautified and trembling with joy. Mrs Vincent met the landlady near the door, and stopped to speak to her. "My daughter is a great deal better," said the minister's mother. "I have been so anxious, I have never been able to thank you as I ought to have done for your kindness and attention. We have been as quiet as if we had been at home. We will all remember your attention, though I have never been able to thank you before; and I am sure it is very gratifying to my son to think it is one of his own flock who has taken so much pains for us. Mr Vincent has been very anxious about his sister," continued the widow; "I fear he has not been taking his food, nor keeping his regular time for meals.

You would oblige me very much if you would try to have something nice for his breakfast. We were all much shaken yesterday, being so anxious; – some new-laid eggs perhaps – though I know they are scarce in a town at this time of the year – or anything you can think of that will tempt him to eat. I would not say so much," said Mrs Vincent, smiling upon the astonished landlady, and leaning to support her own weakness on the rail of the passage upon which the staircase opened, "but that I know your kind interest in your minister. I am sure you will take all the pains you can to get him to attend to his precious health. Thank you. I am very much obliged."

With this the little woman passed on, feeling indeed too weak to stand longer; and leaving the landlady, who had intended to mingle some statement of her own grievances with her congratulations, with the plea quietly taken out of her hands, and the entire matter disposed of. Mrs Vincent was moving back again to the sick-room, when the door opened down-stairs, and some one asked for Mr Vincent, and came up hurriedly. The minister's mother recognised Tozer's voice, and made a pause. She was glad of the opportunity to make sure that all was well in the flock. She leant over the railing to shake hands with the butterman, moved to a little effusion of thankfulness by the recollection of the state of anxiety she was in when she saw him last.

"My son is not up yet," she said. "We were very anxious yesterday. It was the crisis of the fever, and everything depended upon it. I daresay you would see how anxious Mr Vincent was; but, thank heaven, now all is going on well."

"You see, ma'am," said Tozer, "it must have all been on the nerves, and to be sure there ain't nothing more likely to be serviceable than good news. It's in the paper this morning. As soon as I see it, I said to my missis, 'This is why the minister was so pecooliar yesterday.' I divined it in a moment, ma'am; though it wasn't to say prudent, Mrs

Vincent, and not as you would have advised no more nor myself, to fly off like that out of chapel, without as much as shaking hands with one o' the deacons. But I make allowances, I do; and when I see it in the paper, I said to my missis, 'It's all along o' this Mr Vincent was so queer.' I don't doubt as it'll be quite looked over, and thought no more of, when it's known what's the news."

"What news?" said Mrs Vincent, faintly, holding fast by the railing. "You mean the news of my dear child's recovery," she added, after a breathless pause. "Have they put it in the papers? I am sure it is very good, but I never heard of such a thing before. She has been very ill to be sure – but most people are very ill once in their lives," said the widow, gasping a little for breath, and fixing her eyes upon the paper which Tozer held in his hand.

"Poor soul!" said the deacon, compassionately, "it ain't no wonder, considering all things. Phoebe would have come the very first day to say, Could she be of any use? but her mother wasn't agreeable. Women has their own ways of managing; but they'll both come to-day, now all's cleared up, if you'll excuse me. And now, ma'am, I'll go on to the minister, and see if there's anything as he'd like me to do, for Pigeon and the rest was put out, there's no denying of it; but if things is set straight directly, what with this news, and what with them sermons yesterday, I don't think as it'll do no harm. I said to him, as this Sunday was half the battle," said the worthy butterman, reflectively; "and he did his best – I wouldn't say as he didn't do his best; and I'm not the man as will forsake my pastor when he's in trouble. Good morning, ma'am; and my best respects to miss, and I hope as she'll soon be well again. There ain't no man as could rejoice more nor me at this news."

Tozer went on to Vincent's room, at the door of which the minister had appeared summoning him with some impatience and anxiety. "News? what news?" said Mrs

Vincent, faintly to herself, as she held by the rail and felt
the light forsaking her eyes in a new mist of sudden dread.
She caught the look of the landlady at that moment, a look
of half pity, curiosity, and knowledge, which startled her
back to her defences. With sudden firmness she gathered
herself together, and went on to the sick-room, leaving
behind her, as she closed the door, the whole troubled
world, which seemed to know better about her most
intimate affairs than she did; and those newspapers, which
somehow mentioned Susan's name, that sweet maiden
name which it was desecration to see so much as named in
print. Rather the widow carried that uneasy world in with
her to the sick-room which she had left a few minutes
before in all the effusion of unhoped-for joy. Everything
still was not well though Susan was getting better. She sat
down by the bedside where Susan lay languid and pale,
showing the change in her by little more than quietness
and a faint recognition of her mother, and in her troubled
heart began to look the new state of affairs in the face, and
to make up her mind that more of the causes of Susan's
illness than she had supposed known, must have become
public. And then Arthur and his flock, that flock which he
evidently had somehow affronted on the previous day.
Mrs Vincent pondered with all the natural distrust of a
woman over Arthur's imprudence. She almost chafed at
her necessary confinement by her daughter's bedside; if
she herself, who had been a minister's wife for thirty
years, and knew the ways of a congregation, and how it
must be managed, could only get into the field to bring her
son out of the difficult passages which she had no faith in
his own power to steer through! So the poor mother
experienced how, when absorbing grief is removed, a host
of complicated anxieties hasten in to fill up its place. She
was no longer bowed down under an overwhelming dread,
but she was consumed by restless desires to be doing –
cravings to know all – fears for what might at the moment
be happening out of her range of influence. What might

Arthur, always incautious, be confiding to Tozer even
now? – perhaps telling him those "private affairs" which
the widow would have defended against exposure with her
very life – perhaps chafing at Salem and rejecting that
yoke which, being a minister, he must bear. It was all Mrs
Vincent could do to keep herself still on her chair, and to
maintain that quietness which was necessary for Susan. If
only she could have been there to soften his impatience
and make the best of his unnecessary confidences! Many a
time before this, the widow had been compelled to submit
to that female tribulation – to be shut up apart, and leave
the great events outside to be transacted by those incautious masculine hands, in which, at the bottom of her
heart, a woman seldom has perfect confidence when her
own supervising influence is withdrawn. Mrs Vincent felt
instinctively that Arthur would commit himself as she sat
resigned but troubled by Susan's bed.

Tozer went directly to the door of Vincent's room,
where the minister, only half-dressed, but much alarmed
to see the colloquy which was going on between his mother
and the butterman, was waiting for him. The deacon
squeezed the young man's hand with a hearty pressure.
His aspect was so fatherly and confidential, that it brought
back to the mind of the young Nonconformist a certain
rueful half-comic recollection of the suppers in the back
parlour, and all the old troubles of the pastor of Salem,
which heavier shadows had driven out of his mind. Tozer
held up triumphantly the paper in his hand.

"You've seen it, sir?" said the butterman; "first thing I
did this morning was to look up whether there wasn't
nothing about it in the latest intelligence; for the 'Gazette'
has been very particular, knowing, at Carlingford, folks
would be interested – and here it is sure enough, Mr
Vincent; and we nigh gave three cheers, me and the lads
in the shop."

To this Vincent listened with a darkening brow and an
impatience which he did not attempt to conceal. He took

the paper with again that quick sense of the intolerable which prompted him to tear the innocent broadsheet in pieces and tread it under foot. The 'Gazette' contained, with a heading in large characters, the following paragraph: –

"THE DOVER TRAGEDY.

"Our readers will be glad to hear that the unfortunate young lady whose name has been so unhappily mixed up in this mysterious affair, is likely to be fully exonerated from the charge rashly brought against her. In the deposition of the wounded man, which was taken late on Saturday night, by Mr Everett, the stipendiary magistrate of Dover, he distinctly declares that Miss— was not the party who fired the pistol, nor in any way connected with it – that she had accompanied his daughter merely as companion on a hasty journey, and that, in short, instead of the romantic connection supposed to subsist between the parties, with all the passions of love and revenge naturally involved, the ties between them were of the simplest and most temporary character. We are grieved to add, that the fright and horror of her awful position had overpowered Miss— some time before this deposition was made, and brought on a brain-fever, which, of course, made the unfortunate young lady, who is understood to possess great personal attractions, quite unable to explain the suspicious circumstances surrounding her. We have now only to congratulate her respectable family and friends on her exoneration from a very shocking charge, and hope her innocence will soon be confirmed by full legal acquittal. Our readers will find Colonel Mildmay's deposition on another page. It will be perceived that he obstinately refuses to indicate who was the real perpetrator of the deed. Suspicion has been directed to his groom, who accompanied him, in whom, however, the wounded man seems to repose perfect confidence. He is still in a precarious state, but little doubt is entertained of his ultimate recovery."

"There, Mr Vincent, that's gratifying, that is," said Tozer, as Vincent laid down the paper; "and I come over directly I see it, to let you know. And I come to say besides," continued the butterman with some diffidence, "as I think if you and me was to go off to Mr Brown the solicitor, and give him his orders as he was to put in bail for Miss or anything else as might be necessary – not meaning to use no disagreeable words, as there ain't no occasion now," said the good deacon; "but only to make it plain, as you and me is responsible for her, if so be as she was ever to be called for again. It would be the thing to do, that would, sir, if you take my advice. It ain't altogether my own notion, but was put into my head by one as knows. The gentleman as come here from Dover inquiring into the business was the one as suggested it to me. He turned out uncommon obliging, and wasn't to say no trouble in the house; and when word came as the Colonel wasn't dead, he went away as civil as could be. I'll go with you cheerful to Mr Brown, if you'll take my advice, afore Mrs Vincent gets moving about again, or the young lady knows what's a-going on; that's what I'd do, sir, if it was me."

Vincent grasped the exultant butterman's hand in an overflow of gratitude and compunction. "I shall never forget your kindness," he said, with a little tremor in his voice. "You have been a true friend. Thank you from the bottom of my heart. I will go at once, and accept this other great kindness from you. I shall never forget what I owe to you as long as I live."

"I never was the man to forsake my pastor in trouble – not to say a young man like you as is a credit to the connection, and the best preacher I may say as I ever heard in Salem," said Tozer, with effusion, returning the grasp; "but we ain't a-going a step till you've had your breakfast. Your good mother, Mrs Vincent, as is a real lady, sir, and would never advise you different from what I would myself, being for your own interests, would have little opinion of me if I took you out on a Monday mornin' after your labours without so much as a bit o'breakfast to sustain you. I'll sit by you while you're a-eating of your bacon. There's a deal to consider of concerning Salem as I couldn't well bring before you as long as you were in such trouble. Them were uncommon sermons, sir, yesterday; I don't know as I ever heard anything as was just to be compared with the mornin' discourse, and most of the flock was of my opinion; but what is the good of standing up for the pastor – I ask you candid, Mr Vincent – when he'll not take no pains to keep things square? I'm speaking plain, for you can't mistake me as it's anything but your own interests I am a-thinking of. We was all marching in, deacons and committee and all, to say as we was grateful to you for your instructions, and wishing you well out of your trouble – and I was in great hopes as matters might have been made up – when behold, what we finds was the vestry empty and the pastor gone! Now, I ain't a-finding fault. Them news would explain anything; but I don't deny as Pigeon and the rest was put out; and if you'll be guided by one as wishes you well, Mr Vincent, when you've done our business as is most important of all, you'll go and make some visits, sir, and make yourself agreeable, if you'll excuse me. It ain't with no selfish thoughts as I speak," said Tozer, energetically. "It's not like asking of you to come a-visiting to me, nor setting myself forward as the minister's great friend – though we *was* remarking as the pastor was unknown in our house this fortnight and more – but it's for peace and union, Mr Vincent, and the good of the flock, sir, and to keep – as your good mother well knows ain't easy in a congregation – all things straight."

When this little peroration was delivered, Vincent was seated at table, making what he could of the breakfast, in which both his mother and Tozer had interested themselves. It was with a little effort that the young man accepted this advice as the character and intentions of his adviser deserved. He swallowed what was unpalatable in the counsel, and received the suggestion, "in as sweet a frame of mind as I could wish to see," as Tozer afterwards described.

"I will go and make myself agreeable," said the minister, with a smile. "Thank heaven! it is not so impossible to-day as it might have been yesterday; I left the chapel so hurriedly, because—"

"I understand, sir," said Tozer, benevolently inter-posing as Vincent paused, finding explanation impossible. "Pigeon and the rest was put out, as I say, more nor I could see was reasonable – not as Pigeon is a man that knows his own mind. It's the women as want the most managing. Now, Mr Vincent, I'm ready, sir, if you are, and we won't lose no time."

Before going out, however, Vincent went to his sister's room. She was lying in an utter quietness which went to his heart; – silent, no longer uttering the wild fancies of a disordered brain, recovering, as the doctor thought; but stretched upon her white couch, marble white, without any inclination apparently to lift the heavy lids of her eyes, or to notice anything that passed before her – a very sad sight to see. By her sat her mother, in a very different condition, anxious, looking into Arthur's eyes, whispering counsels in his ears. "Oh, my dear boy, be very careful," said Mrs Vincent; "your dear papa always said that a minister's flock was his first duty; and now that Susan is getting better, O Arthur! you must not let people talk about your sister; – and have patience, O have patience, dear!" This was said in wistful whispers, with looks which only half confided in Arthur's prudence; and the widow sank into her chair when he left her, folding her hands in a little agony of self-restraint and compulsory quietness. She felt equal for it herself, if she had been at liberty to go out upon the flock once more in Arthur's cause; but who could tell how he might commit himself, he who was a young man, and took his own way, and did not know, as Tozer said, how to keep all things straight? When Mrs Vincent thought of her son in personal conflict with Mrs Pigeon, she lost faith in Arthur. She herself might have conquered that difficult adversary, but what weapons had he to bring forth against the deacon's wife, he who was only a minister and a man?

CHAPTER XXXI.

"AND now that's settled, as far as we can settle it now," said Tozer, as they left the magistrate's office, where John Brown, the famous Carlingford solicitor, had accompanied them, "you'll go and see some of the Chapel folks, Mr Vincent? It'll be took kind of you to lose no time, especially if you'd say a word just as it's all over, and let them know the news is true."

"I will go with you first," said Vincent, who contemplated the butterman's shop at that moment through a little halo of gratitude and kindness. He went into the back parlour with the gratified deacon, where Mrs Tozer sat reading over again the same 'Gazette' in which poor Susan's history was summed up and ended. It seemed like a year to Vincent since he had dined with his mother at this big table, amid the distant odours of all the bacon and cheese. Mrs Tozer put down the paper, and took off her spectacles as her visitor came in. "It's Mr Vincent, Phoebe," she said, with a little exclamation. "Dear, dear, I never thought as the pastor would be such a strange sight in my house – not as I was meaning nothing unkind, Tozer, so there's no occasion to look at me. I'm as glad as ever I can be to see the minister; and what a blessing as it's all settled, and the poor dear getting well, too. Phoebe, you needn't be a-hiding behind me, child, as if the pastor was thinking of how you was dressed. She has on her morning wrapper, Mr Vincent, as she was helping her mother in, and we didn't expect no visitors. Don't be standing there, as if it was any matter to the minister how you was dressed."

"Oh, ma, as if I ever thought of such a thing!" said Phoebe, extending a pink uncoverd arm out of the loose sleeve of her morning dress to Vincent, and averting her face; "but to see Mr Vincent is so like old times – and everything *has* seemed so different – and it *is* so pleasant to feel as if it were all coming back again. Oh ma! to imagine that I ever supposed Mr Vincent could notice my dress, or think of poor me!" added Phoebe, in a postscript under her breath. The minister heard the latter words quite as well as the first. After he had shaken the pink, plump hand, he sat down on the opposite side of the table, and saw Phoebe, relieved against the light of the window, wiping a tender tear from her eye. All at once out of the darker and heavier trials which had abstracted him from common life, the young Nonconformist plunged back into the characteristic troubles of his position. As usual, he made no response to Phoebe, found nothing civil to say, but turned with desperation to Mrs Tozer, who was luckily about to speak.

"Don't pay no attention to her, Mr Vincent; she's a deal too feelin'. She oughtn't to be minded, and then she'll learn better," said Mrs Tozer. "If we had been your own relations, we couldn't have been more took up; and where should a minister seek for sympathy if it isn't in his own flock? There ain't nobody so safe to put your trust in, Mr Vincent, as Salem folks. There's a many fine friends a young man may have when he's in a prosperous way, but it ain't to be supposed they would stand by him in trouble; and it's then as you find the good of your real friends," continued Mrs Tozer, looking with some significance at her husband. Tozer, for his own part, rubbed his hands and stationed himself with his back to the fire, as is the custom of Englishmen of all degrees. The husband and wife contemplated Vincent with complacence. With the kindest feelings in the world, they could not altogether restrain a little triumph. It was impossible now that the minister could mistake who were his true friends.

But just then, strangely enough, a vision of a tender smile, a glance up in his face, the touch of a soft hand, came to Vincent's mind. His fine friends! he had but one, and she had stood by him in his trouble. From Tozer's complacence the minister's mind went off with a bound of relief to that sweet, fruitless sympathy which was dearer than help. From her soft perfumy presence to Mrs Tozer's parlour, with that pervading consciousness in it of the shop hard by and its store of provisions, what a wonderful difference! It was not so easy to be grateful as he had at first thought.

"Mr Tozer has been my real friend indeed, and a most honest and thorough one," said Vincent. "But I don't think I have any other in Salem so sure and steady," added the minister, after a little pause, half gratefully, half in bitterness. This sentiment was not, however, resented by the assembled family. Phoebe leaned over her mother's chair, and whispered, "Oh, ma, dear! didn't I always say he was full of feeling?" somewhat to the discomfiture of the person commented on; while Tozer himself beamed upon the minister from before the blazing fire.

"I said as we'd pull you through," said Tozer, "and I said as I'd stand by you; and both I'll do sir, you take my word, if you'll but stick to your duty; and as for standing bail in a hundred pound or two," continued the butter-man, magnanimously, "for a poor young creature as couldn't be nothing but innocent, I don't mind that, nor a deal more than that, to keep all things straight. It's nothing but my duty. When a man is a responsible man,

and well known in a place, it's his business to make use
of his credit, Mr Vincent, sir, and his character, for the
good of his friends."

"It may be your duty, but you know there ain't a many
as would have done it," said his straightforward wife, "as
Mr Vincent sees himself, and no need for nobody a-telling
of him. There ain't a many as would have stood up for the
pastor, right and wrong, and finished off with the likes of
this, and the minster don't need us to say so. Dear, dear!
Mr Vincent, you ain't a-going away already, and us hasn't
so much as seen you for I can't tell how long? I made sure
you'd stop and take a bit of dinner at least, not making no
ceremony," said Mrs Tozer, "for there's always enough
for a friend, and you can't take us wrong."

Vincent had rising hurriedly to his feet, under the
strong stimulant of the butterman's self-applause.
Conscious as he was of all that Tozer had really done,
the minister found it hard to listen and echo, with due
humility and gratitude, the perfect satisfaction of the pair
over their own generosity. He had no thanks to say when
thus forestalled. "Oh, ma, how can you make so much of
it?" cried Phoebe. "The minister will think us *so* selfish;
and, oh, please Mr Vincent, when you go home, will you
speak to your mother, and ask her to let me come and help
with her nursing? I should do whatever she told me, and
try to be a comfort to her – oh, I should indeed!" said
Phoebe, clasping those pink hands. "Nobody could be
more devoted than I should be." She cast down her eyes,
and stood the image of maidenly devotedness between
Vincent and the window. She struck him dumb, as she
always did. He never was equal to the emergency where
Phoebe was concerned. He took up his hat in his hands,
and tried to explain lamely how he must go away – how he
had visits to make – duties to do – and would have stuck
fast, and lost Mrs Tozer's favour finally and for ever, had
not the butterman interposed.

"It's me as is to blame," said the worthy deacon. "If it

hadn't have been as the pastor wouldn't pass the door without coming in, I'd not have had him here to-day; and if you women would think, you'd see. We're stanch – and Mr Vincent ain't no call to trouble himself about us; but Pigeon and them, you see, as went off in a huff yesterday – that's what the minister has got to do. You shan't be kep' no longer, sir, in my house. Duty afore pleasure, that's my maxim. Good mornin', and I hope as you won't meet with no unpleasantness; but if you should, Mr Vincent, don't be disheartened, sir – we'll pull you through."

With this encouraging sentiment, Vincent was released from Mrs Tozer's parlour. He drew a long breath when he got out to the fresh air in the street, and faced the idea of the Pigeons and other recusants whom he was now bound to visit. While he thought of them, all so many varieties of Mrs Tozer's parlour, without the kindness which met him there, the heart of the young Nonconformist failed him. Nothing but gratitude to Tozer could have sent him forth at all on this mission of conciliation; but now on the threshold of it, smarting from even Tozer's well-intentioned patronage, a yearning for a little personal comfort seized upon Vincent's mind. It was his duty to go away towards Grove Street, where the poulterer's residence was; but his longing eyes strayed towards Grange Lane, where consolation dwelt. And, besides, was it not his duty to watch over the real criminal, for whose mysterious wickedness poor Susan had suffered? It was not difficult to foresee how that argument would conclude. He wavered for a few minutes opposite Masters's shop, gave a furtive glance back towards the butterman's, and then, starting forward with sudden resolution, took his hasty way to Lady Western's door; only for a moment; only to see that all was safe, and his prisoner still in custody. Vincent sighed over the thought with an involuntary quickening of his heart. To be detained in such custody, the young man thought, would be sweeter than heaven; and the wild hope which came and went like a meteor about his path, sprang up with sudden intensity, and took the breath from his lips, and the colour from his cheek, as he entered at that green garden-door.

Lady Western was by herself in the drawing-room — that room divided in half by the closed doors which Vincent remembered so well. She rose up out of the low chair in which she reposed, like some lovely swan amid billows of dark silken drapery, and held out her beautiful hand to him — both her beautiful hands — with an effusion of kindness and sympathy. The poor young Nonconformist took them into his own, and forgot the very existence of Salem. The sweetness of the moment took all the sting out of his fate. He looked at her without saying anything, with his heart in his eyes. Consolation! It was all he had come for. He could have gone away thereafter and met all the Pigeons in existence; but more happiness still was in store for him — she pointed to a chair on the other side of her work-table. There was nobody else near to break the charm. The silken rustle of her dress, and that faint perfume which she always had about her, pervaded the rosy atmosphere. Out of purgatory, out of bitter life beset with trouble, the young man had leaped for one moment into paradise; and who could wonder that he resigned himself to the spell?

"I am so glad you have come," said Lady Western. "I am sure you must have hated me, and everything that recalled my name; but it was impossible for any one to be more grieved than I was, Mr Vincent. Now, will you tell me about Rachel? She sits by herself in her own room. When I go in she gives me a look of fright which I cannot understand. Fright! Can you imagine Rachel frightened, Mr Vincent — and of me!"

"Ah, yes. I would not venture to come into the presence of the angels if I had guilt on my hands," said Vincent, not very well knowing what he said.

"Mr Vincent! what can you mean? You alarm me very much," said the young Dowager; "but perhaps it is about

her little girl. I don't think she knows where her daughter
is. Indeed," said Lady Western, with a cloud on her
beautiful face, "you must not think I ever approved of my
brother's conduct; but when he was so anxious to have his
child, I think she might have given in to him a little – don't
you think so? The child might have done him good,
perhaps. She is very lovely, I hear. Did you see her? Oh,
Mr Vincent, tell me about it. I cannot understand how you
are connected with it at all. She trusted in you so much,
and now she is afraid of you. Tell me how it is. Hush! she
is ringing her bell. She has seen you come into the house."

"But I don't want to see Mrs – Mrs Mildmay," said
Vincent, rising up. "I don't know why I came at all, if it
were not to see the sun shining. It is dark down below
where I am," said the young man, with an involuntary
outburst of the passion which at that moment suddenly
appeared to him in all its unreasonableness. "Forgive me.
It was only a longing I had to see the light."

Lady Western looked up with her sweet eyes in the
minister's face. She was not ignorant of the condition of
mind he was in, but she was sorry for him to the bottom of
her heart. To cheer him a little could not harm any one.
"Come back soon," she said, again holding out her hand
with a smile. "I am *so* sorry for your troubles; and if we
can do anything to comfort you, come back soon again, Mr
Vincent." When the poor Nonconformist came to himself
after these words, he was standing outside the garden-
door, out of paradise, his heart throbbing, and his pulse
beating in a kind of sweet delirium. In that very moment
of delight he recognised, with a thrill of exaltation and
anguish, the madness of his dream. No matter. What if his
heart broke after? Now, at least, he could take the consolation. But if it was hard to face Mrs Pigeon before, it
may well be supposed that it was not easy now, with all
this world of passionate fancies throbbing in his brain, to
turn away from his elevation, and encounter Salem and its
irritated deacons. Vincent went slowly up Grange Lane,

trying to make up his mind to his inevitable duty. When
he was nearly opposite the house of Dr Marjoribanks, he
paused to look back. The garden-door was again open,
and somebody else was going into the enchanted house.
Somebody else; – a tall slight figure, in a loose light-
coloured dress, which he recognised instinctively with an
agony of jealous rage. A minute before he had allowed to
himself, in an exquisite despair, that to hope was madness;
but the sight of his rival awoke other thoughts in the mind
of the minister. With quick eyes he identified the companion of his midnight journey – he in whose name all
Susan's wretchedness had been wrought – he whom Lady
Western could trust "with life – to death." Vincent went
back at the sight of him, and found the door now close shut
through which his steps had passed. Close shut – enclosing
the other – shutting *him* out in the cold external gloom. He
forgot all he had to do for himself and his friends – he
forgot his duty, his family, everything in the world but
hopeless love and passionate jealousy, as he turned again
to Lady Western's door.

CHAPTER XXXII.

THUS while Mrs Vincent sat in Susan's sick-room, with her
mind full of troubled thoughts, painfully following her son
into an imaginary and unequal conflict with the wife of the
rebellious deacon; and while the Salem congregation in
general occupied itself with conjectures how this internal
division could be healed, and what the pastor would do,
the pastor himself was doing the very last thing he ought to
have done in the circumstances – lingering down Grange
Lane in the broad daylight with intent to pass Lady

Western's door – that door from which he had himself emerged a very few minutes before. Why did he turn back and loiter again along that unprofitable way? He did not venture to ask himself the question; he only did it in an utterly unreasonable access of jealousy and rage. If he had been Lady Western's accepted lover instead of the hopeless worshipper afar off of that bright unattainable creature, he could still have had no possible right to forbid the entrance of Mr Fordham at that garden-gate. He went back with a mad, unreasoning impulse, only excusable in consideration of the excited state of mind into which so many past events had concurred to throw him. But the door opened again as he passed it. Instinctively Vincent stood still, without knowing why. It was not Mr Fordham who came out. It was a stealthy figure, which made a tremulous pause at sight of him, and, uttering a cry of dismay, fixed eyes which still gleamed, but had lost all their steadiness, upon his face. Vincent felt that he would not have recognised her anywhere but at this door. Her thin lips, which had once closed so firmly, and expressed with such distinctness the flying shades of amusement and ridicule, hung apart loosely, with a perpetual quiver of hidden emotion. Her face, always dark and colourless, yet bearing such an unmistakable tone of vigour and strength, was haggard and ghastly; her once assured and steady step furtive and trembling. She gave him an appalled look, and uttered a little cry. She shivered as she looked at him, making desperate vain efforts to recover her composure and conceal the agitation into which his sudden appearance had thrown her. But nature at last had triumphed over this woman who had defied her so long. She had not strength left to accomplish the cheat. "You!" she cried, with a shrill tone of terror and confusion in her voice, "I did not look for you!" It was all her quivering lips would say.

The sight of her had roused Vincent. "You were going to escape," he said. "Do you forget your word? Must I tell *her* everything, or must I place you in surer custody? You have broken your word."

"My word! I did not give you my word," she cried, eagerly. "No. I – I never said—: and," after a pause, "if I had said it, how do you imagine I was going to escape? Escape! from what? That is the worst – one cannot escape," said the miserable woman, speaking as if by an uncontrollable impulse, "never more; especially if one keeps quiet in one place and has nothing to do," she continued after a pause, recovering herself by strange gleams now and then for a moment; "that is why I came out, to escape, as you say, for half an hour, Mr Vincent. Besides, I don't have news enough – not nearly enough. How do you think I can keep still when nobody sends me any news? How long is it since I saw you last? And I have heard nothing since then – not a syllable! and you expect me to sit still, because I have given my word? Besides," after another breathless pause, and another gleam of self-recovery, "the laws of honour don't extend to women. We are weak, and we are allowed to lie."

"You are speaking wildly," said Vincent, with some compassion and some horror, putting his hand on her arm to guide her back to the house. Mrs Hilyard gave a slight convulsive start, drew away from his touch, and gazed upon him with an agony of fright and terror in her eyes.

"We agreed that I was to stay with Alice," she said. "You forget I am staying with Alice: she – she keeps me safe, you know. Ah! people change so; I am sometimes – half afraid – of Alice, Mr Vincent. My child is like her – *my* child – she did not know me!" cried the wretched woman, with a sob that came out of the depths of her heart; "after all that happened, she did not know me! To be sure, that was quite natural," she went on again, once more recovering her balance, for an instant, "she *could* not know me! and I am not beautiful, like Lady Western, to please a child's eye. Beauty is good – very good. I was once pretty myself; any man would have forgiven me as you did when Alice came with her lovely face; but I daresay your mother would not have minded had it been she. Ah, that reminds me," said Mrs Hilyard, gradually acquiring a little more steadiness, "that was why I came out: to go to your mother – to ask if perhaps she had heard anything – from my child."

"This is madness," said Vincent; "you know my mother could not possibly hear about your child; you want to escape – I can see it in your eyes."

"If you will tell me what kind of things people can escape from, I will answer you," said his strange companion, still becoming more composed. "Hush! I said what was true. The governess, you know, had your address. Is it very long since yesterday when I got that news from Dover? Never mind. I daresay I am asking wild questions that cannot have any answer. Do you remember being here with me once before? Do you remember looking through the grating and seeing—? Ah, there is Mr Fordham now with Alice! Poor young man!" said Mrs Hilyard, turning once more to look at him, still vigilant and anxious, but with a softened glance. "Poor minister! I told you not to fall in love with her lovely face. I told you she was kind, too kind – she does not mean any harm. I warned you. Who could have thought that we should have so much to do with each other?" she resumed, shrinking from him, and trying to conceal how she shrank with another convulsive shiver; "but you were going to visit your people or something. I must not keep you, Mr Vincent; you must go away."

"Not till you have returned to the house; and given me your word of honour," said Vincent, "not to escape, or to attempt to escape; or else I must tell *her* everything, or give you up into stronger hands. I will not leave you here."

"My word! but women are not bound by their honour; *our* honour means – not our word," cried Mrs Hilyard, wildly; "my parole, he means; soldiers, and heroes, and

men of honour give their parole; you don't exact it from
women. Words are not kept to us, Mr Vincent; do you
expect us to keep them? Yes, yes; I know I am talking
wildly. Is it strange, do you think? But what if I give you
my word, and nobody sends me any further news –
nothing about my child? Women are only wild animals
when their children are taken from them. I will forget it,
and go away for news – news! That is what I want.
Escape!" she repeated, with a miserable cry; "who can
escape? I do not understand what it means."

"But you must not leave this house," said Vincent,
firmly. "You understand what *I* mean. You must not
leave Lady Western. Go with her where she pleases; but
unless you promise on your honour to remain here, and
with her, I shall be obliged—"

"Hush!" she said, trembling – "hush! My *honour!* –
and you still trust in it? I will promise," she continued,
turning and looking anxiously round into the dull winter
daylight, as if calculating what chance she had of rushing
away and eluding him. Then her eyes returned to the face
of the young man, who stood firm and watchful beside her
– agitated, yet so much stronger, calmer, even more
resolute than she; then shrinking back and keeping her
eyes, with a kind of fascinated gaze, upon his face, she
repeated the words slowly, "I promise – upon my honour.
I will not go away – escape, as you call it. If I should go
mad, that will not matter. Yes, ring the bell for me. You
are the stronger now. I will obey you and go back. You
have taken a woman's parole, Mr Vincent," she went on,
with a strange spasmodic shadow of that old movement of
her mouth; "it will be curious to note if she can keep it.
Good-bye – good-bye." She spoke with a trembling desperation of calmness, mastering herself with all her power.
She did not remove her eyes from his face, till the door
had been opened. "I promise on my honour," she repeated,
with again a gleam of terror, as Vincent stood watching.
Then the door closed, shutting in that tragic, wretched

figure. She was gone back to her prison, with her misery, from which she could not escape. In that same garden, Vincent, with the sharp eyes of love and despair, even while watching her, had caught afar off a vision of two figures together, walking slowly, one leaning on the other, with the lingering steps of happiness. The sight went to his heart with a dull pang of certainty, which crushed down in a moment the useless effervescence of his former mood. His prisoner and he parted, going in and out, one scarcely less miserable at the moment than the other. In full sight of them both lingered for the same moment these two in the tenderest blessedness of life. Vincent turned sharp round, and went away the whole length of the long road past St Roque's, past the farthest village suburb of Carlingford, stifling his heart that it should say nothing. He had forgotten all about those duties which brought him there. Salem had vanished from his horizon. He saw nothing in heaven or earth but that miserable woman going back to her prison, interwoven with the vision of these two in their garden of paradise. The sight possessed him heart and spirit; he could not even feel that he felt it, his heart lying stifled in his bosom. It *was*, and there was no more to say.

CHAPTER XXXIII.

Mrs Vincent made many pilgrimages out of the sick-room that day; her mind was disturbed and restless; she could not keep still by Susan's side. She went and strayed through her son's rooms, looked at his books, gave a furtive glance at his linen; then went back and sat down for a little, until a renewed access of anxiety sent her wandering forth once more. Then she heard him come in,

and went out to see him. But he was gloomy and uncommunicative, evidently indisposed to satisfy her in any
way, absorbed in his own thoughts. Mrs Vincent came and
sat by him while he dined, thinking, in her simplicity, that
it would be a pleasure to Arthur. But Arthur, with the
unsocial habits of a man accustomed to live alone, had
already set up a book before him while he ate, leaving his
mother to wonder by herself behind what was the world of
unknown thought that rapt her son, and into which her
wistful wonder could not penetrate. But the widow was
wise in her generation: she would not worry him with
questions which it was very apparent beforehand that he
did not mean to answer. She admitted to herself with a
pang of mingled pain, curiosity, and resignation, that
Arthur was no longer a boy having no secrets from his
mother. Once more the little woman looked at the unreasonable male creature shut up within itself, and decided,
with a feminine mixture of pity and awe, that it must be
allowed to take its own time and way of disclosing itself,
and that to torture it into premature utterance would be
foolish, not to say impracticable. She left him, accordingly,
to himself, and went away again, returning, however, ere
long, in her vague restlessness, as she had been doing all
day. The early winter evening had closed in, and the lamp
was lighted – the same lamp which had smoked and
annoyed Mrs Vincent's nice perceptions the first evening
she was in Carlingford. Vincent had thrown himself on a
sofa with a book, not to read, but as a disguise under
which he could indulge his own thoughts, when his mother
came quietly back into the room. Mrs Vincent thought it
looked dark and less cheerful than it ought. She poked the
fire softly not to disturb Arthur, and made it blaze. Then
she turned to the lamp, which flared huskily upon the
table. "It smokes more than ever," said Mrs Vincent, half
apologetically, in case Arthur should observe her proceedings as she took off the globe. He, as was natural, put
down his book and gazed at her with a certain impatient

wonder, half contemptuous of that strange female development which amid all troubles could carry through, from
one crisis of life to another, that miraculous trifling, and
concern itself about the smoking of a lamp. As she screwed
it up and down and adjusted the wick, with the smoky
light flaring upon her anxious face, and magnifying the
shadow of her little figure against the wall behind, her son
looked on with a feeling very similar to that which had
moved Mrs Vincent when she watched him eating his
dinner with his book set up before him. These were points
upon which the mother and son could not understand each
other. But the sight disturbed his thoughts and touched his
temper; he got up from the sofa and threw down his
unread book.

"You women are incomprehensible," said the young
man, with an irritation he could not subdue – "what does it
matter about the lamp? but if the world were going to
pieces you must still be intent upon such trifles – leave
that to the people of the house."

"But, my dear, the people of the house don't understand
it," said Mrs Vincent. "Oh Arthur, it is often the trifles
that are the most important. I have had Mrs Tozer calling
upon me to-day, and Mrs Tufton. I don't wonder, dear, if
you find them a little tiresome; but that is what every
pastor has to expect. I daresay you have been worried to-
day paying so many visits. Hush, there is some one
coming up-stairs. It is Mr Tozer, Arthur. I can hear his
voice."

Upon which the minister, conscious of not being prepared for Tozer's questions, gave vent to an impatient
ejaculation. "Never a moment's respite! And now I shall
have to give an account of myself," said the unfortunate
Nonconformist. Mrs Vincent, who had just then finished
her operations with the lamp, looked up reproachfully
over the light at her son.

"Oh, Arthur, consider how kind he has been! Your dear
father would never have used such an expression – but

you have my quick temper," said the widow, with a little sigh. She shook hands very cordially with the good butter-man when he made his appearance. "I was just going to make tea for my son," said Mrs Vincent. "I have scarcely been able to sit with him at all since Susan took ill. Arthur, ring the bell – it is so kind of you to come; you will take a cup of tea with us while my son and you talk matters over – that is, if you don't object to my presence?" said the minister's mother, with a smile. "Your dear papa always liked me to be with him, Arthur; and until he has a wife, Mr Tozer, I daresay his mother will not be much in the way when it is so kind a friend as you he has to talk over his business with. – Bring tea directly, please. I fear you have forgotten what I said to you about the lamp, which burns quite nicely when you take a little pains. Arthur, will you open the window to clear the atmosphere of that smoke? and perhaps Mr Tozer will take a seat nearer the fire."

"I am obliged to you, ma'am," said the butterman, who had a cloud on his face. "Not no nearer, thank you all the same. If I hadn't thought you'd have done tea, I shouldn't have come troubling Mr Vincent, not so soon;" and Tozer turned a doubtful glance towards the minister, who stood longer at the window than he need have done. The widow's experienced eye saw that some irritation had risen between her son and his friend and patron. Tozer was suspicious, and ready to take offence – Arthur, alas! in an excited and restless mood, only too ready to give it. His mother could read in his shoulders, as he stood at the window with his back to her, that impulse to throw off the yoke and resent the inquisition to which he was subject, which, all conscious as he was of not having carried out Tozer's injunctions, seized upon the unfortunate Nonconformist. With a little tremulous rush, Mrs Vincent put herself in the breach.

"I am sure so warm a friend as Mr Tozer can never trouble any of my family at any time," said the widow, with a little effusion. "I know too well how rare a thing real kindness is – and I am very glad you have come just now while I can be here," she added, with a sensation of thankfulness perhaps not so complimentary to Tozer as it looked on the surface. "Arthur, dear, I think that will do now. You may put up the window and come back to your chair. You don't smell the lamp, Mr Tozer? and here is the little maid with the tea."

Mrs Vincent moved about the tray almost in a bustle when the girl had placed it on the table. She rearranged all the cups and moved everything on the table, while her son took up a gloomy position behind her on the hearthrug, and Tozer preserved an aspect of ominous civility on the other side of the table. She was glad that the little maid had to return two or three times with various forgotten adjuncts, though even then Mrs Vincent's instincts of good management prompted her to point out to the handmaiden the disadvantages of her thoughtlessness. "If you had but taken time to think what would be wanted, you would have saved yourself a great deal of trouble," said the minister's mother, with a tremble of expectation thrilling her frame, looking wistfully round to see whether anything more was wanted, or if, perhaps, another minute might be gained before the storm broke. She gave Arthur a look of entreaty as she called him forward to take his place at table. She knew that real kindness was not very often to be met with in this cross-grained world; and if people are conscious of having been kind, it is only natural they should expect gratitude! Such was the sentiment in her eyes as she turned round and fixed them upon her son. "Tea is ready, Arthur," said the widow, in a tone of secret supplication. And Arthur understood his mother, and was less and less inclined to conciliate as he came forward out of the darkness, where he might look sulky if he pleased, and sat down full in the light of the lamp, which smoked no longer. They were not a comfortable party. Mrs Vincent felt it so necessary that she should talk and keep them separated, that she lost her usual self-command, and subjects failed her in her utmost need.

"Let me give you another cup of tea," she said, as the butterman paused in the supernumerary meal which that excellent man was making; "I am so glad you happened to come this evening when I am taking a little leisure. I hope the congregation will not think me indifferent, Mr Tozer. I am sure you and Mrs Tozer will kindly explain to them how much I have been occupied. When Susan is well, I hope to make acquaintance with all my son's people. Arthur, my dear boy, you are over-tired, you don't eat anything – and you made a very poor dinner. I wish you would advise him to take a little rest, Mr Tozer. He minds his mother in most things, but not in this. It is vain for me to say anything to him about giving up work; but perhaps a little advice from you would have more effect. I spoke to Dr Rider on the subject, and he says a little rest is all my son requires; but rest is exactly what he will never take. It was just the same with his dear father – and you are not strong enough, Arthur, to bear so much."

"I daresay as you're right, ma'am," said Tozer; "if he was to take a little more exercise and walking about – most of us Salem folks wouldn't mind a little less on Sundays, to have more of the minister at other times. I hope as there wasn't no unpleasantness, Mr Vincent, between you and Pigeon when you see him to-day?"

"I did not see him; – I mean I am sorry I was not able to call on Pigeon to-day," said Vincent, hastily; "I was unexpectedly detained," he added, growing rather red, and looking Tozer in the face. "Indeed, I am not sure that I ought to call on Pigeon," continued the minister, after a pause; "I have done nothing to offend him. If he chooses to take an affront which was never intended, I can't help it. Why should I go and court every man who is sulky or ill-tempered in the congregation? Look here, Tozer – you are a sensible man – you have been very kind, as my mother says. I set out to-day intending to go and see this man for your sake; but you know very well this is not what I came to Carlingford for. If I had known the sort of thing that was required of me!" cried Vincent, rising up and resuming his place on the hearthrug – "to go with my hat in my hand, and beg this one and the other to forgive me, and receive me into favour: – why, what have I ever done to Pigeon? if he has anything to find fault with, he had much better come to me, and have it out."

"Mr Vincent, sir," said Tozer solemnly, pushing away his empty teacup, and leaning forward over the table on his folded arms, "them ain't the sentiments for a pastor in our connection. That's a style of thing as may do among fine folks, or in the Church where there's no freedom; but them as chooses their own pastor, and pays their own pastor, and don't spare no pains to make him comfortable, has a right to expect different. Them ain't the sentiments, sir, for Salem folks. I don't say if they're wrong or right – I don't make myself a judge of no man; but I've seen a deal of our connection and human nature in general, and this I know, that a minister as has to please his flock, has got to please his flock whatever happens, and neither me nor no other man can make it different; and that Mrs Vincent, as has seen life, can tell you as well as I can. Pigeon ain't neither here nor there. It's the flock as has to be considered – and it ain't preaching alone as will do that; and that your good mother, sir, as knows the world, will tell you as well as me."

"But Arthur is well aware of it," said the alarmed mother, interposing hastily, conscious that to be thus appealed to was the greatest danger which could threaten her. "His dear father always told him so; yet, after all, Mr Vincent used to say," added the anxious diplomatist, "that nothing was to be depended on in the end but the pulpit. I have heard him talking of it with the leading people in the connection, Mr Tozer. They all used to say that, though visiting was very good, and a pastor's duty, it was the pulpit, after all, that was to be most trusted to; and I have always seen in my experience – I don't know if the same has occurred to you – that *both* gifts are very rarely to be

met with. Of course, we should all strive after perfection,"
continued the minister's mother with a tremulous smile –
"but it is so seldom met with that any one has *both* gifts!
Arthur, my dear boy, I wish you would eat something; and
Mr Tozer, let me give you another cup of tea."

"No more for me, ma'am, thankye," said Tozer, laying
his hand over his cup. "I don't deny as there's truth in
what you say. I don't deny as a family here and there in a
flock may be aggravating like them Pigeons. I'm not the
man to be hard on a minister if that ain't his turn. A pastor
may have a weakness, and not feel himself as equal to one
part of his work as to another; but to go for to say as visiting
and keeping the flock pleased, ain't his duty – it's that,
ma'am, as goes to my heart."

Tozer's pathos touched a lighter chord in the bosom of
the minister. He came back to his seat with a passing sense
of amusement. "If Pigeon has anything to find fault with,
let him come and have it out," said Vincent, bringing, as
his mother instantly perceived, a less clouded countenance
into the light of the lamp. "You, who are a much better
judge than Pigeon, were not displeased on Sunday," added
the minister, not without a certain complacency. Looking
back upon the performances of that day, the young Nonconformist himself was not displeased. He knew now –
though he was unconscious at the time – that he had made
a great appearance in the pulpit of Salem, and that once
more the eyes of Carlingford, unused to oratory, and
still more unused to great and passionate emotion, were
turned upon him.

"Well, sir, if it come to be a question of that," said the
mollified deacon; "but no – it ain't that – I can't, whatever
my feelings is, be forgetful of my dooty!" cried Tozer, in
sudden excitement. "It ain't that, Mr Vincent; it's for your
good I'm a-speaking up and letting you know my mind. It
ain't the pulpit, sir. I'll not say as I ever had a word to say
against your sermons: but when the minister goes out of
my house, a-saying as he is going to visit the flock, and

when he's to be seen the next moment, Mrs Vincent, not going to the flock but a-spending his precious time in Grange Lane with them as don't know nothing, and don't care nothing for Salem, nor understand the ways of folks like us—"

Here Tozer was interrupted suddenly by the minister, who once more rose from his chair with an angry exclamation. What he might have said in the hasty impulse of the moment nobody could tell; but Mrs Vincent, hastily stumbling up on her part from her chair, burst in with a tremulous voice –

"Arthur, my dear boy! did you hear Susan call me? – hark! I fancied I heard her voice. Oh, Arthur dear, go and see, I am too weak to run myself. Say I am coming directly – hark! do you think it is Susan? Oh, Arthur, go and see!"

Startled by her earnestness, though declaring he heard nothing, the young man hastened away. Mrs Vincent seized her opportunity without loss of time.

"Mr Tozer," said the widow, "I am just going to my sick child. Arthur and you will be able to talk of your business more freely when I am gone, and I hope you will be guided to give him good advice; what I am afraid of is, that he will throw it all up," continued Mrs Vincent, leaning her hand upon the table, and bending forward confidential and solemn to the startled butterman, "as so many talented young men in our connection do nowadays. Young men are so difficult to deal with; they will not put up with things that we know must be put up with," said the minister's mother, shaking her head with a sigh. "That is how we are losing all our young preachers; – an accomplished young man has so many ways of getting on now. Oh, Mr Tozer, I rely upon you to give my son good advice – if he is aggravated, it is my terror that he will throw it all up! Good-night. You have been our kind friend, and I have such trust in you!" Saying which the widow shook hands with him earnestly and went away, leaving the worthy deacon much shaken, and with a weight of responsibility upon him. Vincent met her at the door, assuring her that Susan had not called; but with a heroism which nobody suspected – trembling with anxiety, yet conscious of having struck a master-stroke – his mother glided away to the stillness of the sick-room, where she sat questioning her own wisdom all the evening after, and wondering whether, after all, at such a crisis, she had done right to come away.

When the minister and the deacon were left alone together, instead of returning with zest to their interrupted discussion, neither of them said anything for some minutes. Once more Vincent took up his position on the hearthrug, and Tozer gazed ruefully at the empty cup which he still covered with his hand, full of troubled thoughts. The responsibility was almost too much for Tozer. He could scarcely realise to himself what terrors lay involved in that threatened danger, or what might happen if the minister threw it all up! He held his breath at the awful thought. The widow's Parthian arrow had gone straight to the butterman's heart.

"I hope, sir, as you won't think there's anything but an anxious feelin' in the flock to do you justice as our pastor," said Tozer, with a certain solemnity, "or that we ain't sensible of our blessins. I've said, both to yourself and others, as you was a young man of great promise, and as good a preacher as I ever see in our connection, Mr Vincent, and I'll stand by what I've said; but you ain't above taking a friend's advice – not speaking with no authority," added the good butterman, in a conciliatory tone; "it's all along of the women, sir – it's them as is at the bottom of all the mischief in a flock. It ain't Pigeon, bless you, as is to blame. And even my missis, though she's not to say unreasonable as women go – none of them can abide to hear of you a-going after Lady Western – that's it, Mr Vincent. She's a lovely creature," cried Tozer, with enthusiasm; "there ain't one in Carlingford to compare with her, as I can see, and I wouldn't be the one to blame a young man as was carried away. But there couldn't no good come of it, and Salem folks *is* touchy and jealous," continued the worthy deacon; "that was all as I meant to say."

Thus the conference ended amicably after a little more talk, in which Pigeon and the other malcontents were made a sacrifice of and given up by the anxious butterman, upon whom Mrs Vincent's parting words had made so deep an impression. Tozer went home thereafter to overawe his angry wife, whom Vincent's visit to Lady Western had utterly exasperated, with the dread responsibility now laid upon them. "What if he was to throw it all up!" said Tozer. That alarming possibility struck silence and dismay to the very heart of the household. Perhaps it was the dawn of a new era of affairs in Salem. The deacon's very sleep was disturbed by recollections of the promising young men who, now he came to think of it, *had* been lost to the connection, as Mrs Vincent suggested, and *had* thrown it all up. The fate of the chapel, and all the new sittings let under the ministry of the young Nonconformist, seemed to hang on Tozer's hands. He thought of the weekly crowd, and his heart stirred. Not many deacons in the connection could boast of being crowded out of their own pews Sunday after Sunday by the influx of unexpected hearers. The enlightenment of Carlingford, as well as the filling of the chapel, was at stake. Clearly, in the history of Salem, a new era had begun.

CHAPTER XXXIV.

THAT week passed on without much incident. To Vincent and his mother, in whose history days had, for some time past, been counting like years, it might have seemed a very grateful pause, but for the thundrous atmosphere of doubt and uncertainty which clouded over them on every side. Susan's recovery did not progress; and Dr Rider began to look as serious over her utter languor and apathy, which nothing seemed able to disturb, as he had done at her delirium. The Salem people stood aloof, as Mrs Vincent perceived, with keen feminine observation. She could not persuade herself, as she had tried to persuade Mrs Tozer, that the landlady answered inquiries at the door by way of leaving the sick-room quiet. The fact was, that except Lady Western's fine footman, the sight of whom at the minister's door was far from desirable, nobody came to make inquiries except Mrs Tufton and Phoebe Tozer, the latter of whom found no encouragement in her visits. Politic on all other points, the widow could not deny herself, when circumstances put it in her power to extinguish Phoebe. Mrs Vincent would not have harmed a fly, but it gave her a certain pleasure to wound the rash female bosom which had, as she supposed, formed plans of securing her son. As for Tozer himself, his visits had almost ceased. He was scarcely to be seen even in the shop, into which sometimes the minister himself gazed disconsolately when he strayed out in the twilight to walk his cares away. The good butterman was otherwise employed. He was wrestling with Pigeon in many a close encounter, holding little committees in the back parlour. On his single arm and strength he felt it now to depend whether or not the pastor could tide it over, and be pulled through.

As for Vincent himself, he had retired from the conflict. He paid no visits; with a certain half-conscious falling back upon the one thing he could do best, he devoted himself to his sermons. At least he shut himself up to write morning after morning, and remained all day dull and undisturbed, brooding over his work. The congregation somehow got to hear of his abstraction. And to the offended mind of Salem there was something imposing in the idea of the minister, misunderstood and unappreciated, thus retiring from the field, and devoting himself to "study." Even Mrs Pigeon owned to herself a certain respect for the foe who did not humble himself, but withdrew with dignity into the intrenchments of his own position. It was fine; but it was not the thing for Salem. Mrs Brown had a tea-party on the Thursday, to which the pastor was not even invited, but where there were great and manifold discussions about him, and where the Tozers found themselves an angry minority, suspected on all sides. "A pastor as makes himself agreeable here and there, but don't take no thought for the good of the flock in general, ain't a man to get on in our connection," said Mrs Pigeon, with a toss of her head at Phoebe, who blushed over all her pink arms and shoulders with mingled gratification and discomposure. Mrs Tozer herself received this insinuation without any violent disclaimer. "For my part, I can't say as the minister hasn't made himself very agreeable as far as we are concerned," said the judicious woman. "It's well known as friends can't come amiss to Tozer and me. Dinner or supper, we never can be took wrong, not being fine folks but comfortable," said the butterman's wife, directing her eyes visibly to Mrs Pigeon, who was not understood to be liberal in her housekeeping. Poor Phoebe was not so discriminating. When she retired into a corner with her companions, Phoebe's injured feelings disclosed themselves. "I am sure he never said anything to me that he might not have said to any one," she confessed to Maria Pigeon; "it is very hard to have people look so at me when perhaps he means nothing at all," said Phoebe, half dejected, half important. Mrs Pigeon heard the unguarded confession, and made use of it promptly, not careful for her consistency.

"I said when you had all set your hearts on a young man, that it was a foolish thing to do," said poor Vincent's skilful opponent; "I said he'd be sure to come a-dangling about our houses, and a-trifling with the affections of our girls. It'll be well if it doesn't come too true; not as I want to pretend to be wiser nor other folks – but I said so, as you'll remember, Mrs Brown, the very first day Mr Vincent preached in Salem. I said, 'He's not bad-looking, and he's young and has genteel ways, and the girls don't know no better. You mark my words, if he don't make some mischief in Carlingford afore all's done,' – and I only hope as it won't come too true."

"Them as is used to giddy girls gets timid, as is natural," said Mrs Tozer; "it's different where there is only one, and she a quiet one. I can't say as I ever thought a young man was more taking for being a minister; but there can't be no doubt as it must be harder upon you, ma'am, as has four daughters, than me as has only one – and she a quiet one," added the deacon's wife, with a glance of maternal pride at Phoebe, who was just then enfolding the spare form of Maria Pigeon in an artless embrace, and who looked, in her pink wreath and white muslin dress, "quite the lady," at least in her mother's eyes.

"The quiet ones is the deep ones," said Tozer, interfering, as a wise man ought, in the female duel, as it began to get intense. "Phoebe's my girl, and I don't deny being fond of her, as is natural; but she ain't so innocent as not to know how things is working, and what meaning is in some folks' minds. But that's neither here nor there, and it's time as we was going away."

"Not before we've had prayers," said Mrs Brown. "I *was* surprised the first time I see Mr Vincent in your house, Mr Tozer, as we all parted like heathens without a blessing, specially being all Chapel folks, and of one way of thinking. Our ways is different in this house; and though we're in a comfortless kind of condition, and no better than if we hadn't no minister, still as there's you and Mr Pigeon here—"

The tea-party thus concluded with a still more distinct sense of the pastor's shortcomings. There was nobody to

"give prayers" but Pigeon and Tozer. For all social pur-
poses, the flock in Salem might as well have had no
minister. The next little committee held in the back
parlour at the butter-shop was still more unsatisfactory.
While it was in progress, Mr Vincent himself appeared,
and had to be taken solemnly up-stairs to the drawing-
room, where there was no fire, and where the hum of the
voices below was very audible, as Mrs Tozer and Phoebe,
getting blue with cold, sat vainly trying to occupy the
attention of the pastor.

"Pa has some business people with him in the parlour,"
explained Phoebe, who was very tender and sympathetic,
as might be expected; but it did not require a very brilliant
intelligence to divine that the business under discussion
was the minister, even if Mrs Tozer's solemnity, and the
anxious care with which he was conveyed past the closed
door of the parlour, had not already filled the mind of the
pastor with suspicion.

"Go down and let your Pa know as Mr Vincent's here,"
said Mrs Tozer, after this uncomfortable *séance* had lasted
half an hour; "and he's not to keep them men no longer
than he can help; and presently we'll have a bit of supper
– that's what I enjoy, that is, Mr Vincent; no ceremony
like there must be at a party, but just to take us as we are;
and we can't be took amiss, Tozer and me. There's always
a bit of something comfortable for supper; and no friend as
could be made so welcome as the minister," added the
good woman, growing more and more civil as she came to
her wits' end; for had not Pigeon and Brown been asked to
share that something comfortable? For the first time it was
a relief to the butterman's household when the pastor
declined the impromptu invitation, and went resolutely
away. His ears, sharpened by suspicion, recognised the
familiar voices in the parlour, where the door was ajar
when he went out again. Vincent could not have imagined
that to feel himself unwelcome at Tozer's would have had
any effect whatever upon his preoccupied mind, or that to

pass almost within hearing of one of the discussions which must inevitably be going on about him among the managers of Salem, could quicken his pulse or disturb his composure. But it was so notwithstanding. He had come out at the entreaty of his mother, half unwillingly, anticipating, with the liveliest realisation of all its attendant circumstances, an evening spent at the big table in the back parlour, and something comfortable to supper. He came back again tingling with curiosity, indignation, and suppressed defiance. The something comfortable had not this time been prepared for him. He was being discussed, not entertained, in the parlour; and Mrs Tozer and Phoebe, in the chill fine drawing-room up-stairs, where the gas was blazing in a vain attempt to make up for the want of the fire – shivering with cold and civility – had been as much disconcerted by his appearance as if they too were plotting against him. Mr Vincent returned to his sermon not without some additional fire. He had spent a great deal of time over his sermon that week; it was rather learned and very elaborate, and a little – dull. The poor minister felt very conscious of the fact, but could not help it. He was tempted to put it in the fire, and begin again, when he returned that Friday evening, smarting with those little stinging arrows of slight and injury; but it was too late: and this was the beginning of the "coorse" which Tozer had laid so much store by. Vincent concluded the elaborate production by a few sharp sentences, which he was perfectly well aware did not redeem it, and explained to his mother, with a little ill-temper, as she thought, that he had changed his mind about visiting the Tozers that night. Mrs Vincent did Arthur injustice as she returned to Susan's room, where again matters looked very sadly; and so the troubled week came to a close.

CHAPTER XXXV.

SUNDAY! It came again, the inevitable morning. There are pathetic stories current in the world about most of the other professions that claim the ear of the public; how lawyers prepare great speeches, which are to open for them the gates of the future, in the midst of the killing anxieties of life and poverty – how mimes and players of all descriptions keep the world in laughter while their hearts are breaking. But few people think of the sufferings of the priest, whom, let trouble or anxiety come as they please, necessity will have in the inexorable pulpit Sunday after Sunday. So Vincent thought as he put on his Geneva gown in his little vestry, with the raw February air coming in at the open window, and his sermon, which was dull, lying on the table beside him. It *was* dull – he knew it in his heart; but after all the strain of passion he had been held at, what was to preserve him any more than another from the unavoidable lassitude and blank that followed? Still it was not agreeable to know that Salem was crowded to the door, and that this sermon, upon which the minister looked ruefully, was laboured and feeble, without any divine spark to enlighten it, or power to touch the hearts of other men. The consciousness that it was dull would, the preacher knew, make it duller still – its heaviness would affect himself as well as his audience. Still that was not to be helped now; there it lay, ready for utterance; and here in his Geneva gown, with the sound in his ears of all the stream of entering worshippers who were then arranging themselves in the pews of Salem, stood the minister prepared to speak. There was, as Vincent divined, a great crowd – so great a crowd that various groups stood during the whole service, which, by dint of being more laboured and feeble than usual, was longer too. With a certain dulness of feeling, half despairing, the minister accomplished the preliminary devotions, and was just opening his Bible to begin the work of the day when his startled eye caught a most unlooked-for accession to the flock. Immediately before him, in the same pew with Mrs Tozer and Phoebe, what was that beautiful vision that struck him dumb for the moment? Tozer himself had brought her in during the prayers, through the groups that occupied the passage, to his own seat, where she sat expanding her rustling plumage, and looking round with all her natural sweetness, and a kind of delightful unconscious patronage and curiosity, upon the crowd of unknown people who were nobody in Carlingford. The sight of her struck the young Nonconformist dumb. He took some moments to recover himself, ere, with a pang in his heart, he began his dull sermon. It mattered nothing to Lady Western what kind of a sermon he preached. She was not clever, and probably would never know the difference; but it went to the young man's heart, an additional pang of humiliation, to think that it was not his best he had to set before the unexpected hearer. What had brought the beauty here? Vincent's dazzled eyes did not make out for some time the dark spare figure beside her, all sunned over with the rays of her splendour. Mrs Tozer and Phoebe on one side, proud yet half affronted, contemplating with awe and keen observation the various particulars of Lady Western's dress, were not more unlike her, reposing in her soft beauty within the hard wooden enclosure of the pew, beaming upon everybody in sweet ease and composure – than was the agitated restless face, with gleaming uncertain eyes that flashed everywhere, which appeared at her other side when Vincent came to be able to see. He preached his sermon with a certain self-disgust growing more and more intense very time he ventured to glance at that strange line of faces. The only attentive hearer in Tozer's pew was

Lady Western, who looked up at the young minister
steadily with her sweet eyes, and listened with all the
gracious propriety that belonged to her. The Tozers, for
their part, drawn up in their end of the seat, gave a very
divided attention, being chiefly occupied with Lady
Western; and as for Mrs Hilyard, the sight of her restlessness and nervous agitation would have been pitiful had
anybody there been sufficiently interested to observe it.
Mr Vincent's sermon certainly did not secure that wandering
mind. All her composure had deserted this strange woman.
Now and then she almost rose up by way apparently of
relieving the restless fever that possessed her; her nervous
hands wandered among the books of the Tozer pew with an
incessant motion. Her eyes gleamed in all directions with a
wistful anxiety and suspicion. All this went on while
Vincent preached his sermon; he had no eyes for the other
people in the place. Now and then the young man became
rhetorical, and threw in here and there a wild flourish to
break the deadness of his discourse, with no success as he
saw. He read tedium in all the lines of faces before him as
he came to a close with a dull despair – in all the faces
except that sweet face never disturbed out of its lovely calm
of attention, which would have listened to the Dissenting
minister quite as calmly had he preached like Paul. With a
sensation that this was one of the critical moments of his
fate, and that he had failed in it, Vincent dropped into his
seat in exhaustion and self-disgust, while his hearers got up
to sing their hymn. It was at this moment that Tozer walked
up through the aisle, steadily, yet with his heart beating
louder than usual, and ascended the pulpit-stairs to give
forth that intimation which had been agreed upon in the
back parlour on Friday. The minister was disturbed in his
uncomfortable repose by the entrance of the deacon into
the pulpit, where the worthy butterman seated himself by
Vincent's side. The unconscious congregation sang its
hymn, while the Nonconformist, rousing up, looked with
surprised eyes upon his unexpected companion; yet there

were bosoms in the flock which owned a thrill of emotion as
Tozer's substantial person partially disappeared from view
behind the crimson cushion. Phoebe left off singing, and
subsided into tears and her seat. Mrs Pigeon lifted up her
voice and expanded her person; meanwhile Tozer whispered
ominously, with a certain agitation, in his pastor's ear –

"It's three words of an intimation as I'd like to give –
nothing of no importance; a meeting of the flock as some of
us would like to call, if it's quite agreeable – nothing as you
need mind, Mr Vincent. We wouldn't go for to occupy your
time, sir, attending of it. There wasn't no opportunity to tell
you before. I'll give it out, if it's agreeable," said Tozer,
with hesitation – "or if you'd rather—"

"Give it to me," said the minister quickly. He took the
paper out of the butterman's hand, who drew back uncomfortable and embarrassed, wishing himself anywhere
in the world but in the pulpit, from which that revolutionary
document menaced the startled pastor with summary
deposition. It was a sufficiently simple notice of a meeting
to be held on the following Monday evening, in the
schoolroom, which was the scene of all the tea and other
meetings of Salem. This, however, was no tea-meeting.
Vincent drew his breath hard, and changed colour, as he
bent down under the shadow of the pulpit-cushion and the
big Bible, and read this dangerous document. Meanwhile
the flock sang their hymn, to which Tozer, much discomposed, added a few broken notes of tremulous bass as
he sat by the minister's side. When Mr Vincent again raised
his head, and sat erect with the notice in his hand, the
troubled deacon made vain attempts to catch his eye, and
ask what was to be done. The Nonconformist made no
reply to these telegraphic communications. When the
singing was ended he rose, still with the paper in his hand,
and faced the congregation, where he no longer saw one
face with a vague background of innumerable other faces,
but had suddenly woke up to behold his battle-ground and
field of warfare, in which everything dear to him was

suddenly assailed. Unawares, the assembled people, who had received no special sensation from the sermon, woke up also at the sight of Vincent's face. He read the notice to them with a voice that tingled through the place; then he paused. "This meeting is one of which I have not been informed," said Vincent. "It is one which I am not asked to attend. I invite you to it, all who are here present; and I invite you thereafter," continued the minister, with an unconscious elevation of his head, "to meet me on the following evening to hear what I have to say to you. Probably the business will be much the same on both occasions, but it will be approached from different sides of the question. I invite you to meet on Monday, according to this notice; and I invite you on Tuesday, at the same place and hour, to meet me."

Vincent did not hear the audible hum and buzz of surprise and excitement which ran through his startled flock. He did not pay much attention to what Tozer said to him when all was over. He lingered in his vestry, taking off his gown, until he could hear Lady Western's carriage drive off after an interval of lingering. The young Dowager had gone out slowly, thinking to see him, and comfort him with a compliment about his sermon, concerning the quality of which she was not critical. She was sorry in her kind heart to perceive his troubled looks, and to discover that somehow, she could not quite understand how, something annoying and unexpected had occurred to him. And then this uneasy companion, to whom he had bound her, and whose strange agitation and wonderful change of aspect Lady Western could in no way account for – But the carriage rolled away at last, not without reluctance, while the minister still remained in his vestry. Then he hurried home, speaking to no one. Mrs Vincent did not understand her son all day, nor even next morning, when he might have been supposed to have time to calm down. He was very silent, but no longer dreamy or languid, or lost in the vague discontent and dejection with which she was familiar. On the contrary, the minister had woken up out of that abstraction. When he sat down to his writing-table it was not to muse, with his pen in his languid fingers, now and then putting down a sentence, but to write straightforward with evident fire and emphasis. He was very tender to herself, but he did not tell her anything. Some new cloud had doubtless appeared on the firmament where there was little need for any further clouds. The widow rose on the Monday morning with a presentiment of calamity on her mind – rose from the bed in Susan's room which she occupied for two or three hours in the night, sometimes snatching a momentary sleep, which Susan's smallest movement interrupted. Her heart was rent in two between her children. She went from Susan's bedside, where her daughter lay in dumb apathy, not to be roused by anything that could be said or done, to minister wistfully at Arthur's breakfast, which, with her heart in her throat, the widow made a pitiful pretence of sharing. She could not ask him questions. She was silent, too, in her great love and sorrow. Seeing some new trouble approaching – wistfully gazing into the blank skies before her, to discover, if that were possible, without annoying Arthur, or compromising him, what it was; but rather than compromise or annoy him, contenting herself not to know – the greatest stretch of endurance to which as yet she had constrained her spirit.

Arthur did not go out all that Monday. Even in the house a certain excitement was visible to Mrs Vincent's keen observation. The landlady herself made her appearance in tears to clear away the remains of the minister's dinner. "I hope, sir, as you don't think what's past and gone has made no difference on me," said that tearful woman in Mrs Vincent's hearing; "it ain't me as would ever give my support to such doings." When the widow asked, "What doings?" Arthur only smiled and made some half-articulate remark about gossip, which his mother of course treated at its true value. As the dark wintry afternoon closed in, Mrs Vincent's anxiety increased under the influence of the landlady's Sunday dress, in which she was visible progressing about the passages, and warning her husband to mind he wasn't late. At last Mrs Tufton called, and the minister's mother came to a true understanding of the state of affairs. Mrs Tufton was unsettled and nervous, filled with a not unexhilarating excitement, and all the heat of partisanship. "Don't you take on," said the good little woman; "Mr Tufton is going to the meeting to tell them his sentiments about his young brother. My dear, they will never go against what Mr Tufton says: and if I should mount upon the platform and make a speech myself, there shan't be anything done that could vex you; for we always said he was a precious young man, and a credit to the connection; and it would be a disgrace to us all to let the Pigeons, or such people, have it all their own way." Mrs Vincent managed to ascertain all the particulars from the old minister's wife. When she was gone, the widow sat down a little with a very desolate heart to think it all over. Arthur, with a new light in his eye, and determination in his face, was writing in the sitting-room; but Arthur's mother could not sit still as he did, and imagine the scene in the Salem schoolroom, and how everybody discussed and sat upon her boy, and decided all the momentous future of his young life in this private inquisition. She went back, however, beside him, and poured out a cup of tea for him, and managed to swallow one for herself, talking about Susan and indifferent household matters, while the evening wore on and the hour of the meeting approached. A little before that hour Mrs Vincent left Arthur, with an injunction not to come into the sick-room that evening until she sent for him, as she thought Susan would sleep. As she left the room the landlady went down-stairs, gorgeous in her best bonnet and shawl, with all the personal satisfaction which a member of a flock naturally feels when called to a bed of justice to decide the future destiny of its head. The minister's fate was in the hands of his people; and it was with a pleasurable sensation that, from every house

throughout Grove Street and the adjacent regions, the good
people were going forth to decide it. As for the minister's
mother, she went softly back to Susan's room, where the
nurse, who was Mrs Vincent's assistant, had taken her
place. "She looks just the same," said the poor mother.
"Just the same," echoed the attendant. "I don't think
myself as there'll be no change until—" Mrs Vincent
turned away silently in her anguish, which she dared not
indulge. She wrapped herself in a black shawl, and took out
the thick veil of crape which she had worn in her first
mourning. Nobody could recognise her under that screen.
But it was with a pang that she tied that sign of woe over her
pale face. The touch of the crape made her shiver. Perhaps
she was but forestalling the mourning which, in her age and
weakness, she might have to renew again. With such
thoughts she went softly through the wintry lighted streets
towards Salem. As she approached the door, groups of
people going the same way brushed past her through Grove
Street. Lively people, talking with animation, pleased with
this new excitement, declaring, sometimes so loudly that
she could hear them as they passed, what side they were
on, and that they, for their part, were going to vote for the
minister to give him another trial. The little figure in those
black robes, with anxious looks shrouded under the crape
veil, went on among the rest to the Salem schoolroom. She
took her seat close to the door, and saw Tozer and Pigeon,
and the rest of the deacons, getting upon the platform,
where on occasions more festive the chairman and the
leading people had tea. The widow looked through her veil
at the butterman and the poulterer with one keen pang of
resentment, of which she repented instantly. She did not
despise them as another might have done. They were the
constituted authorities of the place, and her son's fate, his
reputation, his young life, all that he had had or could hope
for in the world, was in their hands. The decision of the
highest authorities in the land was not so important to
Arthur as that of the poulterer and the butterman. There

they stood, ready to open their session, their inquisition, their solemn tribunal. The widow drew her veil close, and clasped her hands together to sustain herself. It was Pigeon who was about to speak.

CHAPTER XXXVI.

MR PIGEON was a heavy orator; he was a tall man, badly put together, with a hollow crease across his waistcoat, which looked very much as if he might be folded in two, and so laid away out of mischief. His arms moved foolishly about in the agonies of oratory, as if they did not belong to him; but he did not look absurd through Mrs Vincent's crape veil, as she sat gazing at the platform on which he stood, and taking in with eager ears every syllable that came from his lips. Mr Pigeon said it was Mr Vincent as they had come there to discuss that night. The managers had made up their minds as it was a dooty to lay things before the flock. Mr Vincent was but a young man, and most in that congregation was ready to make allowances; and as for misfortunes as might have happened to him, he wasn't a-going to lay that to the pastor's charge, nor take no mean advantages. He was for judging a man on his merits, he was. If they was to take Mr Vincent on his merits without no prejudice, they would find as he hadn't carried out the expectations as was formed of him. Not as there was anything to be said against his preaching; his preaching was well enough, though it wasn't to call rousing up, which was what most folks wanted. There wasn't no desire on the part of the managers to object to his preaching: he had ought to have preached well, that was the truth, for every one as had been connected with Salem in Mr Tufton's time knew as there was a deal of difference between the new pastor and the old pastor, as far as the work of a congregation went. As for Pigeon's own feelings, he would have held his peace cheerful, if his dooty had permitted him, or if he had seen as it was for the good of the connection. But things was come to that pass in Salem as a man hadn't ought to mind his own feelings, but had to do his dooty, if he was to be took to the stake for it. And them were his circumstances, as many a one as he had spoken to in private could say, if they was to speak up.

To all this Mrs Vincent listened with the profoundest attention behind her veil. The schoolroom was very full of people – almost as full as on the last memorable tea-party; but the square lines of the gasburners, coming down with two flaring lights each from the low room, were veiled with no festoons this time, and threw an unmitigated glare upon the people, all in their dark winter-dresses, without any attempt at special embellishment. Mrs Pigeon was in the foreground, on a side-bench near the platform, very visible to the minister's mother, nodding her head and giving triumphant glances around now and then to point her husband's confused sentences. Mrs Pigeon had her daughters spread out on one side of her, all in their best bonnets, and at the corner of the same seat sat little Mrs Tufton, who shook her charitable head when the poulterer's wife nodded hers, and put her handkerchief to her eyes now and then, as she gazed up at the platform, not without a certain womanly misgiving as to how her husband was going to conduct himself. The Tozers had taken up their position opposite. Mrs Tozer and her daughter had all the appearance of being in great spirits, especially Phoebe, who seemed scarcely able to contain her amusement as Mr Pigeon went on. All this Mrs Vincent saw as clearly as in a picture through the dark folds of her veil. She sat back as far as she could into the shade, and pressed her hands close together, and was noways amused, but listened with as profound an ache of anxiety in her heart as if Pigeon had been the Lord Chancellor. As for the audience in general, it showed some signs of weariness as the poulterer stumbled on through his confused speech; and not a restless gesture, not a suppressed yawn in the place, but was apparent to the minister's mother. The heart in her troubled bosom beat steadier as she gazed; certainly no violent sentiment actuated the good people of Salem as they sat staring with calm eyes at the speaker. Mrs Vincent knew how a congregation looked when it was thoroughly excited and up in arms against its head. She drew a long breath of relief, and suffered the light clasp of her hands to relax a little. There was surely no popular passion there.

And then Mr Tufton got up, swaying heavily with his large uncertain old figure over the table. The old minister sawed the air with his white fat hand after he had said, "My beloved brethren" twice over; and little Mrs Tufton, sitting below, in her impatience and anxiety lest he should not acquit himself well, dropt her handkerchief and disappeared after it, while Mrs Vincent erected herself under the shadow of her veil. Mr Tufton did his young brother no good. He was so sympathetic over the misfortunes that had befallen Vincent's family, that bitter tears came to the widow's eyes, and her hands once more tightened in a silent strain of self-support. While the old minister impressed upon his audience the duty of bearing with his dear young brother, and being indulgent to the faults of his youth, it was all the poor mother could do to keep silent, to stifle down the indignant sob in her heart, and keep steady in her seat. Perhaps it was some breath of anguish escaping from her unawares that drew towards her the restless gleaming eyes of another strange spectator there. That restless ghost of a woman! – all shrunken, gleaming, ghastly – her eyes looking all about in an obliquity of furtive glances, fearing yet daring everything. When she found Mrs Vincent out, she fixed her suspicious desperate gaze upon the crape veil which hid the widow's face. The deacons of Salem were to Mrs Hilyard but so many wretched masquers playing a rude game among the dreadful wastes of life, of which these poor fools were ignorant. Sometimes she watched them with a reflection of her old amusement – oftener, pursued by her own tyrannical fancy and the wild restlessness which had brought her here, forgot altogether where she was. But Mrs Vincent's sigh, which breathed unutterable things – the steady fixed composure of that little figure while the old minister maundered on with his condolences, his regrets, his self-glorification over the interest he had taken in his dear young brother, and the advice he had given him – could not miss the universal scrutiny of this strange woman's eyes. She divined, with a sudden awakening of the keen intelligence which was half crazed by this time, yet vivid as ever, the state of mind in which the widow was. With a half-audible cry the Back Grove Street needlewoman gazed at the minister's mother; in poignant trouble, anxiety, indignant distress – clasping her tender hands together yet again to control the impatience, the resentment, the aching mortification and injury with which she heard all this maudlin pity overflowing the name of her boy – yet, ah! what a world apart from the guilty and desperate spirit which sat there gazing like Dives at Lazarus. Mrs Hilyard slid out of her seat with a rapid stealthy movement, and placed herself unseen by the widow's side. The miserable woman put forth her furtive hand and took hold of the black gown – the old black silk gown, so well worn and long preserved. Mrs Vincent started a little, looked at her, gave her a slight half-spasmodic nod of recognition, and returned to her own absorbing interest. The interruption made her raise her head a little higher under the veil, that not even this stranger might imagine Arthur's mother to be affected by what was going on. For everything else, Mrs Hilyard had disappeared out of the widow's memory. She was thinking only of her son.

As for the other minister's wife, poor Mrs Tufton's handkerchief dropped a great many times during her husband's speech. Oh, if these blundering men, who mis-manage matters so, could be made to hold their peace! Tears of vexation and distress came into the eyes of the good little woman. Mr Tufton meant to do exactly what was right; she knew he did; but to sit still and hear him making such a muddle of it all! Such penalties have to be borne by dutiful wives. She had to smile feebly, when he concluded, to somebody who turned round to congratulate her upon the minister's beautiful speech. The beautiful speech had done poor Vincent a great deal more harm than Pigeon's oration. Salem folks, being appealed to on this side, found out that they had, after all, made great allowances for their minister, and that he had not on his part shown a due sense of their indulgence. Somebody else immediately after went on in the same strain: a little commotion began to rise in the quiet meeting. "Mr Tufton's 'it it," said a malcontent near Mrs Vincent; "we've been a deal too generous, that's what we've been; and he's turned on us." "He was always too high for *my* fancy," said another. "It ain't the thing for a pastor to be high-minded; and them lectures and things was never nothing but vanity; and so I always said." Mrs Vincent smiled a wan smile to herself under her veil. She refused to let the long breath escape from her breast in the form of a sigh. She sat fast, upright, holding her hands clasped. Things were going against Arthur. Unseen among all his foes, with an answer, and more than an answer, to everything they said, burning in dumb restrained eloquence in her breast, his mother held up his banner. One at least was there who knew Arthur, and lifted up a dumb protest on his behalf to earth and heaven. She felt with an uneasy half-consciousness that some haunting shadow was by her side, and was even vaguely aware of the hold upon her dress, but had no leisure in her mind for anything but the progress of this contest, and the gradual overthrow, accomplishing before her eyes, of Arthur's cause.

It was at this moment that Tozer rose up to make that famous speech which has immortalised him in the connec-

tion, and for which the Homerton students, in their
enthusiasm, voted a piece of plate to the worthy butterman. The face of the Salem firmament was cloudy when
Tozer rose; suggestions of discontent were surging among
the audience. Heads of families were stretching over the
benches to confide to each other how long it was since they
had seen the minister; how he never had visited as he
ought; and how desirable "a change" might prove. Spiteful
glances of triumph sought poor Phoebe and her mother
upon their bench, where the two began to fail in their
courage, and laughed no longer. A crisis was approaching.
Mrs Tufton picked up her handkerchief, and sat erect,
with a frightened face; she, too, knew the symptoms of the
coming storm.

Such were the circumstances under which Tozer rose in
the pastor's defence.

"Ladies and gentlemen," said Tozer, – "and Mr Chairman, as I ought to have said first, if this meeting had been
constituted like most other meetings have been in Salem;
but, my friends, we haven't met not in what I would call
an honest and straightforward way, and consequently we
ain't in order, not as a free assembly should be, as has met
to know its own mind, and not to be dictated to by nobody.
There are them as are ready to dictate in every body of
men. I don't name no names; I don't make no suggestions;
what I'm a-stating of is a general truth as is well known to
every one as has studied philosophy. I don't come here
pretending as I'm a learned man, nor one as knows better
nor my neighbours. I'm a plain man, as likes everything
fair and above-board, and is content when I'm well off.
What I've got to say to you, ladies and gentlemen, ain't no
grumbling nor reflecting upon them as is absent and can't
defend themselves. I've got two things to say – first, as I
think you haven't been called together not in an open
way; and, second, that I think us Salem folks, as ought to
know better, is a-quarrelling with our bread-and-butter,
and don't know when we're well off!

"Yes, ladies and gentlemen! them's my sentiments! *we don't know when we're well off!* and if we don't mind, we'll find out how matters really is when we've been and disgusted the pastor, and drove him to throw it all up. Such a thing ain't uncommon; many and many's the one in our connection as has come out for the ministry, meaning nothing but to stick to it, and has been drove by them as is to be found in every flock – them as is always ready to dictate – to throw it all up. My friends, the pastor as is the subject of this meeting" – here Tozer sank his voice and looked round with a certain solemnity – "Mr Vincent, ladies and gentlemen, as has doubled the seat-holders in Salem in six months' work, and, I make bold to say, brought one-half of you as is here to be regular at chapel, and take an interest in the connection – Mr Vincent, I say, as you're all collected here to knock down in the dark, if so be as you are willing to be dictated to – the same, ladies and gentlemen, as we're a-discussing of to-night – told us all, it ain't so very long ago, in the crowdedest meeting as I ever see, in the biggest public hall in Carlingford – as we weren't keeping up to his standard of the old Non-conformists, nor showing, as we ought, what a voluntary church could do. It ain't pleasant to hear of, for us as thinks a deal of ourselves; but that is what the pastor said, and there was not a man as could contradict it. Now, I ask you, ladies and gentlemen, what is the reason? It's all along of this as we're doing to-night. We've got a precious young man, as Mr Tufton tells you, and a clever young man, as nobody tries for to deny; and there ain't a single blessed reason on this earth why he shouldn't go on as he's been a-doing, till, Salem bein' crowded out to the doors (as it's been two Sundays back), we'd have had to build a new chapel, and took a place in our connection as we've never yet took in Carlingford!"

Mr Tozer paused to wipe his heated forehead, and ease his excited bosom with a long breath; his audience paused with him, taking breath with the orator in a slight universal rustle, which is the most genuine applause. The worthy butterman resumed in a lowered and emphatic tone.

"But it ain't to be," said Tozer, looking round him with a tragic frown, and shaking his head slowly. "Them as is always a-finding fault, and always a-setting up to dictate, has set their faces again' all that. It's the way of some folks in our connection, ladies and gentlemen; a minister ain't to be allowed to go on building up a chapel, and making hisself useful in the world. He ain't to be left alone to do his dooty as his best friends approve. He's to be took down out of his pulpit, and took to pieces behind his back, and made a talk and a scandal of to the whole connection! It's not his preaching as he's judged by, nor his dooty to the sick and dyin', nor any of them things as he was called to be pastor for; but it's if he's seen going to one house more nor another, or if he calls often enough on this one or t'other, and goes to all the tea-drinkings. My opinion is," said Tozer, suddenly breaking off into jocularity, "as a young man as maybe isn't a marrying man, and anyhow can't marry more nor one, ain't in the safest place at Salem tea-drinkings; but that's neither here nor there. If the ladies haven't no pity, us men can't do nothing in that matter; but what I say is this," continued the butterman, once more becoming solemn; "to go for to judge the pastor of a flock, not by the dooty he does to his flock, but by the time he calls at one house or another, ain't a thing to be done by them as prides themselves on being Christians and Dissenters. It's not like Christians – and if it's like Dissenters the more's the pity. It's mean, that's what it is," cried Tozer, with fine scorn; "it's like a parcel of old women, if the ladies won't mind me saying so. It's beneath us as has liberty of conscience to fight for, and has to set an example before the Church folks as don't know no better. But it's what is done in our connection," added the good deacon with pathos, shaking his forefinger mournfully at the crowd. "When there's a young man as is clever and talented, and fills a chapel, and gives the connection a chance of standing up in the world as it ought, here's some one as jumps up and says, 'The pastor don't come to see me,' says he – 'the pastor don't do his duty – he ain't the man for Salem.' And them as is always in every flock ready to do a mischief, takes it up; and there's talk of a change, and meetings is called, and – here we are! Yes, ladies and gentlemen, here we are! We've called a meeting, all in the dark, and give him no chance of defending himself; and them as is at the head of this movement is calling upon us to dismiss Mr Vincent. But let me tell you," continued Tozer, lowering his voice with a dramatic intuition, and shaking his forefinger still more emphatically in the face of the startled audience, "that this ain't no question of dismissing Mr Vincent; it's a matter of disgusting Mr Vincent, that's what it is – it's a matter of turning another promising young man away from the connection, and driving him to throw it all up. You mark what I say. It's what we're doing most places, us Dissenters; them as is talented and promisin', and can get a better living working for the world than working for the chapel, and won't give in to be worried about calling here and calling there – we're a-driving of them out of the connection, that's what we're doing! I could reckon up as many as six or seven as has been drove off already; and I ask you, ladies and gentlemen, what's the good of subscribing and keeping up of colleges and so forth, if that's how you're a-going to serve every clever young man as trusts hisself to be your pastor? I'm a man as don't feel no shame to say that the minister, being took up with his family affairs and his studies, has been for weeks as he hasn't crossed my door; but am I that poor-spirited as I would drive away a young man as is one of the best preachers in the connection, because he don't come, not every day, to see me. No, my friends! them as would ever suspect such a thing of me don't know who they're a-dealing with; and I tell you, ladies and gentlemen, as this is a question as must come home to every one of your bosoms. Them as is so set upon their own way that they can't hear reason – or them as is led away by folks as like to dictate – may give their voice again' the minister, if so be as they think fit; but as for me, and them as stands by me, I ain't a-going to give in to no such tyranny! It shall never be said in our connection as a clever young man was drove away from Carlingford, and I had part in it. There's the credit o' the denomination to keep up among the Church folks – and there's the chapel to fill, as never had half the sittings let before – and there's Mr Vincent, as is the cleverest young man I ever see in our pulpit, to be kep' in the connection; and there ain't no man living as shall dictate to me or them as stands by me! Them as is content to lose the best preaching within a hundred miles, because the minister don't call on two or three families in Salem, not as often as they would like to see him," said Tozer, with trenchant sarcasm, "can put down their names again' Mr Vincent; but for me, and them as stands by me, we ain't a-going to give in to no such dictation: we ain't a-going to set up ourselves against the spread of the Gospel, and the credit o' the connection, and toleration and freedom of conscience, as we're bound to fight for! If the pastor don't make hisself agreeable, I can put up with that – I can; but I ain't a-going to see a clever young man drove away from Salem, and the sittings vacant, and the chapel falling to ruin, and the Church folks a-laughing and a-jeering at us, not for all the deacons in the connection, nor any man in Carlingford. And this I say for myself and for all as stands by me!"

The last sentence was lost in thunders of applause. The "Salem folks" stamped with their feet, knocked the floor with their umbrellas, clapped their hands in a *furore* of enthusiasm and sympathy. Their pride was appealed to; nobody could bear the imputation of being numbered among the two or three to whom the minister had not paid sufficient attention. All the adherents of the Pigeon party deserted that luckless family sitting prominent upon their bench, with old Mrs Tufton at the corner joining as heartily as her over-shoes would permit in the general commotion. There they sat, a pale line of faces, separated, by their looks of dismay and irresponsive silence, from the applauding crowd, cruelly identified as "them as is always ready to dictate." The occasion was indeed a grand one, had the leader of the opposition been equal to it; but Mrs Pigeon only sat and stared at the new turn of affairs with a hysterical smile of spite and disappointment fixed on her face. Before the cheers died away, a young man – one of the Young Men's Christian Association connected with Salem – jumped up on a bench in the midst of the assembly, and clinched the speech of Tozer. He told the admiring meeting that he had been brought up in the connection, but had strayed away into carelessness and neglect – and when he went anywhere at all on Sundays, went to church like one of the common multitude, till Mr Vincent's lectures on Church and State opened his eyes, and brought him to better knowledge. Then came another, and another. Mrs Vincent, sitting on the back seat with her veil over her face, did not hear what they said. The heroic little soul had broken down, and was lost in silent tears, and utterances in her heart of thanksgiving, deeper than words. No comic aspect of the scene appeared to her; she was not moved by its vulgarity or oddity. It was deliverance and safety to the minister's mother. Her son's honour and his living were alike safe, and his people had stood by Arthur. She sat for some time longer, lost in that haze of comfort and relief, afraid to move lest perhaps something untoward might still occur to change this happy state of affairs – keen to detect any evil symptom, if such should occur, but unable to follow with any exactness the course of those addresses which still continued to be made in her hearing. She was not quite sure, indeed, whether anybody had spoken after Tozer, when, with a step much less firm than on her entrance, she went forth, wiping the tears that blinded her from under her veil, into the darkness and quiet of the street outside. But she knew that "resolutions" of support and sympathy had been carried

by acclamation, and that somebody was deputed from the
flock to assure the minister of its approval, and to offer
him the new lease of popularity thus won for him in
Salem. Mrs Vincent waited to hear no more. She got up
softly and went forth on noiseless, weary feet, which
faltered, now that her anxiety was over, with fatigue and
agitation. Thankful to the bottom of her heart, yet at
the same time doubly worn out with that deliverance,
confused with the lights, the noises, and the excitement of
the scene, and beginning already to take up her other
burden, and to wonder by times, waking up with sharp
touches of renewed anguish, how she might find Susan,
and whether "any change" had appeared in her other
child. It was thus that the great Salem congregational
meeting, so renowned in the connection, ended for the
minister's mother. She left them still making speeches
when she emerged into Grove Street. The political effect
of Tozer's address, or the influence which his new doctrine
might have on the denomination, did not occur to Mrs
Vincent. She was thinking only of Arthur. Not even the
darker human misery by her side had power to break
through her preoccupation. How the gentle little woman
had shaken off that anxious hand which grasped her old
black dress, she never knew herself, nor could any one
tell; somehow she had done it: alone, as she entered, she
went away again – secret, but not clandestine, under that
veil of her widowhood. She put it up from her face when
she got into the street, and wiped her tears off with a
trembling, joyful hand. She could not see her way clearly
for those tears of joy. When they were dried, and the crape
shadow put back from her face, Mrs Vincent looked up
Grove Street, where her road lay in the darkness, broken
by those flickering lamps. It was a windy night, and Dr
Rider's drag went up past her rapidly, carrying the doctor
home from some late visit, and recalling her thoughts to her
own patient whom she had left so long. She quickened her
tremulous steps as Dr Rider disappeared in the darkness;

but almost before she had got beyond the last echoes of the Salem meeting, that shadow of darker woe and misery than any the poor mother wist of, was again by Mrs Vincent's side.

CHAPTER XXXVII.

"You are not able to walk so fast," said Mrs Hilyard, coming up to the widow as she crossed over to the darker side of Grove Street, just where the house of the Miss Hemmings turned its lighted staircase-window to the street; "and it will not harm you to let me speak to you. Once you offered me your hand, and would have gone with me. It is a long long time ago – ages since – but *I* remember it. I do not come after you for nothing. Let me speak. You said you were a – a minister's wife, and knew human nature," she continued, with a certain pause of reverence, and at the same time a gleam of amusement, varying for a moment the blank and breathless voice in which she had spoken. "I want your advice."

Mrs Vincent, who had paused with an uncomfortable sensation of being pursued, recovered herself a little during this address. The minister's mother had no heart to linger and talk to any one at that moment, after all the excitement of the evening, with her fatigued frame and occupied mind; but still she was the minister's mother, as ready and prepared as Arthur himself ought to have been, to hear anything that any of the flock might have to say to her, and to give all the benefit of her experience to anybody connected with Salem who might be in trouble. "I beg your pardon," said Mrs Vincent; "my daughter is ill – that is why I was making so much haste; but I am sure, if I can be of any use to any member of – I mean to any of my son's friends" – she concluded rather abruptly. She did not remember much about this woman, who was strangely unlike the other people in Salem. When was that time in which they had met before? The widow's mind had been so swept by the whirlwind of events and emotions, that she remembered only dimly how and where it was she had formerly seen her strange companion.

"Your daughter is ill?" said Mrs Hilyard; "that is how trouble happens to you. You are a good woman; you don't interfere in God's business; and this is how your trouble comes. You can nurse her and be about her bed; and when she wakes up, it is to see you and be grateful to you. But *my* child," she said, touching the widow's arm suddenly with her hand, and suppressing painfully a shrill tone of anguish in her voice which would break through, "does not know *me*. She opens her blue eyes – they are not even my eyes – they are Alice's eyes, who has no right to my child – and looks at me as if I were a stranger; and for all this time, since I parted with her, I have not heard – I do not know where she is. Hush, hush, hush!" she went on, speaking to herself, "to think that this is me, and that I should break down so at last. A woman has not soul enough to subdue her nerves for ever. But this is not what I wanted to say to you. I gave Miss Smith your son's address—"

Having said this, she paused, and looked anxiously at the widow, who looked at her also in the windy gleams of lamplight with more and more perplexity. "Who are – you? Indeed, I am very sorry to seem rude; but my mind has been so much occupied. Arthur, of course, would know if he were here, but Susan's illness has taken up all my thoughts; and – I beg your pardon – she may want me even now," she continued, quickening her steps. Even the courtesy due to one of the flock had a limit; and the minister's mother knew it was necessary not to yield too completely to all the demands that her son's people might make upon her. Was this even one of her son's people?

Such persons were unusual in the connection. Mrs Vincent, all fatigued, excited, and anxious as she was, felt at her wits' end.

"Yes, your son would know if he were here; he has taken my parole and trusted me," said the strange woman; "but a woman's parole should not be taken. I try to keep it; but unless they come, or I have news— Who am I? I am a woman that was once young and had friends. They married me to a man, who was not a man, but a fine organisation capable of pleasures and cruelties. Don't speak. You are very good; you are a minister's wife. You don't know what it is, when one is young and happy, to find out all at once that life means only so much torture and misery, and so many lies, either done by you or borne by you – what does it matter which? My baby came into the world with a haze on her sweet soul because of that discovery. If it had been but her body!" said Mrs Vincent's strange companion, with bitterness. "A dwarfed creature, or deformed, or— But she was beautiful – she *is* beautiful, as pretty as Alice; and if she lives, she will be rich. Hush, hush! you don't know what my fears were," continued Mrs Hilyard, with a strange humility, once more putting her hand on the widow's arm. "If he could have got possession of her, how could I tell what he might have done? – killed her – but that would have been dangerous; poisoned what little mind she had left – made her like her mother. I stole her away. Long ago, when I thought she might have been safe with you, I meant to have told you. I stole her out of his power. For a little while she was with me, and he traced us – then I sent the child away. I have not seen her but in glimpses, lest he should find her. It has cost me all I had, and I have lived and worked with my hands," said the needlewoman of Back Grove Street, lifting her thin fingers to the light and looking at them, pathetic vouchers to the truth of her story. "When he drove me desperate," she went on, labouring in vain to conceal the panting, long-drawn breath which impeded her utterance, "you know? I don't talk of that. The child put her arms round that old woman after her mother had saved her. She had not a word, not a word for me, who had done— But it was all for her sake. This is what I have had to suffer. She looked in my face and waved me away from her, and said, 'Susan, Susan!' Susan meant your daughter – a new friend, a creature whom she had not seen a week before – and no word, no look, no recognition for me!"

"Oh, I am very sorry, very sorry!" said Mrs Vincent, in her turn taking the poor thin hand with an instinct of consolation. Susan's name, thus introduced, went to the mother's heart. She could have wept over the other mother thus complaining, moaning out her troubles in her compassionate ear.

"I left them in a safe place. I came home to fall into your son's hands. He might have been sure, had it come to *that*, that no one should have suffered for *me*," said Mrs Hilyard, with again a tone of bitterness. "What was my life worth, could any man suppose? And since then I have not heard a word – not a word – whether the child is still where I left her, or whether some of *his* people have found her – or whether she is ill – or whether – I know nothing, nothing! Have a little pity upon me, you innocent woman! I never asked pity, never sought sympathy before; but a woman can never tell what she may be brought to. I am brought down to the lowest depths. I cannot stand upright any longer," she cried, with a wailing sigh. "I want somebody – somebody at least to give me a little comfort. Comfort! I remember," she said, with one of those sudden changes of tone which bewildered Mrs Vincent, "your son once spoke to me of getting comfort from those innocent young sermons of his. He knows a little better now; he does not sail over the surface now as he used to do in triumph. Life has gone hard with him, as with me and all of us. Tell him, if I get no news I will break my parole. I cannot help myself – a woman's honour is not her word. I told him so. Say to your son—"

"My son? what have you to do with my son?" said Mrs Vincent, with a sudden pang. The poor mother was but a woman too. She did not understand what this connection was. A worn creature, not much younger than herself, what possible tie could bind her to Arthur? The widow, like other women, could believe in any "infatuation" of men; but could not understand any other bond subsisting between these two. The thought went to her heart. Young men had been known before now to be mysteriously attracted by women, old, un-beautiful, unlike themselves. Could this be Arthur's fate? Perhaps it was a danger more dismal than that which he had just escaped in Salem. Mrs Vincent grew sick at heart. She repeated, with an asperity of which her soft voice might have been thought incapable, "What have you to do with my son?"

Mrs Hilyard made no answer – perhaps she did not hear the question. Her eyes, always restlessly turning from one object to another, had found out, in the lighted street to which they had now come, a belated postman delivering his last letters. She followed him with devouring looks; he went to Vincent's door as they approached, delivered something, and passed on into the darkness with a careless whistle. While Mrs Vincent watched her companion with doubtful and suspicious looks through the veil which, once more among the lights of Grange Street, the minister's mother had drawn over her face, the unconscious object of her suspicion grasped her arm, and turned to her with beseeching eyes. "It may be news of my child?" she said, with a supplication beyond words. She drew the widow on with the desperation of her anxiety. The little maid had still the letter in her hand when she opened the door. It was not even for Mr Vincent. It was for the mistress of the house, who had not even returned from the meeting at Salem. Mrs Vincent paused upon the threshold, compassionate but determined. She looked at the unhappy woman who stood upon the steps in the light of the lamp, gazing eagerly in at the door, and resolved that she should penetrate no farther; but even in the height of her determination the widow's heart smote her when she looked at that face, so haggard and worn with passion and anxiety, with its furtive gleaming eyes, and all the dark lines of endurance which were so apparent now, when the tide of emotion had grown too strong to be concealed. "Have you – no – friends in Carlingford?" said the widow, with hesitation and involuntary pity. She could not ask her to enter where, perhaps, her presence might be baleful to Arthur; but the little woman's tender heart ached, even in the midst of her severity, for the suffering in that face.

"Nowhere!" said Mrs Hilyard; then, with a gleam out of her eyes which took the place of a smile, "Do not be sorry for me; I want no friends – nobody could share my burden with me. I am going back – home – to Alice. Tell Mr Vincent; I think something must happen to-night," she added, with a slight shiver; "it grows intolerable, beyond bearing. Perhaps by the telegraph – or perhaps— And Miss Smith has this address. I told you my story," she went on, drawing closer, and taking the widow's hand, "that you might have pity on me, and understand – no, not understand; how could she? – but if you were like me, do you think you could sit still in one place, with so much upon your heart? You never could be like me – but if you had lost your child—"

"I did," said Mrs Vincent, drawing a painful breath at the recollection, and drawn unwittingly by the sight of the terrible anxiety before her into a reciprocation of confidence – "my child who had been in my arms all her life – God gave her back again; and now, while I am speaking, He may be taking her away," said the mother, with a sudden return of all her anxiety. "I cannot do you any good, and Susan may want me: good-night – good-night."

"It was not God who gave her back to you," said Mrs Hilyard, grasping the widow's hand closer – "it was I – remember it was I. When you think hardly of me, recollect –

I did it. She might have been – but I freed her – remember; and if you hear anything, if it were but a whisper, of my child, think of it, and have pity on me. You will? – you understand what I say?"

The widow drew away her hand with a pang of fear. She retreated hurriedly, yet with what dignity she could, calling the little maid to shut the door. When that strange face, all gleaming, haggard, and anxious, was shut out into the night, Mrs Vincent went up-stairs very hastily, scarcely able to give her alarmed withdrawal the aspect of an orderly retreat. Was this woman mad to whom she had been speaking so calmly? In her agitation she forgot all the precautions with which she had intended to soften to her son the fact of her attendance at the meeting of which he had not even informed her. Pursued by the recollection of that face, she hastened to Arthur, still in her bonnet and veil. He was seated at the table writing as when she left him; but all the minister's self-control could not conceal a certain expectancy and excitement in the eyes which he raised with a flash of eager curiosity to see who it was that thus invaded his solitude. "Mother! where have you been?" he asked, with irritation, when he perceived her. His impatience and anxiety, and the great effort he had made to subdue both, betrayed him into a momentary outburst of annoyance and vexation. "Where have you been?" he repeated, throwing down his pen. "Surely not to this meeting, to compromise me, as if I had not trouble enough already!" This rude accost put her immediate subject out of Mrs Vincent's mind: she went up to her son with deprecating looks, and put her hand fondly on his head. The tears came into her eyes, not because his words offended or grieved her, but for joy of the good news she had to tell; for the minister's mother was experienced in the ways of man, and knew how many things a woman does for love which she gets no thanks for doing. Her boy's anger did not make her angry, but it drove other matters, less important, out of her head.

"Oh, Arthur, no one saw me," she said; "I had my veil down all the time. How could I help going when I knew of it? I did not tell you – I did not mean you to know; but it was impossible to stay away," cried the widow, perceiving her son's impatience while she explained herself, and growing confused in consequence, "when I heard what was going on. Oh, Arthur dear, don't look so disturbed; they know better than you imagine – they appreciate you, though they have not the way of showing it. I have seen things happen so differently, that I know the value of such friends as you have in the flock. Oh, my dear boy, don't look so strange! It has been a great triumph, Arthur. There is a deputation coming to offer you their support and sympathy. All this dreadful business has not harmed *you*. Thank God for that! I think I shall be able to bear anything now."

The minister got up hastily from his chair, and took refuge on the hearthrug. He changed colour; grew red and grew pale; and by way of escaping from the complication of feelings that moved him, once more broke out into impatient exclamations. "Why did you go? Why did not you tell me you were going?" he said. "Why did you leave Susan, who wanted you? Mother, you will never understand that a man's affairs must not be meddled with!" cried the Nonconformist, with an instinctive effort to conceal the agitation into which this unexpected news threw him. Then he began to pace about the room, exclaiming against the impatience of women, who can never wait for a result. The young man was too proud to acknowledge the state of feverish suspense in which he had been, or the wonderful tumult suddenly produced in his mind. He seized upon this ready safety-valve of irritation, which was half real and half fictitious. It gave him time to collect his troubled thoughts.

"Arthur dear, hush! no one saw me at the meeting. I had my veil down, and spoke to nobody," said the widow:

"and oh! don't you think it was only natural that your mother should be there? No one in the world is so much interested in what concerns you. I spoke to no one – except," said Mrs Vincent, with a little effort, "that strange woman, Arthur, whom you have had so much to do with. Who is she? Oh, my dear boy, I hope you have not formed any connections that you will repent? She said something about a promise, and having given her word. I don't know why you should have her word, or what she has to do with you. She came here to the door with me to-night."

"Mrs Hilyard!" cried the minister, suddenly roused. "Mrs—; no matter what her name is. Where is she? Do you mean that she came here? They keep no watch over her. To-night of all nights in the world! If you had but stayed at home, I should not have known of her wanderings at least," he said, with vexation. "Now I shall have to go and look after her – she must be sent back again – she must not be allowed to escape."

"Is she mad?" said Mrs Vincent, alarmed, yet relieved. "Don't go away, Arthur; she is not here. She said I was to tell you that she had gone back – to Alice. Who is Alice? – who is this woman? What have you to do with her? Oh! my dear boy, you are a minister, and the world is so ready to make remarks. She said you had her word. Oh, Arthur, I hope it does not mean anything you will live to repent?" cried the anxious mother, fixing her jealous eyes on her son's face. "She is not like you. I cannot tell what you can have to do with such a woman – you who might—" Mrs Vincent's fright and anxiety exhausted both her language and her breath.

"It does not matter much after all," said the Non-conformist, who had been busy with his own thoughts, and had only half heard his mother's adjurations. "Like me? – what has that to do with the matter? But I daresay she will go back, as she said; and now that he is out of danger, and has not accused her, things must take their chance. Mad? It would not be wonderful if she were mad. I can sympathise with people when they are driven out of their wits. Who is this next? Another messenger from the meeting, or perhaps your deputation? I think *I* shall go mad after a while if I get no rest."

But as the minister stood in ill-concealed excitement by the fire, not without expectation that it might be somebody with an official report from Salem, Mr Vincent's landlady, still in her bonnet and shawl, just returned from the meeting, came in to tell the widow of the approach of the doctor. "He's a-coming directly, ma'am; he's gone in for a minute to Smith's, next door, where they've got the hooping-cough. And oh, Mr Vincent, sir," cried the woman, who had made this a pretence to express her sentiments on the more important subject, "if there hasn't a-been a sweet meeting! I'd have giv' a half-year's rent, ma'am, the pastor had been there. All as unanimous and as friendly! – all but them Pigeons, as are the poison of the place; and sweet Miss Phoebe Tozer a-crying of her pretty eyes out; but there ain't no occasion for crying now," said the triumphant landlady, who had a real stake in the matter. At this touch the minister regained his composure. He went back to his seat at the table, and took up the pen he had thrown down. A bishop could not have looked more grandly indifferent than did the Nonconformist as he turned his back upon his anxious partisan. "Tell the doctor to let me know how Susan is, mother, for I am busy to-night," said the young man. "I cannot leave my work just now even for Dr Rider." He began again to write in the excitement of his mind, and produced a sentence which was not one of the least successful of his sentences, while the two women, with a certain awe, stood silent behind his chair.

"I will not disturb you any longer, my dear boy. Goodnight," said Mrs Vincent. She went away, followed by the discomfited landlady, who was overwhelmed, and did not know what to make of it. The widow could not but improve such an opportunity. "The minister must not be disturbed in his studies," she said, with importance and in a whisper as she closed the door. "When he is engaged with a subject, it does not answer to go in upon him and disturb his attention. Neither meetings nor anything else, however important, should interrupt a pastor when he is engaged in composition," said the little woman grandly. But while the mistress of the house departed to her own quarter much overawed, the minister's mother went to the sick-room with no such composure as she assumed. Something she did not understand was in Arthur's mind. The Salem meeting did not appear to her so conclusive as it had done an hour ago. He was young and high-spirited and proud, and had not that dutiful subjection to the opinions of the flock which became a minister of Salem. What if that visionary horror with which she had frightened Tozer might turn out a real danger? Though she had made such skilful use of it, the possibility she had herself invented had not really alarmed her; but the thought thrilled through her now with a fear which had some remorse in it. She had invoked the ghost, not much believing in any such supernatural climax; but if the apparition really made itself visible, the widow recognised at once her entire want of any power to lay it. She took off her shawl and bonnet with little comfort in her mind on that subject to support her under the returning pangs of anxiety about Susan, which overwhelmed her again as she opened the door of the sick-room. The two troubles united in her heart and aggravated each other, as with a sick throb of expectation she went in to Susan's bedside. Perhaps there might be "a change" – for better or for worse, something might have happened. The doctor might find something more conclusive to-night in that languid pallid face. The noiseless room struck her with a chill of misery as she went to her usual place, carrying the active life of pain and a troubled heart into that melancholy atmosphere from which life seemed to have fled. With a faltering voice she spoke to Susan, who showed no signs of hearing her except by a feeble half-lifting of her heavy eyelids and restless motion of her frame. No change! Never any change! or, at least, as the nurse imagined, until— The widow's heart heaved with a silent sob of anguish – anguish sharp and acute as it is when our misery breaks suddenly upon us out of a veil of other thoughts, and we feel it intolerable. This sudden pang convulsed Mrs Vincent's much-tried heart as she wiped the bitter tears out of her eyes and looked at her child, thus gliding, in a hopeless apathy and unconsciousness, out of the arms that strained themselves in vain to hold her. After so much as she had borne in her troubled life, God knows it was hard. She did not rebel, but her heart lifted up a bitter cry to the Father in heaven.

It was just then, while her anxious ear caught the step of the doctor on the stair, that Mrs Vincent was aware also of a carriage driving rapidly up to the door. Preoccupied as she was, the sound startled her. A passing wonder who it could be, and the vague expectation which influences the mind at the great crises of life, when one feels that anything may happen, moved her dimly as she rose to receive the doctor. Dr Rider came in with his noiseless step and anxious face; they shook hands with each other mechanically, she gazing at him to see what his opinion was before it could be formed – he looking with solicitous serious eyes on the sick-bed. The light was dim, and Dr Rider held it up to see his patient. There she lay, moving now and then with the restlessness of weakness, the pale large eyelids half closed, the pale lips dropping apart, – a solemn speechless creature, abstracted already out of this world and all its influences. The light that streamed over her for the moment made no difference to Susan. There was nothing here powerful enough to rouse the soul which horror and passion had driven into one terrible corner of memory, obliterating all the rest of her life. Dr Rider looked at her with eyes in which the impatience of powerless strength overcame even his professional reserve. He wrung the widow's hand, which she laid on his arm in a trembling appeal to him to tell her the worst. "The worst is that she is dying before our eyes, and that she might be saved," he said, leading the poor mother to the other end of the room. "All her heart and soul are concentrated upon that time when she was away from you; unless we can rouse her by something that will recall that time, she will never know you more. Think! is there nothing that would wake her up even to remember the misery she endured? Where is your servant who was with her? – but she has seen her lately, and nothing has come of that. If you have the courage and strength," said the doctor, once more grasping Mrs Vincent's hand tight, "to talk of that man under the name she knew him by – to talk of him so as perhaps she might hear; to discuss the matter; anything that will recall her mind. Hush! what is that noise downstairs?"

Even while listening to the doctor's dreadful suggestion, Mrs Vincent had been aware of the opening of the door down-stairs, and a sound of voices. She was trembling so that she could scarcely stand, principally, no doubt, on account of this strange demand which he made upon her strength, but with a nervous expectation besides which she could not explain even to herself. But when, out of the confused commotion below, there rose faint but audible the sound of a voice calling "Susan! Susan!" the two anxious people started apart, and turned a wondering momentary gaze upon each other, involuntarily asking what was that? what did it mean? Then the doctor rushed to the door, where the widow followed him as well as her trembling limbs would permit. She saw him dash downstairs, and herself stood grasping the railing, waiting for what was about to happen, with her heart so beating and fluttering in her breast that she could scarcely breathe for it. She could make nothing of the rapid interrogation that went on down-stairs. She heard the voice of the doctor in hasty questions, and the slow, agitated, somewhat confused utterance of a strange voice, which appeared to answer him; and once or twice through these sounds came the strange cry, "Susan! Susan!" which went to the widow's heart. Who could this be that called upon Susan with so pathetic a repetition! It seemed a very long interval to Mrs Vincent before the doctor reappeared, and yet so short was the time, that the door by which the new-comers, whoever they were, had entered, was still open, admitting some strange familiar sounds from the street into the bewildering maze of wonder and expectation. Mrs Vincent held fast by the rails to support herself, when she saw the doctor returning up the stair, leading by the hand a girl whom he grasped fast, and carried along with him by a kind of gentle but strong compulsion. It was she who was calling Susan, gazing round her with large dilated blue eyes, looking everywhere for something she had not yet found. A beautiful girl – more beautiful than anything mortal to the widow's surprised and wondering eyes. Who was she? The face was very young, sadly simple, framed by long curling locks of fair hair, and the broad circle of a large flapping Leghorn hat and blue veil. A bewildered half-recognition came to Mrs Vincent's mind as this blue veil waved in her face in the wind from the open door; but excitement and anxiety had deprived her of speech: she could ask no questions. "Here is the physician," said Dr Rider, with a kindred excitement in his voice. He went into the room before her, leading the girl, behind whom there followed slowly a confused and disturbed woman, whose face Mrs Vincent felt she had seen before. The mother, half jealous in her wonder, pressed in after the doctor to guard her Susan even from experiments of healing. "Doctor, doctor, who is it?" she said. But Dr Rider held up his hand imperatively to silence her. The room was imperfectly lighted with candles burning dimly, and a faint glow of firelight. "Susan!" cried the eager child's voice, with a weary echo of longing and disappointment. "Susan! – take me to Susan; she is not here." Then Dr Rider led her round to the bedside, closely followed by the widow, and, lifting a candle, threw its light fully upon the stranger. "Is it Susan?" said the girl. "Will she not speak to me? – is she dead? Susan, oh Susan, Susan!" It was an outcry of childish impatience and despair, rising louder than any voice had risen in that room for many a day. Then she burst forth into tears and sobs. "Susan! – she will not speak to me, she will not look at me!" cried the stranger, drawing her arm out of the doctor's hold, and clasping her hands together. There was a slight movement in the bed; not the restless tossing with which her nurse was familiar, but a trembling shiver came over that dying frame. The sound had reached to the dull ears of the patient. She lifted her heavy eyelids, and looked round with half-awakened eyes. "Call her again, again!" said the doctor, in an intense whisper, which seemed to thrill through the room. The girl, who was engaged with a much more engrossing interest of her own, took no notice of the doctor. She knew nothing about Susan's danger – she was bent on gaining succour for herself. "Susan! tell her to look at me – at me! Susan! I care for nobody but you!" said the lovely helpless creature, with strange half-articulate cries, pressing closer to the bed. "*You* are to take care of me." Mrs Vincent pressed forward with pangs of anxiety, of terror, of hope, and of a mother's tender jealousy through all, as these strange entreaties filled the room. She too cried aloud, as she perceived the awakening in that pallid face, the faint movement as if to raise herself up, which indicated a conscious effort on the part of Susan. The clouds were breaking on that obscured and hopeless firmament. The light, which trembled in the doctor's hand, caught a gleam of understanding and life in Susan's eyes, as her mother flew to raise her up, obeying the suggestion of that unhoped-for movement. "Susan! you said you would take care of me!" cried the young stranger, throwing herself upon the bedside and grasping at the weak arm which once had protected her. The touch of her hands awoke the slumbering soul. Slowly the light grew in Susan's

eyes. She who had not moved for days except in the
restless tossings of languor, lifted those white feeble arms
to put them round the appealing child. Then Susan struggled up, faint, yet inspired, unconscious of her mother's
help that enabled her to do so, and confronted the strange
people in her room, whom she had seen for weeks past,
but did not know, with living eyes. "Nobody shall touch
her – we will protect each other," said the voice that had
grown strange even to her mother's ears. Mrs Vincent
could hardly be restrained from breaking in with a thousand caresses and outcries of joy and thankfulness. But Dr
Rider quieted the poor mother with a touch of his hand.
"Let them alone," he said, with that authority which no
one in a sick-room can resist. Mrs Vincent kept back with
unspeakable pangs in her heart, and watched the wakening
up of that paralysed life which, alike in its loss and its
recovery, had been swept apart from her into another
world. Without any help from her mother, without even
recognising her mother or distinguishing her from the
strangers around, Susan's soul awoke. She raised herself
more and more among those pillows where a little while
ago she lay so passively – she opened her eyes fully and
looked round upon the man by her bedside, and the other
indistinct figures in the room, with a look of resistance and
conscious strength. "We will protect each other," said
Susan, slowly; "nobody shall harm her – we will keep each
other safe." Then, after another interval, other instincts
awoke in the reviving soul. She cast a wistful look from
one to another, always drawing her faint white arm round
the girl who clung to her and found security in her clasp.
"Hush, hush! there are women here," she said in a whisper,
and with a tone of strange confusion, light breaking through
the darkness. Then there followed a long pause. Dr Rider
stood by the bedside holding up his candle, attracting the
wandering wistful glances of his patient, who ceased to
look at him with defiance as her eyes again and again
returned to the face, of which, often as it had bent over

her, she had no knowledge. All over the unknown room wandered those strange looks, interrogating everything with a wistfulness beyond words. What was this strange unfamiliar world into which, after her trance of suffering, Susan had awakened? She did not know where she was, nor who the people were who surrounded her. But the recollection of deadly peril was not more distinct upon her confused mind than was the sentiment of safety, of love, and watchfulness which somehow abode in this strange dim room, in the little undecipherable circle of faces which surrounded her bed. "Hush!" said Susan again, holding the stranger close. "Here are women – women! nobody will harm us;" then, with a sudden flush over all her face and cry of joy as the doctor suddenly threw the light full upon Mrs Vincent, who was bending over her, her mind struggled into possession of itself, – "Here is my mother, she has come to take us home!"

Mrs Vincent remembered nothing more; she did not faint, for her child wanted her – she sat all the night through on the bed, with Susan leaning against her shoulder, clinging to her, holding her fast – starting again and again to make sure that all was safe, and that it was, indeed, her mother's arms that held her. Her soul was recalled out of that trance of death. They laid the beautiful child upon the sofa in her young guardian's sight, to keep up that happy influence; and when the night was about half spent, the widow, throbbing all over her wearied frame with exhaustion, pain, and joy, perceived that her Susan had fallen deep and sweet asleep, clasping close, as if never again to lose hold of them, her mother's tender hands.

CHAPTER XXXVIII.

THE after-events of the evening naturally lessened, in the minister's family at least, the all-absorbing interest of the meeting at Salem. Even Mr Vincent's landlady, in her wondering narrative of the scene in the sick-room which, all Mrs Vincent's usual decorums being thrust aside by that unexpected occurrence, she had witnessed – forgot the other public event which was of equally great importance. The house was in a state of agitation as great as on Susan's return; and when the exulting doctor, whose experiment had been so rarely successful, turned all supernumerary persons out of the sick-room, it fell to Vincent's part to take charge of the perplexed governess, Miss Smith, who stood outside, anxious to offer explanations, a fatigued and harassed, but perfectly virtuous and exemplary woman. Vincent, who had not realised his sister's extreme peril, and who was rather disconcerted by this fresh invasion of his house, opened the door of his sitting-room for her with more annoyance than hospitality. His own affairs were urgent in his mind. He could not keep his thoughts from dwelling upon Salem and what had occurred there, though no one else thought of it. Had he known the danger in which his sister lay, his heart might have rejected every secondary matter. But the minister did not know that Susan had been sinking into the last apathy when this sudden arrival saved her. He gave Miss Smith the easy-chair by the fire, and listened with an appearance of attention, but with little real understanding, to her lengthy and perplexed story. She was all in a flutter, the good governess said: everything was so mysterious and out of the way, she did not know what to think. Little Alice's mamma, Miss Russell that was, Mrs Mildmay she meant, had brought the child back to her after that dreadful business at Dover. What was the rights of that business, could Mr Vincent tell her? Colonel Mildmay was getting better, she knew, and it was not a murder; and she was heartbroken when she heard the trouble poor dear Miss Vincent had got into about it. Well, Alice's mamma brought back the child, and they started with her at once to France. They went up beyond Lyons to the hills, an out-of-the-way little place, but Mrs Mildmay was always so nervous. "And then she left us, Mr Vincent," said the afflicted governess, as the minister, in grievous impatience, kept pacing up and down the room thus occupied and taken possession of – "left us without a soul to speak to or a church within reach; and if there is one thing I have more horror of than another for its effect upon the youthful mind, it is Popery, which is so seductive to the imagination. Alice did not take to her mamma, Mr Vincent. It was natural enough, but it was hard upon Mrs Mildmay: she never had a good way with children; and from the moment we started till now, it has been impossible to get your sister out of the child's mind. She took a fancy to her the moment she saw her. Girls of that age, if you will not think it strange of me to say so, very often fall in love with a girl older than themselves – quite fall in love, though it is a strange thing to say. Alice would not rest – she gave me no peace. I wrote to say so, but I think Mrs Mildmay could not have got my letter. The child would have run away by herself if I had not brought her. Besides," said Miss Smith, apologetically, "the doctors have assured me that, if she ever became much interested in any one, or attached to anybody in particular, she was not to be crossed. It was the best chance for her mind, the doctors said. What could I do? What do you think I could do, Mr Vincent? I brought her home, for I could not help myself – otherwise she would have run away. She has a very strong will, though she looks so gentle. I hope you will help me to explain the circumstances to Mrs

Mildmay, and how it was I came back without her authority. Don't you think they ought to call in the friends on both sides and come to some arrangement, Mr Vincent?" said the excellent woman, anxiously. "I know she trusts you very much, and it was she herself who gave me your address."

To this speech Vincent listened with an impatience and restlessness which he found it impossible to conceal. He paced about the darker end of his room, on the other side of that table, where the lamp shone vacantly upon his open desk and scattered papers, answering now and then with a monosyllable of reluctant courtesy, irritated and disturbed beyond expression by the perfectly serious and proper figure seated by the fire. Somebody might come from that assembly which had met to discuss him, and he could not be alone to receive them. In the annoyance of the moment the minister almost chafed at his sister and her concerns. His life was invaded by these women, with their mysteries and agonies. He listened to the steps outside, thinking every moment to hear the steady tramp of the deputation from Salem, or at least Tozer, whom it would have been balm to his mind, in the height of the good man's triumph, to cut short and annihilate. But how do that, or anything else, with this woman seated by his fire explaining her unintelligible affairs? Such was Vincent's state of mind while his mother, in an agony of joy, was hearing from Susan's lips, for the first time, broken explanations of those few days of her life which outbalanced in terrible importance all its preceding years. The minister did not know that his sister's very existence, as well as her reason, hung upon that unhoped-for opening of her mouth and her heart.

Matters were not much mended when Dr Rider came in, beaming and radiant, full of congratulations. Susan was saved. It was the most curious psychological puzzle, the doctor said; all her life had got concentrated into the few days between her departure from Lonsdale and her arrival at Carlingford. Neither her old existence, nor the objects that surrounded her at the moment, had any significance for Susan; only something that belonged to that wonderful interval in which she had been driven desperate, could win back consciousness to her mind. It was the most singular case he had ever met with; but he knew this was the only way of treating it, and so it had proved. He recognised the girl with the blue veil the moment he saw her – he knew it could be no other. Who was she? where had she sprung from at that critical moment? where had she been? what was to be done with her? Dr Rider poured forth his questions like a stream. He was full of professional triumph, not to say natural satisfaction. He could not understand how his patient's brother, at that wonderful crisis, could have a mind pre-occupied or engaged with other things. The doctor turned with lively sympathy and curiosity from the anxious Non-conformist to Miss Smith, who was but too willing to begin all her explanations over again. Dr Rider, accustomed to hear many personal narratives, collected this story a great deal more clearly than Vincent, who was so much more interested in it, had, with all his opportunities, been able to do. How long the poor minister might have suffered under this conversation, it is impossible to tell. But Mrs Vincent, in all the agitation of her daughter's deliverance, could not forget the griefs of others. She sent a little message to her son, begging that he would send word of this arrival to "the poor lady." "To let her know – but she must not come here to-night," was the widow's message, who was just then having the room darkened, and everything arranged for the night, if perhaps her child might sleep. This message delivered the minister; it recalled Miss Smith to her duty. She it was who must go and explain everything to her patroness. Dr Rider, whose much-excited wonder was still further stimulated by hearing that the child's mother was at Lady Western's, that she was Mrs Mildmay, and that the Nonconformist was in her confidence, cheerfully undertook to carry the governess in his drag to Grange Lane, not without hopes of further information; and it was now getting late. Miss Smith made Vincent a tremulous curtsy, and held out her hand to him to say good-night. "The doctor will perhaps explain to Mrs Mildmay why I have left little Alice," said the troubled woman. "I never left her before since she was intrusted to me – never but when her papa stole her away; and you are a minister, Mr Vincent, and oh, I hope I am doing quite right, and as Alice's mamma will approve! But if she disapproves I must come back and—"

"They must not be disturbed to-night," said Dr Rider promptly; "I will see Mrs Mildmay." He was not reluctant to see Mrs Mildmay. The doctor, though he was not a gossip, was not inaccessible to the pleasure of knowing more than anybody else of the complications of this strange business, which still afforded matter of talk to Carlingford. He hurried her away while still the good governess was all in a flutter, and for the first time the minister was left alone. It was with a troubled mind that the young man resumed his seat at his desk. He began to get utterly weary of this business, and all about it. If he could only have swept away in a whirlwind, with his mother and sister, where the name of Mildmay had never been heard of, and where he could for ever get rid of the haunting woman with her gleaming eyes, who had pursued even his gentle mother to the door! but this new complication seemed to involve him deeper than ever in those strange bonds. It was with a certain disgust that the minister thought it all over as he sat leaning his head on his hands. His way was dark before him, yet it must speedily be decided. Everything was at a crisis in his excited mind and troubled life – even that strange lovely child's face, which had roused Susan from her apathy, had its share in the excitement of her brother's thoughts; for it was but another version, with differences, of the face of that other Alice, who all unwittingly had procured for Vincent the sweetest and the hardest hours he had spent in Carlingford. Were they all to pass like a dream – her smiles, her sweet looks, her kind words, even that magical touch upon his arm, which had once charmed him out of all his troubles? A groan came out of the young man's heart, not loud, but deep, as that thought moved him. The very despair of this love-dream had been more exquisite than any pleasure of his life. Was it all to pass away and be no longer? Life and thought, the actual and the visionary, had both come to a climax, and seemed to stand still, waiting the decision which must be come to that night.

From these musings the entrance of Tozer roused the minister. The excellent butterman came in all flushed and glowing from his success. To him, the meeting, which already the Nonconformist had half lost sight of under the super-structure of subsequent events, had newly concluded, and was the one occurrence of the time. The cheers which had hailed him master of the field were still ringing in Tozer's ears. "I don't deny as I am intoxicated like," said the excellent deacon; "them cheers was enough to carry any man off his legs, sir, if you'll believe me. We've scattered the enemy, that's what we've been and done, Mr Vincent. There ain't one of them as will dare show face in Salem. We was unanimous, sir – *un*animous, that's what we was! I never see such a triumph in our connection. Hurrah! If it warn't Miss as is ill, I could give it you all over again, cheers and all."

"I am glad you were pleased," said Vincent, with an effort; "but I will not ask you for such a report of the proceedings."

"Pleased! I'll tell you one thing as I was sorry for, sir," said Tozer, somewhat subdued in his exultation by the pastor's calmness – "I did it for the best; but seeing as things have turned out so well, I am as sorry as I can be – and that is, that you wasn't there. It was from expecting some un-pleasantness as I asked you not to come; but things turning out as they did, it would have done your heart good to see 'em, Mr Vincent. Salem folks has a deal of sense when you put things before them effective. And then you'd only have had to say three words to them on the spur of the moment, and all was settled and done with, and everything put straight; which would have let them settle down steady, sir, at once, and not kept no excitement, as it were, hanging about."

"Yes," said the minister, who was moving about his papers, and did not look up. The butterman began to be alarmed; he grew more and more enthusiastic the less response he met with.

"It's a meeting as will tell in the connection," said Tozer, with unconscious foresight; "a candid mind in a congregation ain't so general as you and me would like to see, Mr Vincent; and it takes a bit of a trial like this, sir, and the opposition, to bring out the real attachment as is between a pastor and a flock."

"Yes," said Vincent again. The deacon did not know what to make of the minister. Had he been piqued and angry, Tozer thought he might have known how to manage him, but this coldness was an alarming and mysterious symptom which he was unequal to. In his embarrassment and anxiety the good butterman stumbled upon the very subject from which, had he known the true state of affairs, he would have kept aloof.

"And the meeting as was to be to-morrow night?" said Tozer; "there ain't no need for explanations now – a word or two out of the pulpit is all as is wanted, just to say as it's all over, and you're grateful for their attachment, and so forth; you know a deal better, sir, how to do it nor me. And about the meeting as was called for to-morrow night? – me and the missis were thinking, though it's sudden, as it might be turned into a tea-meeting, if you was agreeable, just to make things pleasant; or if that ain't according to your fancy, as I'm aware you're not one as likes tea-meetings, we might send round, Mr Vincent, to all the seat-holders to say as it's given up; I'd do one or the other, if you'd be advised by me."

"Thank you – but I can't do either one or the other," said the Nonconformist. "I would not have asked the people to meet me if I had not had something to say to them – and this night's business, you understand," said Vincent, with a little pride, "has made no difference in me."

"No, sir, no – to be sure not," said the perplexed

butterman, much bewildered; "but two meetings on two nights consecutive is running the flock hard, it is. I'd give up to-morrow, Mr Vincent, if I was you."

To this insinuating address the minister made no answer – he only shook his head. Poor Tozer, out of his exultation, fell again into the depths. The blow was so unlooked-for that it overwhelmed him.

"You'll not go and make no reflections, sir?" said the troubled deacon; "bygones is bygones. You'll not bring it up against them, as they didn't show that sympathy they might have done? You'll not make no reference to nobody in particular, Mr Vincent? When a flock is conscious as they've done their duty and stood by their pastor, it ain't a safe thing, sir, not to turn upon them, and rake up things as is past. If you'll take my advice, sir, as wishes you well, and hasn't no motive but your good, I'd not hold that meeting, Mr Vincent; or, if you're bent upon it, say the word, and we'll set to work and give 'em a tea-meeting, and make all things comfortable. But if you was prudent, sir, and would go by my advice, one or the other of them two is what I would do."

"Thank you, Tozer, all the same," said Vincent, who, notwithstanding his preoccupation, saw the good butterman's anxiety, and appreciated it. "I know very well that all that is pleasant to-night is owing to you. Don't suppose I don't understand how you've fought for me; but now the business is mine, and I can take no more advice. Think no more of it; you have done all that you could do."

"I have done my humble endeavour, sir, as is my dooty, to keep things straight," said the deacon, doubtfully; "and if you'd tell me what was in your mind, Mr Vincent—?"

But the young Nonconformist gathered up his papers, closed his desk, and held out his hand to the kind-hearted butterman. "My sister has come back almost from the grave to-night," said Vincent; "and we are all, for anything I can see, at the turning point of our lives. You have done all you can do, and I thank you heartily; but now the business is in my hands."

This was all the satisfaction Tozer got from the minister. He went home much discouraged, not knowing what to make of it, but did not confide his fears even to his wife, hoping that reflection would change the pastor's mind, and resolved to make another effort to-morrow. And so the night fell over the troubled house. In the sick-room a joyful agitation had taken the place of the dark and hopeless calm. Susan, roused to life, lay leaning against her mother, looking at the child asleep on the sofa by her, unconscious of the long and terrible interval between the danger which that child had shared, and the delicious security to which her mind had all at once awakened. To Susan's consciousness, it appeared as if her mother had suddenly risen out of the mists, and delivered the two helpless creatures who had suffered together. She could not press close enough to this guardian of her life. She held her arms round her, and laid her cheek against the widow's with the dependence of a child upon her mother's bosom. Mrs Vincent sat upon the bed supporting her, herself supported in her weariness by love and joy, two divine attendants who go but seldom together. The two talked in whispers, – Susan because of her feebleness, the mother in the instinct of caressing tenderness. The poor girl told her story in broken syllables – broken by the widow's kisses and murmurs of sympathy, of wonder and love. Healing breathed upon the stricken mind and feeble frame as the two clung together in the silent night, always with an unspoken reference to the beautiful forlorn creature on the sofa – that visible symbol of all the terrors and troubles past. "I told her my mother would come to save us," said poor Susan. When she dropt to sleep at last, the mother leant her aching frame upon some pillows, afraid to move, and slept too, supreme protector, in her tender weakness, of these two young lives. As she woke from time to time to see her child sleeping by her side, thoughts of her son's deliverance stole across Mrs Vincent's mind to sweeten her repose. The watch-light burned dimly in the room, and threw a gigantic shadow of her little figure, half erect on the side of the bed, still in her black gown and the close white cap, which could not be less than dainty in its neatness, even in that vigil, upon the further wall. The widow slept only in snatches, waking often and keeping awake, as people do when they grow old; her thoughts, ever alive and active, varying between her projects for the future, to save Susan from all painful knowledge of her own story, and the thankful recollection of Arthur's rescue from his troubles. From echoes of Tozer's speech, and of the cheers of the flock, her imagination wandered off into calculations of how she could find another place of habitation as pleasant, perhaps, as Lonsdale, and even to the details of her removal from thence, what portions of her furniture she would sell, and which take with her. "For now that Arthur has got out of his troubles, we must not stay to get him into fresh difficulties with his flock," she said to herself, with a momentary ache in her thankful heart; and so dropped asleep for another half-hour, to wake again presently, and enter anew into the whole question. Such was the way in which Mrs Vincent passed that agitated but joyful night.

In the adjoining room Arthur sat up late over his papers. He was not writing, or doing any work; for hours together he sat leaning his head on his hands, gazing intently at the lamp, which his mother had adjusted, until his eyes were dazzled, and the gloom of the room around became spotted with discs of shade. Was he to permit the natural gratification into which Tozer's success had reluctantly moved him, to alter his resolve? Was he to drop into his old harness and try again? or was he to carry out his purpose in the face of all entreaties and inducements? The natural inclination to adopt the easiest course – and the equally natural, impetuous, youthful impulse to take the leap to which he had made up his mind, and dash forth in the face of his difficulties – gave him abundant occupation for his thoughts as they contended against each other. He sat arguing the question within himself long after his fire had sunk into ashes. When the penetrating cold of the night drove him at last to bed, the question was still dubious. Even in his sleep the uneasy perplexity pursued him; – a matter momentous enough, though nobody but Tozer – who was as restless as the minister, and disturbed his wife by groans and murmurs, of which, when indignantly woke up to render an account, he could give no explanation – knew or suspected anything. Whether to take up his anchors altogether and launch out upon that sea of life, of which, much as he had discussed it in his sermons, the young Nonconformist knew next to nothing? The widow would not have mused so quietly with her wakeful eyes in the dim room next to him, had she known what discussions were going in Arthur's mind. As for the congregation of Salem, they slept soundly, with an exhilarating sensation of generosity and goodness – all except the Pigeons, who were plotting schism, and had already in their eye a vacant Temperance Hall, where a new preaching station might be organised under the auspices of somebody who would rival Vincent. The triumphant majority, however, laughed at the poulterer, and anticipated, with a pleasurable expectation, the meeting of next night, and the relief and delight of the pastor, who would find he had no explanations to make, but only his thanks to render to his generous flock. The good people concluded that they would all stop to shake hands with him after the business was over. "For it's as good as receiving of him again, and giving him the right hand of fellowship," said Mrs Brown at the Dairy, who was entirely won over to the minister's side. Only Tozer, groaning in his midnight visions, and disturbing the virtuous repose of his wedded partner, suspected the new cloud that hung over Salem. For before morning the minister's mind was finally made up.

CHAPTER XXXIX.

The next day dawned amid the agitations natural to such a crisis of affairs. Almost before it was daylight, before Susan had woke, or the young stranger stirred upon her sofa, Miss Smith, troubled and exemplary, had returned to see after her charge. Miss Smith was in a state of much anxiety and discomfort till she had explained to Mrs Vincent all the strange circumstances in which she found herself; and the widow, who had ventured to rise from Susan's side, and had been noiselessly busy putting the room in order, that her child might see nothing that was not cheerful and orderly when she woke, was not without curiosity to hear, and gladly took this opportunity, before even Arthur was stirring, to understand, if she could, the story which was so connected with that of her children. She ventured to go into the next room with Miss Smith, where she could hear every movement in the sick-chamber. The widow found it hard to understand all the tale. That Mrs Hilyard was Mildmay's wife, and that it was their child who had sought protection of all the world from Susan Vincent, whom the crimes of her father and mother had driven to the very verge of the grave, was so hard and difficult to comprehend, that all the governess's anxious details of how little Alice first came into her hands, of her mother's motives for concealing her from Colonel Mildmay, even of the ill-fated flight to Lonsdale, which, instead of keeping her safe, had carried the child into her father's very presence – and all the subsequent events which Miss Smith had already confided to the minister, fell but dully upon the ears of Susan's mother.

"*Her* daughter – and *his* daughter – and she comes to take refuge with *my* child," said the widow, with a swelling heart. Mrs Vincent did not know what secret it was that lay heavy on the soul of the desperate woman who had followed her last night from Grove Street, but somehow, with a female instinct, felt, though she did not understand, that Mrs Hilyard or Mrs Mildmay, whatever her name might be, was as guilty in respect to Susan as was her guilty husband – the man who had stolen like a serpent into the Lonsdale cottage and won the poor girl's simple heart. Full of curiosity as she was, the widow's thoughts wandered off from Miss Smith's narrative; her heart swelled within her with an innocent triumph; the good had overcome the evil. This child, over whom its father and mother had fought with so deadly a struggle, had flown for protection to Susan, whom that father and mother had done their utmost to ruin and destroy. They had not succeeded, thank God! Through the desert and lions the widow's Una had come victorious, stretching her tender virgin shield over this poor child of passion and sorrow. While Miss Smith maundered through the entire history, starting from the time when Miss Russell married Colonel Mildmay, the widow's mind was entirely occupied with this wonderful victory of innocence over wickedness. She forgot the passionate despair of the mother whose child did not recognise her. She began immediately to contrive, with unguarded generosity, how Susan and she, when they left Carlingford, should carry the stranger along with them, and nurse her clouded mind into full development. Mrs Vincent's trials had not yet taught her any practical lessons of worldly wisdom. Her heart was still as open as when, unthinking of evil, she admitted the false Mr Fordham into her cottage, and made a beginning of all the misery which seemed now, to her sanguine heart, to be passing away. She went back to Susan's room full of this plan – full of tender thoughts towards the girl who had chosen Susan for her protector, and of pride and joy still more tender in her own child, who had overcome evil. It was, perhaps, the sweetest solace which could have been offered, after all her troubles, to the minister's mother. It was at once a vindication of the hard "dealings" of Providence, and of that strength of innocence and purity, in which the little woman believed with all her heart.

The minister himself was much less agreeably moved when he found the governess in possession of his sitting-room. Anything more utterly vexatious could hardly have occurred to Vincent than to find this troubled good woman, herself much embarrassed and disturbed by her own position, seated at his breakfast-table on this eventful morning. Miss Smith was as primly uncomfortable as it was natural for an elderly single woman, still conscious of the fact that she was unmarried, to be, in an absolute *tête-à-tête* with a young man. She, poor lady, was as near blushing as her grey and composed non-complexion would permit. She moved uneasily in her seat, and made tremulous explanations, as Vincent, who was too young and inexperienced to be absolutely uncourteous, took his place opposite to her. "I am sure I feel quite an intruder," said poor Miss Smith; "but your mother, Mr Vincent, and little Alice – and indeed I did not know I was to be left here alone. It must seem so odd to you to find a lady – dear, dear me! I feel I am quite in the way," said the embarrassed governess; "but Mrs Mildmay will be here presently. I know she will be here directly. I am sure she would have come with me had she known. But she sat up half the night hearing what I had to tell her, and dropped asleep just in the morning. She is wonderfully changed, Mr Vincent – very, very much changed. She is so nervous – a thing I never could have looked for. I suppose, after all, married ladies, however much they may object to their husbands, can't help feeling a little when anything happens," continued Miss Smith, primly: "and there is something so dreadful in such an accident. How do you think it can have happened? Could it be his groom, or who could it be? but I understand he is getting better now?"

"Yes, I believe so," said Vincent.

"I am so glad," said Miss Smith, "not that if it had been the will of Providence. – I would make the tea for you, Mr Vincent, if you would not think it odd, and I am sure Mrs Mildmay will be here directly. They were in a great commotion at Grange Lane. Just now, you know, there is an excitement. Though she is not a young girl, to be sure it is always natural. But for that I am sure they would all have come this morning; but perhaps Mr Fordham—"

"Not any tea, thank you. If you have breakfasted, I will have the things removed. I have only one sitting-room, you perceive," said the minister, rather bitterly. He could not be positively uncivil – his heart was too young and fresh to be rude to any woman; but he rang the bell with a little unnecessary sharpness when Miss Smith protested that she had breakfasted long before. Her words excited him with a touch beyond telling. He could not, would not ask what was the cause of the commotion in Grange Lane; but he walked to the window to collect himself while the little maid cleared the table, and, throwing it open, looked out with the heart beating loud in his breast. Were these the bells of St Roque's chiming into the ruddy sunny air with a confused jangle of joy? It was a saint's day, no doubt – a festival which the Perpetual Curate took delight in proclaiming his observance of; or – if it might happen to be anything else, what was that to the minister of Salem, who had so many other things on his mind? As he looked out a cab drove rapidly up to the door – a cab from which he saw emerge Mrs Hilyard and another figure, which he recognised with a start of resentment. What possible right had this man to intrude upon him in this moment of fate? The minister left the window hastily, and stationed himself with a gloomy countenance on the hearthrug. He might be impatient of the women; but Fordham, inexcusable as his intrusion was, had to be met face to face. With a flash of sudden recollection, he recalled all his previous intercourse with the stranger whose name was so bitterly interwoven with the history of the last six months. What had he ever done to wake so sharp a pang of dislike and injury in Vincent's mind? It was not for Susan's sake that her brother's heart closed and his countenance clouded against the man whose name had wrought her so much sorrow. Vincent had arrived at such a climax of personal existence that Susan had but a dim and secondary place in his thoughts. He was absorbed in his own troubles and plans and miseries. On the eve of striking out for himself into that bitter and unknown life in which his inexperienced imagination rejected the thought of any solace yet remaining, what malicious influence brought this man here?

They came in together into the room, "Mrs Mildmay and Mr Fordham" – not Mrs Hilyard: that was over; and, preoccupied as the minister was, he could not but perceive the sudden change which had come over the Back Grove Street needlewoman. Perhaps her despair had lasted as long as was possible for such an impatient spirit. She came in with the firm, steady step which he had observed long ago, before she had begun to tremble at his eye. Another new stage had commenced in her strange life. She went up to him without any hesitation, clear and decisive as of old.

"I am going away," she said, holding out her hand to him, "and so I presume are you, Mr Vincent. I have come to explain everything and see your mother. Let me see your mother. Mr Fordham has come with me to explain to *you*. They think in Grange Lane that it is only a man who can speak to a man," she went on, with the old movement of her thin lips; "and that now I have come to life again, I must not manage my own affairs. I am going back to society and the world, Mr Vincent. I do not know where you are going, but here is somebody come to answer for me. Do they accept bail in a court of honour? or will you still hold a woman to her parole? for it must be settled now."

"Why must it be settled now?" said Vincent. He had dropped her hand and turned away from her with a certain repugnance. She had lost her power over him. At that moment the idea of being cruel, tyrannical to somebody – using his power harshly, balancing the pain in his own heart by inflicting pain on another – was not unagreeable to the minister's excited mind. He could have steeled himself just then to bring down upon her all the horrible penalties of the law. "Why must it be settled?" he repeated; "why must you leave Carlingford? I will not permit it." He spoke to her, but he looked at Fordham. The stranger was wrapped in a large overcoat which concealed all his dress. What was his dress, or his aspect, or the restrained brightness in his eyes, to the minister of Salem? But Vincent watched him narrowly with a jealous inspection. In Fordham's whole appearance there was the air of a man to whom something was about to happen, which aggravated to the fever-point the dislike and opposition in Vincent's heart.

"I will be answerable for Mrs Mildmay," said Fordham, with an evident response on his side to that opposition and dislike. Then he paused, evidently perceiving the necessity of conciliation. "Mr Vincent," he continued, with some earnestness, "we all understand and regret deeply the in-convenience – I mean the suffering – that is to say, the injury and misery which these late occurrences must have caused you. I know how well – that is, how generously, how nobly – you have behaved—"

Here Mr Fordham came to a pause in some confusion. To express calm acknowledgements to a man for his conduct in a matter which has been to him one of unmitigated disaster and calamity, requires an amount of composure which few people possess when at the height of personal happiness. The minister drew back, and, with a slight bow, and a restraint which was very natural and not unbecoming in his circumstances, looked on at the confusion of the speaker without any attempt to relieve it. He had offered seats to his visitors, but he himself stood on the hearthrug, dark and silent, giving no assistance in the explanation. He had not invited the explanation – it must be managed now as the others might, without any help from him.

"I have seen Colonel Mildmay," continued Mr Fordham, after a confused pause. "If it can be any atonement to you to know how much he regrets all that has happened, so far as your family is concerned – how fully he exonerates Miss Vincent, who was all along deceived, and who would not have remained a moment with him had she not been forcibly detained. Mildmay declares she met with nothing but respect at his hands," continued the embarrassed advocate, lowering his voice; "he says—"

"Enough has been said on the subject," said Vincent, restraining himself with a violent effort.

"Yes – I beg your pardon, it is quite true – enough has been said," cried Fordham, with an appearance of relief. Here, at least, was one part of his difficult mediation over. "Mildmay will not," he resumed, after a pause, "tell me or any one else who it was that gave him his wound – that is a secret, he says, between him and his God – and another. Whoever that other may be," continued Fordham, with a quick look towards Mrs Mildmay, "he is conscious of having wronged – him – and will take no steps against – him. This culprit, it appears, must be permitted to escape – you think so? – worse evils might be involved if we were to demand – his – punishment. Mr Vincent, I beg you to take this into consideration. It could be no advantage to you; the innocent shall not suffer – but – the criminal – must be permitted to escape."

"I do not see the necessity," said Vincent, between his teeth.

"No, no," said Mrs Mildmay, suddenly. "Escape! who believes in escape? Mr Vincent knows better. Hush, you are a happy man just now – you are not qualified to judge; but *we* know better. Escape! – he means from prisons, and suchlike," she continued, turning to Vincent with a half-disdainful wave of her hand towards her companion. "But you know, and so do I, that there is no escape – not in this world. I know nothing about the next," said the strange woman, curbing once more the flush of excitement which

had overpowered her as she spoke – "nothing; neither do
you, although you are a priest. But there is enough of
retribution here. The criminal – Mr Vincent – you know –
will not escape."

She spoke these last words panting, with pauses between,
for breath. She was afraid of him again; his blankness, his
passive opposition, drove her out of her composure. She
put her hands together under her shawl with a certain dumb
entreaty, and fixed upon him her eager eyes. They were a
strange group altogether. Miss Smith, who had still lingered
at the door, notwithstanding Mrs Mildmay's imperative
gesture of dismissal – out of hearing, but not out of sight –
suffered some little sound to escape her at this critical
moment; and when her patroness turned round upon her
with those dreadful eyes, fled with precipitation, taking
refuge in Mrs Vincent's room. The table, still covered with
its white cloth, stood between that dismayed spectator
before she disappeared finally, and the little company who
were engaged in this silent conflict. Beside it sat Mrs
Mildmay, with a renewed panic of fear rising in her face.
Fordham, considerably disturbed, and not knowing what to
say, stood near her buttoning and unbuttoning his overcoat
with impatient fingers, anxious to help her, but still more
anxious to be gone. The minister stood facing them all, with
compressed lips, and eyes which looked at nobody. He was
wrapt in a silent dumb resistance to all entreaties and
arguments, watching Fordham's gestures, Fordham's looks,
with a jealous but secret suspicion. His heart was cruel in its
bitterness. He for whom Providence had no joys in store, to
whom the light was fading which made life sweet, was for
this moment superior to the happy man who stood embarrassed and impatient before him; and generous as his real
nature was, it was not in him, in this moment of darkness, to
let the opportunity go.

"The innocent have suffered already," said Vincent, "all
but madness, all but death. Why should the criminal
escape? – go back into society, the society of good people,

perhaps strike someone else more effectually? Why should
I betray justice, and let the criminal escape? My sister's
honour and safety are mine, and shall be guarded, whoever
suffers. I will not permit her to go."

"But I offer to be answerable for her appearance," said
Fordham, hastily. "I undertake to produce her if need be.
You know me. I am a – a relation of the family. I am a man
sufficiently known to satisfy any magistrate. You have no
legal right to detain her. What would you have more? Is not
my guarantee enough for you?"

"No," said Vincent, slowly. The two men stood defiant
opposite to each other, contending for this woman, whom
neither of them looked at, for whom neither of them cared.
She, in the mean time, sat still in an agony of suspense and
concealed anguish, with her eyes fixed on Vincent's face.
She knew very well it was not of her that either of the two
was thinking; yet it was her fate, perhaps her very life,
which hung trembling in the balance. A smothered sighing
sob came from her breast. She was silenced for the first time
in her life. She had escaped her crime; but all its material
consequences, shame and punishment, still hung over her
head. After God himself had freed her from the guilt of
blood – after the injured man himself had forgiven her –
when all was clear for her escape into another life – was this
an indignant angel, with flaming sword and averted face,
that barred the way of the fugitive? Beyond him, virtue and
goodness, and all the fruits of repentance, shone before the
eyes which had up to this time seen but little attraction in
them – all so sweet, so easy, so certain, if but she were free.
Her worn heart sighed to get forth into that way of peace.
She could have fallen on her knees before the stern judge
who kept her back, and held over her head the cloud of her
own ill-doings, but dared not, in her paroxysm of fear and
half-despair. A groaning, sighing sob, interrupted and
broken, came from her exhausted breast. Just as she had
recovered herself – as she had escaped – as remorse and
misery had driven her to yearn after a better life, to be cast

down again into this abyss of guilt and punishment! She trembled violently as she clasped her poor hands under her shawl. Composure and self-restraint were impossible in this terrible suspense.

Her cry went to Fordham's heart; and, besides, he was in desperate haste, and could afford to sink his pride, and make an appeal for once. He made a step forward, and put out his hand with an entreating gesture. "Do you hear her?" he cried, suddenly. "You have had much to bear yourself; have pity on *her*. Let her off – leave her to God. She has been ill, and will die if you have no mercy. You who are a minister—"

In his energy his overcoat fell back for a moment; underneath he was in full dress, which showed strangely in that grey spring morning. Vincent turned round upon him with a smile. The young man's face was utterly pale, white to the lips. The bells were jangling joy in his ears. He was not master of himself. "We detain you, Mr Fordham; you have other affairs in hand," he said. "I am a minister only – a Dissenting minister – unworthy to have such an intercessor pleading with me; but you, at least," cried poor Vincent, with an attempt at sarcasm, "do not want my pity; there is nothing between us that requires explanation. I will arrange with Mrs Mildmay alone." He turned away and went to the window when he had spoken. There he stood with his back to them, listening to the bells of St Roque's, as they came and went in irregular breaks upon the wind. His heart was bursting with wild throbs of bitterness and despair; it was all he could do to keep the tumult down, and contain himself in that flush of passion. He turned away from them, and stood gazing out at that tedious window into the blank world. What did it matter? Let her escape if she would – let things go as they might; nothing was of any further importance – certainly on earth – perhaps even in heaven.

"I will go away – I can do you no good – I should only lose my temper; and time presses," said Mr Fordham, with a flush of resentment on his face, as he turned to the

anxious woman behind him. What could he do? He could
not quarrel with this angry man in his own house on such a
day. He could not keep happier matters waiting. He
would not risk the losing of his temper and his time at this
moment of all others. He went away with a sensation of
defeat, which for half an hour materially mitigated his
happiness. But he *was* happy, and the happy are indulgent
judges both of their own conduct and of others. As for the
minister, he was roused again when he saw his rival jump
into the cab at the door, and drive off alone down the
street, which was lively with the early stir of day. The sun
had just broken through the morning clouds, and it was
into a ruddy perspective of light that the stranger disappeared as he went off towards Grange Lane. Strange
contrast of fate! While Fordham hastened down into the
sunshine to all the joy that awaited him there, Tozer, a
homely, matter-of-fact figure in the ruddy light, was crossing the street towards the minister's door. Vincent went
away from the window again, with pangs of an impatience
and intolerance of his own lot which no strength of mind
could subdue. All the gleam of impossible joy which had
lighted his path in Carlingford had now gone out, and left
him in darkness; and here came back, in undisturbed
possession, all the meaner circumstances of his individual
destiny. Salem alone remained to him out of the wreck of
his dreams; except when he turned back and discovered
her – the one tragic thread in the petty history – this
woman whose future life for good or for evil he held in his
avenging hands.

Mrs Mildmay was still seated at the table. She had
regained command of herself. She looked up to him with
gleaming eyes when he approached her. "Mr Vincent, I
keep my parole – I am waiting your pleasure," she said,
never removing her eyes from his face. It was at this
moment that Mrs Vincent, who had from the window of
Susan's chamber seen the cab arrive and go away with
some curiosity, came into the room. The widow wanted to

know who her son's visitors were, and what had brought them. She came in with a little eagerness, but was brought to a sudden standstill by the appearance of Mrs Mildmay. Why was this woman here? what had she to do with the minister? Mrs Vincent put on her little air of simple dignity. She said, "I beg your pardon; I did not know my son was engaged," with a curtsy of disapproving politeness to the unwelcome visitor. With a troubled look at Arthur, who looked excited and gloomy enough to justify any uncomfortable imaginations about him, his mother turned away somewhat reluctantly. She did not feel that it was quite right to leave him exposed to the wiles of this "designing woman;" but the widow's own dignity was partly at stake. All along she had disapproved of this strange friendship, and she could not countenance it now.

"Your mother is going away," said Mrs Mildmay, with a restrained outcry of despair: "is no one to be permitted to mediate between us? You are a man and cruel; you are in trouble, and you think you will avenge yourself. No, no – I don't mean what I say. Your son is a – a true knight, Mrs Vincent; I told you so before. He will never be hard upon a woman: if I had not known that, why should I have trusted him? I came back, as he knows, of my own will. Don't go away; I am willing you should know – the whole," said the excited woman, with a sudden pause, turning upon Vincent, her face blanching into deadly whiteness – "the whole – I consent; let her be the judge. Women are more cruel than men; but I saved her daughter – I am willing that she should hear it all."

She sat down again on the seat from which she had risen. A certain comfort and relief stole over her face. She was appealing to the general heart of humanity against this one man who knew her secret. It might be hard to hear the story of her own sin – but it was harder to be under the stifling sway of one who knew it, and who had it in his power to denounce her. She ceased to tremble as she looked at the widow's troubled face. It was a new tribunal before which

she stood; perhaps here her provocations might be acknowledged – her soul acquitted of the burden from which it
could never escape. As the slow moments passed on, and
the minister did not speak, she grew impatient of the
silence. "Tell her," she said, faintly – it was a new hope
which thus awoke in her heart.

But while Mrs Mildmay sat waiting, and while the widow
drew near, not without some judicial state in the poise of
her little figure, to hear the explanation which she felt she
was entitled to, Tozer's honest troubled face looked in at
the door. It put a climax upon the confusion of the morning.
The good butterman looked on in some surprise at this
strange assemblage, recognising dimly the haze of an
excitement of which he knew nothing. He was acquainted,
to some extent, with the needlewoman of Back Grove
Street. He had gone to call on her once at the solicitation of
the anxious Brown, who had charge of her district but did
not feel himself competent to deal with the spiritual necessities of such a penitent; and Tozer remembered well that
her state of mind had not been satisfactory – "not what was
to be looked for in a person as had the means of grace close
at hand, and attended regular at Salem." He thought she
must have come at this unlucky moment to get assistance of
some kind from the minister – "as if he had not troubles
enough of his own," Tozer said to himself; but the deacon
was not disposed to let his pastor be victimised in any such
fashion. This, at least, was a matter in which he felt fully
entitled to interfere.

"Good mornin', ma'am," said the worthy butterman;
"good mornin', Mr Vincent – it's cold, but it's seasonable
for the time of year. What I wanted was a word or two with
the pastor, ma'am, if he's disengaged. It ain't what I
approve," continued Tozer, fixing his eyes with some
sternness upon the visitor, "to take up a minister's time in
the morning when he has the work of a flock on his hands.
My business, being such as can't wait, is different; but them
as are in want of assistance, one way or another, which is a

thing as belongs to the deacons, have no excuse, not as I can
see, for disturbing the pastor. It ain't a thing as I would put
up with," continued Tozer, with increasing severity; "the
charities of the flock ain't in Mr Vincent's hands; it's a
swindling of his time to come in upon him of a morning if
there ain't a good reason; and, as far as I am concerned, it
would be enough to shut my heart up again' giving help –
that's how it would work on me."

Mrs Mildmay was entirely inattentive to the first few
words of this address, but the pointed application given by
the speaker's eyes called her attention presently. She
gazed at him, as he proceeded, with a gradual lightening of
her worn and anxious face. While Mrs Vincent did all she
could, with anxious looks and little deprecatory gestures, to
stop the butterman, the countenance of her visitor cleared
by one of those strange sudden changes which the minister
had noted so often. Her lips relaxed, her eyes gleamed with
a sudden flash of amusement. Then she glanced around,
seeing with quick observation not only the absurdity of
Tozer's mistake, but the infallible effect it had in changing
the aspect of affairs. The minister had turned away, not
without a grim, impatient smile at the corner of his mouth.
The minister's mother, shocked in all her gentle politeness,
was eagerly watching her opportunity to break in and set
the perplexed deacon right. The culprit, who had been on
her trial a moment before, drew a long breath of utter
relief. Now she had escaped – the crisis was over. Her quick
spirit rose with a sense of triumph – a sensation of amusement. She entered eagerly into it, leaning forward with
eyes that shone and gleamed upon her accuser, and a mock
solemnity of attention which only her desperate strain of
mind and faculties could have enabled her to assume so
quickly. When the butterman came to a pause, Mrs
Vincent rushed in breathlessly to the rescue.

"Mr Tozer – Mr Tozer! this lady is – a – a friend of ours,"
cried the minister's mother, with looks that were much
more eloquent of her distress and horror than any words.

She had no time to say more, when the aggrieved individual herself broke in –

"Mr Tozer knows I have been one of the flock since ever Mr Vincent came," said the strange woman. "I have gone to all the meetings, and listened faithfully to the pastor every time he has preached; and would you judge me unworthy of relief because I once came to see him in a morning? That is hard laws; but the minister will speak for me. The minister knows me," she went on, turning to Vincent, "and he and his mother have been very charitable to a poor woman, Mr Tozer. You will not exclude me from the Salem charities for this one offence? Remember that I am a member of the flock."

"Not a church-member as I know," said the sturdy deacon – "not meaning no offence, if I've made a mistake – one sitting, as far as I remember; but a – lady – as is a friend of Mrs Vincent's—"

Here Tozer paused, abashed but suspicious, not disposed to make any further apology. That moment was enough to drive this lighter interlude from the vigilant soul which, in all its moods, watched what was going on with a quick apprehension of the opportunities of the moment. All her perceptions, quickened as they were by anxiety and fear, were bent on discovering an outlet for her escape, as she saw her chance now. She got up wearily, leaning on the table, as indeed she needed to lean, and looked into Mrs Vincent's face: "May I see my child?" she said, in a voice that went to the heart of the widow. The minister's mother could not resist this appeal. She saw the trembling in her limbs, the anxiety in her eye. "Arthur, I will see to Mrs Mildmay. Mr Tozer has something to say to you, and we must not occupy your time," said the tender little woman, in whose gentle presence there was protection and shelter even for the passionate spirit beside her. Thus the two went away together. If there had ever been any revengeful intention in Vincent's mind, it had disappeared by this time. He too breathed deep with relief. The criminal had

escaped, at least out of his hands. He was no longer
compelled to take upon himself the office of an avenger.

CHAPTER XL.

"I hope, sir, as I haven't said anything to give offence?
– it was far from my meaning," said Tozer; "not as the
person – is a church-member, being only a seat-holder
for one sittin', as is down in the books. I wouldn't have
come over, not so early, Mr Vincent, if it wasn't as I
was wishful to try if you'd listen to reason about the
meetin' as is appointed to be tonight. It ain't no interest
of mine, not so far as money goes, nor nothing of that kind.
It's you as I'm a-thinking of. I don't mind standing the
expense out of my own pocket, if so be as you'd give
in to make it a tea-meetin'. I don't know as you'd need
to do nothing but take the chair and make yourself agreeable. Me and Brown and the women would manage the
rest. It would be a pleasant surprise, that's what it
would be," said the good butterman; "and Phoebe and
some more would go down directly to make ready: and
I don't doubt as there's cakes and buns enough in Carlingford, Mr Vincent, sir, if you'd but bend your mind to it
and consent."

"I am going out," said Vincent; "I have – something to
do; don't detain me, Tozer. I must have this morning to
myself."

"I'll walk with you, sir, if I ain't in the way," said the
deacon, accompanying the young man's restless steps
down-stairs. "They tell me Miss is a deal better, and all
things is going on well. I wouldn't be meddlesome, Mr
Vincent, not of my own will; but when matters is settling,

sir, if you'd but hear reason! there can't be nothing but harm come of more explanations. I never had no confidence in explanations, for my part; but pleasant looks and the urns a-smoking, and a bit of green on the wall, as Phoebe and the rest could put up in no time! and just a speech as was agreeable to wind up with – a bit of an anecdote, or poetry about friends as is better friends after they've spoken their minds and had it out – that's the thing as would settle Salem, Mr Vincent. I don't speak, not to bother you, sir, but for your good. There ain't no difficulty in it; it's easier a deal than being serious and opening up all things over again; and as for them as would like to dictate—"

"I am not thinking of Salem," said the minister; "I have many other things to distract me; for heaven's sake, if you have any pity, leave me alone to-day."

"But you'll give in to make it a tea-meetin'?" said the anxious butterman, pausing at his own door.

Tozer did not make out the minister's reply. It is difficult to distinguish between a nod and a shake of the head, under some circumstances – and Vincent did not pause to give an articulate answer, but left his companion to his own devices. It seemed to Vincent to be a long time since Fordham left his house – and he was possessed with a fever of impatience to see for himself what was being transacted down yonder in the sunshine, where the spire of St Roque's appeared in the distance through the ruddy morning haze. The bells had ceased, and all was quiet enough in Grange Lane. Quite quiet – a few ordinary passengers in the tranquil road, nursemaids and children – and the calm green doors closing in the concealed houses, as if no passion or agitation could penetrate them. The door of Lady Western's garden was ajar. The minister crossed over and looked in with a wistful, despairing hope of seeing something that would contradict his conclusion. The house was baking in the spring sunshine – the door open, some of the windows open, eager servants hovering about, an air of expectation over all. With eyes full of memories, the minister looked in at the half-open door, which one time and another had been to him the gate of paradise. Within, where the red geraniums and verbenas had once brightened all the borders, were pale crocuses and flowers of early spring – the limes were beginning to bud, the daisies to grow among the grass. The winter was over in that sheltered and sunny place; Nature herself stood sweet within the protecting walls, and gathered all the tenderest sweets of spring to greet the bride in the new beginning of her life. It was but a glance, but the spectator, in the bitterness of his heart, did not lose a single tint or line; and just then the joy-bells burst out once more from St Roque's. Poor Vincent drew back from the door as the sudden sound stung him to the heart. Nothing had any pity for him – all the world, and every voice and breath therein, sided with the others in their joy. He went on blindly, without thinking where he was going, with a kind of dull, stubborn determination in his heart, not to turn back in his wretchedness, even from the sight of the happy procession which he knew must be advancing to meet him. A pang more or less, what did it matter? And for the last time he would look on Her who was nothing in the world to him now – who never could have been anything – yet who had somehow shed such streams of light upon the poor minister's humble path, as no reality in all his life had ever shed before. He paused on the edge of the road as he saw the carriage coming. It was one of those moments when a man's entire life becomes apparent to him in long perspective of past and future, he himself and all the world standing still between. The bells rang on his heart, with echoes from the wheels and the horses' feet coming up in superb pride and triumph. Heaven and earth were glad for her in her joy. He, in his great trouble, stood dark in the sunshine and looked on.

It was only a moment, and no more. He would have seen nothing but the white mist of the veil which surrounded her, had not she in her loveliness and kindness perceived him, and bent forward in the carriage with a little motion of her hand calling the attention of her unseen bridegroom to that figure on the way. At sight of that movement, the unhappy young man started with an intolerable pang, and went on heedless where he was going. He could not control the momentary passion. She had never harmed him – never meant to dazzle him with her beauty, or trifle with his love, or break his heart. It was kind as the sunshine, this sweet bridal face leaning out with that momentary glance of recognition. She would have given him her kind hand, her sweet smile as of old, had they met more closely – no remorseful consciousness was in *her* eyes; but neither the bells, nor the flowers, nor the sunshine, went with such a pang to poor Vincent's heart as did that look of kindness. It was all unreal then – no foundation at all in it? not enough to call a passing colour to her cheek, or to dim her sweet eyes on her bridal day? He went down the long road in the insensibility of passion – seeing nothing, caring for nothing – stung to the heart. No look of triumph, no female dart of conscious cruelty, could have given the poor minister so bitter a wound. All her treasured looks and smiles – the touch of her hand – her words, of which he had scarcely forgotten one – did they mean nothing after all? nothing but kindness? He had laid his heart at her feet; if she had trodden on it he could have forgiven her; but she only went on smiling, and never saw the treasure in her way. And this was the end. The unfortunate young man could not give way to any outbreak of the passion that consumed him; he could but go on hotly – on past St Roque's, where flowers still lay in the porch, and the open doors invited strangers, to the silent country, where the fields lay callow under the touch of spring. Spring! everlasting mockery of human trouble! Here were the hedgerows stirring, the secret grain beginning to throb conscious in the old furrows; but life itself standing still – coming to a sudden end in this heart which filled the young man's entire frame with pulsations of anguish. All his existence had flowed towards this day, and took its termination here. His love – heaven help him! he had but one heart, and had thrown it away; his work – that too was to come to nothing, and be ended; all his traditions, all his hopes, were they to be buried in one grave? and what was to become after of the posthumous and nameless life?

CHAPTER XLI.

WHEN the minister fully came to himself, it was after a long rapid walk of many miles through the silent fields and hazy country. There the clouds cleared off from him in the quietness. When he began to see clearly he turned back towards Carlingford. Nothing now stood between him and the crisis which henceforward must determine his personal affairs. He turned in the long country road, which he had been pursuing eagerly without knowing what he was doing, and gazed back towards the distant roofs. He had a consciousness that it stirred within his breast, still smarting and thrilling with that violent access of agony – but the climax was over. The strong pulsations fell into dull beats of indefinite pain. Now for the other world – the neutral-coloured life. Vincent did not very well know which road he had taken, for he had not been thinking of where he was going; but it roused him a little to perceive that his homeward way brought him through Grove Street, and past Siloam Cottage, where Mr Tufton lived.

Mrs Tufton was at the window, behind the great geranium, when the minister came in sight. When she saw him she tapped upon the pane and beckoned him to go in. He obeyed the summons, almost without impatience, in the languor of his mind. He went in to find them all by the fire, just as they had been when he came first to Carlingford. The old minister, in his armchair, holding out his flabby white hand to his dear young brother; the invalid daughter still knitting, with cold blue eyes, always vigilant and alert, investigating everything. It was a mild day, and Mrs Tufton herself had shifted her seat to the window, where she had been reading aloud as usual the 'Carlingford Gazette.' The motionless warm air of the little parlour, the prints of the brethren on the walls, the attitudes of the living inhabitants, were all unchanged from the time when the young minister of Salem paid his first visit, and chafed at Mr Tufton's advice, and heard with a secret shiver the prophecy of Adelaide, that "they would kill him in six months." He took the same chair, again making a little commotion among the furniture, which the size of the room made it difficult to displace. It was with a bewildering sensation that he sat down in that unchangeable house. Had time really gone on through all these passions and pains, of which he was conscious in his heart? or had it stood still, and were they only dreams? Adelaide Tufton, immovable in her padded chair, with pale blue eyes that searched through everything, had surely never once altered her position, but had knitted away the days with a mystic thread like one of the Fates. Even the geranium did not seem to have gained or shed a single leaf.

"I have just been reading in the 'Gazette' the report of last night's meeting," said good Mrs Tufton. "Oh, Mr Vincent, I was so glad – your dear mother herself, if she had been there, could not have been happier than I was. I hope she has seen the 'Gazette' this morning. You young men always like the 'Times;' but they never put in anything that is interesting to me in the 'Times.' Perhaps, if she has not seen it, you will put the paper in your pocket. Indeed, it made me as happy as if you had been my own son. I always say that is very much how Mr Tufton and I feel for you."

"Yes, it went off very well," said the old minister. "My dear young brother, it all depends on whether you have friends that know how to deal with a flock; nothing can teach you that but experience. I am sorry I dare not go out again to-night – it cost me my night's rest last night, as Mrs Tufton will tell you; but that is nothing in consideration of duty. Never think of ease to yourself, my dear young friend, when you can serve a brother; it has always been my rule through life—"

"Mr Vincent understands all that," said Adelaide; "that will do, papa – we know. Tell me about Lady Western's marriage, Mr Vincent. I daresay you were invited, as she was such a friend of yours. It must have been an awkwardness between you when she turned out to be Colonel Mildmay's sister; but, to be sure, those things don't matter among people in high life. It was delightful that she should marry her old love after all, don't you think? Poor Sir Joseph would have left a different will if he had known. Parted for ten years and coming together again! it is like a story in a book—"

"I do not know the circumstances," said poor Vincent. He turned to Mr Tufton with a vain hope of escaping. "I shall have to bid you good-bye shortly," said the minister; "though it was very good of the Salem people not to dismiss me, I prefer—"

"You mean to go away?" said Adelaide; "that will be a wonderful piece of news in the connection; but I don't think you will go away: there will be a deputation, and they will give you a piece of plate, and you will remain – you will not be able to resist. Papa never was a preacher to speak of," continued the dauntless invalid, "but they gave him a purse and a testimonial when he retired; and you are soft-hearted, and they will get the better of you—"

"Adelaide!" said Mrs Tufton, "Mr Vincent will think you out of your senses: indeed, Mr Vincent, she does not mind what she says; and she has had so much ill-health, poor child, that both her papa and I have given in to her too much; but as for my husband's preaching, it is well known he could have had many other changes if his duty had not called him to stay at Salem; invitations used to come—"

CHRONICLES OF CARLINGFORD

"Oh, stuff!" said the irreverent Adelaide – "as if Mr Vincent did not know. But I will tell you about Lady Western – that is the romance of the day. Mr Fordham was very poor, you know, when they first saw each other – only a poor barrister – and the friends interfered. Friends always interfere," said the sick woman, fixing her pale eyes on Vincent's face as she went on with her knitting; "and they married her to old Sir Joseph Western; and so, after a while, she became the young Dowager. She must have been very pretty then – she is beautiful now; but I would not have married a widow, had I been Mr Fordham, after I came into my fortune. His elder brother died, you know. I would not have married her, however lovely she had been. Mr Vincent, would you?"

"Adelaide!" cried Mrs Tufton, again in dismay. The poor minister thrust back his chair from the table, and came roughly against the stand of the great geranium, which had to be adjusted, and covered his retreat. He glanced at his conscious tormentor with the contemptuous rage and aggravation which men sometimes feel towards a weak creature who insults them with impunity. But she did not show any pleasurable consciousness of her triumph; she kept knitting on, looking at him with her pale blue eyes. There was something in that loveless eagerness of curiosity which appalled Vincent. He got up hastily to his feet, and said he had something to do and must go away.

"Good-bye, my dear brother," said Mr Tufton slowly, shaking the young minister's hand; you will be judicious to-night? The flock have stood by you, and been indulgent to your inexperience. They see you never meant to hurt any of their feelings. It is what I always trained my people to be – considerate to the young preachers. Take my advice, my beloved young brother, and dear Tozer's advice. We do all we can for you here, and dear Tozer is a tower of strength. And you have our prayers; we are but a little assembly – I and my dear partner in life and our afflicted child – but two or three, you know – and we never forget you at the throne of grace."

With this parting blessing Vincent hastened away. Poor little Mrs Tufton had added some little effusion of motherly kindness which he did not listen to. He came away with a strange impression on his mind of that knitting woman, pale and curious, in her padded chair. Adelaide Tufton was not old – not a great many years older than himself. To him, with the life beating so strong in his veins, the sight of that life in death was strange, almost awful. The despair, the anguish, the vivid uncertainty and reality of his own existence, appeared to him in wonderful relief against that motionless background. If he came back here ten years hence, he might still find as now the old man by the fire, the pale woman knitting in her chair, as they had been for these six months which had brought to the young minister a greater crowd of events than all his previous years. When he thought of that helpless woman, with her lively thoughts and curious eyes, always busy and specu-lating about the life from which she was utterly shut out, a strange sensation of thankfulness stole over the young man; though he was miserable, he was alive. Between him and the lovely figure on which his heart had dwelt too long, rose up now this other figure which was not lovely. He grew stronger as he went home along the streets in the changed light of the afternoon. Siloam Cottage interposed between him and that ineffable moment at the bridal doors; presently Salem too would interpose, and all the difficulties and troubles of his career. He had taken up life again, after that pause when the sun and the moon stood still and the battle raged. Now it was all over, and the world's course had begun anew.

Mrs Vincent was looking out for him when he reached his own door. He could see her disappear from the window above, where she had been standing watching. She came to meet him as he went up to the sitting-room. There was nobody now in that room, where the widow had been making everything smile for her son. The table was spread; the fire bright; the lamp ready to be lighted on the

table. Mrs Vincent had been alarmed by Arthur's long
absence, but she did not say so. She only made haste to
tell him that Susan was so much better, and that the doctor
was in such high spirits about her. "After we come back
from the meeting you are to go in and sit with your sister
for an hour, my dear boy," said his mother. "Till that was
over, we knew your mind would be occupied, and Susan
would like to see you. Oh, Arthur! it will make you happy
only to look at her. She remembers everything now; she
has asked me even all about the flock, and cried with joy
to hear how things had gone off last night – not for joy
only," said the truthful widow, "with indignation too, that
you ever should have been doubted – for Susan thinks
there is nobody like her brother; but, my dear, we ought
to be very thankful that things have happened so well.
Everybody must learn to put up with a little injustice in
this world, particularly the pastor of a flock. If you will go
and get ready for dinner, Arthur," said Mrs Vincent, "I
will light the lamp. I have taken it into my own hands,
dear; it is better to put it right at first than to be always
arranging it after it has been put wrong. Dinner is quite
ready; and make haste, my dear boy. I have got a little
fish for you, and you know it will spoil if you keep it
waiting; and I have so much to tell you before we go out to
the meeting to-night."

Vincent made no answer to the wistful inquiring look
which his mother turned to his face as she mentioned this
meeting. He went away with an impatient exclamation
about that lamp, which seemed to him to occupy half her
thoughts. Mrs Vincent was full of many cares and much
news which she had to give her son; she was always deeply
anxious and curious to know what he was going to do that
night; but still she spared a little time for the lamp, to set
the screw right, and light to a delicate evenness the well-
trimmed wick. When she had placed it on the table, it
gave her a certain satisfaction to see how clearly it burned,
and how bright it made the table. "If I only knew what

Arthur was going to do," she said to herself, with a little sigh, as she rang the bell for the dinner, and warned the little maid to be very careful with the fish; "for if it is not put very nicely on the table Mr Vincent will not have any of it," said the minister's mother, with that feminine mingling of small cares and great which was so incomprehensible to her son. When he came back and seated himself listlessly at the table, he never thought of observing the light, or taking note of the brightness of the room. To think of this business of dinner at all, interjected into such a day, was almost too much for Arthur; and he was half disgusted with himself when he found that, after all, he could eat, and that not only for his mother's sake. Mrs Vincent talked only of Susan while the little maid was going and coming into the room; but when they were alone she drew her chair a little nearer and entered upon other things.

"Arthur, I had a great deal of conversation with Mrs Mildmay; she told me – everything," said the widow, growing pale. "Oh, my dear! when God leaves us alone to our own devices, what dreadful things a sinful creature may do! I said you would do nothing to harm her now when Susan was safe. Hush, dear! we must never breathe a word of it to Susan, or any one. Susan is changed, Arthur; sometimes I am glad of it, sometimes I could cry. She is not an innocent girl now. She is a woman – oh, Arthur! a great deal stronger than her mother: she would clear herself somehow if she knew; she would not bear that suspicion. She is more like your dear papa," said the mother, wiping her eyes, "than I ever thought to see one of my children. I can see his high-minded ways in her, Arthur – and steadier than you and me; for you have my quick temper, dear. Wait just another moment, Arthur. This poor child dotes upon Susan; and her mother asked me," said poor Mrs Vincent, pausing, and looking her son in the face, "if – I would keep her with me."

"Keep her with *you!* Let us be rid of them," cried the

minister; "they have brought us nothing but misery ever since we heard their names."

"Yes, Arthur dear; but the poor child never did any one any harm. They have made her a ward in Chancery now. It should have been done long ago but for the wickedness and the disputes; and, my dear boy," said Mrs Vincent, anxiously, "I will have to leave Lonsdale, you know; my poor child could not go back there; and we will not stay with you in Carlingford to get you into trouble with your flock," continued the widow, gazing wistfully in his face to see if she could gather anything of his purpose from his looks; "and with my little income, you know, it would be hard work without coming on you; but all the difficulty is cleared away if we take this child. I was thinking I might take Susan abroad," said the widow, with a little sigh; "it is the best thing, I have always heard, after such trouble; and it would be an occupation for her when she got better. My dear boy, don't be hasty; your dear father always took a little time to think upon a thing before he would speak; but you have always had my temper, Arthur. I won't say any more; we will speak of it, dear, in your sister's room, when we come home from the meeting to-night."

"I think you had better not go to the meeting to-night; there will be nothing said to please you, mother," said the minister, rising from the table, and taking his favourite position on the hearthrug. His mother turned round frightened, but, afraid to show her fright, determined still to look as if she believed everything was going well.

"No fine speeches, Arthur? My dear boy, I always like to hear you speak. I know you will say what you ought," said the widow, smiling, with a patient determination in her face. Then there was a pause. "Perhaps you will give me a little sketch of what you are going to say," she went on, with a tender artifice, concealing her anxiety. "Your dear papa often did, Arthur, when anything was going on among the flock."

But Arthur made no reply. His clouded face filled his mother with a host of indefinite fears. But she saw, as she had seen so often, that womanish entreaties were not practicable, and that he must be left to himself. "He will tell me as we go to Salem," she said in her heart, to quiet its anxious throbbing. "Perhaps you would like to have the room to yourself a little, dear," she said aloud. "I will go to Susan till it is time to leave; and I know my Arthur will ask the counsel of God," she added softly, just touching his hand with a tender momentary clasp. It was all the minister could do to resist the look of anxious inquiry with which this little caress was accompanied; and then she left him to prepare for his meeting. Whether he asked advice or not of his Father in heaven, the widow asked it for him with tears in her anxious eyes. She had done all that she could do. When the minister was left to himself, he opened his desk and took out the manuscript with which he had been busy last night. It was the speech he had intended to deliver, and he had been pleased with it. He sat down now and read it over to himself, by the white-covered table, on which his mother's lamp burned bright. Sheet by sheet, as he read it over, the impatient young man tossed into the fire, with hasty exclamations of disgust. He was excited; his mind was in fiery action; his heart moved to the depths. No turgid Homerton eloquence would do now. What he said must be not from the lips, but from the heart.

CHAPTER XLII.

MRS VINCENT was ready in very good time for the meeting; she brought her son a cup of coffee with her own

hand when she was dressed in her bonnet and shawl. She
had put on her best bonnet – her newest black silk dress.
Perhaps she knew that device of Tozer's, of which the
minister yet was not aware; but Arthur for once was too
peremptory and decided for his mother. She who knew
how to yield when resistance was impossible, had to give
in to him at last. It was better to stay at home, anxious as
her heart was, than to exasperate her boy, who had so
many other things to trouble him. With much heroism the
widow took off her bonnet again and returned to Susan's
room. There could be little doubt now what the minister
was going to do. While she seated herself once more by her
daughter's bedside, in a patience which was all but unbearable, her son went alone to his last meeting with his
flock. He walked rapidly through Grove Street, going
through the stream of Salem people, who were moving in
twos and threes in the same direction. A little excitement
had sprung up in Carlingford on the occasion. The public
in general had begun to find out, as the public generally
does, that here was a man who was apt to make disclosures
not only of his opinions but of himself wherever he
appeared, and that a chance was hereby afforded to the
common eye of seeing that curious phenomenon, a human
spirit in action – a human heart as it throbbed and changed
– a sight more interesting than any other dramatic performance under heaven. There was an unusual throng
that night in Grove Street, and the audience was not less
amazed than the minister when they found what awaited
them in the Salem schoolroom. There Phoebe Tozer and
her sister-spirits had been busy all day. Again there were
evergreen wreaths on the walls, and the stiff iron gaslights
were bristling with holly. Phoebe's genius had even gone
further than on the last great occasion, for there were pink
and white roses among the green leaves, and one of the
texts which hung on the wall had been temporarily elevated
over the platform, framed in wreaths and supported by
extempore fastenings, the doubtful security of which filled

Phoebe's artless soul with many a pang of terror. It was the tender injunction, "Love one another," which had been elevated to this post of honour, and this was the first thing which met Vincent's eye as he entered the room. Underneath, the platform table was already filled with the *élite* of the flock. The ladies were all in their best bonnets in that favoured circle, and Tozer stood glorious in his Sunday attire – but in his own mind privately a little anxious as to the effect of all this upon the sensitive mind of the minister – by the side of the empty chair which had been left for the president of the assembly. When Vincent was seen to enter, it was Tozer who gave the signal for a burst of cheering, which the pleased assembly, newly aware of the treat thus provided for it, performed heartily with all its boots and umbrellas. Through this applause the minister made his way to the platform with abstracted looks. The cheer made no difference upon the stubborn displeasure and annoyance of his face. Nothing that could possibly have been done to aggravate his impatient spirit and make his resolve unalterable, could have been more entirely successful than poor Tozer's expedient for the conciliation of the flock. Angry, displeased, humbled in his own estimation, the unfortunate pastor made his way through the people, who were all smiles and conscious favour. A curt general bow and cold courtesy was all he had even for his friends on the platform, who beamed upon him as he advanced. He was not mollified by the universal applause; he was not to be moved to complaisance by any such argument. He would not take the chair, though Tozer, with anxious officiousness, put it ready for him, and Phoebe looked up with looks of entreaty from behind the urn. In the sight of all the people he refused the honour, and sat down on a little supernumerary seat behind, where he was not visible to the increasing crowd. This refusal sent a thrill through all the anxious deacons on the platform. They gathered round him to make remonstrances, to which the minister paid no regard. It was a dreadful moment. Nobody knew what to do in the emergency. The throng streamed in till there was no longer an inch of standing ground, nor a single seat vacant, except that one empty chair which perplexed the assembly. The urns began to smoke less hotly; the crowd gave murmurous indications of impatience as the deacons cogitated – What was to be done? – the tea at least must not be permitted to get cold. At last Mr Brown stood up and proposed feebly, that as Mr Vincent did not wish to preside, Mr Tozer should be chairman on this joyful occasion. The Salem folks, who thought it a pity to neglect the good things before them, assented with some perplexity, and then the business of the evening began.

It was very lively business for the first half-hour. Poor Mrs Tufton, who was seated immediately in front of the minister, disturbed by his impatient movements, took fright for the young man; and could not but wonder in herself how people managed to eat cake and drink tea in such an impromptu fashion, who doubtless had partaken of that meal before leaving home, as she justly reflected. The old minister's wife stood by the young minister with a natural *esprit de corps*, and was more anxious than she could account for. A certain cloud subdued the hilarity of the table altogether; everybody was aware of the dark visage of the minister, indignant and annoyed, behind. A certain hush was upon the talk, and Tozer himself had grown pale in the chair, where the good butterman by no means enjoyed his dignity. Tozer was not so eloquent as usual when he got up to speak. He told the refreshed and exhilarated flock that he had made bold to give them a little treat, out of his own head, seeing that everything had gone off satisfactory last night; and they would agree with him as the minister had no call to take no further trouble in the way of explanations. A storm of applause was the response of the Salem folks to this suggestion; they were in the highest good-humour both with themselves and the minister – ready to vote him a silver tea-service on the spot, if anybody had been prompt enough to suggest it.

But a certain awe stole over even the delighted assembly
when Mr Vincent came forward to the front of the table
and confronted them all, turning his back upon his loyal
supporters. They did not know what to make of the dark
aspect and clouded face of the pastor, relieved as it was
against the alarmed and anxious countenances behind
him. A panic seized upon Salem: something which they
had not anticipated – something very different from the
programme – was in the minister's eye.

The Pigeons were in a back seat – very far back, where
Mrs Vincent had been the previous evening – spies to see
what was going on, plotting the Temperance Hall and an
opposition preacher in their treacherous hearts; but even
Mrs Pigeon bent forward with excitement in the general
flutter. When the minister said, "My friends," you could
have heard a pin drop in the crowded meeting; and when,
a minute after, a leaf of holly detached itself and fluttered
down from one of the gaslights, the whole row of people
among whom it fell thrilled as if they had received a blow.
Hush! perhaps it is not going to be so bad after all. He is
talking of the text there over the platform, in its evergreen
frame, which Phoebe trembles to think may come down
any moment with a crash upon her father's anxious head.
"Love one another!" Is Mr Vincent telling them that he is
not sure what that means, though he is a minister – that he
is not very sure what anything means – that life is a great
wonder, and that he only faintly guesses how God, being
pitiful, had the heart to make man and leave him on this
sad earth? Is that what he says as he stands pale before the
silent assembly, which scarcely dares draw breath, and is
ashamed of its own lightness of heart and vulgar satisfaction
with things in general? That is what the minister says.
"The way is full of such pitfalls – the clouds so heavy
overhead – the heavens, so calm and indifferent, out of
reach – cannot we take hands and help each other through
this troubled journey?" says the orator, with a low voice
and solemn eyes. When he pauses thus and looks them all

in the face, the heart of Salem fails. The very gaslights seem to darken in the air, in the silence, and there is not one of the managers who does not hear the beating of his own heart. Then suddenly the speaker raises his voice, raises his hand, storms over their heads in a burst of indignation not loud but grand. He says "No." – "No!" exclaims the minister – "not in the world, not in the church, nowhere on earth can we be unanimous except by moments. We throw our brother down, and then extend a hand to him in charity – but we have lost the art of standing side by side. Love! it means that you secure a certain woman to yourself to make your hearth bright, and to be yours for ever; it means that you have children who are yours, to perpetuate your name and your tastes and feelings. It does not mean that you stand by your brother for him and not for you!"

Then there followed another pause. The Salem people drew a long breath and looked in each other's faces. They were guilty, self-convicted; but they could not tell what was to come of it, nor guess what the speaker meant. The anxious faces behind, gazing at him and his audience, were blank and horror-stricken, like so many conspirators whose leader was betraying their cause. They could not tell what accusation he might be going to make against them, to be confirmed by their consciences; but nobody except Tozer had the least conception what he was about to say.

The minister resumed his interrupted speech. Nobody had ventured to cheer him; but during this last pause, seeing that he himself waited, and by way of cheering up their own troubled hearts, a few feeble and timid plaudits rose from the further end of the room. Mr Vincent hurriedly resumed to stop this, with characteristic impatience. "Wait before you applaud me," said the Nonconformist. "I have said nothing that calls for applause. I have something more to tell you – more novel than what I have been saying. I am going to leave Carlingford. It was you who elected me, it is you who have censured me, it was you last night who consented to look over my faults and give me a new trial. I am one of those who have boasted in my day that I received my title to ordination from no bishop, from no temporal provision, from no traditionary church, but from the hands of the people. Perhaps I am less sure than I was at first, when you were all disposed to praise me, that the voice of the people is the voice of God; but, however that may be, what I received from you I can but render up to you. I resign into your hands your pulpit, which you have erected with your money, and hold as your property. I cannot hold it as your vassal. If there is any truth in the old phrase which calls a church a cure of souls, it is certain that no cure of souls can be delegated to a preacher by the souls themselves who are to be his care. I find my old theories inadequate to the position in which I find myself, and all I can do is to give up the post where they have left me in the lurch. I am either your servant, responsible to you, or God's servant, responsible to Him – which is it? I cannot tell; but no man can serve two masters, as you know. Many of you have been kind to me – chief among all," said Vincent, turning once round to look in Tozer's anxious face, "my friend here, who has spared no pains either to make me such a pastor as you wished, or to content me with that place when he had secured it. I cannot be content. It is no longer possible. So there remains nothing but to say good-bye – good-bye! – farewell! I will see you again to say it more formally. I only wish you to understand now that this is the decision I have come to, and that I consider myself no longer the minister of Salem from this night."

Vincent drew back instantly when he had said these words, but not before half the people on the platform had got up on their feet, and many had risen in the body of the room. The women stretched out their hands to him with gestures of remonstrance and entreaty. "He don't mean it; he's not going for to leave us; he's in a little pet, that's all,"

cried Mrs Brown, loud out. Phoebe Tozer, forgetting all
about the text and the evergreens, had buried her face in
her handkerchief and was weeping, not without demonstration of the fact. Tozer himself grasped at the minister's
shoulder, and called out to the astonished assembly that
"they weren't to take no notice. Mr Vincent would hear
reason. They weren't a-going to let him go, not like this."
The minister had almost to struggle through the group of
remonstrant deacons. "You don't mean it, Mr Vincent?"
said Mrs Tozer; "only say as it's a bit o' temper, and you
don't mean it!" Phoebe, on her part, raised a tear-wet
cheek to listen to the pastor's reply; but the pastor only
shook his head, and made no answer to the eager appeals
which assailed him. When he had extricated himself from
their hands and outcries, he hastened down the tumultuous
and narrow passage between the benches, where he would
not hear anything that was addressed to him, but passed
through with a brief nod to his anxious friends. Just as
Vincent reached the door, he perceived, with eyes which
excitement had made clearer than usual, that his enemy,
Pigeon, had just got to his feet, who shouted out that the
pastor had spoken up handsome, and that there wasn't
one in Salem, whatever was their inclination, as did not
respect him that day. Though he paid no visible attention
to the words, perhaps the submission of his adversary
gave a certain satisfaction to the minister's soul; but he
took no notice of this nor anything else, as he hurried out
into the silent street, where the lamps were lighted, and
the stars shining unobserved overhead. Not less dark than
the night were the prospects which lay before him. He did
not know what he was to do – could not see a day before
him of his new career; but, nevertheless, took his way out
of Salem with a sense of freedom, and a thrill of new
power and vigour in his heart.

Behind he left a most tumultuous and disorderly meeting.
After the first outburst of dismay and sudden popular
desire to retain the impossible possession which had thus

slid out of their hands – after Tozer's distressed entreaty
that they would all wait and see if Mr Vincent didn't hear
reason – after Pigeon's reluctant withdrawal of enmity and
burst of admiration, the meeting broke up into knots, and
became not one meeting, but a succession of groups, all
buzzing in different tones over the great event. Resolutions,
however, were proposed and carried all the same. Another
deputation was appointed to wait on Mr Vincent. A proposal
was made to raise his "salary," and a subscription instituted
on the spot to present him with a testimonial. When all
these things were concluded, nothing remained but to
dismiss the assembly, which dispersed not without hopes
of a satisfactory conclusion. The deacons remained for a
final consultation, perplexed with alarms and doubts. The
repentant Pigeon, restored to them by this emergency,
was the most hopeful of all. Circumstances which had
changed *his* mind must surely influence the pastor. An
additional fifty pounds of "salary" – a piece of plate – a
congregational ovation – was it to be supposed that any
Dissenting minister bred at Homerton could withstand
such conciliatory overtures as these?

CHAPTER XLIII.

But the deputation and the increased salary and the silver
salver were all ineffectual. Arthur would not hear reason,
as his mother knew. It was with bitter restrained tears of
disappointment and vexation that she heard from him,
when he returned to that conference in Susan's room, the
events of the evening. It came hard upon the widow, who
had invited her son to his sister's bedside that they might
for the first time talk together as of old over all their plans.

But though her heart ached over the opportunity thus thrown away, and though she asked herself with terror, "What was Arthur to do now?" his mother knew he was not to be persuaded. She smiled on Tozer next morning, ready to cry with vexation and anxiety as she was. "When my son has made up his mind, it will be vain for any one to try to move him," said the widow, proud of him in spite of all, though her heart cried out against his imprudence and foolishness; and so it proved. The minister made his acknowledgements so heartily to the good butterman, that Tozer's disclaimer of any special merit, and declaration that he had but tried to "do his dooty," was made with great faltering and unsteadiness; but the Nonconformist himself never wavered in his resolve. Half of Carlingford sat in tears to hear Mr Vincent's last sermon. Such a discourse had never been heard in Salem. Scarcely one of the deacons could find a place in the crowded chapel to which all the world rushed; and Tozer himself listened to the last address of his minister from one of the doors of the gallery, where his face formed the apex and culminating point of the crowd to Mr Vincent's eyes. When Tozer brushed his red handkerchief across his face, as he was moved to do two or three times in the course of the sermon, the gleam seemed to the minister, who was himself somewhat excited, to redden over the entire throng. It was thus that Mr Vincent ended his connection with Salem Chapel. It was a heavy blow to the congregation for the time – so heavy that the spirit of the butterman yielded; he was not seen in his familiar seat for three full Sundays after; but the place was mismanaged in Pigeon's hands, and regard for the connection brought Tozer to the rescue. They had Mr Beecher down from Homerton, who made a very good impression. The subsequent events are so well known in Carlingford, that it is hardly necessary to mention the marriage of the new minister, which took place about six months afterwards. Old Mr Tufton blessed the union of his dear young brother with the blushing Phoebe, who made a most suitable minister's wife in Salem after the first disagreeables were over; and Mr Beecher proved a great deal more tractable than any man of genius. If he was not quite equal to Mr Vincent in the pulpit, he was much more complaisant at all the tea-parties; and, after a year's experience, was fully acknowledged, both by himself and others, to have made an 'it.

Vincent meanwhile plunged into that world of life which the young man did not know; not that matters looked badly for him when he left Carlingford – on the contrary, the connection in general thrilled to hear of his conduct and his speech. The enthusiasm in Homerton was too great to be kept within bounds. Such a demonstration of the rightful claims of the preacher had not been made before in the memory of man; and the enlightened Non-conforming community did honour to the martyr. Three vacant congregations at least wooed him to their pulpits; his fame spread over the country: but he did not accept any of these invitations; and after a while the eminent Dissenting familes who invited him to dinner, found so many other independencies cropping out in the young man, that the light of their countenances dimmed upon him. It began to be popularly reported that a man so apt to hold opinions of his own, and so convinced of the dignity of his office, had best have been in the Church, where people knew no better. Such, perhaps, might have been the conclusion to which he came himself; but education and prejudice and Homerton stood invincible in the way. A Church of the Future – an ideal corporation, grand and primitive, not yet realised, but surely *real*, to be come at one day – shone before his eyes, as it shines before so many; but, in the mean time, the Nonconformist went into literature, as was natural, and was, it is believed in Carlingford, the founder of the 'Philosophical Review,' that new organ of public opinion. He had his battle to fight, and fought it out in silence, saying little to any one.

Sundry old arrows were in his heart, still quivering by times as he fought with the devil and the world in his desert; but he thought himself almost prosperous, and perfectly composed and eased of all fanciful and sentimental sorrows, when he went, two or three years after these events, to Folkestone, to meet his mother and sister, who had been living abroad, away from him, with their charge, and to bring them to the little house he had prepared for them in London, and where he said to himself he was prepared, along with them – a contented but neutral-coloured household – to live out his life.

But when Mr Vincent met his mother at Folkestone, not even the haze of the spring evening, nor the agitation of the meeting, which brought back again so forcibly all the events which accompanied the parting, could soften to him the wonderful thrill of surprise, almost a shock, with which he looked upon two of the party. The widow, in her close white cap and black bonnet, was unchanged as when she fell, worn out, into his arms on her first visit to Carlingford. She gave a little cry of joy as she saw her son. She trembled so with emotion and happiness, that he had to steady her on his arm and restrain his own feelings till another time. The other two walked by their side to the hotel where they were to rest all night. He had kissed Susan in the faint evening light, but her brother did not know that grand figure, large and calm and noble like a Roman woman, at whom the other passengers paused to look as they went on; and his first glance at the younger face by her side sent the blood back to his heart with a sudden pang and thrill which filled him with amazement at himself. He heard the two talking to each other, as they went up the crowded pier in the twilight, like a man walking in a dream. What his mother said, leaning on his arm, scarcely caught his attention. He answered to her in monosyllables, and listened to the voices – the low, sweet laughter, the sound of the familiar names. Nothing in Susan's girlish looks had prophesied that majestic figure,

that air of quiet command and power. And a wilder
wonder still attracted the young man's heart as he listened
to the beautiful young voice which kept calling on Susan,
Susan, like some sweet echo of a song. These two, had
they been into another world, an enchanted country?
When they came into the lighted room, and he saw them
divest themselves of their wrappings, and beheld them
before him, visible tangible creatures and no dreams,
Vincent was struck dumb. He seemed to himself to have
been suddenly carried out of the meaner struggles of his
own life into the air of a court, the society of princes.
When Susan came up to him and laid her two beautiful
hands on his shoulders, and looked with her blue eyes into
his face, it was all he could do to preserve his composure,
and conceal the almost awe which possessed him. The
wide sleeve had fallen back from her round beautiful arm.
It was the same arm that used to lie stretched out uncovered upon her sick-bed like a glorious piece of marble.
Her brother could scarcely rejoice in the change, it struck
him with so much wonder, and was so different from his
thoughts. Poor Susan! he had said in his heart for many a
day. He could not say poor Susan now.

"Arthur does not know me," she said, with a low, liquid
voice, fuller than the common tones of women. "He
forgets how long it is ago since we went away. He thinks
you cannot have anything so big belonging to you, my
little mother. But it is me, Arthur. Susan all the same."

"Susan perhaps, since you say so – but not all the same,"
said Arthur, with his astonished eyes.

"And I daresay you don't know Alice either," said his
sister. "I was little and Alice was foolish when we went away.
At least I was little in Lonsdale, where nobody minded me.
Somehow most people mind me now, because I am so big, I
suppose; and Alice, instead of being foolish, is a little wise
woman. Come here, Alice, and let my brother see you. You
have heard of him every day for three years. At last here is
Arthur; but what am I to do if he has forgotten me?"

"I have forgotten neither of you," said the young man. He was glad to escape from Susan's eyes, which somehow looked as if they were a bit of the sky, a deep serene of blue; and the little Alice imagined he did not look at her at all, and was a little mortified in her tender heart. Things began to grow familiar to him after a while. However wonderful they were, they were real creatures, who did not vanish away, but were close to him all the evening, moving about – this with lovely fairy lightness, that with majestic maiden grace – talking in a kind of dual, harmonious movement of sound, filling the soft spring night with a world of vague and strange fascination. The window was opened in their sitting-room, where they could see the lights and moving figures, and, farther off, the sea – and hear outside the English voices, which were sweet to hear to the strangers newly come home. Vincent, while he recovered himself, stood near this window by his mother's chair, paying her such stray filial attentions as he could in the bewilderment of his soul, and slowly becoming used to the two beautiful young women, unexpected apparitions, who transformed life itself and everything in it. Was one his real sister, strange as it seemed? and the other——? Vincent fell back and resigned himself to the strange, sweet, unlooked-for influence. They went up to London together next day. Sunshine did not disperse them into beautiful mists, as he had almost feared. It came upon him by glimpses to see that fiery sorrow and passion had acted like some tropical tempestuous sun upon his sister's youth; and the face of his love looked back upon him from the storm in which it died, as if somehow what was impossible might be possible again. Mrs Mildmay, a wandering restless soul as she was, happened to be absent from London just then. Alice was still to stay with her dearest friends. The Nonconformist went back to his little home with the sensation of an enchanted prince in a fairy tale. Instead of the mud-coloured existence, what a glowing, brilliant firmament!

Life became glorious again under their touch. As for Mrs Vincent, she was too happy in getting home – in seeing Susan, after all the anguishes and struggles which no one knew of fully but herself, rising up in all the strength of her youth to this renewed existence – to feel as much distressed as she had expected about Arthur's temporary withdrawal from his profession. It was only a temporary withdrawal, she hoped. He still wore his clerical coat, and called himself "clergyman" in the Blue Book – and he was doing well, though he was not preaching. The Nonconformist himself naturally was less sober in his thoughts. He could not tell what wonderful thing he might not yet do in this wonderful elevation and new inspiring of his heart. His genius broke forth out of the clouds. Seeing these two as they went about the house, hearing their voices as they talked in perpetual sweet accord, with sweeter jars of difference, surprised the young man's life out of all its shadows; – one of them his sister – the other—. After all his troubles, the loves and the hopes came back with the swallows to build under his eaves and stir in his heart.

THE END

VIRAGO MODERN CLASSICS

The first Virago Modern Classic, *Frost in May* by Antonia White, was published in 1978. It launched a list dedicated to the celebration of women writers and to the rediscovery and reprinting of their works. Its aim was, and is, to demonstrate the existence of a female tradition in fiction which is both enriching and enjoyable. The Leavisite notion of the 'Great Tradition', and the narrow, academic definition of a 'classic', has meant the neglect of a large number of interesting secondary works of fiction. In calling the series 'Modern Classics' we do not necessarily mean 'great' — although this is often the case. Published with new critical and biographical introductions, books are chosen for many reasons: sometimes for their importance in literary history; sometimes because they illuminate particular aspects of womens' lives, both personal and public. They may be classics of comedy or storytelling; their interest can be historical, feminist, political or literary.

Initially the Virago Modern Classics concentrated on English novels and short stories published in the early decades of this century. As the series has grown it has broadened to include works of fiction from different centuries, different countries, cultures and literary traditions. In 1984 the Victorian Classics were launched; there are separate lists of Irish, Scottish, European, American, Australian and other English speaking countries; there are books written by Black women, by Catholic and Jewish women, and a few relevant novels by men. There is, too, a companion series of Non-Fiction Classics constituting biography, autobiography, travel, journalism, essays, poetry, letters and diaries.

By the end of 1986 over 250 titles will have been published in these two series, many of which have been suggested by our readers.